Amid Secrets

Amid Secrets, the third novel in the Falling Castles series, is definitely a tale filled with suspense, multiple dilemmas, and lots of twists and turns in the plot. Just about everyone we have met in the first two books of this series ends up in some sort of crisis or life-changing event. In other words, this is another exceptional mystery, intrigue, and romantic thriller by Stacy Lynn Miller.

-Betty H., *NetGalley*

Absolutely brilliant. The whole series has kept me engaged, and on my toes and hooked me in. Great storyline, fantastic characters throughout the book, gripping suspense storyline, cannot fault this author at all.

-Jo R., *NetGalley*

Blind Suspicion

4.25 stars. With the first book ending on a cliffhanger, I was very much looking forward to reading this sequel and it was so satisfying. Lynn Miller knows how to keep things interesting and I'm learning that the different volumes in her series never feel repetitive...In summary, drama, romance, and mystery – what's not to like? I hope to see more books in this series.

-Meike V., *NetGalley*

Honestly? Stacy Lynn Miller is probably one of the better authors I've come across in the last few years. If you want something fresh, gripping, entertaining and keeps you guessing to the end, this author is for you. *Blind Suspicion* is the sequel to *Despite Chaos*, another fantastic read, I recommend you read it first.

-Jo R., *NetGalley*

This novel is a very enticing and captivating story full of love, drama, loyalty, family dynamics (both good and bad ones), romance, mystery and so many other things...

-Laurie D., *NetGalley*

Despite Chaos

I honestly do not know what to say! Fantastic story. Everything I've read by Stacy Lynn Miller has been entertaining, engaging and gripping. *Despite Chaos* is yet another amazing story, it's a must book to own in 2022. It's a 5/5. And with a cliffhanger like that...Can't wait for that sequel.

-Emma S, *NetGalley*

4.25 Stars. Stacy Lynn Miller has a great ability to write messy, complicated people that are easy to like. With this first book in the "Falling Castles" series, she does it again with Alexandra Castle and Tyler Falling.

-Colleen C., *NetGalley*

This is a well-written, slow-burn romance. There's romance, competition, blackmail, embezzlement and jealousy. The story was fast-paced, and I enjoyed every minute of it. The love, support and understanding of Tyler's husband was astounding. Hands down a great read and I recommend getting a copy. 4.5 stars.

-Bonnie K., *NetGalley*

Beyond the Smoke

This was really good! This is the third book in Miller's Manhattan Sloane Thriller series and is the best written book of the series. I was caught up in the mystery, it kept me turning the pages, but so did the romance.

-Lex Kent's Reviews, *goodreads*

I loved the first two novels, but I think this one might be the best yet...I've enjoyed all the mystery, excitement, action, and intrigue in the plots of these books, but I've fallen in love with these characters, and want to know what's happening in their lives. This is the mark of an exceptionally talented author.

-Betty H., *NetGalley*

From the Ashes

I have been looking forward to reading *From the Ashes* by Stacy Lynn Miller since I read her first Manhattan Sloane novel back in April. I fell in love with Sloane, Finn, and all the other characters in this story while reading the first book, and I wanted more, especially since the story didn't completely end with the first novel. I'm happy to say I loved this book as much as the first one.

I highly recommend both novels, though, so get them both. You won't be disappointed.

-Betty H., *NetGalley*

This was the sequel to this author's very good debut book, *Out of the Flames*.

I enjoyed how the author developed this sequel with realistic problems the characters faced after the loss of loved ones... This book was very engaging with tense moments, emotional breakdowns and recovery, and most of all, tender loving scenes.

-R. Swier, *NetGalley*

From the Ashes is the sequel to *Out of the Flames* with SFPD Detective Manhattan Sloane and DEA [Agent] Finn Harper... Miller is a wonderful storyteller and this story had me sitting on the edge of my seat from start to finish. The first book in the series, *Out of the Flames*, was a 5-star read and *From the Ashes* is the same as it ducks and weaves and thrills and spills all the way to the end. The chemistry between Sloane and Harper is palpable...Miller certainly knows how to write angst into her characters. This book is a thrill a minute and I can't wait for the next one.

-Lissa G., NetGalley

I read Stacy Lynn Miller's debut novel *Out of the Flames* back in May, and couldn't wait to read the sequel to learn what happens to San Francisco police detective Manhattan Sloane and DEA Agent Finn Harper's relationship as well as the drug cartel they were chasing. *From the Ashes* resumes from the point that *Out of the Flames* ended.

The book was fast-paced with quite a few anxious and emotional moments. I don't think that you have to read the first book to enjoy this one, but I recommend it since it is a good story and it will introduce the background and characters in a more complete manner. I'd definitely recommend both books to other readers.

-Michele R., NetGalley

Out of the Flames

This is the debut novel of Stacy Lynn Miller and it's very, very good. The book is a roller coaster of emotion as you ride the highs and lows with Sloane as she navigates her way through her life which is riddled with guilt, self blame, and eventually love. It's easy to connect with all the main characters and sub-characters, most of them are all successful, strong women so what's not to love? The story line is really solid.

-Lissa G., NetGalley

If you are looking for a book that is emotional, exciting, hopeful, and entertaining, you came to the right place. There are characters you will love, and characters you will love to hate. And the important thing is that Miller makes you care about them so, yes, you might need the tissues just like I did. I see a lot of potential in Miller and I can't wait to read book two.

-Lex Kent's 2020 Favorites List.
Lex Kent's Reviews, goodreads

If you are looking for an adventure novel with mystery, intrigue, romance, and a lot of angst, then look no further.

...I'm really impressed with how well this tale is written. The story itself is excellent, and the characters are well-developed and easy to connect with.

-Betty H., NetGalley

DEVIL'S SLIDE

STACY LYNN MILLER

About the Author

A late bloomer, Stacy Lynn Miller took up writing after retiring from the Air Force. Her twenty years of toting a gun and police badge, tinkering with computers, and sleuthing for clues as an investigator form the foundation of her Lexi Mills crime thriller series and Manhattan Sloane romantic thriller series. She is visually impaired, a proud stroke survivor, mother of two, tech nerd, chocolate lover, and terrible golfer with a hole-in-one. When you can't find her writing, she'll be golfing or drinking wine (sometimes both) with friends and family in Northern California.

For more information about Stacy, visit her website at stacylynnmiller.com. You can also connect with her on Instagram @stacylynnmiller, Twitter @stacylynnmiller, or Facebook @ stacylynnmillerauthor

DEVIL'S SLIDE

STACY LYNN MILLER

BELLA
BOOKS

2023

Acknowledgments

Thank you, Louise, Kristianne, Diane, Sue, and Sabrin. This incredible crew of beta readers pushes me to be a better writer.

Thank you, Linda and Jessica Hill, for believing in my work and making my dream come true.

Thank you, Medora MacDougall, my editor who brings out the best in me.

Finally, to my family. Thank you for loving and encouraging me.

Dedication

To my family.

CHAPTER ONE

Alameda, California, 1920

Rose Hamilton arrived at school nearly late for her first class of the day for no reason other than she dawdled because it was Friday—a habit she needed to break, according to her mother. She ran up the steps, clasping her textbooks close to her chest, but slowed once through the main doors. The sea of students milling about meant the first bell had yet to ring.

Walking down the corridor, she noticed a boy she hadn't seen before, a senior maybe, shamelessly flirting with the class beauty queen near the attendance office door. He appeared handsome enough with a blond crew cut, broad shoulders, and new clothes, but when Rose passed him, the overpowering scent of oakmoss nearly made her choke. Clearly, he didn't understand the meaning of moderation when applying Aqua Velva.

Rose snickered. On his first day, this young man already appeared no different from the other boys in her high school. They were all out for one thing—S.E.X. But that didn't interest her, at least not with boys. That fact, though, was a tightly held secret. Thinking such things was a sin, and as far as Rose knew, she was the only one in her high school who did. However, she hoped that one particular girl might think the same way.

The warning bell rang, and Rose searched the hallway for her best friend of the last five years. Dax was easy to spot, not because she was athletic and six inches taller than Rose, but because she was the only girl in school with hair cropped short around her ears.

Rose glimpsed Dax's dark hair as she stepped into their eleventh-grade history class and took off after her. Following a quick "good morning," both took their traditional seats next to each other, the same ones they'd chosen on the first day of class. Rose's position in the second-to-the-last desk in the row furthest from the teacher's desk had its benefits. With Mrs. Bowman's rule of filling in every seat, starting from the front, Rose had no one sitting behind her. For the past three weeks, she and Dax had passed notes to each other with impunity.

To Rose's horror, Aqua Velva walked in at the final bell. She buried her head in her arms atop her desk. "Please, just be looking for directions," she whispered to herself, but then the teacher welcomed Billie to class and directed him to take the first empty seat. Rose popped her head up, nauseated by his toothy grin first and then by his aftershave when he reached the desk right behind her.

She tried pushing him out of her head, but the cloud of oakmoss made it impossible until Mrs. Bowman made a second horrifying announcement. She introduced a new student-led teaching method she wanted to try. Instead of her lecturing today, five students would take turns reading aloud sections from a chapter on the Civil War. The walls then started a slow, steady march, closing in on Rose the moment Mrs. Bowman said she would begin with the row furthest to her left—Rose's row. That meant Dax would be the fourth reader, and Rose would be the fifth.

What unforgivable offense did she commit to tip fate and earn such a cruel punishment? Rose had gotten through ten years of school without asking a single question or speaking in front of the class. A simple "Here" during attendance call, a respectful "Yes, ma'am" or "No, ma'am," and a reciting of the alphabet one letter at a time were the most she'd uttered in school since her first day of kindergarten. That record was about to come to a terrifying, abrupt end. Besides her parents and her older brother, Conroy, who died two years ago from the Spanish Flu, Dax was the only person she felt comfortable talking to. Heck, Conroy had once told her that besides toddler grunts, Rose didn't speak to other people until she was four, preferring to let him do the talking for her.

Minute by minute, the pounding in Rose's head magnified, muffling each student's voice as they read and making them all sound like they were talking through pillows. She followed along in her textbook until Billie tapped her on the shoulder and dropped something into her lap. By the time she determined it was a piece of paper folded into a tiny triangle and returned her concentration to the book, she'd lost her place. Panic set in, but she remembered what Dax had once told her when she got frustrated before speaking. *"Take a deep breath, relax, and focus on the first word."* Rose did, and within a few seconds, found her place again and followed along.

Moments later, there was a second tap on her shoulder. Rose was never one to lose her temper after making it out of the terrible twos, according to her mother, but the Neanderthal behind her was testing her patience. He leaned in until his warm breath tickled her ear and aftershave curled her nose. "Read it," he said.

That was it. The terrible twos returned with a vengeance. Rose snapped her head around so hard her neck cracked. She yelled loud enough to grind a speeding train to a halt. "Stop it!" Billie leaned back in his chair with the stupidest grin, reminding her of the mischievous cat Lewis Carroll had written about. His confidence boiled her blood to the temperature of a volcano. She flung the note at him, square in the nose. Words flowed fluently from her like hot lava, destroying everything in its path. "You are a bothersome halfwit."

"Miss Hamilton!" Mrs. Bowman barked. "Need I send you to the principal's office?"

Rose's stomach churned her morning pancakes into a bubbling, burning concoction that threatened to make a reappearance. Her mother would never stand for her being singled out for punishment. *"Insolence and insubordination were the devil's work,"* she would say. *"God reserved a special place in hell for unmanageable little girls,"* her mother had often told her after Sunday church service.

Rose inched her head in the chalkboard's direction, afraid to lock eyes with the fuming taskmaster. Without a doubt, Mrs. Bowman had steam blasting from both ears like a train whistle. The teacher was now the train Rose had impulsively brought to a stop right at her feet. Her chin pinned to her chest, Rose answered, "No, ma'am."

"Very well. Thank you for a fine reading, Miss Xander. You may finish the chapter, Miss Hamilton."

Besides Rose not knowing where Dax had left off, a lump the size of the apple Rose had waiting for her in the lunch sack below her desk formed in her throat. She hadn't felt this shaky since the day her father returned home to say that Conroy had died. "I-I—"

"I'd like to keep going, Mrs. Bowman, if it's all the same." Dax volunteering to save Rose from inevitable humiliation was no surprise, and like her kindness did a hundred times before, the offer warmed her heart.

Since meeting on the first day of secondary school, Dax had been Rose's sworn protector from the playground bullies. It didn't seem to bother Dax that Rose hadn't said a word to her for the first three days. In fact, she appeared to feed on it. The more embarrassment-filled smiles and grateful grins Rose had issued for coming to her rescue, the more time Dax had spent with her. They were inseparable by the end of the first week during and after school unless Rose had to be home or Dax had a carpentry job with her father.

"I applaud your zeal, Miss Xander, but it is Miss Hamilton's turn."

Rose sunk deep into her chair, dreading the equivalent of being stripped bare in the public square. Dax twisted at the waist, shifted her stare over her shoulder, and squeezed Rose's hand. Her sad eyes and reassuring nod momentarily eased Rose's trembling.

Rose shook her head, unsure where to begin reading, and mouthed, "Where?"

Dax pointed to the passage labeled "Battle of Antietam." *Crap. Crap. Crap.* A problem sound on the third word. She'd never get through this without making a fool of herself. Rose glimpsed at Dax again for an extra dose of courage, but instead, her eyes gave her the softest caress she'd ever felt. And when Rose cleared her throat, she still felt its echo on her cheeks.

"Battle of Ah-Ah-Ah-Ah." Rose's trembling returned tenfold. Her worst enemies were *R*s, *W*s, *L*s, and multisyllable words beginning with vowels. They had the power to make her feel incapable, inferior, embarrassed, and furious all at once. Not even her overbearing mother could do that. Everyone she knew spoke as smooth as glass, some more elegantly than others. However, Rose couldn't get out two words in front of people without stumbling on one. She was a little better with Dax but not perfect like her, and today, she learned she could speak flawlessly when blowing her stack. If only she could sing her reading. For some unknown reason, Rose could string together every word in the dictionary when alone or singing.

"The word is Antietam, Miss Hamilton," Mrs. Bowman said with an added hint of superiority when she stressed the word Antietam. And in an instant, embarrassment took a front seat. A chorus of snickers made Rose want to crawl into a hole for the next seventy-five years.

"Who's the halfwit now?" Billie rolled to the floor into an ear-bursting belly laugh, turning the room's snickers into a mortifying mix of shrieks and guffaws.

Short of dropping dead, nothing could take away the hurt Rose felt at that moment. Not even Dax. She picked up her books and ran out the door, leaving her lunch and every ounce of self-respect behind. Tears fell as fast as her feet were moving, the fastest they'd ever come and the fastest she'd ever run. She wanted out of this nightmare and never to step foot in this school again.

The moment the door shut, the laughter inside the classroom crested to a roar. It was an unthinking, uncaring reaction that turned Dax's stomach. They didn't realize they were ridiculing the girl she loved. Dax had heard all she could bear. Making matters worse, Mrs. Bowman stood statue-like following Rose's hasty departure, mouth agape, doing nothing to quell the mob of bullies.

"Enough!" Dax yelled, leaping to her feet. The room came to a sudden hush. "You should be ashamed of yourselves. For God's sake, she's a straight A student with a malady."

Dax scanned the room of tormentors and found suitable targets to drive her point home. This would unfold as a distasteful lesson, but she had to do it after how cruel they were to her sweet Rose.

"I wouldn't laugh at you, Tommy, for the pits left on your face after your bout with chickenpox even though they make you look like a corpse. Or you, Sally. I wouldn't laugh at your head-to-toe freckles that look as if you haven't bathed for months. Or you, Mrs. Bowman. I wouldn't laugh at that nasty mole on your cheek that looks like a rat gnawed it half off."

At the students' collective gasp, Mrs. Bowman turned fiery eyes on Dax. "That's quite enough, Miss Xander. Report to the principal's office right this instant."

"My pleasure." Dax stuffed her book into her satchel with an exaggerated huff. Before leaving, she gave Billie, who had returned to his chair, a bone-crushing stomp on his foot. She heard something crack. The ensuing sharp bang confirmed she'd yanked the door open with the force of a tornado. Dax stepped down the hallway with an added strut, chin held out in both indignation for that disgraceful show and satisfaction for unveiling it for what it was.

Ignoring that awful teacher's orders, Dax continued past the principal's office to the main entrance without one ounce of concern for the punishment the principal would pile on for skipping out. Every minute of detention spent writing sentences would be worth it because she had one vital task on her mind: Find Rose.

The previous five years as each other's only friend gave Dax a pretty good idea of where Rose might go to lick her wounds. She wouldn't dare go home in the middle of the school day. Nor would she sneak into Neptune Beach on a Friday with all the tourists. That left only three options. The drug store soda fountain on Webster Street, which she and Rose frequented for a soda when they each scraped up a dime, would likely be too crowded. The same went for the movie house. Rose didn't like being around people when she was upset, so that left Sweeney Park.

Slipping into the girls' bathroom, Dax removed the uniform skirt the school made her wear, which was punishment itself, and stuffed it into her satchel with her books. The wool knickerbockers she had on underneath were much more her style. The white shirt she had to wear under her dark, heavy blazer wasn't too bad, but the way the school had her tie the dark blue scarf around her collar was silly. She removed it too and instantly felt more like herself.

Dax jogged the mile to Sweeney Park but kept her pace slow. Rose's protector shouldn't show up smelling like a mule. Several young mothers had set up in a circle on the grassy field. Some tended to infants on their picnic blankets while a group of toddlers engaged in mayhem in the center. Walking past the maternal scene Dax couldn't fathom for herself in any universe, she set her sights on the grove of poplar trees at the far end of the park.

Her heart broke when she spotted Rose sitting against a tree trunk deep inside the grove, with her head buried in crossed arms resting atop her raised bent knees. Rose and Dax had been in this position before—Rose devastated by a bully and Dax consoling her after dealing with the browbeater. It was a dynamic she didn't mind. In fact, it made her feel as if she had a purpose in life beyond being her father's assistant on big carpentry jobs.

Dax lowered her satchel and then herself to the ground, leaning against the same tree trunk as Rose. She scooted closer. The moment their thighs and shoulders touched, Rose quaked, sniffles coming from beneath her arms. The silence between them, Dax figured, was all Rose needed for now.

Dax inspected the gray sky between the delicate leaves when the crying stopped, discovering the marine layer had never lifted. "I think it might rain today."

Rose finally lifted her head and stared up into the trees. "I think you're right." Her words came out nearly perfect, a shift Dax noticed about a year after they'd become friends. When it was only the two of them, Rose's speech improved so much that Dax often forgot about the malady.

"Why don't you stutter much around me anymore?"

"I don't know. Maybe because it's just you."

Dax shifted her position until she knelt in front of Rose. "What do you mean, just me?" Dax feigned taking offense. "Just as in, I'm a nobody? Or it's just the two of us and you prefer it that way? I don't think I could live with the first choice." Dax placed both hands over her chest in dramatic Lillian Gish fashion. "It would stab me through the heart."

The slightest grin formed on Rose's lips, precisely what Dax had hoped to extract. Rose didn't know it, but her cute button nose, long brunette curls, and a smile that could guide ships into San Francisco Bay had her mesmerized at first sight. And when Rose spoke to her for the first time days later, her sweet, unique voice stuck in the most disarming fashion, capturing her heart. No one knew her secret, not even her older sister, May, her confidant in all things except Rose.

"You know which one." Rose's grin inched wider. "You're my best friend."

"I'm your only friend." Dax gave Rose's knees a playful shove. The sparkle in Rose's eyes that had been missing since history class partially returned.

"Well, I'm your only friend, too. Who else would want to be friends with a strange one like you?"

Dax returned her bottom to the ground with a thump. "No one after what I did today."

"What did you do, Darlene Augusta Xander?"

"I hate it when you call me that." Why on earth did her parents name her after her grandmother? The only thing she remembered of her mother's mother before she died was she'd wrap her long hair in a bun and wear a white apron that covered her dress from the waist down. Dax looked nothing like her. If anything, she looked like the grandfather whose middle name she shared. Dax much preferred her chosen nickname based on her initials.

"Then tell me what you did," Rose ordered.

Dax released a deep sigh. Unlike Rose, Dax had narrowed her friend list to one out of choice. Before Rose came along, popularity wasn't an issue. Dax had the same group of boys and girls she'd grown up with since kindergarten. But none of them held her interest once she'd laid eyes on her sweet Rose.

Conversely, Rose was new to town. She'd refused to talk to anyone and stayed to herself. Heck, it took three days of persistence to get a "hello" out of her, but once Rose spoke, Dax was hooked. Dax was sure none of her old friends would have her back after what she'd unleashed today, though. She'd likely burned every bridge in that school, all but the one she had with Rose.

Dax rubbed the back of her neck, pushing back her regret. "I pointed out Tommy's pox face and how it made him look like a corpse, Sally's freckles and how it seemed like she hadn't bathed, and Mrs. Bowman's nasty mole that looked half-chewed."

Rose slapped Dax on the arm with the unmistakable force of shock and disappointment. It stung both inside and out. "You didn't."

"I know it was wrong." Dax dipped her head. "But I had to make a point about making fun of people for things they can't change about themselves because that was exactly what they did to you. I couldn't let it stand."

Rose raised Dax's chin with her small, slender hand, sending shivers up and down her spine. Rose had never touched her like that before. The informal familiarity of being best friends receded, giving way to a gentleness that sparked an ache in her chest. She wanted that breath-stopping caress to never end.

"You did that for me?" Rose asked in the softest, sweetest tone Dax had ever heard.

"Of course, I did. You're my best friend. I love you." Those last three words tumbled out of Dax's mouth before she could stop them. She knew they were true, but according to church, school, and her parents, loving Rose in that way was wrong. Dax couldn't help herself. Everything about this angel had her floating in the clouds.

"Well, thank you." Rose dropped her hand, its touch still tingling Dax's skin where it had touched. "But it was still wrong."

"I know." Dax fought back the disappointment that Rose didn't say she loved her too, and forced a grin. "But you might be pleased to hear that Billie might return to school on Monday using crutches."

Rose's mouth fell open wide enough that Dax could fit an apple in there. "What did you do?"

"I may have broken his foot when I stomped it."

"That's horrible." Rose's hand flew to her mouth to hide a growing smile.

"Just horrible." Dax's cheeky tone matched Rose's.

Raindrops spritzed Dax's hair. She craned her neck to check the expansive green she'd passed earlier. The group of mothers had packed up their children and were making their way to the street. Except for a loose dog scurrying toward the other end of the grove, Dax and Rose were the only ones remaining in the park.

The rain picked up, quickly bursting into a full-out shower. The poplar trees helped block a fraction of the rain with their sparse leaves, but most of it got through. Dax and Rose would be soaked in no time. She removed her school blazer, scooted next to Rose, and draped it over their heads.

The wind picked up, and Dax considered seeking better shelter, but being this close to Rose came with a new sensation, one she didn't want to stop. She'd known for years that she loved Rose and until today hadn't the inclination to say or do anything about it. She suspected the reason for the sudden change but feared admitting it. Even to herself. Especially to Rose. She was no longer satisfied with simply being friends.

Dax shivered.

"Are you cold?" Rose asked.

The innocent question laid a dilemma at Dax's feet. Telling each other the truth had become the bedrock of her and Rose's friendship, but until now, the truth had never scared her. The heart-pounding truth was that she'd shivered at the prospect of caressing Rose's face like she'd done to her. But this novel sensation she felt for Rose had her convinced that one touch wouldn't be enough. How could it? Rose was the most beautiful creature in the world.

"No," Dax replied. A nugget of the truth would have to suffice.

"I just learned something about you."

"What's that?"

"You're a terrible liar." Rose wrapped her arms around Dax's torso and pressed their bodies together. *Dear Lord.* The sensations Rose's earlier caress had kindled returned a hundred times stronger. Every nerve ending sparked like fireworks on the Fourth of July, making that heartbending truth impossible to hide.

"Rose."

"Yes."

"Look at me." Dax dizzied, saying those three words. Her chest thumped at the leap she was about to take. The next minute would make their friendship strong as granite or forever fracture it. Rose loosened her hold and raised her head to meet Dax's gaze.

Dax swallowed the lump in her throat to summon the final bit of courage. She inched her head down until their lips touched. *Please don't pull away,* she thought. *Please let this moment linger.* Every childhood dream and fantasy about a first kiss was about to be tested. Would Rose's lips feel as pillowy soft as she'd imagined since her first hello? Would they taste like sweet fruit freshly picked from the vine?

Rose flinched, and in that instant, every thought Dax had conjured up about sharing a magical kiss went up in smoke. She'd never know if a kiss compared to a summer's day because Rose was the only one who made her want to discover its properties. Dax pulled back, the weight of her egregious error crushing every good feeling flat.

Rose narrowed her brow. A prominent crease formed between her eyes. "Why did you stop?"

"You flinched."

"Because you made my heart stop." Rose's gaze dropped to the level of Dax's lips, breathing life into her dreams. Rose leaned in, pressing their lips together into a soft kiss.

Each muscle relaxed in succession, starting from Dax's chest. Her long exhale released every expectation. Her inhale tingled both lungs with the savory scent of Rose. No drug store perfume. No earthy soap or shampoo. Only her. A moan escaped. Then another. Both were hers, and both were Rose's. One kiss turned into two. Then three. Then four. Dax could do this forever, but an ache formed in each arm from holding up her rain-soaked blazer.

Dax pulled back reluctantly and adjusted their makeshift shelter to relieve the crick in her arms. The sparkle in Rose's eyes had transformed into something Dax had only seen on the movie screen. They seemed to smile and wrap Dax in their warmth at the same time.

"Remember when we were fourteen, and we fantasized about falling in love with someone?" Dax asked.

"Yeah."

"I love you, Rose."

"I love you too." But for a slight grin, Rose's expression remained unchanged. Either she didn't understand the meaning of Dax's confession, or she didn't return the feelings. Dax's instinct was to not press her luck, but the way Rose's body felt against hers demanded otherwise.

"I mean, I really love you. You're my fantasy."

Rose's grin slowly expanded until her teeth showed. Then she said the sweetest three words Dax had ever heard. "You're mine too."

CHAPTER TWO

Following that life-changing first kiss, Dax could think of doing nothing else. They'd met the next day, Saturday, at the department store soda counter and split a Coca-Cola and ham sandwich—Dax's treat. The best fifty cents she'd ever spent. Her daily scenic route home from school, combing the shoreline outside the fence of Neptune Beach, had paid off. At least one or two wasteful vacationers of that amusement park threw a soda bottle into the bay every day. It had become a race between the local kids to snatch up the bottles and turn them into the grocery store for the ten-cent deposit.

After their lunch, when the clouds turned dark and let loose an even stouter rainstorm than yesterday's, everyone on the street but Dax ducked inside for cover. She took Rose by the hand and led her down a narrow dead-end alley between two brick buildings where their only company was feral cats feasting on trash can scraps. The setting was far from ideal, but Dax couldn't wait a minute longer to feel Rose's lips against hers again.

She stopped behind a head-high stack of crates, pulling Rose against her. The force reawakened the familiar sensation she craved more than the biscuits May used to bake before she married and moved away. Dax's legs nearly buckled in the rain. "You feel so good."

"You feel wonderful." Rose wrapped her arms tighter around Dax's neck, pressing their bodies together like lovers. Dax thought she'd melt into a puddle and drift out to the street along with the rainwater. The only thing that could feel better would be Rose's lips.

Dax relaxed her hold enough to capture Rose in a searing kiss. And like their first, this kiss woke every part of her, from her toes to the heartbeat echoing in her head. She was no longer in control, an instinct she never knew existed now driving every movement and breath.

Dax flattened her hands against the wet cotton of Rose's light jacket, treasuring how every back muscle contracted and released with each deep breath. The heat between them was nearly enough to snap dry their clothing. It grew until Dax could no longer keep her lips together, the need to taste more overpowering her. She parted them, hoping Rose would do the same. And she did. Dax eased her tongue forward, past the confines of her mouth. The shift felt like crossing the line from darkness to light, where every color imaginable existed. Then their tongues touched, and those colors danced in the sky.

The first moist caress sent a jolt to Dax's core, producing a throbbing ache. It was the same ache she had in bed last night while reliving their first kiss in her head. The pulsing intensified well beyond any she'd experienced and screamed for swift attention. Dax lowered her hands to Rose's bottom and pressed their centers together, making the need more acute. She pressed harder in an upward motion. The added pressure made her wonder how it would feel if their wet clothing were gone, but Rose ripped their mouths apart and pressed both palms against Dax's chest.

"Wait." The fright swirling in Rose's eyes instantly doused Dax's ache and drove regret through her heart like a stake. Dax took a step back.

"I'm so sorry, Rose."

"You're going too fast." Rose's shaky tone left no room for debate or doubt—Dax had taken things too far.

"I don't know what got into me. You must hate me." Dax lowered her head, ashamed she'd done something nearly as brutish as Tommy McAdams had done to ruin Rose's very first kiss.

"I don't hate you."

"But I ruined things." At least Dax didn't shove her tongue down Rose's throat and fondle a breast in the first ten seconds like Tommy had.

"You did no such thing. Unlike Tommy, I want you to touch me." Rose raised Dax's chin with two fingers like she did yesterday. Thankfully, the same affection Dax saw yesterday had replaced the fear in her eyes. "But I need to take this slow because I'm not sure how things work between two girls."

Dax slumped against a brick wall, the weight of the world lifting for more reasons than she'd previously considered. Then her cheeks flushed at the cause. "That's a relief. But, to be honest, I'm not sure how it would work either." She understood how sex worked between a man and a woman, but she was at a loss beyond the things she'd fantasized about Rose doing to her.

Rose pressed against Dax again and gave her a brief, yet toe-curling kiss. "I'd like to figure it out with you." Her lower seductive tone sent a shiver down Dax's spine.

* * *

Dax had woken on Sunday, eager to carry out the plan she and Rose had made yesterday, but minutes ago her father said he had a job for her. She regretted not having a brother, especially a teenage one, for the first time. Maybe then her father might not have given in when she was ten and begged to watch him in his woodshop. And maybe Dax wouldn't have taken an interest in following in his footsteps, and he wouldn't have taught her everything about his job.

Instead, she had learned framing to flooring to cabinetry to trim work. Two years ago, he'd told her she'd become more skilled than he was. *"You're a fine carpenter, even better than me in most things with those small hands. It's a shame no one will hire a woman carpenter, but you can be my apprentice. With that small chest of yours, no one will be able to tell you're a girl if you wear a hat. We can rename the company Xander and Son."*

Until today, Dax didn't mind that he depended on her. The work put some money in her pocket, though only a fraction of what he would pay a real apprentice. Those few dollars and the ability to earn a living made her barely concerned when she nearly failed tenth grade for lack of attendance. Her principal, thankfully, had considered her ability to make up the work and solid "B" average and passed her along with her classmates.

Today, though, Dax wished she'd never picked up a jack plane. She had had the day all planned out. Her father would be installing a new floor across town, and her mother would be at the church, helping with the late service. Rose would come over after finishing her chores following the morning church service. They'd go into Dax's room and pick up where they'd left off in the alley. But then her father ruined everything. If she didn't come up with a way out of this, she'd spend the morning cutting and hauling planks of wood for him and Rose would think she'd chickened out or, worse, had changed her mind.

After breaking for lunch in her father's jalopy, eating the sandwiches and apples her mother had packed for them, Dax feigned a stomach cramp.

"Was it the food, Darlene?" her father asked. She rolled her eyes. Her given name was too girly for her taste, but thankfully, school was formal, and her teachers called her Miss Xander all day.

"I don't think so, Papa. It's my time, and I didn't bring anything today. I need to go home."

"This is why no one will ever hire a woman as a carpenter. They're unreliable." He waved his hand dismissively. "Go, girl. Take care of things. I'll expect your help tomorrow. No school for you until this job is done."

"Yes, Papa." Dax took off on foot at a slow jog. Once out of her father's view, she settled into a faster pace all the way home.

Upstairs, Dax stripped off her sweaty clothes, estimating she had a few minutes until Rose would arrive. After handwashing the smell away, she put on the shirt she'd worn to church that morning and her favorite knickerbockers. They were loose, so she added suspenders to keep them in place. A peek in the bathroom mirror necessitated a quick run of the comb through her chin-length, straight brown hair. Finally, blowing into both hands found her breath on the safe side.

Before falling asleep last night, she'd fantasized about how she wanted their first time to transpire, down to everything she wanted her and Rose to do to each other and how she wanted her bedroom to look and smell. The lacy pillow from Mama's couch and a sprig of lavender from the garden were the perfect touches.

She looked good in her Sunday best, and her room was neatly picked up. She was ready. The state of being ready, though, brought out an enormous case of the nerves. She sat on the bottom stair, bouncing a leg up and down like a piston in her father's Tin Lizzie, as he liked to call his Model T. What she and Rose were about to do would forever change their lives and friendship.

A double, double tap on the door, her and Rose's secret code, meant Dax had run out of time. Her fretting was over. She opened the door to the most beautiful sight in the world—Rose in her floral blouse and rose-colored church skirt. Dax had seen her in it a dozen times, but today Rose had never looked more stunning. She'd done nothing different. Her hair and shoes were the same, but the glow about her had Dax's hand glued to the doorknob and feet nailed to the floorboards.

"Y-Y-You g-g-gonna l-l-let me in?" Rose asked. The glow, Dax realized, wasn't an amorous effect. Rose's stutter had returned, which meant she was as nervous as Dax. Gentle reassurance was in order.

Dax pulled Rose inside, double-checking across the street to confirm the neighborhood busybody didn't have her sights set on her house before closing the front door. Once safely inside, Dax rubbed Rose's arms and softened her tone. "Nothing will happen that we both aren't ready for. Okay?" Rose's silent, rapid nod wouldn't have been encouraging without her faint grin. "Would you like to go upstairs? My folks won't be home for hours."

The instant Dax laced their fingers together, Rose rewarded her with a tender squeeze and a soft whisper in her ear. "Yes."

That one word sent Dax's heart into a tumult so loud she heard it thumping in her chest. Her knees turned weak, but that didn't deter her. Instead, she tugged Rose along, one stair at a time, until they reached the top landing. Pulling their clasped hands against her chest, she searched Rose's eyes for any sign of doubt. She found none but had to ask one more time. "Are you sure?"

"With you, yes." Rose stepped closer and craned her neck. The sweet scent of roses wafted upward—a dizzying perfume Rose had worn only once before for Dax at May's wedding reception at the house. The tender kiss she gave Dax signaled that reversing course wasn't on the agenda. Yet.

Twisting the knob to her bedroom, Dax was pleased to find the subtle smell of lavender. It masked the musty smell of her school blazer hanging in her closet after drying. The bed, made with perfect hospital corners any nurse would be proud of, had never looked better with fresh sheets and the living room pillow her grandmother had brought with her on a Conestoga all the way from St. Louis.

She didn't think the thumping in her chest could get more substantial, but a locomotive rumbled through her at full steam when she closed the door. More of her came alive, the parts that ached both times when she and Rose kissed. The same parts she swore had burst when she laid awake thinking of Rose last night.

Rose sat gingerly on the side of the bed, folding her hands in her lap. Her gaze inspected the room from corner to corner. "It l-l-looks a-a-a-and smells different. Is that your m-m-ma's pillow?"

The tips of Dax's ears tingled with embarrassment. Rose had caught her red-handed. Until today, she'd never put on airs for anyone. Not for the pastor. Not for her parents. The closest she'd come was to bite her tongue when May married Logan Foster, some fancy investment man who never looked at May the same way May looked at him. He'd seemed more interested in gaining a wife for what she could do for him than building a life with her.

"It's nothing." Dax snatched the pillow and threw it into the hallway. She leaned against the door, regretting not acting like herself.

"I liked it." Rose grinned. Besides her stutter nearly disappearing, that was the most disarming thing she could have done. She patted a section of the bed next to her. "Sit."

Dax did. The length of their thighs touched, transforming her uneasiness into desire. But diving right into kissing seemed indelicate. Rose was special, and acting like Tommy and the other sex-crazed boys in school was the thing Dax wanted to avoid. Accordingly, she took Rose's hand in hers and focused on the floral pattern of her blouse. "You look pretty."

"You look good in knickerbockers, but your suspenders nearly made me faint."

"How so?"

"They made me want to touch them." Rose shifted, twisting at the waist to face Dax. The hunger behind her eyes matched the wanting lingering in every breath Dax took. "May I?" She raised a hand. Slowly. Tentatively.

Dax nodded in the same slow, tentative fashion.

Rose traced the strong cotton webbing with an index finger in an agonizing, deliberate descent starting at the shoulder. Then, at the top of a breast, she veered off course and grazed the white shirt fabric, pressing lightly enough along the curve to send a jolt to the tips of Dax's breasts.

Sharp intakes of air ended in breathy exhales from them both.

Dax pressed their lips together in their third spellbinding kiss. Tongues caressed in a sensual dance. But where their previous encounter had stopped at this steamy juncture, the private setting emboldened her to take it further. Much further.

Dax encouraged Rose to lie on the bed by leaning forward without breaking their kiss. Every inch down was an eternity in torturous anticipation. The moment Rose stopped flat on the mattress, Dax caught up, pressing her full weight. Her skin tingled beneath her clothes where their bodies touched, giving birth to a field of goose bumps. It was as if a cool breeze had kissed her all over.

Dax couldn't wait a minute longer to turn fantasies into reality. Shifting to one side, she drifted a hand to a breast. It was heavenly suppleness hidden beneath a thin layer of a vibrant floral pattern. A squeeze turned into a rub, which turned into a heart-stopping nipple tease. The heat in her center continued to rise, making it impossible to keep the rest of her still. She rocked her hips into Rose, re-creating the glorious pressure she felt yesterday when she pressed Rose's center against her in the alley. No wonder every adult wanted to have sex. This was beyond exquisite. It knocked her for a loop.

Rose broke the kiss, visibly out of breath. Her chest heaved to the rhythm of Dax's heartbeat. "I want your mouth on it." Not a single stutter, only fluent words wrapped around carnal desire.

Dax curled her toes in her shoes at the imminent prospect of turning another fantasy into reality. She slid further to one side, pulling on fabric to release the lower section of the blouse tucked into Rose's skirt. Rose squirmed beneath her and helped it along, exposing more luscious skin each fraction of a second until she'd revealed a single brassiere cup.

On the verge of her brain overloading, Dax raked her tongue along Rose's soft skin, starting at her waistband. Each lick was like sweet cream, more tantalizing than the last. Abdominal muscles quaked in her wake, urging her to continue her path. When she reached lace sewn over cotton, Rose gasped. "Please."

Dax pushed the remaining fabric out of the way and latched her mouth onto the breast. Between feverish sucks and swirls, she realized every adult in her life was wrong. Anything that felt this good couldn't be evil. No boy ever had her romanticizing for a single day. Rose, on the other hand, had her fantasizing for months. Dax preferred curves over chiseled muscles, soft skin over hair and whiskers, and wanted to give pleasure as much as receive it. She was sure no man could ever live up to her definition of sexy.

The familiar sound of the bedroom door creaked open. Dax froze at her mother's voice. "Why is my pillow—"

Rose instantly covered herself. The deafening silence that ensued crashed the walls on top of Dax. She could take her father's swatting, even a brutal beating within an inch of her life, but not her mother's constant browbeating and words of damnation and going to hell. Dax swung her head around to discover the fury brewing on her mother's face, and right then, she knew her life would never be the same. And knowing her mother, neither would Rose's.

Being caught by a parent while having an intimate encounter was terrible enough, but being caught with Dax by her mother was mortifying. If Dax were a boy, perhaps Rose wouldn't have felt as if life as she knew it was about to end. Her parents would have likely considered it a youthful indiscretion. But Dax was a girl, and so was Rose. That was unforgivable. Both their mothers were volunteers at the same church, and neither had any tolerance for what their pastor called sin and the law deemed immoral.

Terrifying didn't come close to describing the scene Mrs. Xander created. Despite Rose begging for her to stop, she slapped Dax with both hands until both eyes were swollen and her lower lip dripped blood. Rose would have been rendered unconscious, but Dax remained strong. To her credit, Dax had raised her arms only to deflect the continuous blows. She took the beating without lifting a hand to her mother until Mrs. Xander turned her rage on Rose.

Rose retreated to the corner of the bed and curled into a ball with her hands protecting her head.

"Mama, no!" Dax yelled at the first slap. When the second didn't come, Rose looked up to find Dax had placed herself between the bed and her mother, taking the blows intended for her.

"Stop! Stop! I'll leave." Rose's plea created a pause in the attack.

"I will march you home." Mrs. Xander's stern tone and expression left no room for argument.

Rose inched forward. Once she was within reach, Mrs. Xander grabbed her by the upper arm with the crushing force of a vise. She dragged Rose out of Dax's room and down the stairs. When Dax quickstepped down the stairs behind her, Mrs. Xander stopped and pointed an index finger in her face. "Don't you dare leave this house."

Before Mrs. Xander pushed Rose out the door, Rose locked eyes with Dax. The heartache swirling in them matched the anguish enveloping Rose. She was sure this would be the last time she'd see Dax's adorable face. She'd never again kiss her pillowy lips. Never again know how sweet her body felt against hers. Over time, she feared she'd forget what it was like to melt into the strength and softness of Dax's arms around her, so she tried to commit to memory every sensation she'd felt minutes ago.

Rose reached out, hoping for one last touch, a loving caress that could last her a lifetime. Dax extended a hand. They were inches apart, but when Rose leaned to extend her reach, Mrs. Xander yanked her out the door. Dax obeyed and remained at the threshold, tears pooling in her eyes as in Rose's.

"I love you, Rose." The pain in Dax's voice ripped Rose's heart to shreds. Though Rose felt it in her bones, she didn't dare return the words, fearing Mrs. Xander might wrench her arm out of its socket.

Dax's mother kept her word and marched Rose in a humiliating fashion the four blocks home, increasing her grip when entering the walkway leading to her front door. Rather than letting Rose open the door to her own home, Mrs. Xander knocked. Revulsion dripped from her stiff, perfect posture, forming a pool deep enough for Rose to drown in.

When the door opened, Rose dipped her head, unable to meet her mother's eyes. She wasn't ashamed of what she and Dax had done. On the contrary, it was beautiful and made her feel more alive than anything she'd ever experienced. She was, though, petrified of the consequences beyond belief.

Her mother asked, "What is this, Caroline?"

"May I come in?" Mrs. Xander asked.

Her mother replied, "Of course."

Mrs. Xander released her grip and walked several steps inside, but she turned sharp on her heel when Rose didn't follow. "Unless you want the entire neighborhood to learn of your sins, I suggest you get inside this instant, young lady."

Rose minded and followed Mrs. Xander to the parlor, keeping her chin pinned to her chest. She couldn't look her mother in the face because it would change into something more terrifying than Mrs. Xander's once she learned the truth. After that, she would likely no longer have a home here. She had heard how the pastor encouraged parents to deal with unruly children by sending them away to learn discipline. That fate, she feared, would soon become hers.

"Look at me, child, and tell me what you have done to upset Mrs. Xander," her mother demanded, but Rose stood her ground. She wanted a few more moments of knowing that she still had a home near Dax and could still meet up with her somewhere on Alameda Island. "Look at me this instant, or face the belt when your father gets home."

Rose complied by lifting her head, but that was as far as she could go. She said nothing and imagined where her parents might send her. Would she end up in some camp for wayward children, where they worked all day for pennies, producing rope for the shipyards or sewing hats for the wealthy tourists who visit Neptune Beach?

"The belt then." Her mother turned to Mrs. Xander, whose expression implied she'd accept nothing less than seeing Rose burned at the stake. "Caroline, please tell me what has happened."

Mrs. Xander stiffened her spine again as if preparing herself to battle Satan for saying the coming words. "I'm ashamed to say that when I came home, I found our daughters in Darlene's bedroom, engaged in a sin against God."

Those words sealed Rose's fate. She would go somewhere to learn discipline, and Dax would become a distant memory. Settling for what was expected of her would be Rose's only way out.

CHAPTER THREE

Rose got her wish. She would never step foot into Alameda Senior School again. Regrettably, it came true under circumstances more insufferable than the humiliation she'd suffered for desiring it. She had convinced herself she could survive four and a half years of exile. Once she turned twenty-one and could legally decide things for herself, she would return to Alameda and reunite with Dax. But her mother crushed that aspiration with the news that Dax's parents had sent her away. Making the situation worse, each set of parents had pledged to never reveal their daughter's location. She had no way of ever finding Dax.

The sum of Rose's life before three days ago had been reduced to the clothes she had on, the suitcase sitting on the bench seat beside her, and the small steamer trunk stuffed into the back of her father's Model T. Her mother had thrown out any reminder of Dax that was among her belongings. But she managed to hide one photograph Dax had given her in the binding of a book. That one item would have to sustain her.

Rose scanned the streets on both sides when their car rumbled through the neighborhood, hoping to see Dax one last time before leaving Alameda for good, but she had no such luck. The only positive aspect of this entire ordeal, if there was one, was getting to ride the Oakland Harbor Ferry for the first time and ride through the streets of San Francisco in a car like a wealthy tourist.

Rose was unsure of their destination, and asking questions would have earned her the belt. However, before she and her father departed Alameda, she'd overheard her parents talking. Her mother had mentioned, "The ocean air might be what she needs, not the musty smell of the bay." Her father had replied, "Busy hands are what she needs." That meant wherever he was taking her, she'd be put to work. Rose was no stranger to working. She had been in charge of the vegetable garden since she was eight, household laundry since she was ten, and after Conroy died, the cooking duties when her mother volunteered at church. Rose suspected more of the same.

A chill seeped into the car's interior when her father crested a hill an hour after departing Alameda. White tendrils of fog out the window to her left crawled up the cliffside like campfire smoke reaching up to the sky. The mist became patchy in spots to her right, revealing an angry ocean of white-capped waves crashing the cliffs below. The road twisted like the corkscrew her father used to open the Christmas wine and then narrowed, pushing the car wheels dangerously close to the cliff's edge in one turn.

"Gosh. That's scary." Rose's breath caught in her chest.

"It's a long way down from Devil's Slide," her father said. "It gives you too much time to think of your own death if you go over the edge. Unfortunately, the same will happen if you don't straighten up. Do you understand what I'm saying, Rose?"

"Yes, Papa." The pastor and her mother were clear yesterday. Her feelings for Dax were unnatural and would lead to an eternity in hell if left unchecked. Apparently, there was more than one way to slide with the devil.

After passing farms on both sides of the highway and a horse ranch between the road and the shoreline, a sign welcomed Rose to Half Moon Bay, a city she never knew existed. Her father downshifted to slow for pedestrians, arms loaded with picnic baskets and blankets, crossing the road toward the marina. "Tourists." Her father's tone dripped with animus born from years of working the ferry dock and welcoming San Francisco tourists to Neptune Beach, Alameda's grand attraction.

Once the gaggle cleared, he ground the gears to get up to speed again. They passed a two-story hotel decorated with colorful cloth awnings over the entrance and a porch that ran the length of the building. Further down the main road was a smaller two-story building. The sign atop the main door labeling it the Foster House reminded her of Dax. Rose remembered her saying during her sister's wedding reception at her house that her sister, May, had married a man named Foster. She punched herself in the leg, figuring the pain might get her mind off Dax. It didn't work.

Her father pulled his car to a stop in front of a small white house a few blocks inland from the main road. Then, turning off the engine, he said, "Let's go, Rose."

She grabbed her suitcase while he retrieved her trunk from the back of the car. A strong man, he hoisted it over a shoulder and led her up the concrete walkway. A tree she wasn't familiar with kindly provided shade to the front porch.

"Give it a knock." He held onto her trunk like a sack of potatoes.

Rose did. Moments later, the door opened to a short, brown-haired woman she'd never met. Her light blue dress and white stockings were nondescript, but the white bibbed apron meant she was likely a waitress. "Michael, come in. How was the trip?" She opened the door wider, inviting him inside.

"Long. Where do you want her things?"

"Down the hall. The room on the left." While her father trekked down the corridor, the woman gave Rose a glaring inspection from eyelashes to oxfords, like a warden sizing up the new prisoner. Whatever her name was, she didn't appear pleased to be taking in a sixteen-year-old troublemaker.

Pressure grew in Rose's bladder—the perfect excuse to delay the browbeating she appeared ready to unleash on her. "It was a long ride. May I use the bathroom?"

The woman raised her chin, sharp with indignation. "Down the hall to the right."

Once Rose flushed and washed up, she heard her father's voice through the door. "I don't care if you don't want her. You owe us after we took in your bastard son and raised him like our own. I would've never agreed to it if you weren't family. When she turns twenty-one in five years, it's up to you whether you keep her."

What did he say? Did he mean Conroy? It all made sense. It explained why her father was always distant with her brother and wasn't devastated by his death. Rose had a thousand questions, starting with when did her parents take in Conroy and ending with who was his real father.

"You know that wasn't my doing," the woman said.

"You're the one who willingly got pregnant, so it makes no difference. I want no argument from you, or Morris will get an earful."

Secrets apparently ran deep in her family. Rose opened the door and cautiously returned to her father. He handed the woman a twenty-dollar bill. "This should cover expenses until she earns her keep." After she stuffed the money into her apron, he turned her attention to Rose. "Rose, this is your mother's cousin, Ida. Her husband is Morris. You'll stay here at night and work in their diner during the day. You mind your p's and q's. Do you understand?" She nodded, too afraid to open her mouth yet. "I suspect we won't see you for some time, so give your papa a hug."

Rose wrapped her arms around his firm midsection. He smelled of dirt and sweat from the trip, but that didn't bother her in the least. When it was time for her mother to say goodbye, she had stood in the parlor with her arms crossed and refused to look in Rose's direction. At that moment, Rose knew she was no longer her daughter. At least her father offered this much. It made her think she still might have a father.

He kissed her on the top of her head, cleared his throat, and pulled back. "If things work out, I'll try to visit in the spring." The math—spring was nearly six months away—told Rose her childhood was over. The moment he walked out the door, she was on her own, with a distant cousin as an employer and landlord.

"Come with me." Ida's curt tone made it clear that Rose's stay wouldn't be pleasant. She didn't wait for a reply before heading down the hallway. When she turned into the only room on the left, Rose followed, gripping her suitcase for dear life. "This will be your room. I'll expect your bed made every morning and laundry done, including sheets and towels, every Thursday." She walked to the closet, which was the width of a door, and retrieved a dress and apron on a hanger matching her own. She handed it to Rose. "This is your uniform. You'll work the lunch and dinner shifts waitressing and helping cook and clean from noon to ten every day but Monday. We're closed on Mondays except on holidays during tourist season. In exchange, we will provide you three meals a day, a bed, and a place to shower. In addition, you may keep any tips you earn. Do you have questions?"

Rose shook her head no. Opening her mouth seemed unwise, if not a trap.

"Good. One last thing. Morris and I will not tolerate any perversion. Therefore, you may not invite anyone into this home. Is that understood?"

Rose's first impression was dead-on. Ida was the warden, and she was her prisoner.

* * *

One suitcase was all Dax needed to fit the things her mother had allowed her to keep. Her two sets of knickerbockers were now ashes in the backyard burn pile, along with her school uniform. But that last item was Dax's contribution to escalating hostilities in the Xander household. She'd rather see them in flames than have her mother collect a dollar for selling the skirt she hated to another student. Dax especially didn't want anyone else wearing the blazer under which she and Rose had shared their first kiss. That was one invasion she could repel—the one thing she could control. No one would ever desecrate that precious memory.

Besides losing Rose, the one thing that hurt the most was how her father said nothing and did nothing to contradict her mother's edicts. Sadly, it was the first time those two displayed a unified front regarding their daughters in years. Her father never liked the man May married, but her mother had said a stockbroker was a step up in the world. At the same time, her mother never approved of Dax working with her father, calling it unladylike. And when he'd bought her a pair of knickerbockers to make it easier for her to climb up ladders, her mother nearly fainted at the gossip it would generate.

Dax could easily replace the clothes one piece at a time by saving up. The four dollars and thirty-five cents she'd hid in her shoe before her mother had torn apart her room would get her new knickerbockers and she'd still have change left over. But she couldn't replace the most cherished possessions her mother had burned—the only picture she had of Rose and the blue hair ribbon Rose once gave her to wrap around a cut finger. She had nothing but memories of her sweet Rose.

Likewise, the endless hours Dax and her father had spent together on carpentry jobs meant nothing. He didn't bother giving her a hug goodbye before walking out the door this morning. Instead, he left twenty-five cents ferry fare for Dax to get to May's house. "He was too ashamed to face you," her mother had said. *Pathetic*, Dax thought. It was okay for Dax to dress up like a boy when it suited him for work, but when she acted like one in matters of the heart, suddenly, she was the shame of the family.

"You're lucky your sister has agreed to take you in," her mother snarled. "None of my or your father's siblings would have you."

Dax snatched the quarter from the entry table. Then, without a single glance toward her mother, who stood motionless near the bottom stair, she walked out of her home for the last time. She was nearly seventeen and an accomplished carpenter and was sure someone at a woodshop would hire her once she proved her skills. Then she could get a place of her own and track down Rose.

Every step of the two-mile walk to the ferry landing solidified Dax's resolve. She was done with childhood. She was done with living under her mother's thumb. She'd take what her father had taught her and make her way in life.

Dax arrived at the wharf minutes before the next scheduled departure. She was the last to queue to board and pay her fare. The dockworkers heaved at the lines, preparing to cast them off when the captain gave the order. One man looked up and kept his stare on Dax. If she were a man, she suspected he would have risen to his feet and beat her to a pulp for having defiled his daughter. But Dax was a woman, and a beating would raise questions, the type, she hypothesized, he couldn't risk being asked. So instead, he drilled her with his eyes, casting a quiver full of arrows at her heart. She'd never see Rose again.

Dax boarded, handed over the last thing she'd ever accept from her parents, and took a position near the railing at the bow. She refused to look back, only forward to a new life. Once they were underway, she tucked away her recollections of Rose into a safe recess in her mind and let the bay water spraying her face wash away every terrible memory of Alameda. But their kisses, the curve of Rose's face, and the stammer in her voice would be the only thoughts to survive the eighteen-minute ride to San Francisco.

The moment Dax stepped foot off the ferry and took a deep breath, she felt free. But she knew that feeling would only last until she showed up at May's door and Logan laid down the rules. Until then, though, she would take full advantage of her freedom.

Suitcase in hand, she headed for a women's dress shop on Market Street. The racks contained a mix of everyday and party dresses, none of which captured Dax's attention for herself. Several, though, she thought would look fabulous on Rose.

The remains of last year's marked-down knickerbockers were in the back of the store. Two dollars were well worth being able to ditch the stupid dress her mother made her wear. They were a little loose like the pair her mother burned, so another stop was in order. Further up Market Street, she stopped in a men's dress shop and steered toward the markdown bin. One dollar and seventy-five cents later, she walked out with a striped, button-down dress shirt and a handsome pair of suspenders that were near replicas of the ones that had made Rose faint. It was money well spent to look her best when they finally reunited.

Finally, she dipped into a department store a few blocks up and strode directly to the women's bathroom. The stall made for a snug and not the cleanest changing room, but she couldn't stand one more minute in that darn dress. The instant she slipped off the unnecessary undergarments and put on her new outfit, she felt like herself. She walked into that stall as the girl her mother wanted her to be and walked out as the person she was. She was boyish on the outside but still a girl on the inside. Unlike the boys and men Dax knew, her feelings ran deep. She cried when she read *Romeo and Juliet*, was more intuitive and creative than her father, and valued love and relationships like her sister.

The smudged mirror above the sink confirmed her selections from the waist up were on the mark. Rose would swoon if she could see her. She stuffed the dress into the garbage can near the sink and walked out, suitcase in hand and head held high. After the first three miles of battling the steep hills of San Francisco toward Haight Street, where May and Logan had a corner house, Dax decided her next purchase would be a better pair of working shoes to replace the silly school oxfords she had on.

By the time she reached May's house, her feet and legs ached so bad she thought she'd walked for forty days and nights. She trudged up the three steps to the porch and plopped into a chair, leaving her suitcase near the door. The view was beautiful. Across Stanyan Street was the edge of Golden Gate Park. The chatter of children screaming and laughing in the nearby playground outstripped the birds chirping in the trees lining the street. Dax could listen to those soothing sounds all day long.

A hand on Dax's shoulder startled her. She must have fallen asleep.

"Darlene, when did you get here?" At twenty-one, May had shed the round, youthful face in Dax's first memories of her. Nearly three years of married life had been good to her. She looked fit and not worn out, as Dax remembered her when she lived at home. Their mother had been as demanding with May as their father was with Dax.

"Not long ago." Rested now, Dax jumped to her feet. "I like your hair." May had tied her straight brown hair into a relaxed bun, leaving a few strands loose on both sides of her face. It was perfect for the woman of the house, yet quite attractive.

"Not as many chores with a clothes washer and not as many dishes with Logan taking most meals at work. I have time to do my hair every day." May extended her arms. "Do I get a hug?"

"Only if you call me Dax. I hate Darlene."

"You drive a hard bargain." May waved her closer with both hands and gave her a warm, welcoming hug. Other than one from Rose, Dax hadn't received one of those since May's last visit over the holidays. That was nearly ten months ago. May cast her head toward the door. "Let's get you settled, Dax."

"Thanks, May."

May led her upstairs. Her sewing room at the end of the hall had been converted into a tiny bedroom. Her long face suggested she wasn't happy with the accommodations. "I'm sorry, Dax, but Logan insisted on keeping the guest room ready for other guests, especially his parents. This was the best I could do on short notice."

"This will do fine, May." The room was nearly half the size she was accustomed to, but it had a bed and dresser—everything she needed. She didn't plan on becoming a homebody, so the cramped conditions didn't bother her.

May sat on the bed and patted a section of the mattress next to her. "Sit." May continued when Dax plopped down next to her, "Tell me what happened. Mama only said that you sinned."

If there was one person in the world Dax trusted to confide in, it was May. With their four-year age difference, May was her protector as soon as Dax could walk. Until the day she moved away, she had shielded her from their mother's demands, doing Dax's chores over again when Dax didn't get them right. She took the blame several times when a dish or glass got broken despite her not being anywhere in sight. May was the best big sister Dax could have asked for. Telling her about Rose was long overdue.

"I'm not ashamed of what I did. Loving someone can never be wrong."

"Loving? No. But doing something about it can be. I might not agree with everything the church teaches, but I agree you should cling only to each other once you're married."

"It didn't get that far. At least I don't think it did."

"Don't think?"

"Well." Dax rubbed the back of her neck, uneasy with getting too specific. "I'm not sure what counts between two girls."

"Ah. Rose. I always wondered when you two would figure out that you had feelings for each other."

"You knew?"

"The way you looked at her? It wasn't hard to figure out. I'm surprised it took Rose this long to catch up." May patted Dax's thigh. "But Logan won't stand for any of that here."

"Do you plan on telling him?"

"Not on your life."

CHAPTER FOUR

San Francisco, California, 1925

If Dax's mother thought sending her to live with May and Logan was a punishment, she was sorely mistaken. One day under their roof, while not perfect, was an improvement over the seventeen dismal years she'd spent with her parents. Money was regularly scarce with her parents, and Dax often missed school whenever her father needed help. Moreover, he never paid her full wages for her work and never expected her to succeed despite being exceptionally skilled.

She proved him wrong five years ago, within her second month in San Francisco. Putting on her newsboy cap to hide her hair and thick jacket to hide her chest and curves, she'd walked into the woodshop four blocks from May's house. She'd introduced herself as Dax with a firm handshake and then demonstrated her skills with every tool in the shop, intentionally keeping from the owner the fact that she was a girl until he hired her.

"I'll be damned." He'd scratched his head. *"Not a man on my crew can handle a blade or carving tool like you can. Where did you learn carpentry?"*

"My pa. He's been a carpenter all his life, and I've been helping him since I was ten. He said I was really good at finishing work because of my small hands."

The shop owner had rubbed his stubble for several awkward beats as if debating the intelligence of hiring a girl to do a man's job. "Keep that hat on when you're in the shop or on a job site and don't tell anyone, for crying out loud."

The part-time job paid decently but not enough to afford a place of her own in this part of town. Dax got the impression that if she were a man, he'd pay more, but she wasn't in a position to complain. As frustrating as it was five years after women had earned the right to vote, the laws were on his side, and she still couldn't take him to task.

This morning, she put on her blue flannel shirt, work pants, boots, and suspenders and then slipped her newsboy cap over her short hair. Deeming herself properly dressed for work, she grabbed her thick denim jacket and headed to the kitchen. The appetizing smell of bacon and freshly brewed coffee greeted her halfway down the stairs, turning that slight hunger pain in her stomach into an angry growl.

She snatched a piece of toast from the kitchen counter. "Bacon, eggs, *and pancakes*? Must be a special day."

"I wish." May whisked the scrambled egg mixture. "Something is wrong with the icebox again. Much of the food spoiled, so I'm cooking up what's left before it goes to waste."

"That's a lot of food. I don't think you and I can finish all of it."

"Some is for Logan if he can keep it down today."

"Is he any better?"

"He's a big baby." May rolled her eyes. Logan had a weak disposition with ailments. He'd stay home for the sniffles. "It's a stomach bug. I'd be up washing clothes if I were only as sick as he is. If he can't get the food down, I'll take a care package to Mr. Collins next door."

"Did you reach the repairman? I can walk to his shop. It's on the way to my worksite today."

"That won't be necessary. Logan said it's time to replace it with one of those new refrigerators at The Emporium." The smile that had formed on May's face dropped in an instant. "But since he's sick, he wants *me* to pick it out after breakfast."

"But The Emporium is halfway across town, and you hate cable cars." Dax remembered the one time she rode one of those with May. Her sister had held on for dear life, explaining she feared she might fall out and roll to the bottom of Hyde Street.

"I do, but what choice do I have? There's no way Logan is getting out of bed today."

"This is silly. Let me help." Finally, Dax had an opportunity to help May and return the kindness she'd shown her the past five years. "I should finish the job around noon today. I'll hurry home and take you in Logan's Model T."

"That would be wonderful. I'm so glad your boss taught you to drive his pickup because those cable cars scare me like the dickens."

"Me too. Hey, I have an idea. Since all this food you cooked won't keep, I'd like to treat you to a late lunch. That big tip I got last week is burning a hole in my pocket."

"You should save your money."

"I haven't splurged all year. Please let me do this for you." May's face glowed the same way it did whenever she opened a birthday or Christmas present. Her lips crept upward until she smiled with her eyes. Dax didn't have to wait for an answer. "Thank you."

Dax left the house pleased she could finally do more for May than help around the house. She was equally delighted to be working at the Portmans' home, repairing a staircase and handrail her husband said had loosened during last month's tremor. The main draw was Mrs. Portman, a cute redhead not much older than Dax. Yesterday, her pretty blue eyes inspected Dax up and down every time she looked up, far too many times to attribute it to curiosity. Despite enjoying Mrs. Portman's special attention, she had played it safe and limited her part of their conversations to one- or two-word replies. The most disappointing aspect was that she couldn't be sure if Mrs. Portman knew she was eyeing another woman. Dax's clothes and how she carried herself should have led her to believe otherwise.

Dax knocked on the door, inexplicably straightening her hat and smoothing the wisps of hair around her ears. What the heck was she doing? Even if Mrs. Portman extended more glances, she was married, albeit to a man who likely abused her. Despite the woman's claims, Dax was sure the four straight bruises on each arm didn't come from falling down the stairs. She wished she could do something about it but feared anything she said or did would only make things worse for Mrs. Portman. Perhaps minding her own business was the best course of action, and Dax should simply finish the job and be on her way by noon.

The door opened.

The smile Mrs. Portman had greeted Dax with the previous two days was missing, which disappointed Dax more than it should have. Not since Rose had anyone given Dax a smile that made her feel desirable. It was a silly indulgence that would likely end in disaster, so Dax brushed off the letdown and greeted her with a tip of her cap. "Mrs. Portman."

"Please come in, Dax." Mrs. Portman's voice sounded weaker than it had the previous days. She opened the door wider, her face grimacing when she waved Dax inside. "How long do you think you'll be today?"

"About three hours." Dax placed her toolbox on the floor near the bottom of the stairs. The home was by far the nicest she'd been in since her boss started sending her out on jobs instead of working in the woodshop. Her boss had told her that Mr. Portman was a banker and a very important customer, but this house was over-the-top ornate.

"Fine. My husband said he'll be home a little after twelve to inspect your work." Her tone remained flat. "I'll be in the kitchen if you need anything."

Dax followed Mrs. Portman out of the room with her eyes. Her gait contained a stiffness that wasn't there yesterday. It reminded her of the time she walked funny after falling from a tree when she was nine. Her body was sore all over, and her ribs had ached something awful.

She reminded herself that Mrs. Portman's condition was none of her business and went to work. She inspected the railing where she'd left off yesterday and noticed a section of the banister she'd already replaced was loose again. What the heck? She'd told them not to put pressure on it until she'd completed the repairs. Her three-hour job had now turned into four. If she worked fast, she could still make it back home in time to take May to The Emporium.

Dax picked up her pace but didn't sacrifice craftsmanship. Not a single customer had complained to her boss about the quality of her work, and she wasn't about to break that streak. Forgoing a break, Dax had worked up a good sweat by the time she'd finished and packed up her toolbox, leaving it by the front door. A glance at the wall clock in the parlor confirmed Mr. Portman would be home soon. The only thing left was for him to inspect her work to ensure she'd done the repairs to his satisfaction.

Dax went to the kitchen to bother Mrs. Portman for a glass of water. She found her sitting at the small dining table, holding a teacup. Her eyes were tear-filled, red, and puffy as if she'd been crying the entire three and a half hours Dax had been working. The nearly broken railing suddenly made sense and confirmed Dax's earlier suspicions. She kneeled in front of her. "Are you all right?"

The defeated look in Mrs. Portman's eyes broke Dax's heart. No man should ever subject a woman to cruelty, especially the wife he'd sworn to love and protect. She kicked herself for not speaking up to May or Logan or to the neighborhood flatfoot walking his beat yesterday when she returned home after working here.

"He hurts you, doesn't he?" Her continued silence made Dax's heart ache that much more. Dax wiped a tear from an eye. "What can I do to help?"

"I don't know." Mrs. Portman's trembling lips echoed the fear Dax had seen in Rose when she had to read aloud in class. Dax wanted to make her fear go away like she did in school.

Without thinking, Dax caressed and cupped a soft cheek. *At least the brute was careful not to mark up her beautiful face*, she thought. Mrs. Portman leaned into her touch. She closed her eyes to the release of a breathy sigh.

"I haven't been touched like this for a long time."

If Dax were prudent, she'd pull back, grab her toolbox, and get out of there as if the house were on fire, because what she wanted to do next was playing with fire. But prudence was an impossibility once she'd focused on Mrs. Portman's lips. When she looked up, Mrs. Portman had done the same. *Don't do it*, Dax told herself. Saying it in her head on a continuous loop failed to dilute the potent force pulling her toward those tempting pink lips.

Mrs. Portman had every opportunity to flinch, pull back, or turn to the side. To do anything that would tell Dax that she didn't want a kiss equally tender as Dax's caress. But she didn't. Mrs. Portman's eyes fixated on Dax's lips, drawing them further in like a magnet. Dax couldn't break free if she wanted. Then she remembered her mother outlining her fate for kissing another woman. *"You'll burn in hell for playing with the devil."* That was it. She resigned herself to getting burned.

Dax had discounted her mother's rant as religious blathering, but what if Mrs. Portman held the same belief? She couldn't lay that at her feet among the rest of her troubles. So she dug deep, the deepest she'd ever tunneled inside herself, for restraint. She stopped her slow advance and pulled back. "I can't do this to you, Mrs. Portman. I'm not who you think I am."

"It's Heather." She caressed Dax's cheek, still focused on the mouth aching to kiss her. "And I know who you are, Dax. After your first night working here, I saw you at Baxter's Grocery Store with a woman. She called you young lady."

Heather removed Dax's cap and placed it on the table, tying Dax's stomach into a hundred knots. But when her expression turned soft as Rose's did that time in among the poplar trees at Sweeny Park, those knots gave way to a burst of boldness. Dax cupped Heather's cheeks and pulled her closer. Electricity charged the surrounding air, intensifying with each fraction of an inch forward. As it did with Rose.

Their lips touched, the current between them sparking a fire guaranteed to send them to Hell. Every muscle, tendon, and inch of skin ached for Heather's touch, but neither was in the right state of mind for more than a kiss. Heather suffered from her husband's torment, and Dax still pined for her long-lost Rose. Five years had passed, yet every night in bed, her lips tingled for Rose's kiss, and each burning breath she took seared the image of Rose half-naked beneath her into her soul.

Heather deepened the kiss, the third time pressing harder. Their tongues met, caressing in a moist erotic dance that sent jolts to Dax's core. Each gentle stroke awakened dormant parts that hadn't been alive since the day Rose had blown life into them. And when Heather fell to her knees, pulling their bodies together, those parts roared so loud Dax thought of nothing but tending to them.

Dax slid her arms around Heather's back to feel the pressure of their breasts pressed hard together. It felt more magical than every fantasy she'd ever concocted. Then in the next instant, Heather flinched and groaned in pain. Dax drew back.

"Did I hurt you?"

"My ribs are sore from last night."

Dax guided Heather into her chair. She fought back the urge to track down Mr. Portman at that bank of his and give him a taste of his own medicine. But if she did, Dax feared it would only make things worse for Heather, and she'd never see this delicate creature again. "What can I do to make it bearable for you?"

"Kiss me again."

And Dax did. A need to make Heather feel safe replaced the ache in Dax's core. She hoped to remind Heather what it was like for someone to kiss and hold her like lovers should, soft and gentle. They exchanged not a single word, only touches. And when Dax pulled back, the pain behind Heather's eyes receded into the unmistakable look of longing for something more.

A car coasted up in the gravel driveway on the side of the house. Heather's eyes filled with fear again. "It's him."

Dax rose to her feet, hoping for a chance to do something more for her soon. "It will be fine. I'll wait by the door."

Heather grabbed Dax's arm before she stepped out of the kitchen. "Can I see you again?"

If a heart could smile, Dax's did. "I was going to ask the same thing."

An hour later, Dax was behind the wheel of Logan's Model T with her sister by her side, a fat tip from Mr. Portman in her pocket, and a grin on her face. She pulled into the dirt lot next to The Emporium. Historically, parking there was haphazard, but Dax had read in the paper the owners had assigned an attendant to direct people where to go. She followed the teenage boy's hand waving near the lot's exit. Leaving would be a snap after May was done shopping for her new refrigerator. A whopping two hundred and seventy-eight dollars later plus a four-dollar delivery fee, May had her new Kelvinator picked out with the promise that The Emporium's crack crew would have it set up in her kitchen by noon tomorrow.

On their way out, Dax spotted a lunch stand across the street. It looked like the perfect place for her to spend her tip and finally repay May's kindness. She gestured toward it. "Up for some lunch?"

"Absolutely." May linked arms with her sister and crossed the street at the corner with a pep in her step. If Dax had known taking her sister to lunch would elicit this type of reaction from May, she would have done it long ago.

Inside, a row of fifteen red-topped stools stretched alongside a lengthy rectangular, marble- and chrome-faced counter. Mugs and glasses had been stacked in pyramids atop the back counter, creating a mesmerizing geometric pattern against the back wall. Two waitresses buzzed back and forth behind the other side, filling coffee mugs and water cups and serving plates a runner had brought from the kitchen.

Dax and May sat on two neighboring stools. Dax grabbed the stiff paper menu stuffed between a napkin dispenser and a ketchup bottle. The most expensive item was a steak sandwich on a toasted roll for a dollar, including soup, mashed potatoes, and steamed carrots.

The waitress popped by, memo pad and pen in hand. "What will it be, sir?"

Dax never corrected people in public regarding her gender when dressed in her work clothes. Why would she? It only defeated the purpose of her dressing up that way. "I'll have the steak sandwich, and so will my sister."

"That's too much, Dax. I can't."

Under any other circumstance, May's concern would have been valid. When Dax invited her sister to lunch, she'd planned to spend the dollar and fifty cents she'd made in tips on her last few big jobs. But she couldn't wait to blow the silver dollar Mr. Portman had flipped in the air for her to catch on her way out today. Spending it on anything other than something that would be gone in the next half hour would only remind her of that man's cruelty. What better way to get rid of it than to get something frivolous.

"Nonsense. It's your favorite, and that's it." Dax turned her attention to the waitress, raising her index and middle fingers. "That will be two steak sandwiches, two glasses of water, and a banana split for dessert."

"Coming right up, sir."

After the waitress scurried off, May used a playful tone. "You're Miss Money Pants today."

"It's a long story, but I can't wait to spend the tip I got today."

May spun on the stool to face Dax, resting an elbow on the counter. "Well, you have until the end of lunch to spill the beans."

Dax debated how much to tell May, but what was the point of feeling so good if she couldn't share it with the one person in the world closest to her? She couldn't, though, betray Heather's confidence and risk any of what they did together today getting back to her husband. At most, she could couch her news in vague terms.

"I've met someone."

May's face lit up. She cupped Dax's hand that was resting on the counter. "That's wonderful, Dax." She then leaned in, her voice barely loud enough for Dax to hear. "Are you being discreet?"

"We will." Dax thought back to the kisses she and Heather shared earlier today. Her heart hadn't pounded like that since her last day with Rose. She hoped today wouldn't be the last time she'd feel that way with Heather.

"I'm very happy for you." May squeezed her hand before letting it go. "But I don't want to see you hurt again."

"I don't know how this will work out, but I hope it does."

The good feeling Dax had talking about Heather left her the instant she thought of her mother. Living with May and Logan had been good. Until today, she'd considered being sent there as punishment as having backfired. But once Dax kissed Heather and held her in her arms, she realized her mother had succeeded for the last five years. She'd denied Dax the pleasure of sharing bodies and the joy of being with someone she loved.

They finished lunch, chatting about unimportant things. Once they relished the final spoonful of ice cream and syrup and Dax paid the bill, she and May returned to Logan's Model T in The Emporium's dirt lot. She pulled onto Market Street, heading toward Golden Gate Park and May's home. It was the most direct route, and with the new electric stop-and-go traffic signals, it was also the safest route.

"I get that you have to keep things secret, but tell me what you can about this woman you've met." May's interest seemed genuine, a loyalty Dax could rely on from her sister.

"She has beautiful red hair, a smile that melts my heart, and she's sweet as can be." Dax came to a stop at a traffic light.

"I wish things were different and I could meet her. It sounds like she's quite special."

The light switched to "Go," and Dax pressed the gas pedal to move forward, daydreaming about Heather's soft lips. "She is."

A loud honk.

Skidding tires.

A metal-crushing jolt.

Shards of glass flew in the air, forcing Dax to slam her eyes shut.

Logan's Model T came to an abrupt, wobbling halt. When Dax opened her eyes, she realized they'd been hit from the side. May's side. The crash left Dax dazed and able to focus only on the steam or smoke rising from the hood of their car. She shook her head to clear the ringing and looked to her right. May's head and body were slumped toward the middle of the bench seat. Blood was trickling down her right temple.

"May! My God, May!"

The door on May's side was crushed and bent into her side of the cab. Broken glass lay everywhere. Her lower right leg was bent at an unnatural angle. Panic set in. Dax shook May by the shoulder, hoping, praying for a sign of life. When she didn't wake, Dax placed her hand on May's chest. *Thank goodness.* It rose and fell, but slower than Dax expected.

Someone pounded on Dax's side window. A male voice yelled, "Are you all right?" The door opened, and he started to pull her out, but Dax shrugged off his hand.

"I'm fine. Help my sister. She's hurt bad."

"We can't get to the door. It's blocked by the pickup. We need to get you out first."

Dax slid out unassisted. She finally got a good look at the man who had tried to pull her out. His crisp dark-blue uniform with silver buttons running down the front of his jacket matched his seven-point silver badge. His nametag read Decker. He was a police officer. She stood by while he reached inside the crumpled wreck and pulled May out. Mercifully, she was unconscious. Dax couldn't bear it if her sister were in agony.

A second man, likely a butcher judging from his stained white apron and matching cap, helped the officer with May's other arm and dragged her to the pavement several yards from the wreck. Now that May was out, her leg almost appeared normal, but that positive development failed to ease the dread seeping into Dax's pores. May was hurt, and it was her fault. It had to be. Her mind had been on what could be with Heather and not the road.

An hour later, following a bouncy ambulance ride to Bayside Hospital, Dax sat in the blindingly white hallway. She twisted her newsboy cap in her hands, not caring who might recognize her and see that she was a woman. It didn't really matter. The only people in the hallway were a nurse and the police officer who had dragged May from the car.

An antiseptic smell permeated the hallway while Dax waited for news and for Logan to arrive. The scent served as a constant reminder that May was in the fight of her life. Dax hated to think the first time she'd dialed her sister's house phone was to tell her husband she'd been in an awful accident that she had caused.

Soon the swinging doors flew open, and Logan marched toward Dax like a steamroller ready to crush anything in its path. He yanked Dax from her chair by the collar. His scowl alone was enough to frighten Hercules into a quivering mass.

"What did you do, Dax? I knew you were trouble from day one." His words came out spitting mad, enough that Dax smelled bacon on his breath. Likely the bacon May cooked for him earlier this morning. He was such a faker.

The officer approached, puffing out his chest. "Is there a problem here?"

Logan pointed an index finger in Dax's face. "This one here crashed my car and put my wife in the hospital."

The officer nudged Logan back several feet, giving Dax breathing space. "I witnessed the accident, sir. She did nothing wrong. The truck driver ran the traffic signal."

That was news to Dax. So why in the heck didn't the officer speak up sooner? He could have saved her hours of gut-wrenching self-blame. But Logan's death stare gave her the impression the officer's eyewitness account didn't excuse her part in the accident. She felt the same. She'd thought her light read, "Go," but couldn't be absolutely sure because she had been thinking more about Heather's kisses than concentrating on the traffic signals. That was something she could never forgive herself for.

A doctor dressed in all white appeared in the hallway, drawing everyone's attention. He was taller than most and seemed to be exhausted. He looked at Logan. "Are you Mr. Foster?"

"Yes," Logan said plainly. "How is my wife?"

"She's resting now. Luckily, she had no internal injuries. I repaired both broken bones in her lower right leg with plates and screws. I've seen breaks like this before. It should heal, but she'll likely have a noticeable limp for the rest of her life."

Dax slumped in her chair, hands covering her face. A dam of guilt broke, making her fear the wasteful steak lunch she'd shared with May would soon appear on the spotless white hospital floor. She rocked back and forth, unable to come to terms with what the doctor told her.

"What have I done?"

CHAPTER FIVE

Half Moon Bay, California, 1925

Five years of plodding the mile between Ida's home and the café had gotten Rose nowhere. She'd worked for pennies with nothing to show for it but new bedding and towels to replace the ratty ones Ida had provided and four new outfits to better fit how she'd filled out since moving into town. The trench coat, umbrella, and galoshes were necessary purchases to battle the rain, fog, and ocean mist that accompanied her on most trips.

Tips from locals were dismal year around, a dime marking her best take-home pay in a day during the off-season. But from July through September when the vacationers made their trek to Half Moon Bay from San Francisco and other parts of California, Rose could take home as much as a dollar a day. The Fourth of July traditionally marked the opening of tourist season. This year it fell on a Saturday, making it also the perfect day for the grand reopening of the Seaside Hotel after the new owner had made repairs from the New Year's Day storm. Today she expected close to two dollars by closing.

Rose finished pinning her hair up, tied her white apron around her uniform at the waist, and put on her light jacket.

The outer layer wasn't for the warm trip to work but for the chilly walk home in the dark when her shift was over. Then, purse in hand, she locked up and began her daily walk. When she reached Main Street, she stopped in front of Edith's Department Store like she had done every day on her way to work since the week following Easter. Peering through the spotless plate-glass window, she eyed the silver hairbrush and mirror set Edith had put on display several Mondays ago. It was so pretty and looked exactly like the one her mother had passed down to her when she turned sixteen. The same one her mother refused to let Rose take with her. *"It stays with the family,"* her mother had said. *"It was my mother's, and you're no longer a daughter of mine."* Without question, the brush set was a luxury, but when Rose could spare twelve dollars, she'd buy it and hand it down to her daughter when she turned sixteen.

Her gaze drifted to the right side of the display. Edith had put out two beautiful new hair ribbons but hadn't laid out a card with the price. One beautiful strip of blue silk caught her eye, and right then, she had to have it or at least had to ask how much it cost. She opened the door, and the bell fastened along the top of the frame announced her entry. She smiled the instant the bell stopped because Edith had Rose's favorite record playing on the Victrola. The first time she heard the words, the song had reminded her of Dax. For three months straight, Rose came by on her day off and asked Edith to play it until she knew every word by heart.

Rose paused to take in the song "That Thing Called Love" and let the lyrics sweep her away. She grazed a thumb across the top of a breast, remembering the heart-pounding sensation of Dax's mouth against it.

A hand fell to her shoulder. "Still have your eye set on that silver set, Rosebud?" Edith was about Rose's mother's age, maybe a little older, with the same dark wavy hair as her mother's. Her kind face matched her disposition, and her slight pooch said that she enjoyed Rose's pies a little too much. She'd given Rose that nickname to distinguish between her and her daughter, who lived in another town with her own family and who had the same name. The youthful reference was a sweet reminder Rose still had a few more years to marry before the meddlers in town considered her a spinster. If the time ever came, Ida would likely lead the busybody pack. *Funny*, Rose thought. Women had the vote for five years, yet most women still considered each other unproductive unless they had a husband.

"Maybe by the end of tourist season." Rose was likely more optimistic than she should be, but since turning twenty-one last month, she had the feeling her life would change this year. She had reached the age of majority finally and could legally make decisions independently. So the first opportunity that came along, she would jump on it. Anything would be better than working for pennies. "But I was interested in that blue ribbon. How much is it?"

Edith walked to the display window, rolled the ribbon around her index and middle fingers and offered it to Rose. "One slice of your fresh apple pie and a few songs from that beautiful voice of yours. Drop by after you close up tonight."

"You're so sweet, Edith, but I can't." The first night Rose met Morris, he laid down the law—neither charity, alcohol, or perversion would enter his house. Accepting the ribbon would likely bring the law down on her.

"You can, and you will. Besides, you're paying for it with your talent and hard work." Edith placed the ribbon in Rose's hand and cupped it with hers. "But we won't tell Ida."

To hell with it. She accepted Edith's gift and kissed her on the cheek on the way out. Reaching the end of the building, she slipped into the alley and pulled out the photograph she'd kept in a hidden compartment in her purse since her first night in Half Moon Bay. A portion of the image had since rubbed off, so she'd stopped running a thumb across Dax's face years ago to preserve the only reminder of her first love. Every time Rose peeked at Dax dressed in her silly school uniform, showing off her short brown hair and slight smile, she became misty-eyed, pining for what she'd lost. This instance was no exception.

Wiping away the tears, she clutched the ribbon tighter in her other hand, wondering if Dax still had the one she had used to bandage a finger cut six years ago. She remembered that day as if it were yesterday. When she'd held Dax's hand and carefully wrapped the cut finger, her heart had thumped faster and faster like the drum corps competition on the Fourth of July. And when Rose had kissed the finger after tending to it, she knew she had a crush. That was the first time she'd wanted to kiss Dax on the lips. But that was a lifetime ago.

After returning the photograph to its hiding place and depositing the ribbon next to it, she walked to work. The café was bustling, which meant Ida and Morris would be in a cross mood by the end of the day. They preferred the quiet of the off-season and barely tolerated the chaos of tourist season that had started today. Despite operating one of only two sit-down restaurants in Half Moon Bay, they didn't rake in enough money from the local traffic to pay the bills and let them close for one week twice a year for vacation. Rose braced herself for three months of misery, starting today.

"It's about time," Ida barked, balancing three plates of food on her arms. She pointed toward the far wall. "Those tables need bussing."

Never mind that Rose had arrived ten minutes before her shift started. Ida and Morris never gave her credit for hard work and discipline but never failed to gripe if she chipped a plate for rushing to meet their demands.

"Yes, ma'am." Rose bit her tongue and focused on the possibilities tourist season might bring. Someone could offer her their hand in marriage, which Rose would accept in a heartbeat to escape this prison.

Barking orders and snide looks persisted until the end of her shift. Ida had left hours ago, but minutes earlier Morris had closed the kitchen and left after coldly instructing Rose to finish cleaning and lock up for the night.

The main door opened, and two men walked in. With fewer than eight hundred full-time residents in town, Rose knew most of the locals. She recognized Frankie Wilkes, the new owner of the Seaside Hotel, but not the other man. They appeared a lot alike, tall with broad shoulders and dark hair, but Mr. Wilkes appeared a few years younger than the other.

"I'm sorry, Mr. W-W-Wilkes, but M-M-Morris has already gone home for the night."

"Opening day was so busy that my brother and I didn't have time to eat before our little kitchen closed for the night."

"Oh, I d-d-didn't know the Seaside has a place to eat."

"I'm making lots of changes. I plan to make Half Moon Bay *the* vacation destination on the West Coast. Think of it as the Pacific version of Atlantic City."

"That's a tall order, considering this town's track r-r-record." Rose recalled the previous owner of the Seaside Hotel had similar plans. Tourists came, but only from the San Francisco area. He sold two years later.

"You'll see. That day will come. How about some coffee and some of your apple pie?" Mr. Wilkes and his brother sat at the lunch counter.

"That I can do." Rose retrieved two coffee mugs from the wall counter, placed them in front of her customers, and filled them. Then, after saving a piece for Edith, she cut the remaining pie into two generous portions, served them, and left the bill in front of Mr. Wilkes. "Enjoy, fellas. H-H-Holler if you need a-a-anything."

Rose grabbed the last bucket of dirty dishes and retreated to the kitchen. Setting up at the sink, she began the monotonous chore of washing and drying virtually every plate, glass, and piece of flatware in the café. Her mind drifted to the song playing at Edith's. She started with a hum and then broke out into song.

The swing door leading to the dining room jarred open, giving Rose a start. "I didn't mean to frighten you, Rose, but was that you singing?" Frankie Wilkes asked.

Rose's face flushed with embarrassment. Only Dax, Edith, and her best friend, Jules, who worked as a nurse for the town's only doctor, had heard her sing. They'd said she had a beautiful singing voice, but she had chalked it up to each simply being a kind friend. "Yes, sir. I'll stop."

"Please don't. It was quite good," Frankie said. "Have you ever sung in front of a crowd?"

Rose shook her head no. With her stutter, she never considered singing as a profession, and now she wondered why. That was one of the few situations during which her speech was consistently fluid.

"Well, think about it. The singer I hired for my basement club bailed on me. What is a new hotel and club without a singer?"

"I c-c-c-couldn't."

"I'll pay you five dollars for a test run. Then, if the crowd doesn't boo you off the stage, I'll pay forty dollars a week during tourist season. Twenty dollars off-season."

Forty dollars! Rose only saw that much in a month and a half when tourists flocked to town during the summer. That amount of money would be her parole. She could afford a room at the boarding house where Jules lived and never have to obey Ida and Morris again. It was enough for her to ask, "When w-w-w-would I start?"

"Tomorrow night. You'd sing two one-hour sets at seven and nine, four nights a week, Thursday through Sunday. How about it? Yes or no."

Tomorrow night? Her chest fluttered with nerves. She didn't know enough songs to take up an hour. And if she had to talk to the crowd besides singing, she'd crumble like a sandcastle at high tide. "Just sing. No ta-a-alking."

"Just sing." He smiled.

Maybe, just maybe, she could close her eyes and pretend she was in the shower or in Edith's upstairs kitchen long enough to sing a few songs. How could she turn down good pay, three days off, and more than three waking hours to herself a day? Easily. If she didn't show up for her shift on Sunday, she wouldn't have a place to live on Monday. She had every reason in the world to say no, but only one to say yes—her freedom.

"Yes."

Half an hour later, Rose knocked on the door of Edith's darkened department store, holding a wrapped slice of apple pie, along with an entire half of a peach cobbler. She was about to ask the biggest favor of her life and hoped pie would serve as the perfect currency.

The door opened to a smiling Edith. "Right on time, Rosebud. Come in. I thought we could share that slice before you sing for me."

Rose held up the cobbler. "I have another favor to ask."

"Anything for you, Rosebud." Edith led her to the second story of the building, where she and her husband lived, and into the kitchen. Their big house, Edith had explained, was a waste of space and money after their daughter, Rose, moved out, so they sold it and moved above the store. She placed the peach pie in the icebox. "Henry is in bed, so I'll make sure he gets a slice for lunch tomorrow." She gestured toward the kitchen table, already set with two dessert plates, forks, and filled water glasses.

"So thoughtful, Edith."

Once they sat, Edith split the serving in half. "Now, tell me about this favor of yours."

Stuttering, Rose explained Mr. Wilkes's offer and how he expected her to give his piano player, who could play anything, a list of songs before noon so they could rehearse. "Can I listen to your r-r-records tonight? I need to learn the w-w-words."

"This is wonderful news, Rosebud. I've been telling you for years that you have a beautiful voice. It's about time others get a chance to hear it. Let's pick out an hour's worth of music. I'm guessing about sixteen songs. I'll even loan you the records so your piano player can listen along tomorrow."

Sixteen? This was going to be a long night.

By morning, Rose had written down and memorized the words to seventeen songs. Neither Al Jolson nor orchestra music was her style, so she selected bluesy ones. Then, precisely at noon, the time she was supposed to start work at Ida's Café, she reported to the basement club at the Seaside Hotel. The entrance, an inconspicuous door next to the laundry room, was guarded by a large, brawny man, someone she'd never seen before.

The room's red-tufted leather benches and stools with dark rich wood tables, chairs, and counter in the back were like something out of *The Saturday Evening Post*. Rose had heard the stories about the luxurious Neptune Beach Club in Alameda growing up, and this had all the earmarkings of its lavishness. With room for about a hundred patrons, this place was as big as Ida's Café, but it was a thousand times nicer.

The corner stage was big enough for a standup piano and Rose, but not much more. A dark-skinned man, the first she'd seen in Half Moon Bay, was sitting at the piano, eating lunch. "You m-m-must be Lester." She extended her hand. "I'm Rose."

"Frankie said you were pretty." Lester wiped his hand on his pant leg and shook her hand. "He was right."

"W-W-What's up with the guard?"

"You don't know?"

"Know w-w-what?"

"Oh boy. You really are green. Frankie warned me." Lester's tone contained more surprise than frustration, which was an excellent sign. Rose needed all the patience he could offer today. "The club sells whiskey. The guard down here lets in only people with the password, so the prohis can't sneak in."

"Oh boy" was right. Rose was going to be working in a speakeasy, a job she'd never envisioned for herself. Dax maybe, but not her. She knew the law—outside of drinking a private stash collected at home before Prohibition began, it was illegal to make, sell, or transport liquor. She'd read the stories in the *Half Moon Bay Review*, though, detailing how local mayors and sheriffs all over northern California refused to enforce the liquor laws, leaving that task to federal Prohibition agents that some people called "prohis."

"Got it." Rose was satisfied that the risk of getting swept up in a raid was low and worth taking to secure her ticket out of servitude.

"Did you bring a song list?"

Rose raised the stack of records Edith had loaned her. "R-R-Right here. I thought it w-w-would be easier."

Lester thumbed through the records, a big toothy smile forming on his lips. "Now we're talking. I'm gonna like working with you, Rose." He offered her the other half of his sandwich.

"I c-c-c-couldn't." She politely waved him off.

"It's free for employees. We can always get more."

Rose was going to like working here. Ida kept track of every meal she ate at the café and eyed her as if she'd held up the city bank if she took an extra roll for her lunch break.

Over the next few hours, Lester put Rose at ease, remaining patient when she'd forgotten some of the words. "Just hum if that happens on the stage. If you later remember the words, give me a wink, and I'll play the verse over again. If not, we'll move on to the next song."

"Any more tips?"

Lester stepped out from behind the piano and approached Rose. He gestured toward the microphone. "Do you mind?" When she shook her head in the negative, he gently cupped the shiny piece of metal in his hand. "You're a little stiff when you sing. You should sing into the microphone like you're making love to it."

A heat grew in Rose's cheeks, yet Lester appeared as comfortable as he was when she first walked in. Was this how all entertainers talked? Was sex an open topic with them? Surprisingly, she didn't mind the idea.

"We don't have much room up here for dancing." Lester demonstrated as he talked. "But if you add a little sway and occasionally caress the mic, the crowd will love it. Every man in the room will want to take you home."

Rose's eyes widened.

"But it's my job to make sure they don't get close enough to ask."

"You w-w-want me to tease."

"Exactly. I got a question, Rose." Lester shifted to look at her straight on. His eyes were soft and caring. "Don't take this the wrong way, but your words stick a lot when you talk. But when you sing, they flow out like water from a spigot. How is that?"

"I don't know. It just is."

"All right then. This should be a good show tonight."

After taking Edith's records back to her and thanking her, Rose returned to the club. At five minutes before seven, she was standing with Lester in the corridor leading from the club's kitchen to the main floor. She peeked through the small, chin-high glass window on the door and estimated the club was half-full. Still, fifty people were more than she expected. Her hands shook. "Oh boy."

Rose had hoped to perform well and convince Mr. Wilkes not only to hire her but also to give her an advance so she could make today the last day she'd call Ida's house her home. But first she had to get over her nerves. She tried Dax's advice—*"Take a deep breath, relax, and focus on the first word."*—but it didn't help. She'd never gotten up in front of a crowd before.

Lester tapped her on the shoulder and waved a pewter flask in front of her face. "Here. Take a good swig."

Rose hadn't considered drinking a possibility besides a few sips of wine at holiday dinners growing up. It was illegal. But her nervous state required a more flexible way of thinking. She took one good belt and then another, the sweet-tasting liquid burning all the way to her stomach. She returned the flask to Lester. "Thanks."

"You'll do fine. If you get nervous, look at me like we did in rehearsal."

They took the stage, the room humming with conversation and laughter. Mr. Wilkes and his brother occupied the nearest table, telling Rose this performance was her big test. She smoothed the sleeveless red velvet evening dress Edith had loaned her from her inventory for the evening. *"We can't have you looking like a waitress on that stage,"* Edith had said. *"This one matches your name, Rosebud."*

Lester had kindly agreed to do the introductions, so all Rose had to do was sing. He tapped the glass of water sitting atop the piano with a spoon, bringing the warmly lit room to a hush. "Ladies and Gents. The Seaside Club is proud to present a new voice guaranteed to get your toes tapping. So put your hands together for Miss Rose Hamilton."

Rose's mouth went dry as an army of butterflies took flight in her stomach. For a moment, she considered turning tail and running out the secret door, but the second Lester tapped out the opening notes on the piano keys, she took a deep breath and remembered Dax's advice. She sipped from the water glass and then, on a count of eight, she belted out the Mamie Smith song she knew by heart and sang it as if she were alone washing dishes at the café.

Before she knew it, she'd uttered the last word of the seventeenth song and Lester had whispered to her, "Take a bow."

Until then, she'd been too afraid to look at the crowd and see their reaction. To her surprise, every man and woman was clapping. So were the Wilkes brothers, each with a smelly cigar hanging from his lips. Rose even heard a few whistles from the back.

"Thank you, folks," Lester said loud enough for the furthest table of people to hear once the applause died down. "Miss Rose will be back around nine o'clock. So drink up until then."

When Lester scooted his piano bench back, scraping it against the stage floor, Rose exited to another round of applause. Then, after the door leading to the kitchen corridor flapped closed behind her and Lester, she plopped against the wall, feeling like she'd run ten miles on that stage. "That was"—her chest heaved—"amazing."

Lester gripped both of her arms, his face beaming with excitement. "You were incredible, Rose. Everyone loved you."

"They did." A burst of energy shot through Rose. Unlike during rehearsal, when she'd envisioned the audience throwing eggs and tomatoes at her after she belted out the first note, every hand in the room had clapped for her. She bounced up and down like a little schoolgirl.

The door swung open, and Frankie Wilkes walked through, holding a cigar between his middle and index fingers. "That, young lady, was more than I'd hoped for. The job is yours if you want it."

The elation in Mr. Wilkes's voice emboldened Rose. She wouldn't let the opportunity of a lifetime pass through her fingers. "Thank you, but I have a p-p-p-problem."

"What's that?" he asked.

"My r-r-r-room comes with my job at the café. I'll need a place to stay, but I have no m-m-m-money."

Mr. Wilkes pulled a wallet from his inside suit breast pocket and handed Rose a twenty-dollar bill. "A half-week's advance should be enough to get you settled into a room at the boarding house. I own it, so I'll send word to Mrs. Prescott to expect you tomorrow. I'll send a bellhop to your house in the morning to pick up your things."

"How can I th-th-thank you?"

"Thank me by performing tonight's late show as well as you did the first. Then do it all over again starting Thursday. We'll have a packed house every night with a voice like yours."

The second show went better than the first. Thankfully, Rose's nerves had settled without a taste from Lester's flask. He was kind enough to see her home, and they'd agreed to meet up at the club around two on Wednesday to rehearse and maybe pick out different songs.

Rose tiptoed into the darkened house at nearly midnight, expecting Ida and Morris to be sound asleep. Except to freshen up in the morning before showing up at the club for the first time, she hadn't been home since she left for work on Saturday. And she'd missed an entire shift without a word of explanation.

The hallway light directly over Rose flipped on like a stage spotlight. She stopped in her tracks, cringed, and braced herself for the holy hell Ida was about to unleash. Rose had no intention of taking it this time.

Ida screeched behind her, "Where have you been. First, you break curfew, and then you don't show up for work. You made our day impossible."

Rose turned around. She struggled but failed to hold back a snicker. Ida looked like she'd buried her face in a cream pie with the excessive cold cream she'd applied that night. "First, this is the first day of work I've missed in five years. Second, I'm twenty-one. A curfew is laughable."

"We won't stand for you coming and going as you please. We have a business to run, and we need our sleep. So if you want a roof over your head, you'll show up to work when you're expected and be in by midnight."

"Well, I don't. I've had all I can stand from you. I'll clear out my things in the morning." Rose paused to consider every word that came out of her mouth, and they flowed like milk from a bottle. She was spitting mad, which helped, but she was also more confident than she'd ever been. She marched to her room, snatched the uniform and apron she'd come to hate from their hanger, returned to the hallway, and shoved them in Ida's hands. "I quit. Find yourself another girl to boss around."

"Ha! The Foster House has a full staff. You have no other skills. No one will hire you." Ida lathered on the snark as thick as her face cream. "You'll come running back in a day because you can't afford to live anywhere else."

"That's what you think." Rose debated how much to throw back at Ida. She considered bringing up the juicy tidbit about Conroy but decided to table that for a time when she really needed to put Ida in her place. She could brag about a job that paid her more in two weeks than she could make all tourist season in tips. She could go on about being handed enough money in one night to support herself for two weeks. But she wouldn't give Ida the opportunity to fire back with predictions of failure. Instead, she decided, she would take satisfaction by walking into the café next week, having Ida serve her, and leaving a lousy tip.

"Go back to bed, Ida." Rose slammed the door in her face and flopped flat on her bed with a giant smile. Ridding herself of her servitude felt better than she had ever imagined.

CHAPTER SIX

Half Moon Bay, California, Summer, 1926

For five years, Rose had relied on Ida for her survival—a roof over her head, food to eat, and enough money to put clothes on her back. She'd relied on Frankie Wilkes for the same thing for one year and had already been paid more money than she'd seen in all her time under Ida's ruling thumb. Even though she could lose everything with one false step, Rose felt respected working for Frankie.

Rose decided she'd hitched her wagon to a winner. In one year, Frankie was well on his way to making Half Moon Bay the Pacific Coast's answer to Atlantic City. He'd bought the business next door to expand the hotel and had his eye on every property in the marina. His social connections had attracted a regular stream of politicians from Sacramento and movie stars from Los Angeles. But the larger crowds came with drawbacks. A year of singing in an underground speakeasy at a tourist destination during Prohibition had taught Rose one crucial lesson: alcohol brought out an animal instinct in most people. Men or women, it didn't matter. Inhibition went out the window. And with a hotel right upstairs, sex was on the agenda every night for the lucky few who had a room.

Since moving to Half Moon Bay, Rose had either lived under the eye of Ida or Mrs. Prescott at the boarding house. It was impossible to bring anyone home. Still, she refused to debase herself like other locals her age who used every public bathroom, alley, or shed in town as options for impromptu privacy. Rose instead quenched the needs herself. But it wasn't as if she didn't have offers. Nearly every man who got drunk at the Seaside Club, married, dating, or unattached, had at one time tried to get a free touch or made a pass at her.

Not a single patron had caught her eye, but a woman sitting at the front table tonight had a particular way about her. Handsome with slicked-back dirty-blond hair, she was alluring in a men's tuxedo tailored to accentuate every curve. Fortunately, the woman's male companion appeared more interested in the sculpted waitress who had served their drinks.

At the end of Rose's final set of the evening, before she left the stage, a server handed her a folded handwritten note. It read, *Join me for a drink and whatever else you want.* When she asked who had sent her the message, the server pointed toward the tuxedo-clad woman. Rose thanked her but not before eyeing the most intriguing thing she'd seen since Dax.

Rose thanked Lester for another fine session and agreed to meet him the next day an hour earlier to go over a new song he wanted her to try. "Ready to go home?" he asked. He'd been walking her home during tourist season ever since a drunk followed her home last August.

"I'll be fine tonight, Lester. You go home to that pretty wife of yours."

"You be careful, Rosebud." It required only one dinner with Edith before a show for Lester to take to Edith's nickname for her. Even Jules started using it after visiting the department store with Rose. Heck, she split so much of her time between Lester and Jules that sometimes Rose thought her name *was* Rosebud.

"I will." She rubbed his arm, thanking him for his concern, but her instinct told her she wouldn't want to be careful. The woman who had written that note made her want to throw caution into the ocean and let the current take it out to sea. As far as she knew, she was one of only three lesbians in town, was the only one not in a relationship, and was the only one who had yet to discover the joy of sex with a woman. It was about time she changed that sad fact.

The moment Rose stepped toward Tuxedo, the woman whispered into her tablemate's ear. He stood and walked away. Rose stopped at the woman's table and extended her hand. "I'm Rose. You said a drink." Maybe the woman's note had laid to rest the mystery of whether she had desires like Rose. Or perhaps it was the way the woman eyed her like she was the finest cut of meat in all of San Francisco, presenting a sense of inevitability that put Rose at ease. In any case, she wasn't nervous, only anxious.

"I'm Grace." She shook Rose's hand and held on longer than social graces dictated. She glanced at a bottle and two filled glasses on the table. "I took the liberty of ordering champagne. Join me."

Rose sat in the chair directly to the woman's left, matching her relaxed posture by leaning back with her legs crossed at the knees. "I appreciate a w-w-woman with good taste."

"I appreciate one who tastes good." Grace's comment came without warning, but more importantly, it left Rose throbbing. An image of Grace between her legs, lapping her up like long rolling waves against the shoreline, sent a burst of fire to her center no self-stimulation could douse. "Frankie has been holding out on me. When did he hire you?"

"Last July."

"I wish I had made a better effort to change my schedule last year. My husband and I come through here several times during the summer."

"Schedule? W-W-What do you do?"

"I do a little acting."

Rose studied the woman further, cocking her head to the left. Movies didn't interest her, but the fashions the women wore in them did. The magazines had page after page of Hollywood starlets in their gowns and the occasional suit, many of which inspired the outfits Rose wore on stage. Then it dawned on her. "You're Grace Parsons."

"Guilty as charged." Grace dramatically raised her drink before elegantly taking a sip. When Rose emptied her glass in one gulp, Grace added, "Does that bother you?"

"Not in the least, but w-w-what about your h-h-husband?"

"He's off chasing that gorgeous waitress who handed you my note." A picture formed. Rose had read of lavender marriages in the *New Yorker* last year when the magazine first came out but thought the article was an exaggeration. But, considering her interaction with Grace, Rose stood corrected.

"Are you staying at the h-h-hotel?"

"Separate rooms. We have an understanding about our distractions."

"Is that w-w-what I am? A distraction?"

"Does that bother you?"

"Not in the least. I'll grab my things and meet you." Rose's newfound boldness came as a surprise. Spending a year watching bartenders and waitresses leave with guests and one another had apparently rubbed off on her. "W-W-Which room?"

"Three-twelve."

Rose tapped the champagne bottle on the table. "Bring extra."

Backstage, gathering her things, Rose felt like anything else but herself. The Rose Hamilton who left Alameda in shame would never be so forward, never go off to a hotel room for a romantic rendezvous. But that version of her no longer existed. Years of living under Ida's rule had slowly drained the life out of her. Now it was her time to live.

After assuring herself that no one else was in the corridor, she knocked on the door leading to Grace's room without hesitation. When it opened, her mouth watered at a new delicious sight. Grace had removed her jacket, exposing the sexiest pair of suspenders draped over both breasts that rose and lowered with each breath. Her leering was shameless.

"Lord," Rose gutted out, her center clenching on the only word that conveyed her appetite.

Grace guided her inside, giving Rose her first glimpse of a Seaside room. It was plusher than she imagined, with blue velvet drapes and matching bed covers. The crystal bowl filled with fresh fruit atop the small dining table was an unexpected touch. Two champagne bottles and glasses sat beside it. "More champagne?" Grace offered.

"Please." Rose didn't need liquid courage, but she had to lay waste to every ounce of inhibition to make her first time memorable. Accordingly, she demonstrated partial restraint and drank only half in one gulp.

"Nervous?"

"First time."

"First time that you're nervous?" Rose answered Grace's question with a slow headshake. "Ahh. Are you sure you want to do this?" Rose replied with a slow nod. She then downed the remaining champagne in her glass.

Grace finished her drink, took Rose's glass from her hand, and laid both on the table, giving Rose a long questioning look. Rose offered zero doubt and let a building lust-filled smile confirm her desire. She was already pleased with herself, having deflected every offer from a man. The idea of rough, sweaty hands on her and coarse whiskers chafing everywhere he might kiss her had long lost its appeal. Tonight, at long last, she would know the ecstasy of sharing bodies with a woman.

Rose inched forward until their legs touched. She didn't know how to start, but she knew what she wanted Grace to do to her. Several inches shorter than Grace, she wrapped her arms around Grace's neck and wedged her right knee between her legs, raising it until it pressed into her center. Both their mouths hung open.

"For your first time, you certainly know what you're doing." Grace captured Rose's lips in a searing kiss and walked her backward until her back hit a wall and their bodies pressed together. Soft lips relaxed every muscle like warm bath water, while Grace's moist tongue sent a consuming ache to Rose's core. Hips rocked into Rose in an agonizingly slow rhythm, clearly designed to heighten the anticipation. It worked. She wanted Grace's lips and hands everywhere, inside and out.

Grace shifted. Hands cupped each breast, squeezing at the same tormenting, unhurried pace. Her tongue went deep into Rose's mouth, consuming her like a gasoline-fueled fire. Heat built between Rose's legs until it became unbearable. She pressed both hands against Grace's bottom and pushed her hard into herself to smother the heat, but it only increased it tenfold. Finally, she ripped her lips from Grace's.

"Bed."

"You're sure?"

"God, yes."

Grace guided Rose toward the bed. She positioned herself behind Rose and worked the zipper on the back of her stage dress. Feathery kisses trailed the newly exposed skin. Dipping each shoulder, Rose let the loose fabric fall to the floor. Grace unclasped Rose's flapper brassiere. Rose never felt more alive when it fell to the floor, joining her dress. Grace then spun her around and, without warning or hesitation, took both breasts into her hands. Rose no longer controlled her body. It quaked uncontrollably.

Grace stepped back and positioned her hands to lower her suspenders, but Rose stopped her. "Let me." She slid a hand between each suspender and Grace's white shirt at the shoulder, skimming down both breasts to their tips. Her stare followed her hands' path, fueling her need to touch more of Grace. She flipped the suspenders off Grace's shoulders and unbuttoned her shirt as quickly as her dexterity allowed.

The shirt opened, revealing no brassiere and two tempting breasts. Rose took them into her hands for the first time, and they felt like the most precious gems on earth. She could lose herself in them for days. Each squeeze made her more confident than the last, confirming what she'd known since she was sixteen. She was supposed to be with women, not men.

Lowering the zipper on Grace's slacks, Rose kissed her with a hunger that had been unsatisfied for six years. The pants fell unceremoniously to the floor, and Grace stepped out of them while tugging at the waistband of Rose's panties. Rose did the same to Grace's until both garments lay somewhere in the room. They fell to the bed, bodies entwined skin to skin. If bliss had a physical property, this was it.

Grace slid down Rose's torso, taking a breast into her mouth. Alternating between swirls and sucks, she electrified every nerve ending in Rose's body. Rose pushed on her shoulders, hoping she'd get the message to move further down. And she did. Nestling herself between Rose's legs, she caressed an inner thigh with one hand, then nudged Rose's legs wider until she throbbed a painful need. A need that lasted for hours, satisfied by lips, fingers, and a gloriously talented tongue.

From pumping inside her to tasting her essence, Rose experienced pure rapture giving Grace the ultimate pleasure until the sun came up. And when exhaustion took over, she entwined herself with Grace's body to sleep. A deep sleep she'd never before experienced. A sleep that, when she woke, had recharged her energy and spirit and had given her a better understanding of the world. She now appreciated the search for carnal pleasure and how it could drive people to do things they never thought possible.

They dressed unhurriedly. Rose turned her back to her as she did, dreading the end of their physical connection. Watching Grace put her clothes back on would only solidify that their time together was over.

"Are you hungry?" Grace asked, prompting Rose to turn toward her. "I can have the front desk run out and pick us up something."

"I can't stay." Which was a lie. Rose had nowhere to be. If she were honest, she wanted to do this again and again, but she didn't want to appear desperate or needy, so she stuck to her white lie.

"I'll come through town in a month or so." Grace's expression took on a softness as she caressed Rose's cheek. "I'd love to see you again."

"Come to my show then." Rose wanted to say something more seductive or at least something wittier, but she was sure other words would stick. The last thing she wanted was to let Grace leave thinking she was a dunce.

As she walked out, an uncomfortable feeling hung over Rose like a dark cloud. Other than her first time on stage, she hadn't felt self-conscious or insecure about her speech in years. But if that was the worst thing Rose had to put up with to ravage this woman's body again, she considered it a decent trade.

CHAPTER SEVEN

Half Moon Bay, California, 1929

Since Frankie Wilkes had bought nearly every property along Half Moon Bay's marina, a packed house was commonplace at the underground Seaside Club during tourist season. Free-flowing whiskey drew in customers, but Rose kept them in their seats longer than a few drinks with two finely honed performances four nights a week, five if Monday was a holiday.

Off-season nights like tonight were slower, though not as much as they used to be. Rose performed primarily for locals and diehards who couldn't get enough of her, and the occasional wealthy actor or actress like Grace Parsons traveling between Los Angeles and San Francisco. Despite Mr. Wilkes cutting her pay in half this time of year, Rose preferred the sparser crowd. The men were less handsy, and she could use those dead nights to try out new songs.

Taking the stage tonight for her final set of the day, Rose scanned the crowd of a dozen customers. The paltry showing was enough to justify her pay and, thankfully, not enough for the men to rile each other up. She was counting on one particular man showing up, and she wasn't disappointed. During her fall visit last year, Grace had introduced him to Rose as a man from Victor Talking Machine Company. He'd loved her voice but had told her, *"There is no market for a white woman singing the blues."* While Rose considered his comment wholly inaccurate, it didn't insult her. She had no desire to perform anywhere beyond the Seaside Club, but her piano partner's dreams were a different story. So when Grace had mentioned during a summer visit that the Victor man would be through on Halloween, she got an idea.

When Lester took his seat at the piano, she placed a hand over the chin-high microphone and turned to him. "Your songs?"

A toothy smile grew on Lester's face. He was a magnificent piano player who paired well with Rose, but he was also a talented songwriter whose work equaled any RCA Victor record. "You got it, Rosebud."

For the next hour, Rose sang Lester's songs, and he played with a joy that rivaled a father seeing his baby walk for the first time. While the Victor man listened with interest, another man at the bar stood facing Rose, sipping a glass of whiskey. The stage lights made it hard to make him out, but as far as Rose could tell, he never shifted and never took his eyes off her. Rose thought nothing of it for the first half hour, but when it continued during the second half hour, she checked to make sure the bouncer was nearby. His preoccupation with her also made her think of a suggestion that Grace had made the last time they were together.

Mr. Wilkes had questioned her about her three-year friendship with Grace. When she told Grace that, Grace told her that appearance was everything in the entertainment business. Adding that it was time for Rose to find a cover. With no prospect of finding a partner like the one Grace had, finding a boyfriend she could string along might be the diversion she needed to stop the rumors.

Applause followed her final note, including those of the stranger at the bar and the Victor man. It made her proud of

Lester and his excellent songwriting. She stopped at the piano before leaving the stage without being self-conscious about her words sticking. The four years she'd spent with him made her nearly as comfortable as she was with Dax.

"See. They love it," Rose said.

"They love *you*." Lester was too modest for his own good, but Rose was about to remedy the consequence of his finest attribute.

"Th-Th-There's someone you should meet." She led him to the Victor man's table. "Mr. J-J-Johnson."

He stood and shook her hand. "That was some fine singing tonight, Miss Hamilton, but I wasn't familiar with the songs. Whose were they?"

"Lester's." Rose shoved her friend forward to shake Mr. Johnson's hand. "He w-w-wrote them. I'll leave you two to talk."

Rose retreated to the bar for her regular cup of hot tea with honey and lemon that she drank to soothe her throat between sets. The bartender had it waiting for her, as he did after every performance. "Thanks, Jason."

Two sips in, the unfamiliar man at the other end of the bar, the one who had eyed her all set long, downed his whiskey and approached. Tall, muscular, with sandy-brown hair and a chiseled chin, he looked confident. Too confident for her taste.

"I heard you were the prettiest thing in town." Her defenses arose. He was easy to look at and had paid her a sweet compliment, but his staring had made her feel like she was some type of trophy he was trying to win.

Rose harrumphed. "You stare too much." She returned to sipping her tea, wishing Lester was by her side like he was most nights, fending off handsy or flirty customers.

"Can you blame me?" He inched backward, a good sign that Rose had gotten her message across. "Where I come from, girls aren't nearly as pretty, and they certainly can't sing like you."

"And w-w-where's that?"

"Fresno."

Frankie Wilkes sidled next to the man, slinging an arm over his shoulder. "I see you've met my nephew."

"We were just getting to the introductions," the man said.

"Well, let me. Rose Hamilton, this is my sister's son, Riley King."

"It's a pleasure to meet you, Miss Rose." Riley extended his hand. Without thinking, she shook it. It was big and strong, typical for a man's. "That voice of yours is magical." He seemed less forward with his uncle around. "May I get you a drink?"

"I need to get home," Rose replied with the quickest excuse she could think of.

"You should walk her home, Riley. Hooligans are out tonight. Last Halloween, they gave Rose the fright of her life. I can't have that happening again." Mr. Wilkes gave him a playful wink. "Then you can take care of that business we talked about."

"You have a point," Rose said. Chills went down her spine as she recalled her harrowing six-block walk home in the dark that night. The sound of footsteps had cut through the silence and the fog, picking up speed as they came closer and closer. Suddenly four bodies appeared, each with a burlap sack covering its head, wielding sticks. Rose's heart had almost stopped when they ran circles around her, howling like wolves at the moon. Then, without warning, they'd run off into the fog.

She didn't get the impression he was the handsy type, but instinct told her Riley wouldn't give up flirting. Putting up with his weak attempts at getting her attention would be a good trade-off if it meant a trouble-free walk home. After agreeing to his escort home, she gathered her things from her dressing room and accepted his arm before leaving the Seaside Club.

As Riley walked her past the Foster House, he gave it a thorough stare for two solid blocks. She couldn't blame him. It didn't look like the rest of the Wilkes-owned buildings at the marina with their new concrete sidewalks, new awnings, bright signage, and fresh white paint. Conversely, the words "Foster House" obviously had been painted on the front siding along the second story years ago. The letters were fading along with white exterior walls. The wooden walkway in front had several cracked planks, requiring patrons to hopscotch their way past.

During the twenty-minute walk home, Rose discovered two things: Riley was Mr. Wilkes's new whiskey runner, and he could be quite charming when he wanted to. He checked behind every tree, bush, and jalopy and shooed away several imaginary ghosts and goblins along the route to Mrs. Prescott's boarding house. Finally, at the bottom step of the stoop, Riley dramatically waved his arm as if lighting the way up the steps. "Safe and sound, Miss Rose."

Rose considered her escort up and down. Charming and handsome like Grace's husband, he had made an excellent second impression. As Mr. Wilkes's nephew, he could be the answer to her problem. Suddenly, making a good impression mattered. She needed to say good night without her speech making her appear like a joke. The simpler, the better.

"Thank you." She added a shy grin to sell it.

"Before I go…I'm new in town. Can you recommend a place for breakfast since the Seaside Club only offers lunch and dinner?"

Rose picked two practiced words guaranteed not to come out stuck. Two words she was sure Riley was acquainted with. "Foster House." She gestured toward the front door with a thumb. "Gotta go."

Moments before she closed the door, he said, "Perhaps I'll see you there."

When Rose stepped into the darkened entry hall, Mrs. Prescott's testy voice rang out. "Visitors aren't allowed after ten."

Her landlady was pleasant enough most days, but she was a busybody with the residents every day, monitoring the comings and goings of visitors like a jailer.

"He saw me to the door, that's all. Now, go back to bed, Mrs. Prescott." Rose realized she was worked up over Mrs. Prescott's nosiness because her words didn't stick. She trudged upstairs to the women's floor and was relieved to see light seeping through the gap below Jules's door. While Rose's schedule was stable, Jules's wasn't. She assisted the doctor at his clinic whenever he needed her, so Rose took the opportunity to see her whenever their off-time matched.

Rose knocked. The door swung open.

"You're home early." Jules stuck her head into the hallway and looked toward the stairs.

"She went back to her room." Rose snickered. She and Jules had checked that hallway hundreds of times over the last three years, sneaking into each other's room after quiet hours. Quiet hours meant no visitors, no noise, and only coming from or going to work. Three violations of Mrs. Prescott's policy and a resident would be out on their ear. Rose kept a clean slate, but Jules had two strikes against her. After the second one, she learned to meet her visitors elsewhere.

Jules whisked Rose inside and shut the door. Her white nurse's uniform and white stockings were hanging over a clothesline she'd strung diagonally in one corner of the room. Clippings from *Vogue* and *Vanity Fair* covered sections of the wall on either side of her dresser mirror, depicting dresses or swimwear Jules dreamed of buying. With her naturally light brown skin and the toned body she'd developed from lifting patients, Jules would be striking in anything, even one of the burlap sacks those hooligans wore last year. She could tie her straight, long brown hair into a bun and still look as cute as a button.

Jules kept her voice low because sometimes Mrs. Prescott patrolled the halls, looking for violations. "Did the Victor man come tonight?"

"He did." Rose remembered the grateful look on Lester's face when she'd left him with Mr. Johnson tonight. She'd never been prouder nor happier for another person. "I sang Lester's songs for him, and he liked them. When I left, they were still t-t-talking."

"You did a good thing, Rosebud." Jules sat on her bed, back against the wall, and Rose sat on the only chair in the room.

"Yeah, but I might need a new piano man soon."

"Was that a man's voice I heard outside?" Since her room had the window nearest the main door, Jules had a bird's-eye view of everyone coming and going. But unlike Mrs. Prescott, she never used the information against a resident.

"That was Riley, Mr. Wilkes's nephew and his new whiskey runner."

"What was that?"

"What was what?"

"That grin." Rose flushed from her ears to her toes. Nothing got past Jules. Absolutely nothing. "If I didn't know you better, I'd say you had a crush."

"I never said I didn't like men. I said that I liked women." Some days like today, Rose wished Jules didn't have the ability to read every emotion. It was impossible to keep a secret from her.

"Oh, please. You said you once loved a girl and that she curled your toes more than Grace could. Are her visits not enough?"

Jules likely didn't realize it, but she'd gotten to the heart of what had held Rose back since she first met Grace. Their visits served a purpose and left Rose satisfied physically, but not emotionally. Each visit stirred memories of Dax and made her wonder where she was, how her life turned out, and if she ever thought of her. Rose pressed against her chest the purse containing the picture of Dax and the cherished replica blue ribbon from their childhood. She sighed. After all this time, she still held hope that she and Dax would find each other again.

"To be honest, no, but it's not like women are beating down my door."

"Then why Riley?"

"It's time for a cover. People at the hotel are talking about Grace and me."

* * *

Morning came too quickly, but their brief interaction last night didn't give Rose a clear sign of how long Riley might wait, if at all, at the Foster House. Hair tied back in a low bun, she selected her plainest dress. She planned to let Riley kiss her, but first, she wanted him to see not the dolled-up singer she had been last night but what she really looked like.

Rose stepped into the hallway and locked her door. As she turned to go downstairs, Jules reached the top landing. Her eyes were droopy as if she hadn't slept. Her white nurse's uniform was wrinkled as if she'd already been in it for hours.

"Are you coming or going?" Rose asked.

"Coming. I got called in to help with an autopsy before dawn."

"Oh no. Who died?"

"Mister Foster."

Rose gasped. She thought of her limited interaction with Mr. Foster at the restaurant. He wasn't the friendliest person and often rubbed people the wrong way, including her, but she wanted no harm to come to him. "Heart attack?"

"Doc Hughes is calling it accidental. The head waitress at the Foster House found him at the bottom of the stairs in the restaurant."

"That's horrible." Rose detected doubt in Jules when she shook her head. "Do you think it wasn't an accident?"

"Mr. Foster had some bruises on his arms that looked more like grip marks than the result of a nasty fall." Jules flapped her arms in the air. "But he's the doctor."

"Isn't he trained to do autopsies?"

"I went through the same training as his assistant. I always thought he was a competent doctor, but there was no way that was an accidental death. And for the life of me, I can't figure out why he's calling it an accident."

"Maybe some breakfast would help make things clearer." Rose pointed her thumb toward the stairs. "I was just heading out. Would you like to join me?"

Jules inspected Rose up and down. "You're meeting Riley, aren't you? But that's not appropriate first date attire. What were you thinking?"

"I was thinking that he needs to see the real me before I let him kiss me."

"You're really going through with this." Jules had laced her voice with more than a smidgen of disgust. That was bad enough. What was more problematic was that Rose couldn't tell whether Jules disliked Riley or she was disappointed in Rose for settling for a man.

"I'm simply testing the water." Rose rolled her eyes. But if she were honest with Jules, she had plenty of reservations about taking up with Riley King. She'd only met him last night and didn't know if he was a decent man or an unprincipled one.

Leaving Jules at the boarding house, Rose suddenly dreaded her quasi-invitation to Riley for breakfast this morning. The Foster House would likely be closed until Mr. Foster's family sorted things out. That left only one place to test whether she could stomach Riley as her cover.

She crossed the street one block shy of the Foster House. If her feelings before her first kiss with Dax were the benchmark of how the buildup should affect her, she should have been more nervous than she was as she approached the restaurant. She considered turning tail, but time wasn't a luxury. She needed a cover soon.

She walked up to the door, and as expected, the "Closed" sign was still flipped. A paper sign had been taped above it announcing, "Closed until further notice."

"It's closed." Rose turned toward the voice. Riley had stepped out of the Seaside's pickup and to the sidewalk. "The deputy who posted the sign said a waitress found the owner dead at the bottom of the stairs."

"I heard. News t-t-travels fast ar-r-round this town," Rose said. "How l-l-long have you been here?"

The long, sheepish expression meant he'd been there longer than necessary, which meant his interest in Rose extended beyond last night's first impression. "Over an hour, I suppose."

"Still hungry?"

"Starved. Is there any other place to sit down?"

Rose sighed. Another restaurant had opened in town, but it only served lunch and dinner like the Seaside Club. The only other breakfast spot with tables was the last place she wanted to go. Merely thinking about it made her nauseous. "One, but I h-h-haven't been there in y-y-years."

"I'd like to buy you breakfast." Riley dipped at the knees to look Rose in the eyes. "Please say yes." His dimpled smile made it impossible to say no.

"Sure." A foul taste followed that word. Rose sensed that seeing Ida again wouldn't turn out well.

The last time she had walked into Ida's four years ago, she had been on a mission to turn the tables on her former tyrant. She'd left with her belly full and her head held high, knowing she never had to see her again. She'd crossed paths with Ida now and again, but each had continued on their way without exchanging a word. With any luck, she thought, Ida had the late shift today, and Morris would mind his business in the kitchen.

Luck wasn't with her. One step into Ida's Café, she came face-to-face with what had been the main character in a five-year-long nightmare and the temperature in the room plummeted. She instantly regretted her wardrobe choice. She should have selected her Sunday best to reflect how well her life had gone since breaking free from her.

Riley tugged Rose's arm, directing her toward the only unoccupied table. The place was hopping, with several Foster House regulars filling the tables. A scan of the menu confirmed Rose's long-held opinion of Ida and Morris—no imagination. Not one item had changed, only the prices. Their inability to change with the times explained why their café struggled to break even.

"What do you recommend?" Riley asked.

"It depends if M-M-Morris got a good night's sleep. I'd stick with b-b-bacon, eggs, and toast."

"Good tip." Riley waved Ida to the table. "Two coffees and two orders of bacon, eggs over easy, and bacon, crispy."

If Rose hadn't been so focused on the hate pouring from Ida, stronger than the grease smell in the air, she would have been offended by Riley assuming her food preferences. She had waitressed for years, and about half the time, the man ordered for his wife. At first, she'd considered the practice romantic. She presumed the man knew his woman well enough to ask for her favorites, but now she understood the snide looks by women that frequently followed over the years. The men either assumed or were too damn lazy to find out what the women preferred. Rose preferred her eggs over hard.

Ida jotted down the order, dramatically stabbing the notepad with her pen at the end. She pivoted on her heel, but not before skewering Rose with eye daggers.

"What was that about?" Riley asked.

"I used to w-w-work here."

"I take it you didn't leave under good terms."

"No, I didn't."

Riley asked about where Rose was from and how she ended up in Half Moon Bay. She kept her answer truthful yet vague, saying that she grew up near San Francisco and came to work for her cousin. Then one day, his uncle heard her singing to herself and offered her a job at his new club.

"Well, I'm glad he did. Otherwise, I wouldn't have met you." Riley filled the time talking about his two uncles and how important they were, each owning big businesses.

Ida returned. She dropped both plates of food on the table, their orders dancing in midair before bouncing back to earth. That was it. Ida had gotten under her skin, but she bit back the reply she wanted to give. She wasn't one for making a public spectacle, and she wasn't about to start now since Ida knew the real reason Rose came to Half Moon Bay. She couldn't chance Riley finding out. She'd undoubtedly lose her job if word got back to his uncle.

"Let's leave, Riley." Rose sprung from her chair, digging deep to control her temper. "I've lost my appetite."

"Leaving is what you do best." Ida turned her attention to Riley. "Keep a tight leash on this one. She'll disappear without a word of warning and leave you holding the bag."

Ida was baiting Rose, but she refused to give her the satisfaction of a public argument nor a reason to say why Rose's parents sent her to this town. She pulled three one-dollar bills from her purse and tossed them on the table. That amount was way too much for the untouched food, but Rose wanted nothing from Ida, not even her change. She stormed out, digging her fingernails into her palms and marching toward the boarding house as fast as possible. Her anger boiled hotter with each step until she felt like screaming, but a public spectacle would give Ida what she wanted—Rose drowning in humiliation.

"Wait, Rose." Riley ran up from behind until they were shoulder to shoulder. He'd made sandwiches out of the bacon and toast and held one out to Rose. "You paid for it, so I thought better us eat it than have that snoot throw it away."

Rose snorted before coming to an abrupt stop. "Snoot is right. Give me that thing." She snatched the sandwich from his hand and tore off a bite, crumbs dropping wastefully to the sidewalk.

"Let's get out of here." Riley walked her one block down to where he'd parked the Seaside pickup and opened the passenger door for her to slide in. Once he turned on the engine, he turned to her with a devilish smile. "I've seen you at work. How would you like to see what I do?"

During the four years Rose had worked at the Seaside Club, selling liquor was illegal, but whiskey and champagne flowed like water from a hose every night. It was always available, but she never knew how it got there. Riley's offer made her curious. "Sure, why not?"

A smile on his face, Riley drove north out of town, past the half-mile-long split-rail fence of Spencer's Horse Ranch and past one green row after another of growing brussels sprouts. The crops were nearly ripe and ready for harvesting, and the horses were enjoying a much-needed rest after tourist season and the endless hour-long beach runs.

Riley pulled off the road where tourists often parked to sunbathe at Gray Whale Cove. He straightened his wool tie before pointing toward the beach. His smile returned, making him appear eager to please her.

"Once a week, local boat runners get their load from a Canadian ship. They drop off the whiskey barrels at one of two beaches. That's where me and my buddy, Jimmy, come in. We load a dozen of the barrels in the back." Riley gestured his thumb toward the bed of the pickup.

"Are more d-d-delivered?"

"At least a dozen more. Other drivers run the rest into the city, including some to my other uncle's speakeasy."

"Is it dan-g-g-gerous?"

"The real danger is Devil's Slide."

"But we h-h-h-haven't passed it yet."

"The other drop site is Shelter Cove. I had to outrun a prohi around that cliff on my first night. I gunned through it and lost him before I hit town."

"You must be a good d-d-driver." Rose was frustrated with herself. She hadn't stuttered this much in years.

"I'm the best." Riley sat taller in his seat, taking on the confident aura he had last night at the club. "That's why Uncle Frankie hired me. I've been outrunning prohis in Fresno for years."

Riley put his hand on the gear shifter, pulled back to the highway, and continued north. Butterflies awoke in her stomach, stirring up a nauseating storm. Taking curves at high speed, especially those around Devil's Slide, wasn't Rose's idea of Friday fun. "Please don't."

"It's safe, I promise."

He continued to shift gears up the cliffside in the fading mist. After the first hairpin turn, Rose's rapidly increasing pulse matched Riley's speed. The only thing that kept her from jumping out of her seat was the southbound lane between her and sure death. The drop-off and red-stained walls of Devil's Slide jutting out to the ocean were, thankfully, on Riley's side of the truck.

The road crested, and Rose took a deep, relieved breath. The downward climb to Pacifica wasn't nearly as twisty as on the Half Moon Bay side of the cliffs. By the time Riley parked at the end of the road leading to Shelter Cove, though, sweat had soaked Rose's blouse and was dripping from her brow.

"Geez, Rose. Are you okay?" Riley covered her trembling hand with a hand. "You look like you've seen a ghost."

"Drop-offs s-s-scare me."

He slung an arm over her shoulder and gave her a squeeze before rubbing her arm. If he meant to calm her, his effort didn't work. His touch was too strong and lacked the gentleness Grace and Dax had shown her, but his words came out soft. "I'm so sorry. I was an idiot showing off like that."

"It's all right." Rose shook a little less after his apology. There would be no repeat scary performance.

"No, it's not. I'm really sorry." When Rose turned to thank him, he pressed his lips against hers. His kiss wasn't rough like Tommy McAdams's, but it wasn't pillowy soft like Grace's or Dax's. He neither frightened her like Tommy did, nor did he curl her toes like Dax could. It was merely okay. At least she didn't hate it.

He pulled back with a silly grin on his face. "That was nice, Rose. Really nice."

She returned his smile. "Can we head back? A little s-s-slower this time?"

CHAPTER EIGHT

San Francisco, California, 1929

Dax woke to gentle, diffused sunlight warming her face. Unlike workdays, when she'd groan and wish for another hour of sleep, she bounced to a sitting position. It was Saturday— her favorite day of the week. Her boss closed the woodshop on weekends, freeing her to do as she pleased. Her chores would take a few hours, then she would settle into the one thing she looked forward to every week.

She threw on her clean set of work clothes, grabbed the basket of her and Logan's dirty clothes in the hallway, and tiptoed down the stairs, making sure to not wake him too early. He'd been cross since losing his job at the stock exchange two weeks ago following the big crash. Half of the employees there lost their jobs that day, and not a single financial company or bank was hiring, so Logan had been sulking ever since. Dax offered to teach him carpentry, but he refused to "lower himself by performing manual labor." Well, if he didn't lower his expectations, May had said they'd run out of savings in five or six months, and the bank would soon own their house.

Dax continued past the study she'd converted into a bedroom for May following the accident. When she came home from the hospital, stairs were out of the question for May, so Dax swapped the guest room and study and built a small closet for May's things. They'd hoped the downstairs accommodations would be temporary, but after the first year, May seemed to accept her reality—stairs were a thing of the past. Except for one or two.

A loud clang came from the kitchen. Dax rushed in, dropping the clothes basket near the Maytag machine. "Darn it, May. I've told you a thousand times to wait for me before starting breakfast." She guided May to a kitchen chair, kneeled in front of her, and inspected the leg brace Logan had bought when the doctor removed the cast and okayed her to stop using crutches. "The top is still loose. Maybe I should take it to the metal shop and have them fix the rods."

"We can't afford it. Logan said no extras until he finds a job."

Dax harrumphed. Logan had refused to get her things ever since the accident. For over a year, May had been compensating for the lost muscle mass in her right calf by stuffing a folded cloth napkin between her skin and the leather strap around her leg several inches below the knee. Last month, Dax notched an extra hole in the leather to tighten the buckle as far as it would go, but it still wasn't enough. The metal rods had warped.

"Walking isn't extra. It's a necessity. I have a few dollars squirreled away." Dax lowered her head, still blaming herself for not paying more attention to the other drivers. May wouldn't be crippled if she had, and they'd spend their Saturday strolling in the park, not fixing a nearly useless leg brace.

May cupped Dax's hand. "That's your money. You'll need it if carpentry work dries up like Logan's job has."

"I hate this, May." Dax gripped her shirt by the buttons, regretting having spent her savings over the summer on new tools and a locking box for them. If she hadn't, she'd march over to the hospital, buy May a whole new brace, and wrap it up in a shiny bow.

"A new brace equals months of expenses. I'd rather make do than be out on the street months sooner."

Dax rose to her feet, mumbling her frustration with how stubborn her sister could be. Well, Dax could be headstrong too. Somehow, someway, she'd earn the money needed to get May the new brace she deserved.

She picked up the frying pan May had dropped, placed it on the stove, retrieved the items for May to make the eggs and toast, and started their Saturday morning routine. While May prepped and cooked the food, Dax prepped the laundry. She brought a stockpot of water to a boil, poured it into the Maytag tub, which was already half-filled with sink water, loaded it with half the dirty clothes, and turned on the swisher. When the first load was done washing, Dax sent each piece through the wringer, drained and refilled the tub, and started the second load. By that time, May had the food on the plates.

This was the only part of laundry day Dax enjoyed unless the tub sprang a leak. She got to spend the time with her sister, relaxed by the machine's hum and rhythm of water sloshing in the tub while they ate. Without exchanging words, she placed the empty plates in the sink while May filled and placed a dish in the oven warmer for Logan. While May washed the dishes, she finished wringing the laundry and hung the pieces on the clotheslines in the backyard.

Chores done, the sisters retreated to the front porch for the highlight of Dax's week. She elevated May's crippled leg on a stool with a small pillow as a cushion before sitting in the chair next to her. May then shuffled the deck of cards that had been sitting on the table between them.

"Shall we play for desserts first?" May asked and dealt the cards. Their Saturday gin rummy games had become a ritual, playing for what would be on the menu for the week. But May was an expert in the game and could win any hand she put her mind to. She was fair, though, and eased up so Dax could choose several of her favorites.

Dax picked up her cards, keeping an eye on the parade of young families with strollers and dogs on leashes heading to the children's park. May pointed out a handful of ladies in their new hats and dresses as she built her first hand. Meanwhile, Dax waited for one particular lady. If her internal clock was correct, her weekly dose of medicine should stroll by in ten or fifteen minutes.

"Gin." May threw down her cards faceup. A taunting grin formed.

"How do you win every time?" Dax added her cards to the pile and shuffled.

"I keep track."

A familiar ringing sound floated through the screen door. Dax had yet to hear Logan stomp down the stairs, so she needed to answer the phone quickly to avoid waking the man too early. "Saved by the bell. Losing to you again will have to wait." She pushed herself from the chair, flung the screen door open, dashed to the hallway table, and lifted the earpiece by the third ring. "Foster residence."

"I'm looking for Logan Foster," a deep, hoarse male voice croaked.

"He's still sleeping. Who shall I say called?"

"My name is George Butler. I'm a lawyer. This is a matter of some importance. You need to fetch the man."

"Then you need to hold your britches for a few minutes." Since the day Dax's parents kicked her out of her childhood home, she didn't take to anyone telling her what she needed to do. May never did. The only exception was her boss, who paid her to do as she was told. However, Dax avoided Logan like she had avoided church since moving in. He clearly enjoyed bossing people around.

Dax put the phone down and climbed the stairs, taking deep breaths to prepare for the onslaught of curse words. Finally, she knocked on his door.

"Logan, you have a call. It's some lawyer," she yelled through the door, hoping that would be enough to raise him. When Logan still hadn't answered her after ten seconds passed, Dax took one more deep breath and opened the door.

Logan was facedown on the bed, shirtless with his arms stretched over his head. Since the man lost his job, he'd regularly tried sleeping most of the day away, a state of misery Dax understood. After May's accident, Dax would have preferred to hole up in her room rather than face May every morning, but she did. Swallowing her guilt, she doted on her sister every minute she wasn't working. Seeing how Logan had behaved the last two weeks taught her she was ten times stronger than he was. Checking out on her family wasn't an option.

"Logan!" Touching him wasn't an option either. Dax remained at the door when he stirred. "Logan! You have a call. It's some lawyer."

He groaned and pushed himself up. "I'm up."

Dax couldn't turn on her heel fast enough and escape to the porch again. Whoever was on the line and whatever important thing he had to discuss, it was Logan's business, not Dax's. Settling into her chair again, she hoped the call didn't make her miss the event of the week.

"Who was it?" May asked.

"Some lawyer. Logan wasn't happy." Dax rolled her eyes. Unhappy seemed to be his permanent state the last few years, and he made his dislikes abundantly clear. He didn't like Dax living with them. He didn't like May living downstairs. He didn't like relying on Dax to do the chores May used to do. And he certainly didn't like that Dax went off to work and came home with money when he couldn't.

"What else is new?" May sighed.

Dax reshuffled the cards, keeping her gaze focused on the street and silently judging the women's wardrobe choices. They looked pretty enough, but their clothes weren't practical for anything but walking and being admired.

When she dealt the cards, a familiar baby buggy popped into view beneath the neighbor's coastal live oak tree and then the woman pushing it. Dax's breathing shallowed as her heart pumped faster. The red curls bouncing in the buggy perfectly reflected the woman's hair. Beautiful red locks pulled back into a loose bun highlighted her flawless white neck. Every angle and curve drew Dax's attention like a bloom to the sun. It was her sweet Heather.

They'd sneaked kisses for a year before Heather ended things between them out of fear her husband might catch them. But that didn't stop Dax from worrying, nor did it prevent her from slowly falling in love with her with each passing weekly glimpse. Dax had come to care as much for Heather as she did for Rose.

As Heather stepped closer, Dax leaned forward in her chair, waiting for the weekly sign of recognition, but it didn't come. The woman kept her stare straight on the sidewalk ahead, not on Dax on the porch to her left as she'd done every Saturday since giving birth the first time. Seconds later, a young boy appeared on the sidewalk two steps behind, the same red curls bouncing as he skipped. Then a man appeared, paying more attention to the young ladies across the street and the pipe in his hand than to his wife and children.

A rattle or something similar dropped from the buggy, forcing the woman to stop and pick it up. When she did, she turned her gaze toward Dax. Despite her attempt to mask the evidence with makeup, Dax could tell her face was bruised and swollen. It had been years since she'd seen it up close, but Dax knew every inch of that face and how every curve was supposed to appear. When they locked eyes, tears flowed down the woman's cheeks.

Dax didn't need an explanation and threw the cards on the table. Mr. Portman had beat her dear Heather to a pulp, which triggered a volcanic eruption inside Dax. The day she said her last goodbye to Heather, when she'd announced she was pregnant, Dax had sworn to protect her if he ever laid a hand on her again. That oath launched her from her chair and propelled her from the porch. Running full steam down the three wood stairs and the concrete walkway, she landed a powerful right punch square on Mr. Portman's left cheek. He stumbled into the street, holding a hand over the damage Dax had inflicted on him. She landed a second on that hand.

"Dax, no!" Heather screamed, but Dax didn't stop. She couldn't if she wanted. Her blood had boiled, and there was no going back. She landed a third punch right on the eye.

Mr. Portman regained his balance, and when Dax prepared for a fourth punch, he clocked her on the cheek. A sharp sting made Dax stumble, but she continued her charge. Finally, he pushed Dax to the ground and held her in place with a knee to her chest. Punch after punch landed on Dax's face, each more painful than the last. The coppery taste of blood filled her mouth, and the surrounding daylight got darker.

"Benjamin, no. Don't hurt her." Heather's voice was more frantic than before.

"Logan, help. Logan, help," May yelled.

The sound of the screen door slamming against the side of the house echoed. Then something pushed Mr. Portman off Dax and to the sidewalk. Dax rolled to her side, thinking this was how May must have felt after being hit by that truck and how Heather felt after every beating. Every part of her face throbbed with a mix of sharp and dull pain.

"What the hell is going on?" Logan's words came out extra sharp, like when he yelled at Dax for breaking a dinner plate. He'd said they were a wedding gift and she should show more respect.

"This one here"—Mr. Portman pointed at Dax with one hand while nursing his jaw with the other—"started throwing punches. I had to defend myself."

"I don't care what she did. A man should never put a hand on a woman." Logan's voice sounded surprisingly protective. Dax pushed herself off the ground and stood squarely in front of Mr. Portman. She wouldn't give him the satisfaction of knowing he'd given her quite a beating and that it took every ounce of energy to look him in the eye.

"A woman?" Mr. Portman scanned Dax from short hair to boots, clearly confused.

"Yeah, a woman just bested you." Dax clenched her fists, ready to go another round.

Logan turned to Dax. His narrowed eyes meant nothing she'd said so far had helped ease the tension. "What got into your head to start a fight?"

Dax gestured toward Heather, who appeared frozen. She'd picked up her baby, cradled her to her chest with one arm, and held her son's hand with the other. "Look at his wife. Those bruises didn't get there by accident."

"And what business is it of yours?" Mr. Portman asked, testing the mobility of his jaw.

Dax carefully chose her words to protect Heather. "She's a friend. I suspected you were doing it years ago, and those bruises prove it. Someone needed to teach you a lesson."

"Well, it's not your place." Logan pointed toward the house with the subtlety of a riled-up grizzly. "Now, get inside." The stern look he sent Dax gave no room for negotiation.

But it *was* her place, and that duty wasn't negotiable. Speaking up was precisely what people did for the ones they loved. Dax took a few unsteady steps toward Heather, regretting the public spectacle she'd made. A small crowd had gathered across the street, gawking at Dax's brutish method of defending the woman she'd cherished from afar for longer than she should have. At least her attack exposed Mr. Portman as a woman beater. After today, he'd think twice before putting a mark on her again.

"You don't have to live with someone who beats you. You *can* set a brave example for those beautiful children of yours. Did you build that nest egg?" Dax hoped her pleading before they parted ways nearly four years ago got through to her. She'd begged Heather to stash a quarter here, a dollar there, so she could get away from her husband if it ever got to be too much.

Heather offered a tentative nod, clutching her daughter tighter. "Do you have enough?" Heather nodded again. "Good. You can go to your aunt's. He doesn't know where she lives." Dax directed her next words toward the crowd and yelled loud enough for the entire neighborhood to hear. "Spread the word. Benjamin Portman is a wife beater. What man will escort his wife home so she can pack her things and leave this monster?"

"I will." A man stepped forward from the crowd. "I will." A second man stepped closer.

Dax placed both hands on Heather's upper arms, sending

her the strength she'd need to get through this. Heather's eyes spoke of fear but also of relief. Her nightmare would soon be over. "Go. Pack things for you and the children, get on the train, and don't look back."

Mr. Portman grabbed Heather by the arm, but the brave strangers interceded. They pulled him back and warned him not to follow or they'd call for a policeman.

Heather leaned closer to Dax, still holding her children. "I'll never forget you." She disappeared past the coastal live oak, one man pushing the buggy, the other by her side.

Dax choked on the sadness that was overtaking her. She'd never again set eyes on Heather's beautiful red hair. Never again see her smile as she passed by. But that was a sacrifice she would make thousands of times over to know Heather and the children were safe.

A sharp, crushing pain enveloped the side of Dax's face. She stumbled, fell to the sidewalk, and heard the footsteps of several people rushing toward her. When she finally got her bearings, she discovered two men holding Mr. Portman back by his arms.

"You're dead," Mr. Portman spat, struggling to break free. "The next time I see you, you're dead."

"You need to leave, Mr. Portman." Logan used a stern voice. "I don't want any trouble, but if I see you on my property, I'll call the police." Logan grabbed Dax by the arm and pulled her up the walkway toward the house.

Dax finally set her stare on May. The worry on her face was more pronounced than it had been when Dax fell from the tree and broke her wrist when she was nine.

"Let go of her," May ordered when they ascended the porch steps. She inspected Dax's face. "You're bleeding. What were you thinking?"

"I was thinking someone needed to save a defenseless woman from that savage."

"I'm going inside." Logan's words had a bite to them. "Clean her up, and then we need to talk." He yanked the screen door open and disappeared upstairs.

May limped to the kitchen sink and ordered Dax to sit at the table. She wet a dish towel before joining her. She gently dabbed her cheeks, the cool water taking away some of the sting. Her expression and voice softened. "She was the one you met before the accident. The one you gave up to tend to me."

Dax nodded. She'd choke on the word if she said yes.

"I can see why you fell for her." May shifted to wipe Dax's hands. "You did a good thing today."

Grief swelled in Dax's throat. "Why do I lose every woman I love?"

"The world is cruel to people like you." May wiped away a tear. "I wish it weren't so."

"I better go see what Logan wants. I'm sure he'll give me an earful."

Dax peeked in the upstairs bedroom before continuing to the new study to find Logan. She didn't need him to tell her that sucker-punching Heather's tormentor wasn't the best way to go about helping her, but it worked. The woman she loved would be on a train to Chicago and out of Benjamin's life within an hour or two. But now, Dax was in Logan's crosshairs.

She knocked on the open study door, unworried about what he had to say. Instead, she was proud of what she had accomplished today. "You wanted to talk."

"To both of you." Logan had his nose buried in a stack of papers. The anger he'd tossed her way outside was absent. Discombobulation had taken its place. "I'll be right down."

Dax returned to the kitchen, where May had a teapot heating on the stove and three cups and a bowl of honey on the table. "He never wants to talk, so I figured tea might calm him a bit," May said from her traditional kitchen chair.

"I think you're right." The kettle whistled, signaling the water had come to a boil. Dax retrieved it and filled the cups.

Logan walked in, holding a set of papers. He sat, running a hand through his disheveled hair the way he'd do when something from the office had him all worked up. Meaning— whatever he had to say, it wasn't good.

"That was my father's lawyer on the phone. My father died

nearly two weeks ago. I need to settle his affairs."

May cupped her husband's hand. "I'm so sorry, Logan. I know you weren't close, but it still must come as a shock."

"He was a cross man, and now he's left me with a mess to clean up." He withdrew his hand and turned his attention to Dax. "And your temper has made a mess of things here. Benjamin Portman is vice president of the largest bank in the city. I'll be hard pressed to find a bank job anywhere in town with you under my roof. So you need to leave this house by tomorrow."

"But who will take care of May?"

"May can take care of herself." Logan's proclamation rolled off his lips as blithely as if he were ordering bacon and eggs. As if it was of no consequence and he had every expectation that his order would be fulfilled.

"Take care of herself?" Dax's blood boiled again. What was it with men who had influence in her life choosing today to pick at a scab? Her job was to protect the women she loved, but the men made it nearly impossible. "She can barely walk up three steps to get into the house."

May shook her head in crystal clear disappointment. "If you kick her out, you kick me out. I won't have you put my sister on the street for defending a woman in need."

Logan bounced from his chair, pacing the room and running a hand through his hair again. He wasn't the type who took kindly to someone backing him into a corner.

"You leave me no choice. My father owned a restaurant. You two will have to run it until I can find work here. When I do, I'll sell the restaurant and bring you back home."

"Where are we going?" Dax asked.

May turned to her. "Half Moon Bay."

CHAPTER NINE

Dax squeezed everything she owned into a single duffel bag for the long trip to Half Moon Bay. She then helped Logan load his Chrysler Six with May's four chests, three boxes, and two suitcases containing her clothes, linens, and household items they might need. Dax had no way of telling how long they'd be stuck there, but considering the frost storm that had brewed inside the car during most of the drive, she'd bet her last dollar Logan planned to prolong coming back for them as long as he could.

For a tourist destination, Half Moon Bay was smaller than Dax envisioned. Coming from a city with a half-million people and going to one with under one thousand was a massive culture shock. The bustling part of the city comprised a dozen blocks, three or four along the beaches and the rest stretching inland across the coastal highway. The major tourist draw appeared to be the Seaside Hotel, where several cars were parked.

Logan parked his Chrysler two blocks down along the beach side of the highway in front of a building with "Foster House" written across the second-story white siding. Its considerable size suggested it was once at the center of Half Moon Bay's bustle.

"I didn't realize your father's restaurant was this big." May stared out the windshield.

"His home and office are on the top floor. The restaurant is on the bottom." Logan opened the car door.

"Oh." May's unwillingness to complain was admirable and infuriating at the same time. Dax instantly recognized the problem—May wouldn't be able to use the upstairs residence.

"It's all right, May." Dax reached forward, placing a hand on her sister's shoulder. "I can build you a downstairs room. I'm sure the restaurant has a bathroom, and I can tap into the plumbing to add a shower."

"I didn't know you knew about plumbing."

"Don't worry about a thing. I'll set you up in no time." Beyond fixing a leaky faucet and toilet, Dax hadn't a clue about plumbing, but she was a fast learner. She could always trade work with a plumber in town if she couldn't figure it out. But, of course, that was if a town this size had a plumber.

Dax and Logan unloaded the car and brought the first load of bags and chests inside, leaving them near the door. Logan handed May the set of keys. "You'll be in charge. Let's look around."

Dax and May grabbed their pull cords and raised several of the draw-blinds covering the windows of the main dining room. Dust and sand had gathered on the tables and floor and cobwebs had formed in a few places. Otherwise, the room appeared in decent shape with square tables and chairs in the center, booths along the two long walls, the register near the front, and a bar closer to the back. Unfortunately, the décor had a gaudy nautical theme and lacked color, something May would likely address.

Past the bar, a short hallway led to two bathrooms, which appeared up to date, well maintained, and clean. A swing door at the end of the dining room led to the kitchen. The heart of the restaurant was a mix of old and new. The refrigerator and icebox combo appliance was enormous. While the grill and stove were more contemporary, the sinks, cabinets, racks, and floor were well worn. Mixing bowls, pots, dishes, glasses, and flatware were all clean and neatly stacked, ready for use. Besides the need for a light cleaning and fresh produce and meats, the restaurant appeared prepared to reopen.

Two storage rooms lined a side wall, one of which shared a wall with the customer bathrooms. "May, this might be a tight fit, but I think I can make you a bedroom and shower out of the storage room. First, we'll have to figure out another place to keep the extra chairs and such."

"There's a cellar my father used to hold tools and stuff for the pier out back. It has two ways in." Logan pointed toward Dax's left. "That door and one outside. His lawyer said this place barely broke even in the last few years. I already can't afford the taxes. Considering the times, we have to make it a viable business to sell it. That's why I need you two to keep it going while I find work so we won't lose the house in the city to the bank or this place to the county."

Who were we? Dax was sure now. Logan would come back for them when it suited him, not her or May.

"And what if you can't find work?" May's tone left no doubt. She was nervous about fending for herself here.

"Then I'll have to rethink things," Logan said. "May, why don't you sit for a bit while I take Dax upstairs?"

Whoever kept the downstairs clean apparently never set foot upstairs. The clutter there alone posed a fire hazard. However, the ample space—an office, parlor with an extra sink, bathroom, and three bedrooms—had tremendous potential. The bones were good, but the area needed a dumping and deep clean.

"Help me take this small bed downstairs for May." Dax lifted it off the springs without giving Logan a chance to say no. "If you help me clear out the storage room, I can have her set up for tonight."

"Fine." Logan didn't seem pleased with Dax telling him what to do, but it certainly made her feel good. She was tired of taking orders from men and walking on eggshells around them to keep the peace. Logan was leaving her and May here to get this place up and running, so she would act like an equal partner from this point forward.

Logan's physical strength was commensurate to that needed in his profession as a banker. He had to stop to adjust his hold once while coming down the stairs with the frame and three times with the mattress. The mattress needed a good beating to get out the dust, but a few layers of wool between it and May's sheets might turn it into a decent bed.

Once Dax and Logan brought in the groceries they'd picked up in town and the rest of their things and set May up in the storage room, Logan went upstairs to go through his father's office. Dax helped May unpack linens and set up her clothes on a rack she'd dusted off. "It's not much for now, but we have plenty of storage space. I'll build you a nice room that can double as an office."

"You and I grew up together, so we're no strangers to making do." May patted Dax's hand. "But I am grateful for your talent for making things better."

Dax stopped arranging her sister's belongings and hugged her. "It's still my turn to take care of you, May. I'll do whatever it takes to make sure you're safe, fed, and have a roof over your head."

May pulled back, wiping Dax's bangs from her eyes. "We'll do it together."

Logan returned to the main dining room, carrying a box of folders and papers. He placed it on a table and called for May and Dax. "I found employee records, tax records, billers, suppliers, invoices, schedules, and recipes. They should help get this place up and running." He threw Dax a set of keys. "My father had an old jalopy. It should be out back. The lawyer wasn't sure if it works."

Logan pulled out his wallet and laid two hundred dollars on the table. "This is what was left of my father's estate after the lawyer paid off the creditors. It should be enough to keep the restaurant afloat for a few months."

"I'll need to buy supplies to fix May up downstairs." Dax had seen how much cash the lawyer handed over to Logan earlier today, and it was more than Logan had just laid out. He was the one leaving May here, and he'd be the one to pay for fixing it so she could live here.

"How much?"

"Between lumber, sheetrock, plumbing, and other supplies, I guess fifty dollars." Dax estimated high. She wanted to squeeze every penny out of him.

"Fine." He slapped down more money atop the table before turning to May. "I need to wrap up things with the lawyer and head back to the city. Call me if you're in over your head." He kissed her on the cheek, walked out, started the engine of his Chrysler, and left.

That was it. Dax and May were on their own to fend for themselves.

"I'll go through these papers and get things organized." May pulled out a chair at the table.

"Logan mentioned a car and a basement. I'm gonna look around." Dax flipped the wall switch at the top of the interior stairs before descending. One light at the top turned on and more downstairs. The basement smelled musty with a hint of ocean. Logan was right. It was partially filled with old furniture, tools, fishing and boating gear, and lots of cobwebs. But it was spacious, containing about the same amount of floor space as the main dining room upstairs.

Dax exited via the other stairs leading outside. They were wobbly from years of neglect. About six dollars of lumber and nails, though, and she could build a whole new set of stairs in a day. Luckily, she'd bought new tools over the summer and could use them to get right to work, starting with May's room.

The high clouds that had hung overhead when they first arrived had continued their path inland, making the sky brighter but bringing in the briny ocean smell. Dax zipped her light jacket higher to combat the added chill in the air. A black Model T pickup about the same age as the one Logan once owned was parked at the back of the building. It didn't have an engine crank, so it had to be less than ten years old, but the dust and rust it had acquired from sitting near the ocean gave the impression it was older than it was.

Dax unlocked the door, slid into the driver's seat, and inserted the ignition key. The engine sputtered but never turned over. *Damn*, she thought. She should have asked Logan for extra money to get this rust bucket running. Dipping into her savings would be money well spent, though, if it meant she wasn't walking supplies back to the Foster House.

She opened the storage compartment on the dashboard, hoping to find a second set of keys or maybe a gold nugget old Mr. Foster may have left behind, but she had no such luck. She found instead an old pair of work gloves and some crumpled papers that looked like Mr. Foster had stuffed them inside with haste. Their less than pristine appearance was nothing like how she handled the few documents she'd accumulated in her life. She would neatly fold and stack each one with care unless they had her god-awful full name on it. In that unlikely case, she'd wad up those in a ball like these and toss them into a shoebox in case she needed them later. Curiosity tugged at Dax. Wanting to know if Mr. Foster cringed each time he saw his full name in print, she stuffed them in her coat pocket to read later.

After locking up, she walked the twenty-five yards down to the pier Logan had said belonged to his father. She passed a boat no longer than the pickup that was lashed down with chains atop blocks. When she reached the pier, she tested the sturdiness of the first few wood slats, and they seemed to bear weight. Several appeared broken or splintered further down, though, which explained the chain stretching across the entrance with a sign reading, "Danger. Do Not Enter." Since she and May didn't need the pier to run the restaurant, repairing it would have to wait. If Dax found an outboard motor on the property, she might want to fix the pier for entertainment.

She returned inside via the back door leading into the kitchen. May had fixed sandwiches, poured milk, and laid out two apples on the center chopping block. "Thanks, May."

"I figure if I'm hungry, you must be starving."

They chatted over the priority of tasks needed to get them settled in and the restaurant ready to open. The list was long, but they divided the duties along their personal strengths. May had a head for numbers and cooking, and Dax had a head for anything but those things. The biggest obstacle likely would be getting the former employees to return. It had been nearly a month since Logan's father had died, and, in Dax's experience, few wage earners could last that long without being paid.

Once she finished her last bite, Dax retrieved the papers she'd found in the truck, smoothed them out, and studied them. She tried to make sense of the words.

"What do you have there?" May asked.

"I found these in the old truck out back." Dax read more of the documents. "If I understand these correctly, someone made an offer to buy the Foster House earlier this year."

"Let me see those." May scanned the papers. "I can see why he balled these up. Two thousand dollars for this place is an insult. I heard Logan talking to the lawyer, who said it was worth nearly three thousand dollars, but that he needed to settle the taxes and sell quickly to get that price. With the crash, everything is dropping in value."

"Do you plan on telling Logan about this?" Dax asked.

"Not on your life." May grabbed their plates and placed them in the sink. "He'd want to sell and get whatever he could for it. I won't let him sell your new home out from under you."

"Thank you." Dax squeezed May's hand before returning the papers to her pocket.

Dax excused herself to focus on her first task—getting the jalopy working. That meant a mile hike to the garage she spotted when they'd picked up groceries. Charlie's Auto Repairs was a small white building off Main Street. When she spotted it before from the passenger seat of Logan's car, she hadn't noticed the exterior woodwork. Whoever completed the trim work around the facia was a talented carpenter. Dax ran a hand across the carved trim that ran up the corner of the building. The intricate lines and shapes spaced several feet apart gave the structure character.

"Can I help you?"

Dax turned toward the woman's voice and got quite a surprise. A tall, thin brunette with hair cropped around her ears like Dax's was and dressed in greasy coveralls approached, wiping her hands with a shop rag. The cutest, most wrinkled dog with a pushed-in nose waddled between her legs.

"I was admiring the woodwork. Amazing craftsmanship."

"My grandfather's work. He was a builder."

"Well, he's quite talented." Dax kneeled, inviting the lumbering mutt with short, stocky legs to sniff her hand and give her slobbery, wet licks. "Who do we have here?"

"This is Brutus. He runs the place."

"Where are my manners?" Dax wiped her hand on her pant leg and shook the woman's hand. Brutus weaved between Dax's legs in a dizzying figure-eight fashion, brushing against her pants and snorting and bobbing harder with each rotation. "I'm Dax." She glanced down and shifted her legs wider to give Brutus a clearer path. "I'm looking for Charlie."

"You found her. Don't worry about him. That's his way of saying that he likes you. I think he's partial to women in pants."

"It's a pleasure to meet you, Charlie." Dax let a smile grow on her lips. The fewer men she had to deal with, the better her life would be. "My sister and I are taking over the Foster House. I found a Model T pickup in the back, but it won't start. I was hoping you could help?"

"Mr. Foster was a stubborn coot. He left it out back during a spring storm instead of parking it inland like the rest of us. Seawater got into the engine, and it wouldn't start after that. He refused to let a woman work on his truck, so there it sits."

"How much would it cost to get it running again? My sister and I can't spare much right now, but I can trade carpentry work or meals at the restaurant once we're up and going."

"I'd have to take a look, but I'm sure we can work out something."

"Can you come by? I don't think I can push it a mile. We can cook you some dinner."

"Sure thing, but it will have to be tomorrow. I promised to get Mr. Byrne's car back to him today, so I'll be by after the fog lifts."

"About what time is that?"

"It depends on the weather. It could be sunrise, or it could be in the afternoon. I don't want too much moisture dripping into the engine block, so we'll have to wait."

They shook on the promise to see each other tomorrow. Dax returned her hands to her coat pockets, the folded papers in one reminding her about their contents. "What can you tell me about Franklin Wilkes?"

"He owns most of the town, including the hotel," Charlie said. "Why are you asking?"

"I saw his name on some papers at the Foster House."

"That doesn't surprise me. Frankie has bought up every shop along the marina, all but the Foster House. The word around town was that he's been trying to buy it for years, but old man Foster refused to sell."

Once again fearing she'd be homeless once Logan got wind of Frankie Wilkes, Dax left. The day had had one bright spot at least—meeting Charlie. They were kindred spirits. They both performed a man's job, dressed in men's clothes, and shook hands firmly like men did. Dax had yet to meet any other woman who was so much like her. She had a feeling that she and Charlie would become good friends.

* * *

Two weeks later

May's bedroom and shower were done. The upstairs was livable for Dax. The restaurant dining room and kitchen were set up and clean. The menu was set. Three of the servers who had worked for old man Foster were available and ready to work for the grand reopening tomorrow. Thankfully, Ruth was also available. She was the head server and had a wealth of knowledge about operating a restaurant, both in the dining room and the kitchen.

The pantry was fully stocked with dry goods and staples. The final things they needed were the fresh items that didn't last long without refrigeration. Maybe once those items arrived and were stored, Dax could finally explore the town beyond the grocery and hardware stores.

May and Dax busied themselves with last-minute touches while waiting for the grocer to deliver their large order. May had said to give them more time when they were one hour late. She said the same thing at the two-hour mark. A glance at the wall clock confirmed the grocer was overdue with their order by nearly three hours.

Dax tossed her cleaning rag on a dining table and removed her white apron. "That's it. I'm going to the store."

"We're both going." May tossed her rag down, grabbed a copy of the grocery order she'd placed, and followed Dax to the pickup truck Charlie had got running. It still needed new tires but was safe enough to run errands around town.

After days of prepping the restaurant, May's limp had become extra prominent. It made it impossible for her to step up into the cab by herself. "Let me help." Dax lifted May by the waist while she gripped the side cab railing and pulled. When Dax settled her onto the seat, closed the door, and went around to the driver's side, sadness gripped her. This was the worst she'd seen May since right after the accident. Her sister was in pain, yet she worked through it because that was what Xander women did. They ignored whatever might hold them back and pushed forward one day at a time.

Dax pulled up to the front of the grocery store, but the sign on the door was flipped. Her blood went from warm to boiling in an instant. "Closed? What the heck?"

"There are always setbacks to starting a business." May had said the right calming words, but the sudden ashen look on her face suggested she was panicked.

"That's it." Dax was mad enough to punch someone in the face. She exited the truck cab, slamming the door shut. She made a mental note to apologize to May for the ruckus she was about to make. Dax then pounded her fist on the wood frame around the door window. "Hey! Open up in there. We have an order coming!" she yelled loud enough to raise the dead in the cemetery a mile away. She pounded and yelled until a woman emerged from the department store across the street.

"I'm sorry, sir," the woman started but corrected herself when Dax turned around. "I mean, miss. Mr. Thompson had to go home for an emergency. He said someone threw a rock through his front window, and he had to board it up before it rained."

"I'm sorry for making so much noise." Dax gave the woman her best apologetic look. "But my sister and I placed a big order so we can open up the Foster House tomorrow."

"Ah, you're the Foster sisters I've heard about." The woman shook hands with Dax. "I'm Edith. I run the department store. Is there anything I can do to help?"

"Is there another grocer close by?"

Edith placed both hands on the back of her hips. "None that can get you what you need in time unless you want to drive to the city."

"Our old truck won't make it, and we're supposed to open tomorrow. The flyers are up." Dax flapped her hands in the air. "What am I supposed to tell customers when they show up?"

Edith draped an arm over Dax's shoulder. "Let's call Mr. Thompson and see if we can sort this out."

May, Dax, and Edith assembled in the department store back office following introductions. Edith called Mr. Thompson at home and handed May the phone.

"What do you mean canceled? I never canceled the order." May paused to listen, and Dax waited patiently, trying her best to remain calm. "We don't have any men working for us...Can you fill the order?" May went over the order line by line with Mr. Thompson, placing checkmarks beside the items he had in stock. "We'll meet you at the back of the Foster House in a few hours." May returned the earpiece to its resting place.

"Who canceled the order?" Dax asked.

"Some man who said he worked for us." May showed Edith her grocery order, pointing out the items she would still need after Mr. Thompson's delivery. "Can you supply any of these items?"

"Some." Edith pointed an index finger in the air with extra vigor, making Dax think the grand opening might be saved. "But I have a better idea. The town was excited to hear that the Foster House was reopening because it offered the best food. I know several people who'd be willing to help." Edith picked up the telephone. "Let's rally the troops."

Following nearly a dozen calls, Edith tracked down enough produce, meats, eggs, and dairy products to fill every item on May's list. "I can't thank you enough, Edith. How can I repay you?"

"You're quite welcome, but this is what neighbors do. But if you insist, I'm a sucker for apple pie."

"Apple pie it is."

Townspeople appeared at the Foster House within an hour, bearing the items promised. Dax took their names and addresses and noted the items donated with the promise to repay them by the end of the week and a complimentary meal for their kindness.

Once May and Dax washed and stored every item in their chiller, including Mr. Thompson's delivery, Dax pulled up a stool for May to sit at the kitchen's center chopping block. "Can you believe the people in this town?" Dax asked.

"It goes to show you that like us"—May squeezed Dax's hand—"when times get tough, people pull together."

CHAPTER TEN

Following their first week of dating, Rose had successfully convinced Riley to meet her in town for meals and such instead of picking her up at the boarding house. "It's out of your way. Besides, I use that time to memorize new songs," Rose had told him. They'd already exhausted conversation topics that interested her and were left with what interested him. She didn't care about college football, boxing, or chewing tobacco, and she certainly didn't want to hear about his dangerous whiskey runs and eluding federal agents. Rose had even entertained becoming a nag on such topics merely to encourage him to avoid them.

A month after sharing a first kiss with Riley King, Rose still hadn't the courage to take their relationship beyond touching. The cold she had for the last two weeks that made her miss a week of work served was a built-in excuse, but now that she was better, she had a choice to make: call it off or take the next step. Today's breakfast with Riley would be the test.

Riley treated her like a queen, and the idea of him as her cover appealed to Rose more than she thought possible. But she was stuck. Physical intimacy with him was a step too big to take, so she had put him off by saying she was waiting for marriage, but that was a lie. She simply didn't want sex with him or any man. She wished Riley was like Grace's husband. From what she could tell, he understood Grace's desires, and their marriage was an arrangement, nothing more. Grace staved off rumors and her husband enjoyed her riches.

Mr. Wilkes seemed more pleased with their potential coupling than Rose. He'd sent a bottle of champagne from his private stock to her and Riley's table following her last performance two nights ago. He'd mentioned he'd love it if Rose made his sister a grandmother. Nothing like pressure. Rose liked her job and the boarding house where she lived, both of which Mr. Wilkes owned, so she had a fine line to walk. A pleasant singing voice accompanied by a pretty face was no longer an anomaly, and he could easily replace her. Getting on Mr. Wilkes's wrong side was a risk she wasn't willing to take.

One positive development in town had Rose up early today, her last day off for the week, and eager to meet up with Riley. Ida's Café hadn't been an option for the previous five weeks, and she had tired of pastries from the bakery and what canned goods she could heat on the boarding house camp grill. Thankfully, the handwritten flyer she saw stapled to a power pole in town yesterday meant her unfortunate culinary circumstance was about to get better. The Foster House was reopening today under new management.

After brushing her hair with the silver brush she'd bought with her first week's pay as a singer, Rose bundled up and headed down Main Street toward the main highway. Edith's had opened a few minutes earlier, so she stepped in to check on an order she'd placed last week. When Edith finished ringing up a customer, Rose approached the register.

"Rosebud, it's good to see you. Jules said you've been nursing a bad cold." Edith's hair had turned a little grayer, and her pooch had turned out a little more since Rose first met her, and in all that time, she'd remained one of her dearest friends in town.

"Good morning, Edith. I'm all better now."

"It looks like you've lost some weight. You better put some meat on your bones."

"My appetite is finally back, so I'm meeting Riley at the Foster House for opening day."

"Those Foster sisters will give Ida a run for her money. The older one sent over an apple pie as a thank-you for getting her all stocked up for opening day. I'm afraid to say that it's about as delicious as yours, Rosebud."

"Well then, I can't wait to try it. Any idea when those shoes I ordered might come in?"

"They should be in tomorrow's delivery from San Francisco. If not, I'll give my wholesaler holy heck." Edith's version of holy heck was legendary in Half Moon Bay. Put a telephone or a broom in Edith's hand, and the offender would be deaf or picking straw from their rear end for a week.

Rose continued her trek to Foster House, pausing at the sight of Riley leaning against its exterior wall, smoking a cigarette. While she detested its smell, cigarettes were a much less disgusting habit than chewing tobacco—a holdover from Riley's farming days in Fresno.

He perked up as she dashed across the highway at the corner, giving her the same silly, dimpled smile he had the first night they met. He was a grown man and nearly thirty years old, yet he grinned like a twelve-year-old. It was a quirk she'd have to tolerate if he were to become her cover.

"Good morning, beautiful," he said.

Rose braced herself for the inevitable kiss on the cheek, but Riley greeted her with one on the lips this time. He was growing spunkier as their so-called relationship moved along. Despite the need for proper appearances, as Grace had put it, Rose wasn't sure if she could endure his boldness forever.

"Hungry?" Rose asked when he broke the kiss.

"When am I not?"

"You have a point." Rose jutted her chin toward the front door. "Let's go inside."

The new management had made many changes, she saw, and all for the better. Fresh white paint and sheer curtains had brightened the main dining room. Every table and booth was well lit by sunlight or fixtures hung from the ceiling. The board of sailor's knots that used to be behind the bar was gone, along with other seafaring wall decorations. There were nicely done frames of different color pieces of stretched fabric and lace in their place. The room was nearly filled to capacity. The chatter, smiles on customers' faces, and clanking of forks against plates signaled opening day was a big hit.

The three servers running around looked familiar—a good sign that operations would run smoothly today. Ruth, Rose's regular waitress before Mr. Foster died, gestured for her and Riley to sit in the empty booth by the window. Rose replied with a nod.

New menus adorned the table. Each had an eye-catching new hand-drawn logo at the top with "FH" written in the center of a half-moon with an ocean wave beneath it. The menu items had changed. Each appeared simple to prepare from a cook's perspective but, surprisingly, contained a combination of ingredients this restaurant hadn't offered before. A few of the dishes seemed oddly familiar. Rose remembered having something like the Santa Fe Omelet when she was a kid but couldn't recall where.

Ruth popped by Rose's table, setting down two glasses of water. "It's good to see you back, Rose. Who's this handsome fella?"

"Ruth, this is my friend, Riley King. He works with me at the Seaside Hotel."

"Well, I hope to see you two in here regularly. The new owners are a pleasure to work for." Ruth pulled out her order pad and pen. "What will it be?"

Before Riley could order for her again, another annoying habit she had to break him of, Rose handed Ruth her menu. "I'll have the Santa Fe Omelet and coffee."

"Excellent choice." Ruth winked. "It seems to be popular today."

"Make it two." Riley appeared put off by Rose's show of independence and insider knowledge.

Discussion about football became a time filler. Rose didn't care about the upcoming thirty-fifth annual "Big Game" between Stanford and Berkeley. Still, she did her best to appear interested. When the food came, she was grateful Riley's mouth was occupied with an omelet. Rose found hers was simply delicious.

A loud crash near the kitchen suggested that several plates or cups had met their death on the floor.

"Are you all right, Dax?" Ruth called out.

Every muscle in Rose's body tensed simultaneously when the name registered. Her chest ceased to move, making it impossible to take a breath. Every sound and movement in the room bled into one another until the world felt like it had stopped. The only thing she felt or heard was a pounding heartbeat echoing in her ears. She knew of only one person in the world who went by that unique name. Could years of wondering where she was and what had become of her finally be answered?

Rose turned warily toward the crash, unwilling to get her hopes up. And there was Dax, statuesque, with a tub of broken, dirty dishes at her feet. Her hair was still dark and short around her ears, identical to how Rose remembered her. A white apron hid most of her clothes, but Rose guessed she had on slacks and a button-down dress shirt, both highlighting curves that weren't there the last time they were together. Dax likely appeared plain and boyish to most of the world, but she was the most beautiful person in it to Rose.

"Dax," Rose whispered.

Her heart and breathing restarted the instant she said her name. Every muscle relaxed, allowing her to scoot out of the booth and leap to her feet. Each step toward Dax was seamless as if walking on air. The tears pooling in her eyes blurred the path, but Rose didn't need to see past her arms' reach. Dax had closed the distance between them.

Dax's arms wrapped around her, relieving an agonizing nine-year ache. Rose had given up hope of reuniting with her the day she first made love to Grace, but she had never stopped pining for her. Nearly every time she was with Grace and went into her own head, she imagined Dax doing those things to her. And in her dreams, she often conjured up a world where she and Dax could walk together on the beach, run their feet along the cool, wet sand, and lay next to each other in bed, reading stories of love and happy endings.

Rose hugged Dax tighter, hoping she wasn't in one of her dreams. She methodically grabbed and pulled at every inch of fabric on Dax's back to confirm she was real. Rose loosened her hold to get another look at the woman she'd dreamed of seeing for years, but Dax kept a firm grip.

"It's really you," Dax whispered their shared pain and unbelievable joy. She pulled back, keeping her hands on Rose's arms. "How long have you been here?"

"Since the day I left. And you?"

"Ten days. I'm helping May reopen the restaurant."

"*You're* the Foster sisters?" Rose's head spun at the twist of fate that had brought them together. Then it came to her. It had been years since Rose had thought of Dax's sister, but she remembered her marrying a man named Foster. At Dax's nod, Rose added, "Of course, May's husband."

"You have to see May. She'll be so glad to see you." Dax's cheek rose to a delightful smile. Rose gestured toward Riley that she'd be a minute and mouthed for him to wait for her. Without waiting for a response, Dax whisked Rose deeper into the restaurant and into the kitchen. The feel of their hands together made the rest of Rose tingle. She and Grace never held hands, and it had been too long since she'd done so with a woman out of more than a greeting or a brief reassurance. She missed how comforting Dax's hand felt and how it fit so snugly into hers.

"May! You won't believe who's here."

A woman cooking at the grill and leaning most of her weight on a stool turned toward Dax's outburst. The young, vibrant woman with a glowing face that Rose remembered had aged more than one should in nine years. The leg brace likely had something to do with it.

May's eyes danced with recognition. "Rose!" She struggled to push herself from the stool, grimacing in obvious pain, but Rose told her to remain sitting and walked to her. Her hearty hug was no less tight than Dax's but not nearly as stirring. "What on earth are you doing here?"

"I live here."

"My goodness, young lady. Let me look at you." May inspected Rose up and down. "You were cute as a button as a teenager, but you've turned into a knockout."

The tips of Rose's ears heated to May's compliment. Riley had complimented her practically every day, but his attention had grown tiresome. This, coming from someone who had known her as a young girl, brought back the awkward adolescent in her.

"Thank you, May. It's w-w-wonderful seeing you." Rose gestured toward May's brace. "W-W-What happened?"

May patted her right leg. "We were driving, and a truck ran a stoplight a few years back." Some eggs sizzled on the grill, requiring May's attention. She squeezed Rose's hand. "I gotta get back to work. You should come by after closing so we can all catch up."

"I will." Dax took Rose by the hand again, pulling her into a room off the kitchen. It had a bed and dresser and an office desk with stacks of papers and folders. "Do y-y-you live in here?" Rose asked.

"May does. She can't use stairs much, so I built her a room down here. I'm upstairs." Dax closed the door, swept Rose into her arms again, and spun her around like they did in the talkies. She returned Rose to the floor, the wild joy in her eyes taming to a soft caress. "I thought I'd never see you again." She brushed Rose's cheek with the back of a hand.

"I thought the same." Rose leaned into Dax's touch, cupping her hand over the one sending tingles to every limb. Dax began to inch inward, as slow as the time they kissed in the poplar grove. Rose's lips ached to touch hers when she felt Dax exhale on them.

"I've missed you," Dax whispered.

"Rose, I gotta get going." Riley's muffled but loud voice penetrated the closed door, separating Rose from the life she suddenly wanted and the one she had.

"She's catching up with an old friend. I'll send her out. Now, get out of my kitchen before I hit you over the head with a frying pan." May's firm tone left Rose with no doubt she hadn't made an empty threat.

"Who was that?" Dax asked.

"My b-b-boyfriend." Those words nauseated Rose, which was why the words stuck when she'd said them. She'd backed herself into a corner of needing a boyfriend to get Frankie Wilkes off her back, not because she wanted one or specifically wanted Riley. Rose and Dax had much to talk about, but this wasn't the time. Ruth was calling for Dax to come out and help with the orders.

"Oh." Dax's long expression cut Rose's heart to shreds.

"I gotta go, but I'll come by after closing like May suggested. Okay?"

"Okay." Dax had sucked in her lower lip, suggesting Rose had much to explain about Riley.

Rose said goodbye to May before Dax walked her into the dining room while carrying a breakfast plate in each hand. She stopped to say goodbye to Dax but couldn't bring herself to say the words. They never got to say them nine years ago, and now that they'd found each other again, goodbye didn't seem appropriate.

Before she could come up with the right words, Riley came from behind and slung an arm over her shoulder. "Come on, Rose. I paid the check. Uncle Frankie is expecting me."

A lump formed in Rose's throat. The last thing she wanted was to make Dax think she and Riley were closer than his forwardness might suggest, but she couldn't risk giving Riley the same impression of her and Dax. She gave Dax a sheepish look and settled on, "It was nice seeing you, Dax. We'll catch up soon."

Riley ushered Rose out the door and to the corner where they would part ways. Before she could object, he'd pulled her in for a second kiss on the lips. He'd always packed his kisses with a bit of passion, but this one contained an extra wallop. By the time he pulled away, they'd earned the unwanted attention of some locals.

"I was going to tell you over breakfast, but I got nervous, and then you disappeared. Uncle Frankie was so happy to see us together the other night that he's giving me a promotion. He wants me to run the entire club operations, not just do the whiskey runs. That means more pay." He removed a small black velvet box from his coat pocket and opened it, exposing a single-diamond ring. A sinking feeling set in Rose's stomach when he bent to one knee. "I know this is sudden, but I love you, Rose. Will you marry me?"

Her mouth hung open, unsure how to respond with the stare of onlookers pressuring her for an answer. "I d-d-don't know w-w-what to say." A tightness formed in Rose's chest. How was she supposed to let down a man she'd known for only a month without endangering her job and living arrangements? But, more importantly, how was she supposed to explain this to Dax?

Riley rose to his feet and slid the ring onto her finger. "Say that you'll think about it. We can get one of those new row houses off Main Street."

"I don't have that kind of m-m-money."

"Uncle Frankie said he'd help set us up at the bank."

"This is too fast." Rose stared at the ring on her finger, its weight feeling more like chains than a bond of love. If she could, she would take off running down the street and hide in her boarding house room until Riley had forgotten all about her and moved on to the next woman. Any woman would be thrilled to catch a handsome man like him, but Rose wasn't any woman. She was different—like Grace, Dax, Jules, and Charlie were different. No man could ever thrill her physically like Grace had, but Grace would never have her heart. Dax had owned it since she was sixteen.

Riley rubbed Rose's upper arms and bent to stare her in the eye. "Think about it. Can I see you tonight?"

"Not tonight. I need m-m-more time."

Riley kissed her on the cheek, and they parted ways. Rose walked at a fast clip toward her boarding house. She felt light-headed, unable to focus on a single thing. Thoughts of her job, a future with Riley, and a dream life with Dax collided in her head. Why was the world so cruel with expectations of who people were supposed to love and be with? She knew who she wanted, but saying no to Riley would unravel the life she'd built.

Rose was about to walk past Edith's Department Store when a familiar face inside caught her attention through the window, bringing her to an abrupt stop. She detoured inside and, without saying a word, grabbed Jules by the sleeve out of line at the register and dragged her deep inside the store toward the end of a rarely visited aisle.

"I need to talk to you." Rose's head was still pounding at the mindboggling turn of events. She covered her face with both hands and raked them downward to release the frustration.

Jules pointed to Rose's left hand. "What is that?"

"What is what?"

"That ring?"

"Riley proposed, but that's not the important thing."

"Whoa." Jules put her hands up in a stopping motion. "Your boyfriend of all of one month asks you to marry him, and that's not important?"

Jules's question threw Rose off, forcing her to shake her head and change her train of thought. "Of course, it's important."

"So you said yes?"

"I said I'd think about it. The important thing is Dax is in town."

A devious grin formed on Jules's lips. "Your paths finally crossed. And?"

What did Jules say? Rose suspected some deviousness coming from her best friend. "Wait. You knew Dax was in town and didn't tell me. Why didn't you say something?"

"Charlie mentioned her name." Jules shrugged as if she were holding back details on a sale of tuna cans at Edith's, not the news of the decade for Rose. "She worked on Mr. Foster's old truck for her. So, I knew it had to be your Dax with a name like that."

Rose darted her eyes, thinking of the days lost that could have been spent with Dax. Anger overpowered her. She was more furious than when her parents sent her away. Angrier than when Ida made her feel lower than dirt. She formed a fist and punched Jules in the arm hard enough to leave a mark.

"Ow. That hurt." Jules rubbed tomorrow's bruise. She was lucky Rose stopped at one blow. Her omission deserved much more.

"Good. Now tell me why you didn't tell me Dax was in town."

"The way you talked about Grace and the need for a cover, I thought it was better not to say anything and wait for your paths to cross."

"You should have said something. You know how important Dax is to me."

"I'm sorry, Rose, but Charlie and I didn't want to interfere. We agreed to let you two reunite on your own."

"Charlie knew too? You two sure can keep a secret." Rose punched her again.

"Ow. Can you at least alternate arms?" Jules rubbed the spot Rose had been using for target practice. She moved in closer, her tone taking on a mischievous lilt. "So, what was it like seeing her again? Were there fireworks?"

"We were in public for the most part, but yes, there were fireworks until Riley needed to go."

"And propose."

"Don't remind me."

"Let's get back to Dax. Was she what you expected?"

"Better." Rose's breath hitched at the memory of their tight embrace and how she tingled when Dax's body pressed against her. Her soft curves felt more natural, and their near kiss felt more erotic than anything Riley had offered.

"I can't wait to meet her if she has this effect on you with one meeting."

"Humph." The unmistakable sound of displeasure came from behind Rose. She turned to see Ida's disapproving glare.

"I can't believe that woman is here. I'd heard the name around town but didn't put it together until now. Need I remind you of the sin that brought you to my home?"

Rose rolled her eyes, making sure Ida saw every exaggerated movement. "You need to mind your business, Ida."

"You need to mind your p's and q's, young lady." Ida adjusted the wicker shopping handbasket hanging from her left forearm. "If Mr. Wilkes or Mr. King learns of what brought you to Half Moon Bay, they will drop you like a hot potato, and you'll be out on your ear again."

"You don't want to do that, Ida."

"And why wouldn't I? You were nothing but trouble since the day you arrived."

Rose was never so pleased that she'd held back when her father dropped her off. It was time to put Ida in her place. "Because I know the truth. You don't want Morris learning about Conroy, do you? If you say one word about Dax or me, I'll make sure he and everyone else in town knows your dark secret."

Ida's eyes bulged at the mention of Rose's "brother." She and Rose each had much to lose if their secrets were told. "Humph." She raised her chin before turning sharply on her heel and marching out of the store.

Rose scanned the aisle. She'd gathered the attention of at least one other patron, something she couldn't afford. She grabbed Jules by the hand, tugging her down the aisle and toward the door. Jules placed her toothpaste selection on the counter on her way past the register. "Perhaps another time, Edith." Once out the door and marching toward their boarding house, Jules asked, "What secret?"

"Not now, Jules."

"Then what do you plan to do about Riley and Dax? And Grace, for that matter?"

"I don't know. I'm stuck with either losing my job and my home or the love of my life."

CHAPTER ELEVEN

Dax would describe herself as a jumbled mess since Rose walked out of the Foster House minutes ago. Seeing her after nine years had thrown her for a bigger loop than the time she sneaked into Neptune Beach and rode the Whoopee roller coaster on a full stomach. Both were nauseating. The world had stopped spinning when she laid eyes on Rose's unmistakable hair. And when Rose turned and locked gazes with her, her heart stopped. She had spent years daydreaming about each line and curve on Rose's face. The plumpness of youth had left her cheeks, but everything else, from her chin to her eyes, had the same mesmerizing beauty.

Sweeping Rose into her arms had felt like a dream. Dax had done it so many times in her head over the years that she wasn't entirely convinced it was real until breath from a deep sigh had tickled her ear. Then Rose had said the most deflating word in the English language, puncturing Dax's swelling hope. Rose had a boyfriend, and he had proposed to her on the sidewalk, right in front of Dax's eyes. Moments later, Rose disappeared, wearing his ring and pounding the final stake through Dax's heart.

"Dax!" a waitress yelled from somewhere deep inside the restaurant.

What now? Dax thought. She'd reunited with the love of her life minutes earlier, only to learn that she was unobtainable. Going from an emotional high to the lowest of lows was dizzying. She turned on her heel to answer, momentarily losing her balance, then, hearing her name called again, made her way to the voice. She discovered Ruth standing in front of the men's bathroom door as a puddle of water appeared at the threshold.

"The johns both overflowed."

"Great." Dax ran a hand across her forehead, sensing a major headache on the horizon if she didn't keep busy. "I'll handle it."

Thank goodness for plungers. Dax could kiss the person who invented it. She'd cleared both clogs within ten minutes after she fished out of them several dishrags from the bussers' station. The toilets had plenty of paper on the roll, so the rags hadn't ended up in there by accident. Someone had wanted to create havoc. Apparently, not everyone in town was happy to see the Foster House reopen.

The rest of opening day had Dax numb, spending most of the day on her feet, bussing tables, washing dishes, fetching ingredients and pots for May, and helping serve large orders to save the waitresses two trips. By the time the wall clock read two thirty, she was exhausted and dripping with sweat. She wiped her brow, comparing restaurant work to her old job. When she was a carpenter, she could pace herself and sit and rest when it suited her, but running a restaurant was a different type of tiring. Thankfully, the three ladies May had hired were all former waitresses at the Foster House and jumped right in. Dax simply followed their lead. All day.

Dax silently thanked May for settling on serving only breakfast and lunch and closing Mondays unless it was a holiday and Tuesdays until they could afford to hire a second cook and more servers. They had only a half hour until closing. The lunch rush had died down around two o'clock, and the waitresses had gone home for the day, leaving only May, Dax, and two customers at one table on their last few bites. Dax filled the dish bucket with glasses and plates from the group that had left a few minutes earlier and walked it into the kitchen, placing it in the sink. May wasn't at her station nor anywhere in the kitchen. Dax peeked into May's room and found her on the bed, brace off and rubbing her bum leg.

Dax knelt in front of her, concerned about May's haggard appearance. "Let me see."

May's right calf and ankle looked twice as big as her left. They hadn't been that swollen since weeks after the accident. Weighed down again by guilt, she went into caregiver mode, wetting some towels at the sink and returning to May. She leaned back against the head of the bed, positioned a pillow lower on the bed, and placed a dry towel on top of it before propping May's leg on the pillow and wrapping the wet towels around it. "The cold will help. Do you need aspirin?"

"I'll be fine once the swelling is gone."

Dax inspected the brace leaning against the chair next to her bed. One of the metal rods appeared more warped than the last time she checked it. Dax had no doubt it would eventually snap. "You need a new brace, May. It's as simple as that."

"I'll make do. We can add more stools in the kitchen for me to lean on, and I'll start using the cane again."

"You shouldn't have to make do. I'll figure out a way to get you that brace." Dax had spent her savings on parts to get Mr. Foster's old pickup working, so she was starting from nothing. She could offer her carpentry services around town, but few people would want her to work in their homes in the evening. And with only a couple of hundred homes in town, the possibility of earning enough money before the brace broke was more than slim.

The main entry door in the dining room made its distinct sound of opening. May propped herself up, but Dax told her to stay. "If it's another customer, I'll tell them the kitchen is closed for the day."

May patted Dax's hand and gave her a grateful smile. "You're a good sister. I'll get used to this in a few days."

Walking into the dining room, Dax silently renewed her promise to do whatever it took to get May a new brace. The last customer had walked out, leaving a nickel tip. At this rate, living in a small tourist town would force her to get creative.

Dax went to the door to flip the sign but stopped when Charlie and another woman stepped inside. "Hey, Charlie, are the tires in?"

"Not yet. I feel bad about this, but they didn't make today's delivery like my Redwood City supplier had promised. So I raised some holy heck, and now he's making a special run for me tomorrow."

"You're a lifesaver, Charlie. I can't thank you enough for helping me get that thing running and roadworthy. It's made it a lot easier getting the Foster House ready to open." Dax turned her attention to Charlie's friend. "Who do we have here?"

"This is my special friend, Jules." Charlie's extra-wide smile confirmed she was special.

"It's a pleasure to meet you, Jules." Jules shook Dax's hand and offered a pleasant smile.

Jules scanned the dining room. "Are we too late for lunch?"

"I'm sorry, but we had to close the kitchen early. My sister overdid it on her first day."

"I hope she feels better soon," Jules said.

"How about dessert?" Dax offered.

"We wouldn't want to put—" Charlie stopped in midsentence when Jules hit her in the belly with the back of her hand. "That would be great."

Dax dipped into the kitchen, plated, and loaded onto a tray three generous slices of the only remaining dish on the dessert rack, half of an apple pie. She peeked into May's room before returning to the dining room. She was sound asleep. The sight tugged at Dax's conscience. She hoped today's robust receipts accurately predicted that they would be able to afford a second cook in a few short months.

Dax rejoined her guests. "Care to join me in apple pie on me, ladies?" After both cordially agreed, Dax directed them to a booth near a window facing the street where Rose had received her engagement ring earlier. Between bites, they chatted about the Foster House's successful opening day and May's bad leg.

Charlie said, "I can look at May's brace and see if I can straighten and reinforce the metal rods. It won't be a permanent fix, but it could get her through until she can get a new one."

"That would be wonderful." Dax leaned back, taking in her new friend. From the first day they met, she felt a kinship toward Charlie, like they were cut from the same cloth. Looking out for one another and helping without being asked had become the cornerstone of their friendship.

A corner of Jules's lips turned upward in a devilish grin. "Did anything special happen today?"

Her question stirred unpleasant memories of this morning. Seeing Rose's boyfriend drop to one knee had cut her deep like a knife to the gut. Recalling how easily he slipped a ring on her finger twisted the knife every which way.

Charlie snapped her fingers in front of Dax's face, getting her attention. "Where'd you go, Dax?"

Dax pushed back the thoughts that had had her reeling most of the day and focused on her booth mates. "I'm sorry. It's been a long, tiring day."

"That's it?" Jules leaned back in the booth, pressing her lips together tightly.

"Will you stop it, Jules?" Charlie's curt tone left no doubt she was irritated.

"This is ridiculous," Jules said. "They belong together."

"What are you two talking about?" Dax asked, thinking it was cute how much they sounded like an old married couple.

Charlie scanned the empty room and the empty sidewalk in front of the window before directing her attention to Dax. "Let me start by saying that you're not alone, Dax." Charlie took Jules's hand and kissed the back of it. "I have a feeling you're different, like Jules and me. Am I right?"

Dax's stomach went rock hard at the thought of someone figuring out she was different. Every muscle tensed, limiting her to only a nod as her response.

"You're right to be cautious," Charlie continued. "Most people here don't look kindly upon odd girls like us."

A lightness took over. If anyone in Half Moon Bay had to discover Dax's deepest secret, she was glad it was Charlie. "How did you know?"

"I'd like to say I have a special gift in such matters, but I knew as soon as you said your name."

Dax narrowed her eyes in confusion. "My name?"

"It's unique and kinda hard to forget. My girl here is friends with Rose, and Rose mentioned your name to her a few times."

Dax turned her attention to Jules, hopeful she could gain some insight into the woman who had occupied her mind and resided in her heart for years. "She did? What did she say about me?"

"She said she once loved you and that your kiss curled her toes more than anyone else could."

"She said that, huh?" Dax's cheeks warmed at the memory of her and Rose in her bedroom and how she had tingled from head to toe when she took a tantalizing breast into her mouth. However, that sensation quickly left at the reality that Rose was engaged. "What else did she say?"

"Not much until today. Seeing you threw her for a loop."

"It did me too. I'd given up hope of ever seeing her again, and then, there she was, sitting in my restaurant"—Dax swallowed the growing lump in her throat—"with her boyfriend."

"Yeah, about that." Jules squirmed in her seat. "Riley's proposal threw her for a loop too."

"That's his name? Riley?"

"Yeah, they both work at the Seaside Hotel. He's the boss's nephew." Jules's shrug gave Dax the impression she wasn't a fan of Rose's choice of a romantic interest, and conjured up a vital question. Did Rose take up with him because of what he could give her? A stable life and a family of their own? How was Dax supposed to compete with that?

Dax's last ounce of hope left her in a stampede. "I hope he makes her happy."

"That's just it." Jules reached across the table and cupped Dax's hand. "I know he can't. Sure, he's a pip and has a good-paying job."

"You're not helping, Jules." Charlie gave her a look that said to quit while she was behind.

"Right. I'm sorry." Jules gave Dax a sheepish look. "She's been seeing Riley for about a month. Their first date was the morning after Mr. Foster was killed. They were supposed to have breakfast here, but it was closed for obvious reasons."

"Killed?" Dax asked. "Logan said his father fell down the stairs and broke his neck."

"More like pushed if you ask me."

Charlie shot Jules a stern look. "We shouldn't be talking about such things without proof."

"And why not?" Jules shot back a sterner look, one that had fingernail torture written all over it if she wasn't allowed to speak. It was one Dax never wanted to be pointed in her direction. "I was there when Doc Hughes conducted the autopsy. I know what I saw." Jules flailed her arms. "The man had bruises where they shouldn't have been. At the very least, his death should have been listed as suspicious, not accidental."

Dax's suspicions landed on one name. "Do you think Frankie Wilkes may have wanted him dead? He wanted to buy this place."

"I wouldn't put it past him," Jules said without blinking.

"Are you trying to get kicked out of your boarding house?" Charlie's harsh tone set Dax aback and caused Jules to snap her head toward her. However, it wasn't intimidating like the bullies who used to pick on Rose or like Heather's husband. Instead, Charlie's tone contained sharp disappointment. It gave Dax the impression Frankie Wilkes was a major point of contention between Charlie and Jules.

Jules's expression morphed when she looked at Dax, turning softer eyes on her. Clearly, she was about to deescalate. "You don't have to dodge the topic of Rose. She's not seeing Riley for the reason you think. She never talks about him the way she talked about you. If I had to guess, you're the love of her life."

"I sense a 'but' coming." A qualifier was the last thing Dax wanted to hear, but she'd been disappointed by false hope for years and wasn't prepared for more.

"Rose has a hard decision to make, so she wanted me to tell you she's not coming back here today. She's worried if she turns down Riley, she could lose her job and be kicked out of the boarding house."

"Why would she think she'd lose her home?" Dax asked.

"Rose's boss also owns the boarding house. Heck, he owns most of the town."

"It sounds like her boss isn't the type of person Rose wants to cross." Dax chewed on her last words, her stomach churning at the irony. After nearly a decade, she'd finally found Rose again, only to discover she was unobtainable. Fate was a cruel friend.

CHAPTER TWELVE

Rose spent the evening devising her next course of action to keep her job and home, getting Riley to rescind his proposal so she could act as if their breakup was for the best. A single-pronged approach could drag on for months, so she settled on simultaneously annoying him on multiple levels. Remembering how he acted at breakfast yesterday, her best course was to present herself as an independent nag who ran hot and cold, everything Riley disliked in a woman. Rose estimated he would run to the next woman within a week. That would pave the way for her to be with Dax the same way Jules was with Charlie—a couple in private, friends in public. And the next time Grace came through Half Moon Bay, she would explain things about Dax. Two questions remained: Did Dax still want her that way? And was she free to be with Rose?

She'd successfully dodged Riley for the day. Frankie Wilkes had him learning the bar operations at the Seaside Club so he could take it over by the weekend. *Thank goodness for small favors*, she thought. She was counting on Riley's deep sense of obligation to his uncle and a healthy dose of fear toward him, a situation Rose planned to exploit, starting tonight.

She selected her most revealing stage dress for tonight's performances at the Seaside Club. While it would undoubtedly keep Riley's attention, it would also attract the interest of patrons who overindulged and who might make Riley jealous. A little nudge here and there could set off a chain reaction of male instinct and get Riley to question whether Rose was worth the bother.

An hour before her first performance of the night, Rose bundled up in her warm coat and slung her purse over her shoulder to begin her workday walk to the Seaside Hotel in the November twilight. The sun had disappeared over the ocean horizon, adding a chill that penetrated her bones. Clouds had rolled in, warning of a pending storm. *Darn*, she thought. She'd forgotten her umbrella. At least she remembered to wear her galoshes.

When Rose came within a block of Edith's Department Store, she realized she'd neglected to check on the shoes Edith had special ordered for her, so she detoured inside minutes before the Sunday closing time. If they were in, they'd go well with the dress she'd chosen for tonight, and she wouldn't have to use the old ones she kept in a storage room at the club.

Edith acknowledged her with a raised index finger as she rang up a woman who appeared to be the last customer in the store. Rose occupied herself by scanning a collection of cleaning and kitchen items in a produce box near the front door. Edith often gathered items for customers when they called ahead to make sure the things were in stock. This assortment looked like such an order.

After Edith bagged the woman's items and bid her a warm goodbye, she waved Rose over. "I have your shoes right here. I griped so much about the late delivery they took seventy cents off the price." She placed two quarters, two dimes, and a box on the counter.

"How about we split it as a finder's fee?" Rose slid half the change across the counter toward Edith. "You've given me too many discounts over the years, so I won't take no for an answer."

"I never knew you had a stubborn streak, Rosebud."

"It only comes out when I know I'm right." Rose gave her a playful wink.

Edith briefly shifted her gaze toward the front door when it opened. "I hate to rush you off, Rosebud, but I have to help the customer who walked in a minute ago before I close."

"Don't concern yourself, Edith. You have a good night." Rose turned to leave following Edith's goodbye but stopped dead in her tracks. The butterflies that had once filled her stomach in a rain-soaked tree grove had come out of a nine-year dormancy, hoping to experience a second first kiss. "Dax."

"I see you two know each other," Edith said, or something like it. Rose could hardly hear over the thrumming in her ears. Rose opened her mouth to respond, but nothing came out. Her mind was still focused on endless possibilities with Dax.

"Yes, ma'am. We're old friends." Dax's glowing smile added a new meaning to the word friends. It answered Rose's two lingering questions. Dax wanted Rose, and if Dax wasn't already single, she soon would be.

"I think we're past the ma'am stage." Edith smiled. "How about we move past formalities and right into first names?"

Dax finally broke her gaze from Rose and pulled cash from her pocket. "Edith it is. This should cover today's order and our tab. My sister prefers not to run up bills."

"I couldn't agree more. Once you do, chances are, the bank will own everything soon enough. How do you two know each other?" Edith wagged an index finger between Dax and Rose.

"We grew up together." Rose's bland explanation didn't come close to describing their friendship, especially what they shared before falling in love. Dax was the only person who made Rose comfortable in her own skin. She was the only one who put her at ease enough to talk her ear off with the words coming out as smooth as silk. When everyone else made her feel like an oddball because of her speech, Dax made her feel extraordinary.

"I'm glad you have another friend in town, Rosebud." Edith's motherly concern was comforting. It meant Rose had good people around her.

"Rosebud?" Dax raised her eyebrows, her tone becoming playful.

"I have a daughter named Rose, who married and moved away years ago," Edith said. "Your Rose came in so often I had to come up with a name to distinguish between the two."

"It suits you." Dax smiled. "Roses are most beautiful right before they bloom. They're full of color, youth, and mystery." Dax had penned a love letter to Rose in two sentences, conveying longing, desire, and fond memories.

"Thank you." Rose's cheeks warmed to the words she wanted to say. If not for the robust Half Moon Bay rumor mill, she would throw her arms around Dax and tell her she felt the same way.

"Are you heading home?" Dax asked.

"Work. I'm a singer at the Seaside Hotel."

"Of course you are." Dax's chest rose to a deep inhale, and her face glowed with what Rose would describe as beaming pride. "You've had a beautiful voice since we were kids."

Thunder rumbled through Edith's plate glass windows, prompting Rose to glance outside. "I should get going before the rain comes."

"Me too." Dax hoisted the box of goods by the cutout handles and pushed the door open with her backside. "Care to walk with me?"

"Happy to." Rose glanced over her shoulder toward the register. "See you next time, Edith."

"Next time, Edith," Dax shouted before the door closed behind her and Rose. They walked in silence for two blocks without passing another pedestrian, the sky growing darker and the air colder. "I met Jules yesterday. She's a pistol."

"That's an understatement. Nothing gets past that woman, and as one of only two nurses in town, she takes no guff."

Dax briefly looked behind her. "She and Charlie make a great couple."

"That they do."

"Are they the only ones in town like us?"

"We think so. It's not like sapphic women wear name tags, and we certainly can't go around a-a-asking who they enjoy kissing."

"I guess not." Dax snickered. "I've never heard of odd girls described as sapphic. What does that mean?"

"It's French. It refers to the ancient Greece poet Sappho born on the island of Lesbos. She'd fallen in love with a woman." Rose cringed the moment she explained. She only knew its meaning through Grace and hoped Dax wouldn't ask how she learned such a fancy French word. Grace Parsons would be difficult to discuss.

"Aww, lesbian. It makes sense." Dax nodded before turning her expression solemn. "Jules told me about Ida and working at the café. I'm so sorry you went through that. I feel like it's my fault."

Always the protector, Rose thought. Dax had spent most of their childhood chasing bullies who had made fun of Rose. It was good to see she still had that instinct. "Don't feel that way. I w-w-wouldn't have come to your room if I didn't want to be there."

"Still." Dax nudged Rose in the shoulder in midstride. "A singer, huh? How did that happen?"

"The h-h-hotel owner came into the café late one night and heard me singing to myself. A-A-After one show, he offered me the job."

"I bet you gave Ida an earful."

"And then some." Rose nudged her back. "How about you? Where did you end up?"

"With May and Logan in San Francisco. Things were good until the accident." Dax stopped. Rose did too and looked back at her. Dax's eyes misted with tears. "I was driving."

Rose shifted her purse and shoebox into the same hand, freeing the other to rub Dax's lower arm. "I'm so sorry."

"The other driver went through the stoplight, but I should have been paying better attention."

"You blame yourself for things you shouldn't, Dax. Sometimes, bad things happen for no reason." Raindrops sprinkled the top of Rose's head. The sky had turned nearly pitch dark, but the streetlight at the corner provided enough illumination to see more drops were falling. "We should hurry."

They resumed walking in silence. The faster Dax and Rose walked, the quicker the rain fell until it became a downpour. By the time they reached the corner of Main and the highway, their clothes were soaked, and Rose was sure her hair had become a straggly mess. Dax's short hair had clung to the outline of her head, and her bangs had stretched below her eyelids. Rose was sure she could barely see.

They reached the Foster House, and Dax worked the doorknob. "The hotel is blocks away. Come inside until the storm lets up."

Dax disappeared into the dark dining room. The lights were off, and blinds were drawn, the only brightness coming through the open door. Rose placed her shoebox and purse on the nearest table.

The overhead lights near the back of the room flashed on, casting a dim glow near the front where Rose waited. Dax had laid her box of goods on the bar in the rear of the room and was walking back toward Rose, carrying two dish towels. Her stride was full of confidence, and her expression was filled with concern. "Take off that wet coat, and let's get you dried off."

"Where's May?" Rose focused on getting the buttons through the wet holes and eventually slid her jacket off.

"Her light was off, so she must be sleeping. Working the kitchen is wearing her out." Dax handed Rose a towel before taking her coat. She froze, mouth agape, her stare fixed on Rose's dress. "Wow."

"Stage costume." Not once had Rose felt embarrassed wearing a dress that exposed a little skin while performing, until now. Not that she minded Dax seeing her in it, but she didn't want her thinking she dressed like that outside of work.

"Very nice." Dax placed Rose's coat on a hook near the front door before removing her own and hanging it on a hook next to Rose's.

Rose squeezed the excess water from her hair into the towel while watching Dax use the second towel to dry her short hair. She then gestured toward Dax's head. "The benefits of short hair."

"Easy to wash. Easy to dry. Easy to brush. I never have to worry about what to do with it."

"I guess not," Rose laughed. The rain continued to pelt the roof and windows in a soothing rhythm. "I should leave soon. I have a show at seven."

"I'd love to come to hear you sing."

"I'd like that, but I must w-w-warn you. I sing in a speakeasy."

A devilish grin formed on Dax's lips. "Why, Rose Hamilton? Flirting with the law. The next thing you'll tell me is that you've become a drinker."

"Only champagne."

"Well, la de dah, Miss Fancy Pants."

Rose jokingly slapped Dax on the arm. "I don't make enough to buy it. Sometimes the boss or guests o-o-offer me a drink after my show."

Dax's face turned long, her mood changing in an instant. "Like Riley?"

The back of Rose's throat grew thick. Since leaving Edith's, she'd felt like she and Dax were the only two people in the world. That they were best friends again, sharing gossip about the neighborhood comings and goings. Until now. She wanted to be honest with Dax, but explaining Riley meant talking about Grace, and she wasn't ready for this discussion yet.

She dipped her head, unable to form a single word. Dax then lifted her chin with a hand. "Jules didn't say much, but she was clear that you might lose your job and home if you make him mad." Rose confirmed with a slow nod. "Do you love him?"

"No." Rose's heart shriveled at the question. She silently cursed Jules for her steadfast rule of not becoming a buttinsky, wishing she would have explained a little more about Riley but not everything. "It's not like that."

"Then what is it like? Why are you marrying him?" The pain in Dax's voice hurt Rose as well. How could she make Dax understand something that few people in the world would get? She could think of only one way.

"I don't want to marry him."

Rose cupped Dax's face with both hands and drew her into a long-awaited kiss. Their lips and bodies collided at last, unchaining nine years of stifled longing and fantasies. Dax's lips set hers on fire, and Dax's body made every nerve in her tingle. Their tongues feasted on one another as if they had been starved for nearly a decade. Hands roamed, refusing to settle on any single part until Dax lowered her grasp to Rose's bottom. She pressed their centers together with pressure hard enough to crush the diamond Riley had given her.

Rose had noticed earlier today that Dax's arms were more muscular than she remembered. Whatever labor she'd been doing, it had given her Herculean strength. She imagined those arms lifting her for one creative act of passion after another.

Then Rose's mind shifted instantly. If Grace had been pawing her, she would know what to expect and what was expected of her. They'd only seen each other a dozen times, but she and Grace had packed in exhausting hours of raw sex during those few days together. She had become familiar with Grace's cues and how to satisfy her desire at any given moment. But Dax was a mystery. Rose wasn't sure if she'd yet made love to a woman or a man. And if they didn't stop now, she might take things further than what Dax was ready for.

Rose fought the urge to lean Dax atop a table and taste every drop of the essence that was undoubtedly pouring from her. Instead, she slowed her kiss and exploration, hoping Dax would follow her lead, and she did. Rose stopped and pulled back far enough to see a desire burning in Dax's smoky brown eyes.

The patter on the roof had stopped, leaving the pounding in her ears and Dax's heavy breathing as the only sounds in the room. Rose rested a hand on Dax's chest, letting it rise and fall with each breath. The thumping beneath her fingers matched her own racing heartbeat. It beat for the things Rose wanted her and Dax to do to each other. It beat for the knowledge that Dax would always be her protector. It beat for a future where she and

Dax woke every day wrapped in each other's arms until one of them took their final breath.

"I want to be with you."

Dax's breathing slowed. "But."

"But we have much to talk about."

Dax's eyes took on the same confidence behind her walk, her kiss, and how she had carried herself since they reunited. "I love you, Rose. That hasn't changed since the day our parents ripped us apart. If anything, I love you more."

Rose closed her eyes, regretting the choices she'd made. If she hadn't taken up with Grace, she wouldn't need cover in Riley. "I love you too, but before we can be together, I need to untangle the mess I've made." She traced Dax's cheek with a fingertip. "I have to go."

"Can I watch you sing tonight? The restaurant is closed tomorrow, so I don't have to get up early."

"I'd rather you didn't. I'd be thinking of you, not the l-l-lyrics." Besides the distraction, Rose had to settle things with Riley before inviting Dax deeper into her life.

"Soon then?"

"Soon." Rose placed the same index finger on Dax's lips, hoping the barrier would let her walk away. "I want to kiss you again, but I really have to go."

Dax took a step back, but the pull between them remained. This new connection felt different from the one they shared as teenagers. At least for Rose. This one was stronger, with deeper roots stemming from nine years of reliving over and over in her head the few beautiful moments they'd shared as would-be lovers. It was the type of bond that only they could sever.

Rose put on her damp coat, turned, and placed her hand on the doorknob. Dax drew closer, pressing her body into Rose and her hands against the door on either side of Rose's head.

"Don't go." Dax's voice neither begged nor demanded. Instead, it handed Rose a second chance to stay and take this to whatever conclusion she wanted. But what Rose wanted and what she had time for were two distinct options.

Rose turned, gave Dax a brief yet fiery kiss, and ran out the door. Her galoshes splashed puddles on the sidewalk the two long blocks to the entrance of the Seaside Hotel. She continued her fast clip until she reached the storage room in the downstairs kitchen, where she kept things to prepare for her performance. Once inside, she slumped against the door, tracing her lips with two fingers. Her mouth still tingled, and her head spun from that passionate kiss.

"Damn," Rose whispered. Dax could still curl her toes.

A knock on the door followed by Lester's voice dragged Rose to the present. "Five minutes, Rosebud."

"I'll be right out." Rose removed her coat and glanced in the smudged, cracked mirror. She looked like a wet mop. She had no time to dry and poof out her signature wavy curls, so she brushed her hair straight and wrapped it into a tight bun. Some lipstick and rouge added the red that the stage lights loved. She ripped off her galoshes and then realized she'd left her new shoes at the Foster House. "Dammit." She scrounged through her cardboard box of things in the corner and fished out her old black shoes. They didn't complete the look of a vamp, but they would have to do.

She bolted down the corridor leading to the stage. Lester tossed her a questioning look, but Rose couldn't blame him. She'd never had her hair this way and had never been this late for a show. "Do you have your flask with you?" she asked.

Lester removed the silver-plated container from his inside breast pocket and handed it to Rose. She took three long swigs to summon the strength to get through the next two shows despite the fact that every nerve in her body was currently screaming to feel Dax's arms around her.

"Are you all right, Rosebud?"

"I will be." She returned the flask, thinking about how to speed things along with Riley.

They took the stage. Lester took his seat at the piano, adjusted his bow tie, and leaned into his microphone. "Ladies and gentlemen, the Seaside Club is proud to present Miss Rose Hamilton." He placed both hands on the ivory keys and played.

Rose belted out the first verse of Lester's bluesy song while scanning the half-full room. A few couples watched intently from their tables while several men without lady companions appeared focused on Rose's dress. At least the well-dressed one didn't make his leering obvious. Riley was at his usual spot, standing at the end of the bar, leaning one elbow on it.

During several songs, Rose had played up her new hairdo, running her hands against it in a way designed to rev Riley's engine. Each time she did, she thought of sliding her hands down Dax's torso, which had been slickened with sweat from hours of unbridled sex. Rose's center had clenched on stage more than once, an effect that had never resulted from Grace spreading her legs a few inches and licking her lips at Rose from her chair at the front table.

Lester escorted her off the stage into the corridor leading to the kitchen when she finished. "Dang, Rosebud. What's gotten into you tonight? Are you trying to get every man in there to take you home?"

Rose laughed and kissed him on the cheek. "If you only knew. Could you grab us something to eat while I get my tea? I didn't have time to stop before the first show."

"Sure thing, Rosebud. How about a ham sandwich from the kitchen?"

"Perfect." Rose approached the bar and sat on a stool at the end furthest from Riley. She wanted him to come to her before leaving for his weekly whiskey run.

"Thanks, Jason." The bartender had Rose's hot tea with honey and lemon waiting for her. When Jason left, he turned on the Victrola to entertain the guests until her next show.

With Lester not running interference against handsy patrons, Rose sipped on her tea while covertly scanning the room. She hoped at least one would muster the courage to make a pass at her. And there it was. The mysterious well-dressed out-of-towner was making a straight line for her through the rows of round tables. The tall, muscular man rebuttoned the jacket to his crisp black, pinstriped suit when he stopped in front of Rose, bringing his freshly cut dark blond hair and shiny white teeth into view. They would attract any woman in the room. Anyone but Rose, but she had to play it up for Riley's sake. He pulled a silver case from his inside breast pocket and flipped it open with one hand in a clearly practiced motion. He said something.

"Huh?" Rose had trouble hearing over the music. She gestured for him to come closer and positioned her head so he could whisper in her ear.

"Cigarette?" he repeated.

"I don't smoke."

He remained close and asked, "Drink?"

Rose typically declined every offer from a customer she didn't know, but two factors made her consider otherwise. First, Lester's whiskey had worn off, and second, a glance down the bar confirmed the stranger already had Riley's attention. Nothing like a bit of a nudge.

"Champagne."

The man snapped his fingers to attract Jason's attention and ordered two glasses of champagne. "I'm Samuel." He extended his hand.

"Rose." She shook his hand and then sipped her tea to calm her nerves. She'd never played games, and doing so now felt underhanded. But what choice did she have? "W-W-Where's home, Samuel?"

"City of the Angels," he said. "I'm passing through to San Francisco on business."

Jason placed the two glasses atop the bar. Instead of his traditional wink when bringing Rose a beverage, he shook his head from side to side. His eyes darted in Riley's direction. Rose brought her fresh drink to her lips, silently hoping this nudge of hers didn't get out of hand.

Riley stomped up behind Samuel with a fire in his eyes Rose hadn't seen before. Her nudge now seemed like a horrible idea. Riley grabbed him by the jacket at the shoulder and spun him around on his heels. "Hands off the canary."

Samuel didn't back away, yet he didn't retaliate. Instead, he raised his hands, palms forward, to shoulder level. "I'm just having a drink, my friend."

"I am not your friend, chump, and *that* is my girl." Riley poked a stiff index finger into Samuel's chest.

Rose had never considered two things: the word "that" as a demeaning term nor willingly making a public spectacle. The way Riley used the word made her feel like property. Her ire was up. What was she thinking? Unless Riley was like her and Dax, he'd never treat her as an equal like Grace's husband did.

"I am not a thing to possess." She splashed the rest of her champagne in Riley's face, relishing each drop as it dribbled past his chin.

"Who's the chump now?" Samuel snickered. When Riley formed two fists, his expression turned serious. "You don't want to do that, Mac."

"Oh ya?" Riley took a swing but missed. Samuel had bobbed to one side. Once Riley gathered his balance, he took a second but missed that one too.

"That's all you get, pal. Third time's the charm."

Riley unleashed his stubborn streak and swung a third time. This time Samuel weaved and let loose with a rib-crushing blow to the gut, followed by a right hook to the jaw. Riley went down like a paper doll, sending waves of guilt through Rose. She wanted Riley jealous, not beat to a pulp.

"What did you do?" Rose glared at Samuel, and then she tended to Riley on the floor.

"I warned him." Samuel sat on the barstool Rose had vacated and sipped his champagne, assuming a relaxed posture. A bouncer from the main entrance barreled in, a wooden club in his hand, appearing ready to quell a riot.

"Jimmy, wait!" Rose threw up a hand in a stopping motion. "This is all a m-m-misu-u-unders-s-standing."

Jimmy glanced at Samuel before helping Riley to his feet. "Geez, boss. Are you crazy? That's Samuel Baker."

"Who?" Riley wobbled on his legs, pressing one hand against his belly and the other against the swelling, red welt below his left eye.

"The prizefighter from Los Angeles. He's boxing Max Baer Saturday night at the Kezar Pavilion."

"I don't care who he is. He needs to leave."

"Mr. Baker, you have my deepest apologies." Mr. Wilkes came from behind Riley, narrowing an eye at him before returning his attention to Samuel. "My nephew is overly protective of his fiancée. I'm sure you can understand, considering how beautiful she is."

Samuel turned to Rose, smoothing his suit jacket. "My apologies, Miss Rose. I didn't realize you were engaged."

I'm not, she wanted to say, but doing so would only make matters worse. So instead, she simply nodded her response.

"Drinks and room charges are on me, Mr. Baker," Mr. Wilkes said. "If there's anything else I can do to make the rest of your stay more pleasurable, please ask for me personally."

"No harm done, Mr. Wilkes. Your nephew sure can take a punch." Samuel extended his hand to Riley. "No hard feelings?"

Riley eyed Samuel as if deciding if his pride was worth his job. Finally, they shook hands, with Riley offering an unconvincing "Yeah."

When Samuel left the club, Frankie grabbed Riley by the upper arm. "What were you thinking? He's a VIP."

"He was getting too friendly with Rose. That's what I was thinking." Riley grimaced, pressing a hand against the welt again.

"If you like your job, you'll remember one important rule: no picking fights with the guests. Now, get yourself cleaned up and take care of that shiner with a hunk of beef from the kitchen."

"What about the whiskey run?"

"That can wait. I can't have you walking around looking like a two-bit scrapper."

CHAPTER THIRTEEN

When Rose left and ran out in a whirlwind following that toe-curling kiss, the Foster House main door flew open with a vibrating clap, bouncing off the interior wall. Dax glanced toward the kitchen, hoping the noise hadn't woken May, but she had to wait to confirm. *One more glimpse of Rose*, Dax told herself before she rushed out the door and stared in the direction in which Rose had taken off. Each time Rose passed a streetlight, she got smaller and smaller, as did Dax's hope of holding her again anytime soon.

Before Rose disappeared inside the Seaside Hotel, Dax whispered, "I'll wait for you."

Dax retreated to the kitchen, put the towels she and Rose had used in the laundry basket, and stored the new bowls and spatulas May had ordered from Edith. All the while, she was a mix of hope and frustration. Rose still loved her. That much was clear. But was love enough for Rose to give up a traditional life with the possibility of children? Was what she and Rose shared enough to live in the shadows for the rest of their lives?

A knock on the back door stopped her from heading upstairs to alternate between sulking and fantasizing. Dax opened the door, finding Charlie standing in the dark with hands in her coat pocket and a newsboy hat pulled down low. If not for Brutus leaning against her leg with sheets of drool dropping to the gravel, Dax would've mistaken Charlie for a hoodlum ready to pull off a heist.

Dax placed an index finger over her lips and issued a *shh* before gesturing for Charlie to come in. "May's sleeping."

Charlie issued Brutus a *shh* with her index finger against her lips before they tiptoed inside. Well, Charlie tiptoed. Brutus swayed silently into the kitchen, exchanging snorts for more drool. Charlie handed Dax the keys to the Model T. "The new tires are on, and I got her purring like a cat. I even gave her a good polish."

"Thanks, Charlie, but you didn't have to make a special trip." Dax ushered her deeper inside the kitchen toward the chopping block in the center of the room. Brutus began a detailed inspection of the room's perimeter, sniffing at every nook and cranny. If Dax had missed a crumb or splash of sauce, Brutus was on track to find it.

"I wanted to get her in your hands for the Half Moon Bay weekend." Charlie's weekend reference had taken Dax by surprise when she first arrived in town. Because the city was a tourist destination, nearly every business was open on Saturday and Sunday. And when the tourists packed up and left by late Sunday afternoon, the weekend started for the locals.

"You're a lifesaver. I need to start picking up our daily produce to save on the delivery charges. Though…" Dax drifted off, thinking about those head-spinning kisses with Rose earlier this evening.

"That must be one heck of a *though* with that smile of yours."

Dax gestured for Charlie to sit on May's stool. She then dragged over the other one May had positioned in front of the grill. "I saw Rose again today."

"Ahh, that explains the smile. How did it go?"

"Amazing and confusing as heck."

"Aren't all women?" Charlie slapped her knee and chuckled, earning a snort from Brutus.

"I wouldn't know. I've never...I mean...Shoot." A growing embarrassment turned up the heat, starting in Dax's throat, working its way up to her cheeks, and ending at the tips of her ears.

"How old are you, Dax?"

"Twenty-six."

"Being a virgin at that age is nothing to be ashamed about, especially among lesbians. It's hard enough finding a woman we like, let alone one who likes us back."

"And when you do, they're often too scared to do anything about it." For years, Dax had dreamed about her and Heather stealing more than a few kisses when the opportunity presented itself. But Heather was in an impossible situation, and Dax had refused to make it worse until she couldn't stand silent any longer. Knowing Heather and her children were safe now made years of cold showers worth the sacrifice.

"That's why I consider myself lucky to have found Jules." Brutus alerted to the name and rubbed his side against Charlie's leg and then Dax's. Dax petted Brutus on his short fur, apparently convincing him to stay. He leaned against her lower leg, and a glance confirmed he'd drooled on her work boot. Charlie continued, "Of course, it's not ideal with me living in the garage and her at the boarding house, but what other choice do we have?"

"Maybe someday things will change, and people won't care who we love."

"You *are* a dreamer." Charlie patted Dax on the back, sending the message Dax was a fool for thinking such things.

"Dreams were all I had until Rose walked into the restaurant yesterday, and they may be all I'll ever have."

"Why do you think that?"

"Rose said she has a lot to do to untangle the mess she'd made. Riley complicates things."

"So does Grace."

"Who's Grace?"

"Shoot." Charlie rubbed the back of her neck, a nervous tell that Dax had spotted during their previous meetings. "I've said too much. You better ask Rose."

"Oh no, you don't." Dax leaned closer, giving Charlie her best stink eye. "You don't get to drop a grenade in my lap and clam up. Spill it."

Charlie rubbed her neck harder. "Jules will kill me for butting in. We promised each other to not interfere."

"I'm completely in the dark here." Dax's mind flashed to every conceivable obstacle that could prevent her and Rose from getting together. Everything from Grace being a daughter she had out of wedlock to her being the love of Rose's life. "I have to know if I have a chance with her."

"Trust me," Charlie said. "You do."

"That doesn't tell me a darn thing. Now, who the heck is Grace?"

Charlie hung her head low. "Grace Parsons."

"Who's she?"

"You don't know the name Grace Parsons?" Charlie's confused expression made Dax feel like she'd been living under a rock for years.

"I asked, didn't I?"

"She's in the movies." Dax shrugged, the name still not connecting. "*Happy Holiday? Two Faces? The Patsy? The Vikings?*"

A disturbing image formed in Dax's head. Last year, she saw *The Patsy* with May and remembered that the starlet had a masculine vibe with short hair and suspenders. Those qualities didn't interest Dax, but then she remembered Rose once said those things drove her crazy.

"You've got to be kidding. Who is she to Rose?"

Charlie leaned back, ran both hands through her hair, and let out a deep sigh. A gut-wrenching sigh to Dax. "Grace comes through town several times a year, and she and Rose...well, they have a thing."

Dax plummeted her head toward the countertop, thudding it against her folded arms. This was her worst nightmare. Rose's lover was a dreamy Hollywood star with loads of money. How was she supposed to compete with that?

Dax's motion sent Brutus scurrying to the safety of Charlie's feet. "It's all right, boy." Charlie used a calm voice. "He hates sudden loud noises. But if it helps, I don't think she's in love with Grace."

Dax popped her head up. "It doesn't. How long have they had a thing?"

Charlie cocked her head at an angle as if searching for the answer. "Three years, I think."

Even worse. If luck was on Dax's side and she won Rose over, how on earth could she make love to her without making a fool of herself? The answer was that she couldn't. Rose had years of experience and likely had high expectations. Dax's head continued to spin out of control. First, Riley. Now, Grace. But one didn't explain the other.

"Wait." Dax wagged her head like a dog shaking off bathwater. "Why Riley? Rose said she doesn't want to marry him."

"Rose only showed interest because she needed cover."

"Cover?"

"People started talking about Rose and Grace's friendship, and it got back to Rose's boss. Rose figured if she started up with a man, he'd forget all about it. Riley seemed safe."

Dax buried her face in her hands. What little hope she had when Rose kissed her goodbye tonight washed away with the rain that had resumed. "This is a mess."

"Now, you understand why Rose said she had to untangle things." Charlie briefly patted Dax's shoulder. "She loves you, Dax. Trust in that."

"I'll go nuts thinking about this tonight." Dax rubbed her hands down the length of her face, imagining Rose singing at the speakeasy, kissing Riley while eyeing Grace Parsons in the front row.

"Then let's take your new baby for a spin." Charlie snagged the keys to the Model T from the chopping block where Dax had placed them and tossed them in the air.

"I'm driving." Dax snatched them on the way down.

"Let's go, boy. Car ride." Brutus wriggled his entire body and ran for the door, leaving a trail of saliva like a giant, stocky snail.

Dax peeked into May's room, confirming she was still sleeping, locked up, and sat in the front seat of her truck. A smile built on her lips as she ran her hands along the steering wheel as if it were a lover. Before he dumped her and May to fend for themselves, Logan had said, "Anything here is yours to use. So make a go of it, and I'll check on you in a few months." Squeezing the wrap on the wheel, Dax considered the truck hers. It was the first thing other than clothes and her carpentry tools that she'd owned. The sense of power and accomplishment it gave her was more potent than Dax had expected.

She inserted the key and turned the engine over. Its rumbling was deeper and smoother than Logan's Model T. She gunned the engine, earning a mighty growl. Visions of weaving through the sweeping curves of the coastal highway with the ocean on one side and Rose on the seat next to her brought a smile to Dax's lips. "This thing doesn't purr. It roars. This is worth a lot more than five meals for you and Jules."

"Yeah, but it's my fault for going overboard. I've wanted to work on this thing for a long time, and once I started, I couldn't stop. So I won't accept more from you and May."

"In that case, let me build you that new tire rack you mentioned. It should only be five or six dollars in materials, and we could knock it out in a day."

"Deal, my friend." Charlie shook Dax's hand.

"Deal." Besides Rose, Charlie was the only person Dax ever considered a genuine friend. The rest who drifted in and out of her life were acquaintances at most. When she lived in the metropolis of San Francisco, Dax never came across anyone willing to do something for her simply because it was neighborly. This place was different. Whether it was Charlie or small-town living, Dax liked it here and felt like she'd found a home and a friend for life.

Brutus sat on the bench seat between Dax and Charlie, leaning upright against the back with his front paws hanging down like a person. *What kind of dog is this?* Dax thought while she coasted her truck from behind the Foster House and to the edge of the highway. A light rain sprinkled the windshield, blurring her vision. Charlie pointed at the wiper button on the dashboard. "I put on new blades. They should make your window squeaky clean."

"You thought of everything." Dax turned on the wipers, briefly mesmerized by the rhythmic motion and scraping sound as they left two perfect arcs in their wake. She glanced up and down the highway. "North or south?"

"Have you checked out Gray Whale Cove yet?"

"Nope. The most I've seen of Half Moon Bay is the Foster House, the hardware store, the grocer, Edith's department store, and your garage."

"Well, then. You're in for a treat. Let me show you where all the kids go to neck. Head north."

Dax turned left onto the coastal highway. The new tires gripped the wet road, holding like glue on every sweeping turn. They had the road mostly to themselves, passing only one southbound car during the dark nine-mile drive. By the time they reached the beach, the rain had stopped and the clouds had broken apart, revealing a few stars and letting some moonlight through.

Dax parked in a gravel area butting up against the edge of the sand. "I can see why the kids come out here. Dark, yet easy to get to."

"Oh, this isn't the best spot." Charlie exited through the passenger door, and Brutus immediately followed. Dax went through the driver's side. "Follow me."

The push and pull of the surf rolled in and retreated into the Pacific. If not for the soft sand forcing her to concentrate on her steps, the alternating, soothing rhythm of the ocean would have lulled her to sleep. Unfortunately, her work boots made it feel like she was walking on soap suds. Her foot sunk and slipped inches outward with each stride, making it impossible to walk faster than a baby taking its first steps. Thankfully, the closer she got to the shoreline, the harder that sand became and the easier it was to get her footing.

Brutus, on the other hand, was in his element. In the blink of an eye, he transformed from lazy to crazy. His short, stocky body bounced through the uneven sand like a rabbit evading a predator. His snorting took on a joyous chorus like children at a playground. When he reached the smooth, wet sand, he shot off toward the far end of the cove as if Jules Verne's rocket ship was strapped to his back.

"What's gotten into him?" Dax asked.

"He does this almost every night about this time. It's like he flips a switch on and runs until he's drained his tank. I call it crazy dog."

"I was thinking the same thing."

Charlie led them to a massive rock outcropping. The ocean had carved two inlets into the tall cliff, and two semicircles of rock about three feet high hid them from the rest of the beach, creating two cozy, private cutouts. Charlie pointed to the one closest to the waterline.

"That's where I kissed a girl for the first time. The other one is where I lost my virginity."

Dax gave her a playful shoulder shove. "Some friend, making fun of me."

"Just trying to help a friend." Charlie shoved her hands in her coat pocket and lowered her head. "I thought this might make a good spot for your first time if things work out for you and Rose."

Yep. Dax had found a friend for life. Charlie was rooting for her and Rose as much as she was. Dax nudged her again, embarrassment manifesting in a wide grin hiding in the darkness. As awkward as it was having a friend give her advice on where she could lose her virginity, Charlie had made an excellent suggestion. Dax wasn't sure if May would approve of such things under her roof, and the beach under the moonlight would make a romantic setting.

"Thanks, Charlie."

"Want to stay for a while?"

"I should get back to May. She's having a hard time working with that brace."

"Let me take some measurements tonight. Then, when I get a chance, I can weld some new rods to the old ones to strengthen them. I wish we had a shoemaker in town. He could fashion a better-fitting strap. How much is a new brace?"

"The one she really needs is three hundred dollars in San Francisco. It might take me years to save up that much."

"I'd be happy to pitch in."

"I appreciate the offer, but you've done too much already. I'll find a way."

"All right then. Let's head back." Charlie gestured toward the parking area where Dax had left her pickup. Dax couldn't tell whether Charlie was disappointed or okay with her declining the generous offer, but anything more from her friend would feel like charity. Dax had never accepted a handout a day in her life, and she wasn't about to start now.

"Brutus!" Charlie yelled, but the rocket dog didn't appear. However, his snorting in the near darkness overpowered the beat of the ocean waves. Charlie yelled again, but he still didn't come. "Darn that dog. I swear he listens only when he wants to. We better track him down."

Dax followed Charlie and the sound of snorting, walking close to the waterline on the hard sand for as long as she could to minimize the time she'd look like a toddler. Then, twenty yards past the point where Dax would have made her right turn to head toward the truck, Brutus's bobbing silhouette came into view. He was digging furiously at something in the sand.

"Leave that alone. Come on, boy," Charlie ordered, but Brutus refused to mind and continued digging as if he were onto buried treasure. All kinds of things used to roll up on the shores of Alameda Island, some strange, some gruesome. Charlie walked closer as if it didn't scare her in the least. "What do you have, boy?"

Several steps closer, Dax made out a cylindrical shape. "Is that a barrel?"

Charlie stopped a few feet short of the object, scratching her head. "It sure is." She ran a hand down a wood slat, her hand grazing over the metal strap in the center. She then lifted one end a few inches off the sand and returned it to its resting position. "I can't believe this."

"What is it?"

"Whiskey. Likely Canadian."

"Whiskey? But the barrel looks too small."

"I've seen them in the Seaside Club." Charlie gave the barrel another once-over. "I think they make them small enough for a single man to carry."

"But the beach? How did it get here?"

Charlie snickered. "Ships from Canada loaded with the stuff stop a few miles offshore. Then a bunch of motorboats meet them and take the hooch ashore. Some are taken to docks. Some end up on the beaches. Locals then load them into trucks and take them to the cities."

"That's wacky."

"Yeah, but it works. The local coppers don't care much. Only the Coast Guard and Prohibition agents give a hoot."

Dax's brain churned on how she could raise the money for May's brace. "How much do you think this is worth?"

Charlie scratched the side of her face. "Let's see. My guess is that it holds about ten gallons. That's forty quarts. And forty quarts make a hundred-sixty cups. And a hundred-sixty cups makes—"

"One thousand two hundred-eighty ounces."

"The Seaside Club charges two dollars a drink," Charlie said.

"How many ounces in a drink?" Dax asked.

"I'm not sure. One or two."

Headlights from a vehicle heading north on the highway whizzed past, causing both women to crouch. They were, after all, sitting on an illegal gold mine. Brutus, however, was unfazed. If Dax and Charlie were to sell the whiskey one drink at a time, they could make over twelve hundred dollars. May could get her new brace and then some.

"Let's get this back to the Foster House before someone comes looking for it." Dax tested its weight, estimating it was about fifty pounds. As a carpenter, she frequently lifted and carried that amount for short distances, but the sand made her stance unsteady. To be safe, she and Charlie each cradled an end of the two-foot-long barrel and waded through the sand clumsily until they reached the truck. Loading it onto the middle of the bench seat, Dax covered it with her jacket.

"Sorry, boy, but it's the back for you. You have legs. This precious cargo might roll and break." Charlie lowered the truck's tailgate and then hoisted Brutus like a sack of potatoes into the bed.

The silence of the drive back to town was neither strange nor unexpected. Charlie kept both hands on the barrel to prevent it from tumbling to the floor. And when Dax wasn't shifting gears, she too placed a hand on it. Returning to the Foster House, they carried the barrel to the musty basement. Brutus followed, cautiously bouncing down one step with both front paws and then the next until he reached the bottom.

Dax and Charlie laid the barrel in the center of the basement, collapsed into two old, dusty dining chairs, and stared at the treasure they'd stumbled upon. Brutus soon joined them, panting as if he'd run the entire way from the beach and creating a puddle of drool no sane person would touch. Twelve hundred dollars sat across from them. A six hundred-dollar split was significant but not life-changing for most. Yet, that money could change May's life completely.

"We need to sell it by the drink," Dax said.

"Where?" Charlie asked.

"Right here." Dax already had a plan in mind, and with her carpentry skills and Charlie's help, they could make it happen. "But May can't know."

CHAPTER FOURTEEN

Soft lips trailed over Rose's neck, tingling her skin along their moist, titillating path. They finally settled on a breast, causing her to arch her lower back from the mattress. She couldn't stop herself if she wanted. Those lips weren't tentative as she remembered them. Instead, they were determined and glided down her body with the same confidence evident in her downright swoon-worthy stride. Their every suck and lick commanded Rose's attention.

They resumed their trek downward, eliciting every fantasy in Rose's repertoire and some she'd never considered. Rose had long thought they'd never claim her, but with that now an inevitability, she had no control of her body. She didn't want to be in control. When a warm exhale blew between those lips, blanketing her center, Rose relinquished every muscle, breath, and heartbeat to them. They threw her over the edge, leaving her body a quaking mess.

Sweat dripping from every pore, Rose opened her eyes as an annoyingly loud sound invaded her head. It sounded again, but it was accompanied by a muffled voice this time. Still half asleep, Rose looked down her body between her legs. "Riley?" she said in confusion.

The noise sounded a third time, louder than before, jolting Rose out of her dream state and giving her a fright. The lips she'd imagined lavishing her from neck to thigh were Dax's, of course, and not Riley's. Though he was sweet and had defended her in his own immature way last night, nothing on earth could make her fantasize about him bringing her to orgasm.

"Open up, Rose. Riley King is here to see you," the disembodied voice sounded through her bedroom door.

Rose shook her head with the vigor her eight-year-old self had had when she cast off cooties after Lucas Henley kissed her cheek on the playground. "I was asleep, Mrs. Prescott. Give me a minute to get dressed. Tell him I'll be right down."

Putting her landlady's door pounding aside, Riley's morning visit set off alarms in Rose's head. He hadn't set foot in her boarding house since their first week of dating, so coming here from across town from Mr. Wilkes's house meant the likelihood was low that he was there to sweep Rose off her feet.

Rose slipped off her damp sleep things. Her vivid dream of Dax between her legs had left her sweaty and swollen with arousal, but the chilly fall morning air in the house was failing to cool her down. Putting on a loose-fitting day dress and flat shoes, she grabbed a sweater despite not needing one, thinking that walking downstairs without one in the cold air would seem odd.

Mrs. Prescott drank coffee and read the daily *Half Moon Bay Review* from her traditional morning spot—the open study near the stairs. It was the perfect location for gathering gossip about her residents, but Mrs. Prescott got most of her news from Ida. Old friends, they were an excellent match. Both were busybodies who took pleasure in others' misery.

Rose tried tiptoeing by, but Mrs. Prescott belted out, "Your visitor came before eight. That's a violation."

"A violation? I didn't ask him over. He came by unannounced."

"It's your responsibility to tell your acquaintances the rules."

"Fine." Rose turned on her heel toward the parlor, where Mrs. Prescott herded visitors of the opposite sex. She learned a long time ago that arguing with Mrs. Prescott got her nowhere, so she suppressed what she wanted to say. Things like she wished the pile of violations Mrs. Prescott had issued to residents over the years would form a leaky boat and carry her out to sea.

Riley jumped to his feet when Rose entered the room. His left eye was swollen and encircled by various bright and dark red shades. His tight expression and twisting of his cap like an old rag telegraphed his frustration.

"What were you thinking, chatting up Samuel Baker, especially in that flimsy dress you wore last night? That stunt of yours cost me over three hundred dollars in pay. Because of you, I was short a barrel on my pickup at the beach."

The hair tingled on the nape of Rose's neck. She formed fists to tamp down the building heat in her gut, but her effort failed miserably, and words spewed out as fast as she thought of them. "First, it wasn't a stunt. I wanted a drink, and he offered. Second, I never heard you complain about the dress before. Third, who do you think you are lecturing me about who I talk to?"

The muscles in Riley's jaw rippled, clearly fighting as much anger as Rose. "I wasn't your fiancé before, so now it bothers me. And that title gives me the right to lecture you."

"I haven't given you an answer yet, and you're making it plenty hard to say yes."

"Well, you need to give me an answer real soon. Uncle Frankie isn't pleased that you're taking so long."

Those words billowed the heat in Rose like a furnace. "Why is your uncle so concerned about when I give you an answer?"

"Because some VIPs said they'd like to see a change, so he's looking to bring in a new singer. He has an eye on one and wants to hire her before someone else does. But if you're family, he'll have to keep you. Please say yes."

Rose's head spun to the dizzying point. She plopped atop the beat-up couch, unable to keep her balance. The life with Dax she'd thought possible this morning, as limited as it might have been, now seemed unreachable. She'd thought she'd found a way out of the mess she'd made without jeopardizing her job and home, but Riley had made her situation clear. Everything she had rested on marrying a man she neither loved nor could stand touching her and sooner than later.

Riley sat beside her. "I know this sounds harsh, but marrying you was the only way I could think of to keep you around."

"But I don't love you."

"Do you at least like me?"

"You're a nice enough man and easy to look at. Of course, any girl would like you."

"That's a start. You could learn to love me. Until then, I can provide enough love for both of us."

Rose imagined herself making a home with Riley King, living in a row house as he'd suggested when he proposed. The only palatable part of this nightmare was the child or two she envisioned with his sandy brown hair. Rose then saw herself making him breakfast every morning, cleaning up after him every afternoon, and letting him inside her every night. It wasn't a future she could stomach for a day, let alone the rest of her life.

Rose leaped to her feet, ripping the engagement ring from her finger. "I can't, Riley. I can't marry you."

Riley grabbed her by both arms and shook her—a little too hard for her comfort. "Get a hold of yourself, Rose. You'll lose everything."

"Ow! You're hurting me."

Jules burst through the door leading from the kitchen with fire in her eyes. She'd been a force in Rose's life since meeting her at Ida's café years ago but never had she looked capable of murder. Until now. An entire foot shorter than Riley, Jules jumped on his back piggyback style and tightened her arms around his neck until he choked.

"Jules, don't!" Rose screamed.

"No one hurts my friend," Jules yelled.

"Let him go, Jules," Rose pleaded, hoping she'd let go before Riley turned blue.

Jules released her viselike grip, jumped back to the floor, and turned her attention to Rose. "Are you okay? Did he hurt you?"

"I'm fine." Rose placed a hand on Riley's shoulder as he continued to cough. His color hadn't changed, which was a good sign Jules didn't do permanent damage. "He just grabbed me a little hard."

"What on earth is going on?" Mrs. Prescott had left her cave, appearing ready to issue more violations.

"It was a misunderstanding, Mrs. Prescott." Rose was too worked up to use kinder words. "You can go back to your newspaper."

"You know the rules, Rose." Mrs. Prescott raised her nose at Rose and Jules. "No disturbances of any kind. That's a violation for both of you. And if memory serves, that makes your third strike, Jules. So I'll expect you to vacate at the end of the month."

Jules flapped her hands in the air. "Great. Where am I supposed to go? The only rentals are the row houses. I can't afford one of those."

"You should have thought of that before you created a ruckus."

"That's not fair." Rose's ire was fully awake over stupid rules and stupid covers. "She was defending me. I'll take on her violation."

"Then that's three for you. One of you has to go. I don't care which." Mrs. Prescott waved her hand as if shooing the problem out the door.

"Hold on, Mrs. Prescott." Riley's voice was still raspy from the chokehold. "This is all my fault." He pulled out his wallet and handed her two twenty-dollar bills. "Will this resolve the problem? My Uncle Frankie would be very appreciative."

Mrs. Prescott tucked the money into her sweater pocket. "For now. But if either of them violates the rules again, both are out."

Rose gave the back of Mrs. Prescott's head a death stare when she left the room, as did Jules. They'd dodged a bullet, but for how long? If Frankie Wilkes replaced Rose, she could make the rent for a few months. Six if she disciplined her spending.

"I think you should leave, Riley." Rose cast soft eyes on him. "We can talk about this when I return to work Thursday."

"I can put off my uncle for a week or two, but he won't wait forever." He kissed her on the cheek and left.

Jules folded her arms over her chest, giving Rose an icy stare. "What the hell, Rose? Are you seriously considering his proposal? What about Dax?"

"I may not have a choice." Rose fell onto the couch again. The weight of her circumstance crushed any hope of getting out of this with either her job, home, or Dax.

"I don't trust him." Jules's unwavering tone made Rose sense there was something behind her assessment.

"Care to elaborate?" Rose asked. Jules opened her mouth as if to unload every unvarnished opinion she had about Riley King but closed it a second later.

"No." Her one-word response left Rose both curious and frustrated. Jules clearly knew something or at least suspected something juicy.

CHAPTER FIFTEEN

Skimming her lips down soft skin, Dax reached the firmness of a clavicle. She continued down to a tempting, fleshy breast, taking it into her mouth and earning a discernable arch from the body beneath her. Each carefully engineered lick and suck brought out the exact response she wanted—a body that quaked and trembled on command. The body was hers to admire or lavish at will. She had no doubt about how to tease and build the anticipation for them both.

Effortlessly sliding down her torso, Dax continued at an agonizingly slow pace. The only mystery she had yet to solve was what smell and taste she would find when she settled between the two smooth legs waiting for her orders.

"Open a little wider," she rasped. And they did, making her feel like royalty with every whim being met. Dax inhaled, expecting something exotic, but was met with...

Bacon? Dax woke with a start, thinking *bacon?* Bacon had never left her sleep shirt soaked with perspiration. Only fantasies of Rose had. But in an unlikely conclusion, the smell of freshly cooked bacon had interrupted the most erotic dream she'd had in years. If this was in her future every time she and Rose shared a heart-stopping kiss, she'd have to invest in extra sleep shirts or commit to doing laundry nearly every day of the week.

Work pants, a long-sleeved blue flannel shirt, suspenders, and boots completed her uniform for the project she had planned for today. Her father had taught her to always cover herself from head to toe when working with wood because splinters could end up in the worst places. Grabbing her jacket, she made her legs work like pistons down the stairs, eager to start the day. One step into the kitchen revealed May was preparing her a hearty breakfast—bacon, eggs, and pancakes.

"It smells good." Dax snickered. She wasn't sure what appetizing smells awaited her when she made love to Rose for the first time, but she was certain it wasn't going to be bacon.

"I thought you'd need a little something extra for whatever you have planned today." May finished plating their food, adding some to a third dish. "When is Charlie coming?"

"I'm sorry. Did we wake you last night?" Dax cringed at what May might have overheard. May had nothing cross to say about liquor, but she often shared strong opinions about lawbreakers.

"It's not your fault. My leg kept me tossing and turning." May placed Charlie's plate under the heat lamp to keep it warm, grabbed the other two, and set up at the center cutting block. Before Dax forked her first mouthful from the plate, May rested a hand on her forearm and her expression turned soft. "I saw you with Rose last night."

Dax's face turned impossibly hot. She hadn't felt this embarrassed since her mother caught her and Rose in her bedroom. "I'm sorry, May. I thought we were alone."

"You have nothing to apologize for. I'm happy for you two, but you need to be careful."

"We will, but I'm not sure if it will happen again. Rose has a lot to work through."

"Well, you're safe in the Foster House, but I have the impression most people in town aren't too keen on people like you, Rose, and Charlie."

Dax opened her eyes wide. "You heard me talking with Charlie?" A sinking feeling set into her gut. She understood the courage it took for Charlie to come clean about who she was and equally understood how upsetting it would be to discover someone else overheard.

"I did, but I'd already guessed as much. I saw Charlie when she picked up the truck, and I could tell you two were very much alike."

"She's a good friend. I hope you'll keep her secret too."

"That goes without saying."

A car engine rumbled behind the building, followed by a knock on the door a minute later. Dax let Charlie inside. Her coveralls signaled she was ready for a day of dusty work.

"May made you breakfast." Dax ushered Charlie to the chopping block and retrieved her plate from the warming station.

"Thank you, May. This looks delicious. You didn't have to go out of your way."

"I run a restaurant. Don't be silly." May waved her off. "Will your girlfriend be joining us? Should I make her a plate?" Charlie spat out her first bite, returning her scrambled eggs to the plate at lightning speed. She gave Dax a half-questioning, half-angry look. May smacked Charlie lightly on the shoulder, drawing a chuckle from Dax. "Shame on you for thinking your friend would betray your confidence about a thing like that. I overheard you two last night, and I'm happy to hear you've found someone. Now, is she coming?"

"No, ma'am." Charlie's lighthearted grimace conveyed all was forgiven. "She's working at the clinic today."

"We're about the same age, so there's no need for airs." May winked.

"You got it, May." Charlie returned her wink. When May asked what she and Dax had planned for today, Charlie thankfully kept it vague. "I'm helping Dax clean out the basement and inventory what's there."

"You're a good friend, Charlie." May's eyes misted. She'd never say it, but Dax was sure she felt like a burden since the accident. That couldn't be further from the truth. May might have been limited in what she could do, but she worked harder at the things she could do than anyone Dax knew. "I'll expect you to stay for supper." May briefly squeezed her hand.

"Happy to." Charlie added a closed-mouth smile to her reply.

Once they'd cleaned and put away the breakfast dishes, May set off to do laundry while Dax and Charlie escaped downstairs. Dax's first stop was the corner where she and Charlie had hidden the whiskey barrel they'd absconded with last night. She shoved aside the old chairs they'd placed in front of it last night and then removed the dusty tarp she'd draped over it as if she were hiding a corpse. She may have gone overboard, but that ten-gallon container represented May's future. The money she'd split with Charlie would undoubtedly make life easier for them. For May, it would make the difference between suffering and being comfortable.

Dax then eyed the contents of the basement. The four nicked-up tables and dozen chairs from the restaurant gave her an idea. "We could organize and stack all the tools and boating stuff in the corner by the stairs leading to the kitchen. I can add a wall with a door to hide it. That should open up the space." She pointed to a corner on the opposite wall. Fifteen feet away, the exterior door on the wall connecting the other two made for an ideal location. "How about a small bar over there?"

"Perfect," Charlie said. "We can repair and clean the tables and chairs and set them up in the center."

They had the room organized, swept, and dusted with wet rags two hours later. The discovery of an outboard motor was an added surprise, especially after Charlie volunteered to repair it and get it "purring like a kitten."

Dax shifted gears and calculated how much wood and supplies she'd need, including those required to repair the stairs leading outside. She scratched her head. "I figure thirty or forty dollars to fix up the place."

"We can split the cost down the middle," Charlie said.

Dax rubbed the back of her neck. "I don't have twenty dollars to spare. May would know it's missing."

"How about I front you the money? Then I can take your share out of the profits."

"Deal." Dax extended her hand. She didn't know what she did to deserve a friend like Charlie, but she sure as heck was grateful for her. For the first time since setting foot in Half Moon Bay, Dax felt like everything was going right.

After picking up cash at Charlie's, they headed to the hardware store to get the supplies needed to create their own little speakeasy. While the store helper loaded the wood into the bed of Dax's truck, Dax and Charlie picked out the necessary nails, bolts, and whatnot.

Two men walked down the same aisle. One immediately caught Dax's attention, making her stop in her tracks and stop her shopping. She couldn't forget the perfect-looking, tall, muscular man who had kissed Rose right before her eyes after dropping to his knee to propose. His annoyingly chiseled, now bruised, face was seared into her brain. But he didn't notice her in her work clothes, jacket, and newsboy cap. Why would he? To Riley King, Dax was a nobody, only a bothersome old friend who delayed his proposal by a few minutes.

"Dax?" Charlie waved a hand in front of her face, bringing Dax back to the present. "What else do we need?"

"Sorry. The cake-eater over there distracted me." Dax wagged her thumb in Riley's direction.

"Who?" Charlie glanced down the aisle. "Riley? I wouldn't exactly call him a ladies' man. From what Jules tells me, and she knows everything that goes on in this town, the only one he's interested in is Rose."

"Yeah? Well, he rubs me the wrong way." Dax glared his way, unamused at how Riley and his friend acted like they owned the place. Picking up an item only to toss it into the wrong bin was disrespectful and downright arrogant.

"What are we looking for?" Riley's companion asked.

Riley read a piece of paper in his hand. "Lester said he needs a dozen six-penny nails to fix the loose boards on the stage."

His friend looked at the assorted collection of nails, scratching his head. "Which ones?"

"How am I supposed to know, Jimmy? I'm no handyman." Riley shrugged, earning a chuckle from Dax.

"Then how did you get stuck looking for them?"

"Uncle Frankie. He said I'm responsible for keeping the club in top shape." Riley tore his stare from the bins of nails on the shelf and glanced up and down the aisle. "Where in the hell is that store clerk?"

Dax was thoroughly entertained and was glued to their conversation like wallpaper to sheetrock while they sifted through the nails. However, when she heard Riley mention Rose's name, her amusement came to a screeching halt. His friend said, loud enough for the next aisle to hear, heating Dax's temper, "H-H-Has she s-s-said y-y-yes?"

"N-N-Not y-y-yet." Riley snickered.

"What did you say?" Dax yelled. Riley's flippant, thoughtless reply turned her temper into a full rage. She threw the items she had in her hands to the floor, clenched her fists, and marched like a charging bull toward him with steam blasting from her ears.

Riley turned in her direction, his head flinching back slightly. "What's it to you?"

Charlie caught up with Dax and yanked her back before she could throw her first punch. But the shiner he had said that someone had beat her to it. "Don't, Dax." Charlie then whispered into her ear, "Rose might lose her job."

Dax's anger battled her protective nature. She'd spent her youth protecting Rose from bullies like Riley. She hated how others could be so cruel, making fun of something Rose had no control over. As much as Dax wanted to finish the job someone had started by giving him a matching ugly black eye, she held on to her primary role as Rose's protector and dialed down her rage.

Riley squinted. "You're that chump from the Foster House."

"Chump?" Dax squared off with Riley. He had a few inches on her and more muscle, but that didn't scare her. "Who are you calling a chump?"

"How was opening day? I'm surprised you had enough food to open or working shitters to stay open." The half-cocked grin made Dax think he was behind their grocery order debacle and the toilet sabotage.

Charlie ushered Dax up the aisle before she could get answers. "He's not worth it. We can come back for the rest of the stuff."

Dax cursed under her breath each step of the way out of the store and to her truck. The walk didn't lessen her anger in the least. Besides Heather's husband, she'd never wanted to punch a person more in her life. He showed zero respect for his supposed fiancée. She wouldn't be surprised if everything he said and did in front of Rose was an act.

The drive back to the Foster House wasn't much better. In fact, it gave Dax more time to stew on visions of that conniving lug's hands all over Rose. He and Rose had been dating for a month, which was plenty of time for things to happen. Her hand twisted tighter around the steering wheel as each tormenting mental image weaved its way into every corner of her brain. By the time she parked in the back next to the tarped boat, she was more worked up than when they left the hardware store. Dax yanked the first plank from the truck bed with all the force of those disturbing images of Riley and Rose behind them.

"Geez, Dax." Charlie grabbed the other end to stack it near the door leading to the basement. "You might lose a hand if you're not careful."

"I'll be fine. Let's get this load inside."

Hours of sweating and focusing on measuring twice and cutting once kept Dax's mind off Riley playing Rose like a chump—mostly. With Charlie's help, she had shored up the stairs leading outside, built a rudimentary bar with a shelf to store glasses, and was nearly done framing the wall separating the storage area from the future speakeasy. They'd rested a little too long on their last water break, and her thoughts had come back around to Rose. She wanted to warn her off, but she didn't want to interfere. Rose had made it clear that she had a lot to unravel and that much was at risk if she didn't use caution. However, understanding the situation didn't mean it was easy to accept.

Dax pushed herself from the chair to which she'd added a few nails to make it sturdier. "Let's get this wall up and call it a day. We can put up the door tomorrow."

Charlie gingerly rose from her chair, which also needed some extra nails, rubbing and stretching her lower arms. "I thought working on cars was tiring. How did you do this all day?"

"You're using different muscles, that's all. After a few months, you develop powerful arms, especially forearms and hands."

Charlie smirked. "Rose is going to love that."

"How so?"

Charlie laughed harder. "She'll show you why."

A reminder that Rose had a rich sexual history with Grace Parsons was the last thing Dax needed today. Riley King already made it hard to focus. Both Grace and Riley had much to give Rose. Grace could lavish Rose with money and take her to exotic places, while Riley could give Rose a family of her own. The only thing Dax could give Rose was herself. How was she supposed to compete with them?

"Thanks a lot, pal. Thanks for reminding me about Grace." Dax yanked her saw from its resting place atop the next board she planned to cut. Grace and Rose. Rose and Riley. Both combinations simultaneously infuriated and nauseated her. What else could she—

"Ow!" Sharp pain on her index finger nearly doubled Dax over. All thoughts of Rose flew out of the basement in a whirlwind of unbearable throbbing. She hesitated to look, afraid to find her finger missing.

"Geez, Dax!" Charlie wrapped the finger in what Dax hoped was a clean towel and applied pressure. "That looked pretty bad." The pain magnified but stopped short of the throwing-up level when Charlie released her grip and placed Dax's other hand over her injury. "Clamp down on it while I go upstairs and call the doctor at home. It's after hours, so he'll have to open up special."

"I can't afford a doctor." Dax finally looked at her hurt hand and found the towel was already soaked in blood. The intense throbbing around the cut made it impossible to think straight. "I have some bandages upstairs. Let's rinse it off and just wrap it up."

"I saw how deep the slice was. You need stitches."

"Dammit." Dax paced around, hoping to get the pain to stop. "Why now? We were almost done."

"I have an idea." Charlie snatched the truck key from the crate top where they'd left the water pitcher. "Let's go."

Charlie and Dax piled into her pickup with Charlie behind the wheel. Dax held her hurt hand up high to lessen the throbbing while applying pressure with the other hand. The sky was dark, and the evening marine layer had rolled in, casting a strange glow on the primarily vacant city streets.

"Where are we going?" Dax asked.

"To see Jules. She's as good as any doctor with things like this."

Charlie pulled up in front of the Prescott Boarding House and had Dax in the parlor within minutes. "Wait here," Charlie ordered and then dashed up the stairs two at a time, disappearing around the corner. Mumbling voices accompanied two sets of knocking. Moments later, Charlie and then Jules and Rose ran down the stairs, purses in hand, like the joint was on fire.

"Oh no!" Rose cried, gently cradling Dax's injured hand in both of hers. "What happened?"

"I cut my finger." Dax tried to act as if the knee-buckling pain didn't exist.

"It's pretty bad, Jules." Charlie's expression turned long, pleading Dax's case. "She can't afford the doctor, so I thought you could fix her up like you did with me."

"Doc Hughes can't know." Jules turned her attention to Dax. "If he found out I was treating patients without him, he'd fire me for sure."

Dax answered with a nod.

Jules and Charlie led the way for the three-block walk to the clinic. Rose stuck by Dax's side, her arm slung around her back like a mother swan protecting her baby. Each step closer to the clinic, Dax felt closer to Rose. Rose didn't relinquish her touch, not once. And Dax didn't feel any throbbing in her finger, not one. Rose had taken away the pain.

"Jules is the best," Rose said when they were halfway there. "She'll have you patched up in no time."

Jules used her key to enter the clinic through the back entrance. She directed Dax to sit on the table in the first examination room and then collected the items to treat Dax's wound. Rose stood silently by Dax's side, holding her other hand. The rapid beat of their hearts echoed in their palms. Rose cupped their clasped hands with her free one, gently squeezing and telling the tale of her worry. They may have spent the past nine years in different cities, but the concern on Rose's face and in her touch proved they were never truly apart. They were connected at their first kiss.

Jules carefully unwrapped the blood-soaked towel from around Dax's left index finger. "At least the bleeding has stopped." Jules inspected her finger, and Rose gasped. "You have a pretty deep cut. It's a good thing Charlie brought you in. I'll need to clean it out, put in five or six sutures, and bandage it up so it won't get infected. Before I stitch you up, I should numb your finger with Novocain. The shot will hurt a little, but not as much as stitching you up without it. Are you okay with a shot?"

Once Dax agreed, Jules worked cautiously. Dax still couldn't watch. The idea of a needle going in and out of her skin was more nauseating than the injury itself. Rose squeezed her other hand extra hard, making it easy to focus on her, not the ghastly repair Jules was performing.

"How did you cut your hand?" Jules asked while she wrapped Dax's hand—the only part of the procedure Dax could stomach watching.

"I was using a saw and got distracted."

"That's not like you." Rose's voice was more questioning than accusatory. But more importantly, none of her words got stuck—a sure sign Rose was finally comfortable around her again. "You never got hurt while working with your father."

"I've had a lot on my mind." Dax couldn't look Rose in the eye because she shouldn't have let her emotion seep in when she had a saw in her hand. Since she was ten, Dax's father had drilled into her that safety was paramount when using her tools. He'd said a carpenter made a living with his hands and was of no use if he lost a finger.

"Does this have to do with our kiss last night?"

"Kinda."

"I'm sorry about running out like I did, but I have a lot to sort through." A sadness took shape in Rose's eyes. "Riley told me last night that his uncle wants to replace me with another singer, but he'll have to keep me on if I'm family."

"Does that mean you're going to marry him?"

Jules finished wrapping the bandage around Dax's finger and quietly backed away until she was even with Charlie.

"I don't think I have a choice." Rose's head dipped when she let go of her grasp, snapping Dax's heart into tiny pieces. "I have to give him an answer in a week. Until I figure things out, I don't think we should see each other."

Dax didn't know what to do. If she told Rose about how Riley made fun of her, Rose would definitely lose her job after she called it quits and slapped the snot out of him. But if she said nothing, Rose would be stuck in a marriage with a man who had zero respect for her. Like Heather had. If Riley turned out anything like Heather's husband, Dax couldn't stand by and watch Rose in an abusive relationship. It would kill her. If she didn't kill Riley first.

Dax needed time to figure out what was the right thing to do. Whatever course she chose, it had to be what was best for Rose, not her. In the meantime, she'd honor Rose's wishes, focus on putting the finishing touches on her and Charlie's speakeasy, and hope May's brace would hold until she made enough money to replace it.

CHAPTER SIXTEEN

Dax woke with a start for the second time this week. The first time had stemmed from a steamy dream with Rose in it that had her in need of hard work to cool down. Today, though, she'd fallen back asleep after her alarm went off, and she was nearly late for work downstairs. Jules had warned her she'd be extra tired the next few days while her body worked on healing itself, but Dax didn't think finishing the basement would exhaust her. All she had done was hand tools to Charlie and help hold up things with her uninjured hand.

Dax had had no idea how much she used her left hand during the day until she couldn't. She'd expected carrying stuff would be an issue but hadn't anticipated the everyday things. Getting dressed had become a circus act. Items came off a lot easier than when they went on, especially her shoes and unmentionables. Sliding underwear up her legs with one hand was a monumental test of balance. She felt like the Great Wallendas main high-wire act at the Ringling Brothers Circus.

Dax bounded down the stairs, ready to start the day later than she had in years. She'd barely had a taste of what it was like to be disabled and already had a newfound respect for how May had adapted to her limitations. Not being able to do things Dax had done all her life made her feel like a burden, especially since her injury was due to carelessness, not an accident.

"Sorry, I'm late, May."

"Don't concern yourself. Injuries take a lot out of you and need some getting used to." May had the daily produce cleaned and chopped and was binning them for the breakfast crowd when they opened in twenty minutes. "I'm relieved that you'll be as good as new in a few days."

Dax tapped May on the shoulder, and once she turned around, she hugged her in a wave of emotion. Her sister was the strongest, bravest, most giving person in the world, someone who had accepted her and her friends for who they were without a moment of reservation. If Dax could go back in time, she'd trade places with May and take on her lifetime of agony. But she couldn't. The best she could do was get her sister the best brace in San Francisco to make her life easier.

"I love you, May. Thank you for taking me in and for accepting who I am."

May tightened her arms around Dax, enveloping her like a protective mama bear. When she loosened her hold, she locked eyes with Dax. "We're not only sisters. We're each other's rock. Who you love makes no difference."

"Well, you've made a difference for me. Hurting my hand yesterday got me thinking about what would happen if one of us got really hurt or worse? How would the other survive since we both know Logan won't be back anytime soon? We're barely scraping by as is."

"The other will do what we always do—find a way. Besides, we've made some good friends in Half Moon Bay. I'd welcome help from anyone." A devilish grin formed on her lips. "Though I draw the line at that character who came looking for Rose. Anyone who comes into my kitchen uninvited clearly doesn't have manners."

"I hold the same opinion." Dax laughed before turning serious. "I overheard him making fun of Rose's stutter the other day."

May shook her head in her patented slow fashion that meant she'd reached her tolerance for stupidity. "Why on earth does she bother with that oaf?"

"It's complicated." Dax plopped down on the other stool at the chopping block. "At first, she took up with him as cover."

"Cover?"

"Charlie explained women like us sometimes take up with a man for appearances." Dax rubbed her temples. Simply thinking about her next words made her head hurt. "Rose has been seeing a woman who comes through town several times a year and stays at the hotel where she sings. So naturally, people started asking questions, and Riley made a convenient cover."

"I understand her dilemma, but Rose is a pretty girl. She could do a lot better."

"I know she could. He said something to me the other day that makes me think he was the guy who canceled our grocery order and clogged our toilets on opening day."

"If that's true, why would Rose put up with a man like him?" May asked.

Dax further explained about Riley, his uncle, and Rose's job and home hanging in the balance. "So, it looks like she has to marry him. Now I don't know if I should tell Rose about Riley making light of her condition."

"I heard Rose used to work at Ida's Café, baking and serving. If she's worried about a job, I'll give her one. We need a second cook. And if she needs a place to live, she can stay in one of the spare rooms upstairs since I can't use them."

"Thank you, May. I'll talk to Rose today." Dax flung her arms around May again, almost knocking her from her stool. In one conversation, May had solved the impasse that nearly cost Dax her finger. Now only two questions remained: Would Rose accept their offer? And was Rose ready to give up Grace Parsons?

"All right, then. Let's open up for the day."

Dax kissed May on the cheek and entered the main dining room with an extra pep in her step. Their three servers were busy filling water pitchers and coffee carafes, rolling flatware into napkins, and stacking more coffee mugs at the bar they'd turned into a beverage station.

"Good morning, ladies." Dax hooked her thumb from her unhurt hand beneath her right suspender, optimism puffing her chest. "It should be a beautiful day in Half Moon Bay."

"We have a poet, girls," one said, earning laughter from the others and a playful grin from Dax.

"Oh, my. What happened to you?" another asked, pointing at Dax's bandage.

"I had a fight with a saw. It won."

"Now she's a comedian," the first one said. With that, Ruth became Dax's favorite. Besides her dry humor and ability to keep the customers smiling, Ruth commanded the dining room as efficiently as a drill sergeant.

"Are we ready to open, Ruth?"

"What time do we open?" Ruth asked.

"Six."

"And what time is it?"

"Six."

"Then we're ready to open."

"Who can argue with that logic?" Dax shrugged. "Prepare for the stampede, ladies."

Dax unlocked the main door. A line twelve people deep had formed along the exterior wall. That represented a light morning and was typical for midweek. When she and May had their grand opening on Saturday, the line was nearly double because the off-season tourists were still in town. The varying customer flow meant it would take time to assess accurately when they could get ahead and build a little savings for rainy days. That made her and Charlie's whiskey operation that much more critical.

Men poured inside. Based on earlier conversations with Ruth, Dax guessed most were unmarried and had jobs either at the hotel or on one of the fishing boats. She heard some customers remark that rockfish and Pacific halibut were currently in abundance. At the end of the line, one person stood out. Without her beaming smile, Charlie otherwise would have blended in dressed in her mechanic's coveralls, warm wool jacket, and short hair hiding beneath a newsboy cap.

When she reached the door, she waited until the others had taken their tables and the servers were busy taking food orders. "I hope you haven't changed your mind about opening tonight. I told everyone I trusted in line to not spill the beans that they could stop by for a snootful between eight and ten like we talked about. Late enough that May will be asleep, but not so late that we can't get up early the next day."

"Are you sure you can trust them?" A tingle shot up Dax's spine. Selling liquor was a crime. The last thing she needed was the sheriff or the prohis getting wind of their operation. Sister connection or not, May wouldn't accept her getting arrested under her roof.

"These galoots?" Charlie waved Dax off and snorted as if she'd suggested a young man for her to date. "They'd as soon as kiss a fish than talk to a prohi. And this lot will be mighty thirsty after a day on the ocean."

"All right then. We open tonight, partner." Dax extended her right hand with the sense her and May's fortunes were about to change for the better.

"Partner." Charlie shook hands, offering her a toothy grin again.

At the end of the day, Ruth and her crew had finished cleaning, shutting everything down, and placing the last dirty dishes in the deep sink to soak. Dax locked the main door behind them. "Thank you, ladies. See you in the morning."

Once Dax had pulled the blinds down and flipped the sign to "closed," she let her disappointment set in. Rose hadn't stopped by. All Dax needed was a glimpse of her while she ordered breakfast or eye contact when she delivered her lunch plate. Dax wasn't asking for much beyond the opportunity to see for herself that she was all right. That Riley King hadn't said something distasteful to her face, sending her off running into a poplar tree grove to escape the humiliation. Dax decided right then. Since Rose wouldn't come to her, Dax would go to her tonight, but she had to be back in time to open her speakeasy.

Dax had yet to get the last of the dirty dishes to the kitchen, a task she should have completed minutes ago. Being able to use only one hand had slowed her down to the pace of San Francisco traffic at five o'clock. It seemed that every jalopy and new Model T in the city left work at that same time, creating a gridlock that had everyone crawling along like a snail out for a leisurely walk.

She cleared the table used by the last customer of the day and entered the kitchen, discovering May had started washing the previous load of dishes without her. "Darn it, May. That's my job. I said I'd get to those after I locked up."

"I know, but I must be getting used to the hard work because I'm not as tired today. With that injured wing of yours, I thought you could use the extra hand."

Dax had learned during her first week of living with May never to argue with her once she'd set her mind to something. Doing so was a losing battle. She narrowed her eyes, sending her reluctant agreement. "Only until this bandage comes off in a few days." Dax snatched an unused dish towel. "You wash. I'll dry and stack. Then you read your book and get some rest."

Working like a well-practiced assembly line, thanks to years of doing dishes together, May handed Dax the last plate in less than half the time it would have taken Dax to do it alone. May dried her hands. "Are you ever going to tell me what you and Charlie are doing downstairs?"

Dax nearly dropped the saucer she'd been drying. "I told you. I fixed the stairs and built a wall to hide the storage from a large section of the basement. If we continue to grow the restaurant, we might want to move the laundry down there. If not, we can use it for something else."

"I have the impression you already have something in mind for the something else."

"You worry too much, May. I have lots of plans for this place. It's been neglected for years and needs lots of shoring up."

"You certainly take after Papa."

The mention of their father took Dax by surprise. She and May hadn't talked about their parents in years, but they'd become a topic she no longer missed. When her parents first sent her away, she missed her father the most. She'd worked side by side with him for years, learning his trade. They had developed a shorthand form of communication while at a jobsite that only they understood. She once thought that connection was special, but when he didn't come to her defense when her mother sent her away, she'd concluded he only used her for free labor.

Dax was curious about one thing, though. "When was the last time you talked to them?"

"Not since after the accident when they blamed you for it." Moisture pooled in the lower rims of May's eyes. "I never told you, but Mama said you were nothing but trouble and wanted to send you to a cousin in Nebraska to work on his farm. She said working sunup to sundown was what you needed."

"What did you tell her to change her mind?"

"I didn't. I simply refused and told Mama that she gave up her right to have a say in your life the day she sent you to me."

"You did that for me?" Tears formed in Dax's eyes, matching May's. No one had ever stood up to their mother, not even their father.

"It wasn't like you were a criminal. We were both adults at that point, and I wasn't about to let our mother dictate how we lived our lives. But it turns out I did it for me too. I needed you as much as you needed me."

Dax threw her arms around her sister for the third time that day, but this time came with a sense of guilt. May had stood up for her more profoundly than she'd known, and in a few short hours, Dax would repay her by committing a crime while she slept right above her. The county sheriff refusing to enforce the Volstead Act took away most of the sting, but the possibility that she and Charlie could end up in jail gnawed at her conscience. What would May think of her if she got arrested? That would make her a criminal—the very thing May had said she wasn't and the same reason May had wanted her to stay all those years ago.

"I don't deserve you, May."

"Don't be silly." May pulled back enough to lock eyes with Dax again. "I don't know what I would have done without you after the accident, and doubly so since Logan left me here. There's no way I could have survived without you."

"I want you to know that everything I do here is for you. Somehow, I'll make the money to get you that new brace."

May slapped her brace with her right hand. "This old thing still has some life in it. Let's get the restaurant on solid footing first, and then we can look into getting one and paying for it over time."

That could take years, Dax thought. The market crash already had many bankers and investors out of work, Logan being one of them. Hopefully, Heather's husband was another. And according to the newspaper, many companies were bracing for less money available for loans. And less money meant fewer jobs. And fewer jobs meant less spending, which would lead to dwindling customers at the restaurant. Dax was torn between being the sister worthy of May's love and support and getting May what she needed to end her suffering. It was too late to cancel tonight with Charlie, and Dax would keep her word to her new best friend. A discussion, though, was in order.

Dax threw the dirty towel into the laundry basket. "If we're done, I want to catch Rose before her first show tonight and tell her about your offer."

"Go." May shooed Dax toward the door. "I'm going to fall asleep to a dime novel after I shower."

Dax inhaled a new sense of optimism, grabbed her hat and coat, hopped in her pickup, and drove toward Rose's boarding house. Driving was a much better option than walking for what she had in mind. Dax hoped once she presented May's offer, Rose would hop in the truck with her, and she'd take her to the spot on the beach Charlie had pointed out where they'd fulfill a fantasy or two under the stars. If the stars decided to make an appearance tonight.

On the short drive over, Dax envisioned a perfect life. May's presence would provide the perfect cover for her and Rose to work together in the restaurant during the day and live together upstairs at night as if they were a married couple. And by the time Dax parked and walked up to the front door, she had her and Rose creating a family of their own by taking in orphans.

Dax entered the front door and darted upstairs, realizing she hadn't thought this through. She didn't know which of the eight rooms was Rose's. The doors all appeared uniform, without labels or unique decorations. Trying her luck was her only option, so she knocked on the first door. It opened to Jules on the other side.

"Hi, Jules. Thank goodness it's you."

"Is your finger okay?"

"It's fine. I need to talk to Rose. Which room is hers?"

Jules pointed to a particular door down and across the hall from her room. "That one, but she's already left for work. She and Lester are working on a new song."

"Lester?"

"Her piano man."

"Then I'll have to meet her there. How do I get into the club, and how do I get to Rose?"

"Are you sure that's a good idea? She said she needed time." Jules narrowed her brow.

"Yes. I have a way out for her." *And a way for us to be together*, Dax wanted to add but feared saying it aloud might jinx the future she envisioned with Rose.

"This better not blow up. Rose is my girl." Jules wagged an index finger in Dax's face. "The Seaside Club is in the basement. The door is next to the laundry room and is guarded by a very large, intimidating man. Give him the password, Autumn Rose."

"For my Rose?"

"The very one. The password changes but is always the current season and Rose's name. Once you're inside, go through a swinging door next to the stage. It will lead you to the kitchen. Rose gets dressed in a storage room in the hallway."

"Thanks, Jules. You're a lifesaver." Dax kissed her on the cheek and vaulted down the stairs. A lightness filled her chest as she slid behind the steering wheel, as did a boldness when she parked behind the Foster House and walked the two blocks to the Seaside Hotel. Dax was about to propose the perfect solution. Rose had to say yes.

CHAPTER SEVENTEEN

The hotel interior was surprisingly lavish. Marble tiles in the lobby, brass trim on the door, and polished, dark wood at the check-in desk were unexpected touches. They seemed more like something Dax would find in San Francisco than in the small town of Half Moon Bay. But then again, this town existed primarily as the getaway destination for San Francisco's elite and, to a lesser extent, for the starlets of Hollywood. Lavishness was part of that world.

She took confident strides through the lobby so as not to garner unwanted attention by gawking or appearing unsure. Descending the stairs, she got a peek at the behemoth guarding the entrance of the Seaside Club through the balusters. Jules wasn't exaggerating. The bouncer was as big as a tree, and Dax imagined him snapping her in half like a twig if she got out of line. Standing toe to toe with him brought their size difference into clarity. Dax was a few inches taller than most women, but she was still a full head shorter than this giant. Nonetheless, she straightened her spine and squared her shoulders as if she belonged there.

"Good evening. Autumn Rose."

The mighty sequoia eyed Dax up and down, making her self-conscience of her attire. Was Rose's club highbrow, requiring gowns and suits? She timidly zipped her jacket up higher to hide the food and water stains on her shirt and shoved her hands in her pockets to mask her uneasiness. Then, to Dax's relief, he opened the door and moved aside.

The club was darker than she expected. None of the tables were individually lit like at the Foster House. However, every ten feet, wall sconces created a ring of light along the perimeter, while multiple lights from the ceiling highlighted the bar in an amber glow. The stage where Rose should soon perform her first show of the night was opposite the bar. The swinging door Jules had mentioned was to its left. That was her target.

Dax navigated through the two dozen tables but came to a screeching halt when she came to the one closest to the stage. The signature slicked-back dark-blond hair and tailored men's tuxedo were unmistakable, sparking a burning sensation in Dax's stomach. Her breathing became coarse at the thought of Grace Parson's hands on Rose.

Dax must have been staring too long because the woman asked, "May I help you?"

Dax said the safest thing that came to mind. "You're Rose's friend."

"And who are you?" Grace's tilted head implied Dax had gotten her attention.

"An old friend of Rose's. May I sit?" Dax pulled out a chair at Grace's nod and glanced at her male table partner. "May we talk privately?"

Grace whispered into the man's ear, and then he promptly retreated to the bar. "How do you know Rose?" Grace asked.

"We grew up together." Dax sat with her back to the kitchen door.

The light of recognition glowed on Grace's face. "You must be Dax."

"She told you about me?" Dax jerked her head back.

"In detailed terms. Rose must be overjoyed to have you back in her life."

"I'm confused." Dax rubbed the back of her neck, struggling to choose the right word. "Aren't you two…um—"

"Lovers is the word you're searching for," Grace said softly before leaning back in her chair and sipping her champagne.

Dax's breathing came in short, rapid bursts. Grace taunting her with their romantic relationship irritated Dax more than any of Rose's bullies had. "I'm going to fight for her." Grace laughed, turning irritation into wrath. Dax leaned in on instinct but held her temper. "Are you looking for a beating?"

Grace leaned forward and patted the hand Dax had formed into a fist. "Dax, there's no need to fight. Rose and I are distractions to each other, nothing more."

"I'm not sure what that means." Dax relaxed her fist, a nauseated feeling settling into her gut. Grace had eased one fear but sparked another. Rose wasn't in love with Grace but was in lust with her—an equally terrifying nightmare. Was Rose's interest in Dax nothing more than lust?

"It means I'm a substitute for you, and she substitutes for someone I once loved, nothing more. It's no coincidence that you and I share many of the same attributes. We're both masculine and forward, and if my instinct is right about you, we both have an endless drive to protect the ones we care about."

"Do you love her?"

"Yes, but not in the way you think. I want only what's best for her, and that's you, not me. I'm damaged goods."

"How is that?" Dax's question turned Grace's face long as she stared off into space.

"My Dax couldn't bear being apart and took her life years ago." Grace patted Dax's hand again. "I'm relieved that Rose hasn't suffered the same fate as I have."

"What will happen to you if Rose and I get together?" Dax didn't know why she asked, other than she no longer considered Grace the enemy.

"I'll find another substitute." Grace shrugged as if the task were as simple as picking an apple from the tree. "Rose is the third…no, the fourth substitute I've had since receiving the horrible news."

Dax's sympathy for her grew. She covered Grace's hand and squeezed. "I'm so sorry for your loss."

"Ladies and gentlemen, the Seaside Club is proud to present Miss Rose Hamilton," a male voice announced through a speaker from somewhere in the room.

Still grasping Grace's hand, Dax shifted in her chair to view the stage. Rose was stunning in her dark-blue sleeveless sequined gown. Unlike most loose-fitting dresses of the time, Rose's gathered at the waist, silhouetting her slight frame. But the most mesmerizing feature was the neckline that dipped low, exposing the tops of her breasts. *Goodness*, Dax thought. Rose was the most beautiful thing she'd ever seen.

Dax and Rose locked eyes.

Both of Rose's worlds had collided in front of her eyes. Her lover and the woman she loved were both sitting at the same table holding hands. The blast had her frozen. Nothing worked—not her mouth, ears, lungs, arms, or legs. Her first thought weighed the improbability of their meeting. Her second considered the topic of their conversation. What sordid details did Grace pass along? What unseemly notes were they comparing?

She finally woke from her stupor when a hand rested on the small of Rose's back. "Rosebud, are you okay?" Lester asked.

"I c-c-can't." Rose's body trembled, shaken by her greatest fear—that Dax would disappear from her life again. The blank look on Dax's face gave Rose no hint as to what revelations Grace had heaped upon her, nor any sign that Dax wanted an explanation.

Her words stuck inside her chest, making singing impossible even if her life depended on it. Rose ran from the stage through the kitchen door and into the storage room she and Lester used to change clothes. She needed to get as far away as fast as her feet could take her. Shoes. She needed to change out of the new shoes she'd had Lester pick up from the Foster House. They'd cost nearly a week's pay, and she wasn't about to ruin them. She slid one off and then reached for the second, but a knock on the door stopped her.

"Rose, it's Dax. Are you in there?"

Rose slipped, trying to get her second shoe off, crashing into the mop and bucket with a loud *oof*. The door flung open, and Dax rushed to her side.

"Are you okay?" Dax offered her hand to get Rose to her feet.

"No, I'm not." Rose steadied herself and dusted off her stage costume. She'd likely have a few bruises, but those weren't the most worrisome byproducts of the last few minutes. Dax probably knew the full context of her and Grace's relationship, and she'd made a fool of herself in front of an audience and her boss. The latter would be the chief topic of the town's gossip mill by morning. "How did you f-f-find out about Grace?"

"It's not important. What matters is that you're all right." Dax inspected Rose's arms and retrieved a handkerchief from her back pocket. "You're bleeding." She carefully dabbed a spot on her right elbow and then applied pressure. "Why did you run off the stage? You had me worried."

I had you worried? Rose thought. "I didn't expect e-e-either of you tonight. Seeing you both and together threw me for a loop."

"Grace and I had some things to work out."

"And?"

"Dammit, Rose." Riley appeared at the door. "What the hell happened?"

"I w-w-wasn't feeling good," Rose replied.

"Can't you see she's upset?" Dax released her arm and went into protector mode, positioning herself between Rose and Riley. Her squared shoulders and newly formed fists reminded Rose of when Dax had faced bullies who teased Rose about her stutter when they were kids.

"Customers are expecting a show. You need to get out there before Uncle Frankie finds out." Infuriatingly, Riley ignored Dax as if the only thing that mattered was Rose doing as he said.

"I told you. Rose is upset. The show will have to wait." Dax tightened her fists and inched toward Riley.

Riley studied Dax's face and gave her a frosty stare. "You're that Dax character from the Foster House I've heard about. You've been sticking your nose where it don't belong."

"It's 'doesn't' belong," Dax sneered. "And when it comes to Rose, I'll stick my nose wherever I damn well please." If any other person had made such a declaratory, possessive statement, Rose would have told them where they could put their concern. But Dax had said them. They were born out of a connection dating back to their childhood, and they felt like a declaration of eternal love.

"You need to leave." Riley brushed back the flaps of his suit jacket, placed both hands on his hips, and stiffened his posture. "Or I'll have you thrown out on that big nose of yours."

"Says the man who conveniently shows up the night old man Foster died. Let's see how tough you are with someone who can fight back." Dax stood toe to toe with Riley, appearing ready for a fight. While her stance was concerning, her statement perplexed Rose. How would she know when Riley came to town? Was this what Jules held back the other night?

"You better watch what you say in this town." Riley inched forward, staring Dax down as if he would pummel her any second.

Dax turned to Rose when she placed a hand on her arm. Her eyes said she would stay and fight Riley to the bitter end if Rose gave the word. Instead, Rose squeezed Dax's hand until she relaxed the fist she'd made. "Go. We'll talk tomorrow."

"I'll go, but don't believe a word he says. He doesn't respect you. He makes fun of your speech when you're not around. I heard him with my own ears today."

"That's enough." Riley yanked Dax backward by her collar. Dax spun around and swung away with a right cross, landing the punch in the same spot where Samuel had connected his last night. He stumbled backward into the kitchen corridor and onto the floorboards. Dax prepared to defend herself against a retaliatory blow, but Riley was preoccupied with nursing his already bruised left eye.

Rose covered her mouth with a hand, fighting back a roaring belly laugh. Riley had a few inches on Dax and outweighed her by at least fifty pounds, yet she had sent him to the floor like a Raggedy Ann doll with one injured hand. Rose placed a hand on Dax's shoulder. "I'll be fine. Now, go home. I'll drop by the F-F-Foster House later."

"Fine." Dax puffed out her chest, let out a long breath, and walked toward the swinging doors. She looked over her shoulder when Riley yelled, "And don't come back. You're banned." He rose to his feet, cupping his eye. "What is it with your friends and right punches?"

"You bring it on yourself." Rose's ire was up, and her words flowed smoothly like melted chocolate. "Stop sticking your chin out."

"Well, so does your friend, but I'm about to put a stop to it."

"What does that mean?"

"It means your friend is a thief, and I'm going to get back what is mine."

Rose wanted to say that his accusation was preposterous, but she had only a glimpse into Dax's life for the past nine years. Her gut told her that Dax was right and she shouldn't trust a word he said. "A thief? You're lying. What did she supposedly steal?"

"Whiskey." Riley turned pale when he glanced down the hallway. "Uncle Frankie."

"What's going on, Riley?" Frankie Wilkes peeked his head around the doorframe and into the storage room. "Why aren't you singing, Rose? The customers are restless."

"I w-w-wasn't feeling well, but I'm doing b-b-better now." Frankie told Rose to take five more minutes. When he turned to walk out, Rose added, "Mr. W-W-Wilkes, I have a question."

He stopped and pivoted in her direction. "What is it, Rose?"

"R-R-Riley said you might r-r-replace me. That it's time for a change. Is that true?"

"What? Of course not. You're attracting the Hollywood crowd even during the off-season. You're a gold mine."

Rose snapped her head in Riley's direction, casting the coldest, meanest look she'd ever doled out. Riley hunched his shoulders in unmistakable defeat. She'd caught him. "You lied to me? Why?"

Riley shrugged. "I wanted to marry you, but now you've become more trouble than you're worth."

That was all Rose could stand. She clenched a fist, wound up, and walloped Riley in his left eye. Rose's hand stung as if she'd slammed it in a door, but that punch felt more satisfying than a thousand ice cream cones. She was free with that sock to the eye. Free to not marry a man to avoid public scrutiny and save her job and home. Free, as much as she could be in this town, to love Dax the way she deserved. She didn't care what happened next. Frankie said it. Rose was a gold mine. She could find work wherever she wanted. She'd even bring Lester with her. Since the Victor man offered Lester a quarter of what Grace had said white songwriters earned, he'd need the extra money.

Riley tumbled until his back hit the wall. He cupped his eye again. "Geez, Rose. You could have at least hit the other eye."

"You're lucky I threw a punch. I had half a mind to use my knee." Rose ground her back teeth so hard she thought she might crack a tooth. She wished she'd never taken up with Riley King and gotten caught up in his web of lies. If she hadn't, her reunion with Dax would have been without reservation. Instead, the one thing she'd wanted to happen more than anything in her life was convoluted with unnecessary push and pull that made her feel trapped. *That. Will. Never. Happen. Again.*

"I think you better leave, nephew, before she takes your head off completely." Mr. Wilkes appeared unamused, and if Rose had to guess, Riley might be looking for a new job by the end of the week.

"This is upsetting. M-M-May I c-c-cancel tonight?"

"Sure thing, Rose. I'll let Lester know." Mr. Wilkes gave her a reassuring wink before disappearing into the club.

Upsetting was an understatement. Rose barely processed the deceit that had come to light in the last few minutes. She had to see Dax. Rose had to hug her, kiss her, explain about Grace, and then fall into her arms for the rest of her life. Once she heard Lester announce over the microphone that Rose's shows were canceled for tonight, she slipped on her walking shoes, grabbed her coat, and turned toward the door.

Grace occupied the exit, looking ever so sexy in her tux. They locked eyes, and Rose instantly thought of Dax. Every other time when Rose laid eyes on this woman, her mind would focus on the intimate things she wanted to do with her. Over three years, their accumulated time together barely registered a hundred hours, but by the end of the first, it had become clear that their connection was purely physical. They'd packed each waking hour with daring eroticism, testing boundaries, but laid no foundation for emotion beyond friendship. Both were distant. Both preferred to carry the baggage of the past rather than embark on a path into the future.

"Are you all right, Rose?" Grace's pained, uncharacteristic gaze surprised Rose. It contained more emotion than she'd shown in all their time together.

"Seeing you two together was troubling."

"I can see how that would be problematic. What worried you the most?"

Rose took a step back and slumped into the only chair in the storage room. "I am such a fool, Grace."

Grace closed the door behind her, knelt at Rose's feet, and took both hands into hers. "Foolish, maybe, but you certainly are no fool. Why on earth would you think such a thing?"

"I was nearly tricked into m-m-marrying a man."

"Nearly doesn't make you a fool. It makes you human." Grace shifted to her bottom and rested her back against the door. "Now, tell me about Dax. How was it seeing her for the first time in roughly a decade?"

Rose joined Grace on the floor with her back against the door, so their bodies touched from shoulders to knees at several points. "The pull was instant. It was as if time r-r-rewound and the previous nine years never happened. I felt like a teenager again, my stomach in my throat and my heart pounding in both ears."

"It sounds positively dizzying."

"It was. I almost fainted when we kissed the next day."

"And when you made love?"

"We haven't gotten that far yet, but I plan to remedy that now that I've put Riley in his place."

"Ah, the trickster. He is a handsome one, but he has nothing over on Dax. You should have warned me she was downright delectable." Grace was spot on. Rose released a breathy sigh, flashing on the curves and angular arms that Dax had developed since they were kids.

"She turned out well, didn't she?" Rose nudged Grace with a shoulder. "What did you tell her about us?"

"The truth. Dax knows I am no threat to her and that I'm thrilled she's back in your life." The sweet aroma of honesty filled Grace's tone, but after everything she and Rose had shared, it also tugged at Rose's heart, swelling the back of her throat.

"I wish things were different for you."

"Some things cannot be undone." Grace kissed the back of Rose's hand. "I've enjoyed our time together. Of all my distractions, you have been the most enlightening."

"How is that?"

"We're each other's mirror image. We're the same yet the opposite reflection. Each of us clung to the past but for different reasons. Your hope gave you a reason to persevere while my grief made me want to give up." Rose squeezed Grace's hand, hoping she'd realize that they had more than friendship. That they were more than mirror images. That they were each other's shelter in a storm. "I never told you, but I'd always considered your hope a fool's errand. I could not be happier to have been so wrong. But, as I told you today, you are no fool. You've taught me that hope can be a winning proposition and that maybe *I've* been the fool."

"I hope you can find love again."

"There you go hoping again." Grace pushed herself from the floor and offered her hand to help Rose up. Rose hugged her with the certainty that their friendship had taken a different yet stronger form, and they would remain a constant for each other. "Can I offer you a drink?"

"I'd love to, but I need to find Dax."

"Cherish her every day." Grace kissed Rose on the cheek.

"I will." Rose returned the kiss. "How long are you in town? I'd love to have dinner with you before you go."

"I'd planned for three or four days, so we'll have plenty of time."

Rose grabbed her things and locked eyes with Grace for the last time as lovers. She had no regrets. None for being Grace's distraction and none for saying goodbye. When Rose opened the door, she put the past behind her and walked toward her future with Dax.

CHAPTER EIGHTEEN

Dax walked the short distance home and entered through the door leading to the kitchen, noting the need for an exterior light. Her optimism remained high despite failing to pass along May's kind offer. Dax had opened Rose's eyes to Riley's true colors, and there was no chance Rose would marry him after tonight's blowup. Rose would soon see she had options and wasn't trapped between a bad and a worse choice. But if Dax had to choose, squashing Riley wasn't the best part of the night. Her talk with Grace was. While Rose's sexual experience still intimidated Dax, Grace had reassured her she was the only woman Rose loved.

Dax checked on May, confirming she was sound asleep in her bed. She then began preparations for tonight's whiskey sale by hauling two dozen glasses in a burlap sack to the basement in two trips. Both hands were sore, so Dax concentrated on not using her bandaged hand, but she inevitably relied on it for leverage and balancing things. Her right hand wasn't that much better after slugging Rose's almost-fiancé. It hurt, but it was so worth it.

A knock on the basement door stopped her from setting up her last load of glasses. She ascended the stairs leading to the exterior door, slid open the door window she'd installed, and discovered the first flaw in their configuration. The basement door was unlit with the moon hiding behind the clouds and no fixture installed. She could barely make out Charlie's beaming smile through the small window.

Dax swung the door open to Charlie and Brutus. His dense wrinkles made him appear unhappy that his daily companion and food-giver had made him come out after dark again. "Are we all set?" Charlie asked as she stepped inside.

"Almost. If we continue with this thing, we gotta put in a light out there." Dax led Charlie down the stairs. Brutus did his slow-motion bounce routine down them again.

"I was thinking the same thing." Charlie scanned the area she and Dax had put together over two days, while Dax stacked the last few glasses. The room still looked like a basement, but the four tables, chairs, and makeshift bar gave it a café feel. Good enough for Dax and apparently for Charlie too. "The place looks good."

"I grabbed some of today's receipts from the restaurant so we can make change." Dax patted her front pocket as Brutus reached the bottom and waddled to the corner where Dax had laid down a blanket for him to sleep. He then plopped down with a loud snort.

"Good thinking. We should probably come up with a better place other than a shoebox to store the cash." Charlie's tone contained a level of excitement Dax hadn't seen in her before. It made telling her she had second thoughts about running an illegal operation in the basement of May's house and place of business much more challenging.

"Yeah, about that—" A knock on the exterior door interrupted Dax. It was likely their first customer. "Do you want the honors?"

"Absolutely."

"By the way, what's the password for tonight?"

"Rosebud." Charlie needn't explain why she chose that name. Her grin did all the talking, highlighting their growing bond.

"It's perfect." Dax's talk with Charlie could wait until tomorrow. She gestured toward the door with an "after you" motion. "Let them in."

Charlie gave Dax an energetic salute and ascended the stairs two at a time, pulling herself up by the new railing. At the top, she slid the tiny wooden window open. "Password?"

Someone on the other side said in a deep voice, "Rosebud."

Charlie gave Dax a thumbs-up before unlatching the door. It flew open, and Charlie fell backward against the top railing following a distinct thud. She'd been punched and hard. She tumbled down the stairs. Her limbs were limp as if she had no control of them. Two men dressed in dark clothes and hats pulled down low burst through the door and trotted down the stairs, following Charlie as she rolled. Charlie reached the bottom stair but didn't move. Dax couldn't tell whether she was alive.

Dax's heart hammered out of control as she searched frantically with her eyes for something with which to defend herself. Unfortunately, she'd efficiently stored everything but chairs and tables on the other side of the new wall she'd installed. Her survival instinct kicking in, she grabbed the weapon closest to her—a chair. She held it with her right hand like a lion tamer, steadying it with her left. Pain shot through her cut finger, making her think she'd popped the stitches Jules had graciously given her.

The men carried baseball bats. They stepped over Charlie and turned toward Dax. She recognized the one with a black eye when he rushed toward her because she had contributed to it not an hour ago. Riley was here for revenge. The second man was the other dope who was with Riley at the hardware store, mocking Rose. She was silently thankful he wasn't the gorilla she'd left behind at the Seaside Club.

"Come for another ass whooping, Riley?" Dax stabbed the chair at his chest to keep him at bay. He veered toward the tables, wielding his bat like a madman. Splinters flew in every direction as he and his cohort clubbed each table and chair in succession. Brutus went running into the storage area at the first bang. Dax was helpless to stop them and could only watch the thugs destroy everything she and Charlie had built. She backstepped toward her friend while still holding the chair as a shield. Dax crouched, released her left hand, and placed it on Charlie's chest. She was breathing but appeared unconscious. Thank God.

When the ruffians had broken the last chair, Riley turned toward Dax, pointing the bat at her. She wasn't sure if he intended to knock her block off or simply scare her. Either way, the scaring part was working.

"Where is it?" Riley's eyes had turned menacing, even the black and blue one.

"Where is what?"

"My whiskey you stole."

"Stole?" So this wasn't about revenge but something equally base—money. "We found it, and it didn't have your name on it."

"Well, it's ours."

Dax couldn't outpower two angry men with bats, so negotiating was her only option. Fortunately, neither man appeared to be geniuses, so confusing them was an ideal place to start. She lowered the chair she'd been holding to show they hadn't frightened her, though that couldn't be further from the truth.

"Prove it. Do you have a sales receipt? Any merchant would have given you one."

Riley pulled his head back a fraction and tilted it to one side with a grimace. "What are you talking about? You don't get receipts for bootleg."

"Then there's room for negotiation. How about a fifty-fifty split of whatever we make?"

Riley thrusted his bat into her gut. Dax doubled over, sucking in as much air as she could to counter the painful spasm in her stomach and the urge to heave her supper.

"There won't be any splitting. I spread the word that anyone who showed up tonight would get a knuckle sandwich for dinner. Now, where is it?"

"Over there." Dax pointed at the makeshift bar but turned quickly toward Charlie when she shifted on the floor and groaned. Thank goodness. She was coming to.

Riley jutted his chin toward the other man, who retrieved the barrel. "Let this be a lesson. And keep your mouth shut about old man Foster, or I'll be back." He wound up his bat and took out the bar in one swing, sending all twenty-four glasses to the floor in a loud crash.

Once Riley and the other brute disappeared up the stairs and out the door, Dax knelt beside Charlie. She appeared more alert. Her gut clenched again at the thought that her friend might be seriously hurt. If she was, Dax would never forgive herself. "How are you feeling?"

"Like I fell down the stairs after being coldcocked." Charlie pressed a hand against her temple and grimaced.

"Does anything feel broken?"

"I don't think so. I've broken bones before, and this doesn't feel like it."

Dax helped Charlie first to a sitting position and then to her feet. "Can you walk?"

"Dax! Dax!" May yelled from the top of the interior stairs. Her rushed words contained a sense of fear Dax had never heard from May. "There's a ruckus up here."

Dax glanced at Charlie, who told her to "go, go." She then bounded up the stairs, passing Brutus as he huddled in a corner between fishing poles and a stack of old apple crates. May was leaning against the open door with most of her weight on her left leg. The interior metal rod on her brace had snapped in two, and her leg was bleeding below the knee.

"My God, May." Dax lowered to one knee. The cut appeared not too deep but was likely painful, nonetheless. "What happened?"

"I heard crashing noises downstairs, so I got my brace. By the time I put it on, I'd heard glass breaking in the dining room.

Two men were outside with bats and broke some windows. I shooed them away with a broom, but then my brace broke."

"Are they gone?"

"Those cowards took off down the street toward the hotel."

Those cowards, as May called them, were there because of Dax. Seeing Charlie on the ground, holding her head, would have been enough for Dax to learn the lesson Riley had laid out for her, but he had involved May. So now, Riley King had a lesson to learn—no one hurt someone she loved.

"Let me look at you." After helping May to one of her stools in the kitchen, Dax carefully removed her brace, making sure not to scrape the half-inch cut on the side of her calf. Thankfully, she found no further injuries. "I'll wash it out and cut you off a bandage."

May glanced toward the stairs leading to the basement when Brutus snorted from the top of them. "Charlie, what happened to you?"

Dax snapped her head in Charlie's direction. Her jacket and hair were askew, and she walked as stiff as Brutus. Dax shot her a vigorous head shake, replying before Charlie could, "She tumbled down the stairs."

As misleading as it was, the partial truth was much better than the alternative. Withholding nuggets from May was one thing but telling her an outright lie was a path Dax didn't want to wander down. Ever. She deserved better. At the same time, telling her everything might endanger her. May would involve the police, but the sheriff gave bootleggers a pass, according to Charlie. If word got back to Riley that she and May were snitches, that would only invite more trouble.

"Oh no, May." Charlie's stare went to May's broken leg brace, and she picked it up. "At least the strap didn't tear."

"We'll be right back, May. I'll check on the windows and get the bandage." Dax gestured for Charlie to follow. Brutus stuck to Charlie like they were conjoined twins. For such a mean-looking dog, he certainly was a coward. Dax decided right then. If she ever got a dog, it would be one that would have jumped in when Riley was wielding his bat.

Dax clenched both fists when she entered the dining room, finding that Riley had shattered the two six-foot-tall street-facing windows. They would cost at least ten to fifteen dollars to replace. Money Dax didn't have, which meant Riley had gone too far. He'd disrupted her and May's business, so now she'd have to do the same to his.

Rose appeared on the other side of a broken window. She flew a hand to her chest. "My God. What happened, Dax?"

"Riley happened."

"He did this over a black eye?"

"I'm sure it had something to do with it." Telling half-truths tonight had become Dax's defensive mechanism. Her plan to make money had already blown up on her, Charlie, and May. She didn't want the same for Rose. Coming clean was probably the right thing, but she needed time to process everything that had happened.

Dax let Rose inside.

Rose couldn't believe her eyes. The man she let kiss and touch her, whom she once considered safe enough to marry, had wreaked havoc over petty jealousy and a bruised ego. "Riley broke both of these?"

"He had another guy with him. A weaselly curly redhead," Dax said.

"That would be Jimmy. He and Riley are attached at the hip at the club." Every muscle in Rose's neck tensed. Bringing in Jimmy meant Riley wanted to intimidate Dax. If this was the game he wanted to play, she'd give it to him. Uncle Frankie wouldn't be too pleased to learn that he'd vandalized one of the few places other than the Seaside Club where hotel guests could get a decent meal in town.

"Wait here with Charlie. I have to get the bandages for May."

"May was hurt?" Rose glanced at Dax's injured hand when she grasped her hands. "You're bleeding." The reasons to hate Riley King were mounting. She pivoted her head toward Charlie, who appeared stiffer and slower than she typically acted. "Did he hurt you too?"

While Dax darted upstairs, Charlie placed both palms on her flanks and straightened her posture, stretching out the kinks. Brutus was uncharacteristically clingy. He didn't come over, say hello, and then go about his business after receiving a good scratch. Tonight, he nestled his stocky body between Charlie's legs and appeared shaky. "Riley knocked me down the basement stairs."

"My God. Everyone is hurt." Rose's head spun. "I'm getting Jules." She trusted Jules more than the town's only doctor for after-hours emergencies. For one, she had studied medicine at Berkeley for two years and knew as much as Doc Hughes. More importantly, Jules wasn't a regular at the Seaside Club who ran up a hefty liquor tab.

"I don't think that's necessary," Charlie said. "We'll be fine."

Nothing about what had happened tonight was fine. Rose dashed out the door and down the street without replying to Charlie, running faster than she ever had. All of this was her fault, which made her feel angrier and guiltier than she thought possible. If Rose hadn't taken up with Riley, he would never have hurt nearly everyone she cared about. That was it. Rose had to do everything in her power to fix it. She pounded on Jules's door, almost knocking it off the hinges.

"Open up, Jules. Open up."

The door swung open to Jules dressed in a robe and curlers in her hair. "What the heck, Rose? Are you trying to get us kicked out?"

"Charlie and Dax are hurt. So is Dax's sister." Rose rushed her words and grabbed Jules's medical kit.

Jules didn't hesitate, putting on some clothes while Rose changed out of her stage outfit and into a day dress. Minutes later, they sprinted down the street side by side to tend to the women they loved. One thought replayed in Rose's mind like a Victrola stuck at the end of a record. She even mumbled, "Riley has to pay," so many times that Jules stopped her in front of the Foster House and the two broken windows.

"What the hell happened here?" Jules sounded winded. "What did Riley do?"

"What *didn't* Riley do?" Rose muzzled her anger to minister to Riley's trail of destruction. "After you check on everyone, I'll tell you all about it."

Rose led Jules to the kitchen. Dax, Charlie, and May were seated on stools at the room's center's chopping block. Brutus was still at Charlie's feet but appeared more relaxed with his head lying on the floor. Jules first approached Charlie, who had pressed her fingertips against a temple, grimacing in obvious pain.

"Where are you hurt?" Jules lifted Charlie's chin with a hand. Her tone was calm, like when she stitched up Dax, but it contained a hint of worry this time. One by one, she assessed and tended to everyone's injuries.

"Does May need stitches?" Dax asked, biting her nails and hovering over Jules like a nervous father-to-be.

"I don't think so." Jules applied a new bandage. "The cut is narrow and not too deep. You did a fine job cleaning and wrapping it." She patted May on the knee before turning to Dax. "Let's look at that finger."

Thankfully her injury had healed some, but not enough to keep Rose from worrying that Dax was still in pain. The blood-stained bandage didn't help; it made Rose's stomach tighten. The sight of blood never bothered her, but she still hadn't gotten used to seeing Dax's. She wouldn't admit it, but she had been on the verge of tears when she saw Dax hurt the other day. It had taken nine years for Dax to come back into her life, and within hours of sharing an incredible kiss, she'd nearly chopped a finger off. Despite Dax brushing off the cause, Rose was sure she was to blame.

"You've popped one of my beautiful sutures." Jules examined the finger. "Riley must have done a number on you."

"You were right about him," Dax said.

"What do you mean?" Jules scrunched her brow.

"About him arriving the night Mr. Foster died. Riley warned me to keep my mouth shut about him. I got the feeling he was involved."

Rose cocked her head back, and so did May. A flippant comment in the heat of an argument was one thing, but this was a downright accusation of murder.

"Are you suggesting Logan's father was killed?" May asked.

"Dammit, Jules." Charlie shook her head with disappointment in her eyes. "Your suspicious mind is gonna get us all in trouble."

"We need to go to the police." May pushed herself from her chair, flinching when she rose to her feet. She returned to her chair in a hurry.

"I agree," Dax said. "Riley is a bully who likely killed May's father-in-law. He needs to pay for what he's done."

"It won't do any good without proof." Charlie waved her hands in the air. "Riley is Frankie Wilkes's nephew, and the sheriff is in Frankie's pocket. How else do you think he's been able to run a speakeasy for years without being raided?"

"Charlie's right." Rose wanted Riley to pay for what he'd done more than anyone in the room, but she'd seen it firsthand. "The sheriff is a regular at the Seaside Club and never pays for anything. He'd do whatever Frankie Wilkes wants."

"I don't know what Logan's father was like, but no one deserves to be killed." Dax flinched when Jules tightened a new bandage around her hand. "We go to the state police then."

"With what?" Charlie stood and flapped her arms in the air again. "The coincidence that Riley arrived in town the night a man died. And us saying that Riley told us to quit spreading rumors. Even if the sheriff wasn't bought off, we'd be laughed out of the police station."

May covered Dax's uninjured hand. "I'm afraid Charlie's right. Without proof, we have nothing but suspicions."

"We're way too serious, ladies. Let's table this for later." Jules put the last touches on Dax's new bandage. "You're lucky the other sutures held. But if you're not careful, that cut won't heal right. The scar tissue could limit your finger's mobility, and that's a disaster for a lesbian."

Rose cringed.

Everyone stilled except for May. She arched her eyebrows high before saying, "I can see how that would be a problem. You better do as Jules says."

Rose, Charlie, and Jules howled in laughter. Even Brutus snorted.

"I'll be more careful." Dax snatched her hand away when a flush crept across her cheeks. Rose suspected her embarrassment went beyond the topic of sex in front of May. But why?

"Do that." Jules pointed an index finger at Dax before turning to Charlie. "My primary concern is that you may have a concussion. I'll have to wake you every hour tonight to be on the safe side."

"I'm sure she won't mind that." May earned more laughs from everyone, even Dax.

"Well, as long as I have to be awake tonight"—Charlie pulled May's brace across the chopping block—"let me see if I can weld this rod. With any luck, it will be usable by morning."

May squeezed Charlie's hand, tears moistening her eyes. "You're a good friend, Charlie Dawson."

"I'm happy to help, May. I kinda feel like everyone in this room is family."

"I feel the same way. I know it's difficult for your type, but I want you to know"—May scanned each face—"you're always welcome here."

CHAPTER NINETEEN

Charlie left with Jules and Brutus, promising to return with the brace by five o'clock in the morning, an hour before opening. That meant Dax had three hours to board up the broken windows and get the basement cleaned up so she could get at least a half night's sleep. If her hand wasn't still healing, she would have had everything tidied up in an hour or two. However, Jules's warning about her stitches had her spooked. She had an idea what Jules meant by her quip, but wasn't sure of anything beyond her fantasies and experience of satisfying sexual urges herself. She was sure there had to be a lot more to it. Even May seemed to understand more about sex between women than she did.

Dax and Rose helped May into her room. On most days, May could walk short distances and stand briefly without her brace, but the cut and the chilling events of the evening had left her shaky. Dax slung one of May's arms over her shoulder and held on to it while Rose cleared the way, turned on the light in May's room, and untangled the bedding.

May settled into bed before Dax kissed her on the forehead. "Don't worry about a thing. I'll have everything cleaned up for opening and order new windows from the hardware store tomorrow." Dax didn't know where they'd get the money for it, but she had no other choice.

"Did you tell her?" May asked. Dax understood the question without further explanation.

"I haven't had a chance." Dax's temples throbbed at her and Rose's inability to finish a conversation. Dax and Rose had taken turns stumbling over their own feet whenever Riley wasn't butting in, making it impossible.

"Well, the offer stands."

"Thank you." Dax kissed May again before ushering Rose into the kitchen.

"What was that about?"

If not for the unexpected cleanup awaiting Dax, this would have been the perfect time to ask Rose to move in upstairs. "It can wait until later. I first have to board up those windows and clean up the mess Riley made."

"This little bit of glass? I can help."

Unsure whether May had fallen asleep quickly, Dax glanced toward the bedroom and quieted her words. "You haven't seen the basement."

"What did he do down there?" Rose matched Dax's low volume.

"He tore up the place. So it's going to take some time to clean it up."

"I can stay."

"What about your second show tonight?"

"I canceled it. I wanted to spend time with you."

"You did?" A warmth radiated through Dax, giving her a rush of energy.

Rose stepped closer to Dax and held Dax's uninjured hand, causing Dax's heart to drum in her chest. "After how you defended me with Riley tonight? Of course, I did."

A hunger swelled in Dax's chest. She was positive only one thing in the world could satisfy it—Rose. But if she tried to quench it right then, she doubted whether she could stop and still get her work done. Her toes were already tightening at the thought of touching her lips again. Instead of giving in, she tensed every muscle to prevent her from doing so. Otherwise, the work would never get done.

"Then stay the night." Work needed doing, and Dax was sure she'd never get it done if she didn't release Rose's hand and take a step back. So she did. "By the time we finish, it will be late. I'd worry about you walking home in the cold dark night."

"I've been doing it for years." Rose lowered her chin, looking like she was trying to hide a grin. "But I'd prefer to stay with you."

"I'd like that." An uncontrollable smile took over Dax's lips. *Funny*, she thought. Her apprehension about her lack of experience grew small whenever Rose was within kissing distance. It was as if they were sixteen again, and experience didn't matter, only that they loved one another. But that would have to wait until the work was done. She took in a deep breath and focused. "Can you help me measure the broken window frames and pick out wood from downstairs to cover them?"

"Sure."

Dax gestured for Rose to follow her to the dining room. On the way to the front, she grabbed a ball of string from behind the bar and tore off a long strand about twenty feet long, more than what she needed in her estimate. While Rose held one end of the string at a frame corner, Dax let out enough length until the line reached the opposite horizontal corner. Since the measurements didn't need to be precise, only approximately the amount required to cover the frame, she made a butterfly loop to mark the window width at the endpoint. She and Rose repeated the steps for the vertical length and for the second window.

"We're all set." Dax led Rose downstairs, bracing herself for Rose's reaction to what she'd see there and what she'd have to tell her. As she expected, once they passed the wall Dax had installed, Rose gasped, her hand flying to her mouth at the scene. The destruction resembled the aftermath of a tornado.

"Riley and Jimmy did all this? But why down here?"

"They were looking for the whiskey barrel Charlie and I found on the beach the other night."

"So this was about liquor?"

"That and the Foster House. I think he's been trying to sabotage us from the beginning by canceling our grocery order and stuffing up the toilet before he left on opening day."

"He is a weasel." Rose cocked her head to one side, narrowing her brow. "How did Riley know to look for it in the basement?"

"I got the stupid idea to sell the whiskey one drink at a time out of the basement." Dax kicked a splintered chair leg toward the center of the room in frustration. "It was the second-worst mistake of my life."

Rose shifted to face Dax and grabbed her by both arms. "May's accident was not your fault, and neither was this. You had no way of knowing whose whiskey you found. For all you knew, it fell off a ship and floated to shore." Rose flailed her arms and flared her nostrils like a needled bull. "And how dare Riley assume that barrel was his and wreak havoc to get his grubby little hands on it."

Rose went on and on about wasting her time on a sorry excuse of a man, detailing how he'd lied to her all this time and that her job was never in jeopardy. Dax let her complete her rant uninterrupted. Why would anyone stop her? This fiery side of Rose was sexy as heck. Dax simply took a step back, folded her arms over her chest, and watched the show. By the time Rose finished, her cheeks had a warm glow to them, and her chest was heaving like Dax had imagined it doing in her fantasies, only not for the same reason.

"Are you going to say anything?" Rose stood still with her hands on her hips.

"You were doing fine without me."

"Well, I'm not doing fine. If I hadn't been so stupid, thinking that taking up with a man would solve my problems, we wouldn't be in this mess."

Dax reversed roles and grabbed Rose by the arms. "First, stop blaming yourself for choosing between bad and worse.

It's hard for women like us to navigate the world, especially when we have no one to count on. I'm lucky to have May. You were making the best out of a bad situation." Dax paused to appreciate the change in Rose's expression, watching it morph from fuming to pleased in the same minute. "Second, I like how you said we. It makes me hope that we might have a chance."

"I'd say it's a given." Rose's small smile told Dax everything she needed to know. With Riley out of the way and Grace not in the picture, Rose was hers. The silence between them confirmed it. They had belonged together since the poplar grove. Dax resisted the urge to re-create that unforgettable kiss that had sustained her for years. She released her grip and cast her chin toward the misshapen pile of debris.

"Let's get to work," she said.

None of the wood on the floor was sufficiently sized to cover the broken windows, and piecemealing several would appear shoddy. Dax never did sloppy work, so she and Rose carefully removed a section of the room divider she'd put up the day before. If cut in properly, one sheet would be enough to cover both windows. Rose put on a pair of work gloves and insisted on doing most of the physical work to protect the remaining sutures in Dax's finger. Using Dax's clever string measurements, Rose penciled the cut lines.

"What now?" Rose stood straight with her legs spread shoulder-width apart and her arms akimbo.

"I cut." Dax picked up the crosscut saw she'd retrieved from her collection of tools.

"You mean *I* cut." Rose plucked the saw from Dax's hand.

"But you don't know how."

"Teach me." Rose's firm tone and grip meant Dax had no chance of changing her mind.

"Fine."

Dax retrieved the crates she'd used as sawhorses, and she and Rose stretched the plywood across them and clamped a two-by-four along one of the cut lines. Rose grabbed the saw again and positioned herself on one side of the wood. Dax then stepped behind her and inched closer until their bodies pressed together. Everywhere they touched, Dax's skin tingled. Euphoria set in, making it hard to concentrate, let alone stand. Her knees weakened at the thought of letting her hands roam Rose's body, starting at both hips and ending at her breasts. But if she did those things, they'd never get those windows boarded up. She dug deep and focused.

"You're holding a crosscut saw." She cupped a hand over Rose's as she held the tool. "Its smaller teeth cut across the wood grain and leave a smooth edge." Dax guided the saw and rested its teeth against the board's edge, nearly touching the two-by-four on its right side. "Now, extend your index finger and press it against the handle."

"What's that for?"

"It helps to guide the saw as you cut. Now we need to make the first cut. Pull the saw toward you once, gliding it against the edge." Dax angled the saw downward until it was nearly horizontal and then let go. "The idea is to make a shallow starting groove."

"Like this?" Rose leaned forward, pressing her bottom into Dax, and made a flawless cut.

Dax took in a sharp breath and exhaled. *Focus, Dax. Focus.*

"Perfect. Now place the teeth in the notch and angle the saw about forty-five degrees above the wood. Keep your elbows close to your body." Dax pressed Rose's arm against her sides, caressing each before she let go. "This will help counteract the blade's tendency to shift against the perpendicular."

"You're an excellent teacher." Rose slowed her cadence into a seductive tone, making it impossible to think about the next instruction. "I love the personal touch."

"Will you please concentrate? Or we'll never get this done."

"I can't help myself." Rose glanced over her shoulder and gave Dax a look that under any other circumstance would end all work for the day, but they still had much to get done. "It's hard to think about anything but you against me."

"I know the feeling." Dax let out a long, exasperated sigh. She and May couldn't afford to close the restaurant for a day, so she had to fix the windows. Customers might not come in otherwise. "But May is counting on me."

"I'm sorry." Rose's tone changed from tempting to heartfelt. "What's next?"

"Now you cut. Use long, smooth strokes, using the two-by-four as a guide and keeping the angle and pressure steady on both the up and down motion until you reach the end."

"How much pressure?"

"Enough to cut through but not too much, or you'll tire yourself out."

"I never knew sawing was so complicated."

"It's not complicated, but technique matters if you want it done right."

"Like sex."

"I wouldn't know." The words flowed from Dax before she could stop them. But that was how it was with Rose since she came back into her life. Even if she tried holding something back like she did with Riley making light of Rose's stutter, it inevitably came out. And now that she'd said them, she wouldn't take them back if she could. She and Rose were meant to be together. That she was sure of, and sex was now a foregone conclusion. It was useless to hide the fact that she was a virgin.

"I'll teach you," Rose whispered before beginning her cuts. Dax let Rose's comment linger without a response. There was no sense in dwelling on an ego-busting topic.

When Rose finished cutting, Dax complimented her on an excellent job. They carried the pieces upstairs with Dax not putting excessive pressure on her injured finger. Then, holding up the first panel over the larger frame with missing glass, Rose asked, "How did May snap her brace?"

"When she tried to stop Riley from breaking more windows, she must have leaned on it too hard." Dax pounded in the first nail harder than she had to. She couldn't figure out who she was more furious at—Riley for causing it or herself for giving him a reason to be there. "The brace is why Charlie and I were selling the whiskey. We knew she needed a new one, but we didn't have the money."

"That's so like you, setting up your own speakeasy to make money to help May."

"What do you mean by so like me?"

"You grew up protecting me from bullies, and you w-w-weren't afraid to get into trouble for doing so. Now Riley King is a bully and you're protecting May by skirting the law." The angry look in Rose's eye was the same as the one she got right before she broke out in her rant downstairs. "If we can't get the police involved, we need to make him pay for what he's done."

"Before we do that, we need to talk it over with Charlie in the morning." Dax gestured toward the kitchen. "Until then, want to help me clean up the mess in the basement?"

"I would love to."

CHAPTER TWENTY

For the next hour, Rose worked side by side with Dax, hauling splintered wood up the basement stairs and stacking it into a pile behind the restaurant. The work brought Rose back to their childhood when they'd sneak into Neptune Beach in Alameda by swimming into the bay and distracting the lifeguard long enough to jump into the swimming pool. Like today, that had required teamwork and a lot of unspoken cues.

"Are you hungry?" Dax asked after they'd finished and returned to the kitchen.

"I'm more thirsty than hungry." Three years as a club singer had made Rose soft. Except for walking to and from the Seaside Hotel and some memorable nights with Grace, she hadn't sweated this much in years. But considering who she was doing it with, the hard work was worth every drop.

"Why don't you fill up a water pitcher and take it upstairs while I make us sandwiches?" Dax opened their industrial-sized refrigerator. "Is roast beef okay? There's a little left over from May's special today."

"It's perfect."

Dax led Rose upstairs for a late, late dinner in what she told her she'd renamed as the living room, explaining that the term "parlor" brought back painful reminders of her mother. The parlor in her childhood home had been off-limits to kids, and if her mother found anything out of place there, she blamed Dax by default. This room was nothing like Dax's mother's immaculate one. It was tidy and dust-free, but the walls needed a fresh coat of paint, and the furnishings appeared to be late nineteenth century and well-worn.

Dax placed their food on a table matching the ones in the main dining room and laid out two napkin rolls from downstairs. Rose poured two glasses of water before landing in one of the dining chairs, which was likely a mistake. When she sat, her feet tingled from finally being off them. She suspected her legs and back would be equally angry when she tried to get up.

"I don't know how you do carpentry work," Rose said. "I'm exhausted."

"Like I told Charlie when she helped me build out the basement, you're using different muscles. You'll feel fine in a day."

Dax was hungrier than she'd let on, it seemed. By the time Rose ate half her sandwich, Dax had devoured hers. But all the while, they peeked at each other after each bite.

"Are you still hungry?" Rose asked. "This is a bit much for me." Rose's appetite was more focused on Dax, not the food. That hunger had started the moment Dax pressed against her in the basement.

"Are you sure?" Dax asked. "You didn't eat much."

"How about we split what's left?" Rose sliced the half-sandwich in half again with the knife from her napkin roll, cutting Dax's piece slightly bigger than hers as a thank-you.

Four big bites later, Dax threw her napkin on her plate, rubbing her belly as if caressing the food inside. "That hit the spot."

Rose stood, an ache in her back slowing her down and proving her earlier suspicion—she wasn't cut out for carpentry. "I'll take the dishes downstairs."

"Those can wait until morning." Dax cupped Rose's hand, stopping her before she turned on her heel. "Why don't you shower first? I'll hang a nightshirt outside the bathroom door and make up the spare bed."

Rose couldn't tell if Dax's offer was genuine or a pretense. In either case, Rose needed to make her intentions crystal clear. "I'll take that shower, but I'm not ready to be apart from you all night long." She returned her plate to the table and placed a hand under Dax's chin, raising her head until their gazes met. "I'd prefer to stay with you if you'd let me."

Dax searched Rose's eyes, not with hunger, but with the look of yearning. "I'd like that very much, but…" She trailed off. She turned away her gaze and visibly blushed.

"We'll take this at your speed. I want your first time to be special."

Dax looked at her again, this time with more confidence in her eyes. "Okay."

A shower was exactly what Rose needed. She turned the water's temperature down to a cool stream to douse the heat that had simmered during their late-night meal. The alone time allowed her to think about how she would ease Dax into intimacy. She would start with an agonizingly slow exploration of Dax's body, using her fingertips and then her lips, paying particular attention to her breasts to bring her desire to a peak. And when she gauged she had properly prepared Dax, she would take her cues from her.

As promised, Dax had hung a nightshirt on the bathroom doorknob. A striped flannel V-neck that reached past her knees was a surprise, but its lack of dainty trimmings wasn't. It was as masculine as it could be for women's nightwear. Rose pushed the long sleeves past her elbows. They'd agreed to take things slowly, but that didn't mean she couldn't show Dax a little of what she'd missed for nine years.

Floorboards creaked on each step as Rose peeked into one bedroom after another until she found Dax sitting on the foot of a bed. She was as stiff as one of those boards they'd nailed up tonight, still dressed in her work clothes and holding neatly folded nightclothes in her lap. She appeared uncharacteristically nervous, with a blank stare and one bobbing knee.

Rose placed the clothes she'd worn earlier atop the dresser along the same wall as the door. Then, toe to toe with Dax, she raised her chin with a hand again. Dax's excessive swallowing signaled that she might not be ready for sex. "Nothing has to happen tonight," Rose said reassuringly.

Dax wrapped her arms around Rose's midsection and tugged her closer, crumpling the clothes in her lap. Pressing her cheek against Rose's chest, she squeezed tight. Her fingers gripped the cotton on the back of Rose's nightshirt, pulling it taut against her shoulders. "I'm so grateful you came back into my life, but you should know that I once loved someone else."

Rose's heart sank a fraction. She may have had a physical affair with Grace, but Dax had always had her heart. Hearing that Dax had given hers to another person meant she'd given up on Rose. That hurt more than a thousand daggers. She had clung to an unrealistic hope of them finding one another again, but she had no right to expect the same of Dax. Of all people, Rose knew friends were poor substitutes and that nine years was a long time to go without someone to love. Someone to give her whole heart to.

"She must have been special if you loved her."

"She is." Dax's tighter squeeze wrung a little more anguish out of Rose. Present tense meant that whoever she was, she was still living in her heart. Dax loosened her grip, placed the stack of clothes next to her, and patted a section of the mattress on the other side. "Sit."

"All right." An unwanted heat flushed Rose's head and chest. She was sure Dax was about to torment her in a way the thought of Grace had likely done to her, only worse. Dax's affair wasn't physical. When Rose dropped down onto the bed, so did her good spirits about her and Dax. She'd thought the only things they had to get past were Grace and Riley, but she couldn't have been more wrong.

"Her name is Heather," Dax started. She gripped her nightclothes, twisting the regret out of them. "I did some work in her house, and it became apparent her husband was abusing her. There was no mistaking the bruises. I wanted to save her, but I couldn't. She was stuck in a horrible marriage..."

Dax's voice cracked. Of course, she would be drawn to her. Dax had been trying to save every woman in her life—Rose, May, and then Heather.

"She had no one to help her. We stole a few kisses but nothing more because she was afraid her husband would somehow find out. Then she got pregnant. I watched after her for years, offering a shoulder when she needed one. I knew I loved her the first time I saw her with a black eye. I wanted to beat her husband to a pulp, but she wouldn't have it because she and the children had nowhere else to go. That was until this summer. Her aunt moved to Chicago, and she became the only family member whose address he didn't know. She finally had a place to go and had squirreled away enough money if things got unbearable.

"A few months ago, I waited for them to walk past May's house to take the kids to the park like they did every Saturday morning. Then I saw her face. It was horrible, Rose. He'd beaten her so bad I couldn't make out her left eye. I lost it and sucker-punched him. He got the best of me, but the public spectacle I'd created was worth it. I made sure everyone walking on the street knew he was a wifebeater, and a few good men offered to get her out of the house and on the first train out of town."

"Are she and her kids okay?" Rose asked.

"I have no idea. I haven't seen or heard from Heather since. She was supposed to send word when she got to her aunt's, but May's husband sent us here because of the ruckus I'd made. If I didn't leave, Heather's husband, an important bank manager in the city, would have made it impossible for Logan to find a banking or investment job."

"So Logan just left you two here?"

"He wanted to kick me out, but May came to my defense. She said wherever I go, she goes, so he sent us here to run the place until he figures out if he needs to keep it or sell it."

"He sounds like a mistake, like the one I almost made." What kind of husband would leave his crippled wife in a strange city to fend for herself? Logan sounded like he and Riley were cut from the same cloth. Rose would bet her last dollar that Logan had courted May like a proper gentleman, just like Riley had courted her, but his actual plan was to marry a woman he could control. And when he couldn't, he turned tail and ran like Riley.

"But you didn't." Dax's lips settled into a satisfied grin before she lowered her head to inspect her hands folded together into her lap. Moments later, her right knee resumed its nervous bobbing, moving up and down like a piston.

Rose remembered her first time with Grace and how gentle and considerate she was. While Grace had taken the lead, Rose had dictated the boundaries. Dax was a virgin, and Rose would show her the same kindness Grace had shown her. That would start by taking the possibility of an uninvited visit to the bathroom off the table.

She scooted several inches away from Dax, giving her breathing room. "Take your shower. I'll wait right here."

Adjusting the taps, Dax let the water heat before she stepped in. Another shock to her system was the last thing she needed. Meeting Grace, having it out with Riley, May getting hurt, and having the Foster House and her speakeasy broken apart were jarring enough for one night. Keeping her left hand dry, Dax stepped in and let the spray cascade over her. Every tense muscle soaked in the warmth and relaxed in succession, allowing her mind to drift past the infuriating parts of the day.

She settled on Rose and how the world stopped when she first appeared in the dining room days ago. Nine years of fantasizing about reuniting with Rose had failed to account for her heart-stopping inability to breathe when she realized it was her. As the water moistened her skin, her insides swelled at the thought of sliding up next to Rose's porcelain skin and making those fantasies a reality. Her imagination lacked a reference, though, on how to touch Rose and gauge how long their lovemaking would take. Was it supposed to last only minutes like she'd heard it typically was with men? If that were the case, she'd be sorely disappointed. Since procreation wasn't the goal of intimacy between women, her gut told her it was more about mutual satisfaction than anything else and would require much more time.

She throbbed at the thought of spending hours exploring Rose's body and Rose doing the same to her. Dax slid her right hand down her abdomen like she'd done hundreds of times before to satisfy the ache brought on every time she had thought of Rose when she was alone. But this time she stopped, realizing that Rose was waiting in her bed, ready to quench that hunger.

Dax's mind shifted to when she and Rose had met in her childhood home and prepared for intimacy. They were on equal footing then; if the sex was awkward, they could blame it on naïveté. But that was far from the case now, not because of Rose's experience with Grace, but because of Dax's injury. Ready for intimacy again, Dax wanted to give Rose the same pleasure she would undoubtedly give her. However, Jules had her convinced her injury would put that goal out of reach or, at a minimum, would likely make her first time mortifying. That was a risk Dax wasn't willing to take. In an instant, the throbbing stopped.

Dax rinsed the soap from her body and twisted the shower taps until the water ceased to flow. When she slid the shower curtain back, the cool air raised goose bumps on her skin where water droplets remained. The ensuing shivers reminded her of the traumatic events that had unfolded today. Plainly, the shower hadn't cleared her mind. Her shoulders slumped at a mindful conclusion—making love for the first time tonight was a horrible idea.

Dax wrung the excess water from her hair, dried off with a towel, and dressed in her nightclothes—a men's sleeveless undershirt and boxer shorts. Of the two sets Dax owned, she'd purposely picked out the one she'd recently bleached to an eye-catching white. Besides giving the impression of newness, their brightness might hide the fact that Dax rarely got sun.

She smoothed her hair with a brush, less nervous about what might transpire tonight than before the shower, and walked down the narrow hallway. She paused short of the bedroom door for one last pep talk to herself before going in. *This is not the right time*, she thought.

But what if Rose had relieved herself of clothes and lay tantalizingly atop her bed? Dax debated whether she had the weakness of her teenage self or the fortitude to resist such a tempting sight. There was only one way to find out.

When Dax stepped inside the doorway, the weight of worry instantly lifted. She didn't think it possible to love Rose more than she already did because she'd kept her promise by remaining in the same place. Other than drier hair, Rose was precisely as Dax had left her. So if anything were to happen tonight, Dax was sure she would have to be the one to initiate it.

With only three sets of work clothes and no time or desire to do laundry more than once a week, Dax had no other choice but to wear each for two or three days before washing them. She deemed the set she'd worn tonight presentable for at least one more day and headed toward a chair in the corner. More caring than tempting, Rose's gaze followed her across the room. Ironically, the lack of seduction both relieved and disappointed Dax. Part of her wanted to solve the mystery of sex tonight, but her cautious side stopped her from throwing caution out the window and diving in. *Funny*, she thought. She was brave and impulsive when protecting the women she loved, yet restrained with matters involving herself. That was a flaw she would have to work on, but not tonight.

Dax took extra time to hang her clothes on the back of the chair, painstakingly smoothing each wrinkle from her dark gray slacks and then her white, button-down shirt. Her ritual had already inexplicably taken twice as long as it typically did, with no end in sight. She'd already decided that nothing but sleeping would happen tonight, so why was she still nervous? Before she could answer that question, a hand fell softly to her forearm, breaking the delicate tension in the room.

"I think your clothes are as smooth as they're going to get." Rose stopped short of pressing her body against Dax. The imperceptible space she'd left between them was enough to show her respect and enough for Dax to feel her warmth. And that was what Dax wanted most—to fall asleep with Rose's warm body next to her. She wanted a nightlong reminder that her years of hoping were over. That Rose was at long last hers.

Dax stopped her tedious task but kept her gaze focused on the chair. "Can I just hold you tonight?"

"I'd love that." Rose stepped backward, leaving a cold and empty space behind Dax.

A distinctive squeak signaled that Rose had returned to the bed. Counting to ten in her head, Dax mustered the courage to turn around. Rose had crawled beneath the covers and rested on her side, an arm bent and tucked under the pillow. It was a seductive sight Dax could fall asleep to every night.

Once Dax turned off the ceiling light at the switch near the door, she lifted the covers and slid onto the mattress, scooting closer until her body molded against Rose. She wrapped her injured hand over Rose's torso and the other under her head on the pillow and scooted closer until the length of their bodies touched front to back. They fit together perfectly like two pieces of a jigsaw puzzle. For nine years, Dax had conjectured what it would feel like to hold Rose against her, and now that she had, the reality far surpassed the fantasy. What the shower failed to do, holding Rose did. Each muscle relaxed in an instant.

Rose wriggled backward, eliminating the minute gaps between them. If Dax weren't so tired, the movement would have aroused her more than her fantasies. But at the same time, she didn't think she could be more content. Rose then positioned Dax's hand so it covered a breast through the soft cotton of her nightshirt. If heaven existed on earth, this was it.

"Good night, Dax." Rose's words were as soft as the pillows beneath their heads and reassured Dax that Rose was hers to hold until her alarm rang and they'd have to join the world again.

Dax's lids grew heavy and closed of their own accord. On the edge of sleep, she whispered the words she had known were true since their first kiss. "Good night, Rose. I love you."

CHAPTER TWENTY-ONE

Movement against Dax's leg eased her out of deep sleep. Keeping her eyes shut, she took in the muffled ticking from her Big Ben alarm clock on the nearby nightstand, the warmth pressing against the length of her, and…the fact that she was still enveloping a breast. A plump, fantasy-inducing breast. Dax squeezed her hand, the resulting sensation waking her center with a pulsating wave. A second squeeze. Then a third and a fourth. But before she could consider whether she should take this further, Rose let out a faint, intoxicating moan, providing the answer.

Rose leaned her left shoulder backward, pressing her body harder against Dax and offering herself like an irresistible dessert on a platter. Warmth spread past Dax's belly, settling in her chest and making respirations impossible to regulate. She released her left hand and caressed Rose's leg upward beneath the covers, starting at the knee and bringing the nightshirt's trailing edge along for the ride. Surprisingly, Rose's skin wasn't as smooth as she'd envisioned. Instead, slight bumps not unlike her own had populated her thigh.

At that moment, Dax accepted the truth that her fantasies were unrealistic. She'd conjured up a perfect image of Rose over the years, imaging an ideal body and persona, but Rose was far from it. She was beautiful and caring, but she had her blemishes. The bumps on the skin of her upper legs made her flawed, as did nearly marrying a man to conform to social pressure. It was a decision Dax understood but one she would never choose for herself. Those imperfections made her more real.

Strangely, Dax thought, she and Charlie had it easier than Rose and Jules. They each had a high-demand, refined skill typically performed by men, so dressing more masculine and keeping their hair short came with the territory. Dax never cared what other people thought of her and would never change for anyone other than herself. Then again, she wasn't a performer like Rose, whose job depended on an audience's approval, or a nurse like Jules, who could be fired without a doctor's trust.

Rose didn't have the luxury of not conforming, and Dax was grateful for it at this moment. She was feminine, and that alone made her more alluring. Dax continued her hand's ascent, reaching a naked hip. Her heart skipped a beat. If she had known Rose wasn't wearing any undergarments all night long, she wouldn't have gotten a wink of sleep.

Rose rolled her hips once, lifting and pressing hard against Dax again and sparking a deeper craving for her. She then settled, raising and bending her left knee to provide a welcoming path for Dax. But when Rose tilted her head and whispered, "Don't stop," Dax did precisely that. Her injured finger hadn't bothered her until now, and she'd all but forgotten it was still bandaged. And now that it was in the forefront of her mind, it felt stiff. It no longer hurt, but had it healed enough for the exploration she was aching to perform?

"I'm not sure if my finger—"

Rose took Dax's hand by the middle finger, carefully avoiding the neighboring bandaged index finger, and guided it to her center, resting the finger's tip on the warm, swollen nub. Instantly, Dax's insides clenched. She knew what it felt like to touch herself there when she was engorged and anticipated Rose's next moan when she pressed down.

"You feel so good," Dax said softly. Embarrassment over her inexperience had thankfully failed to make an appearance. And now, Rose's soft, rhythmic hip motion laid waste to the last of her insecurities. "Now what?"

"How do you touch yourself?" Rose replied in a husky tone.

Emboldened, Dax began a slow, circular motion, applying light pressure with her middle finger. It wasn't the technique she preferred on herself, forming a V with her index and middle finger, but she had no other choice with her right arm still bracing her head. And stopping to change positions at this point would completely ruin the moment. Though, within a second, she received the answer to her unasked question: Am I doing it right? Rose arched her hips upward, urging Dax on. Now the question was whether Rose—

Big Ben woke with a clang like a school bell marking the start of class. The constant noise was loud enough to wake the dead, which Dax needed some days to get her going. But it couldn't have come at the worst possible moment. If she let it go for too long, May would worry something was wrong.

"Dammit. I'm sorry." Leave it to a stupid alarm clock to interrupt the first time Dax touched a woman. She yanked her hand away, pushed herself to a sitting position, and slid the alarm switch to quiet the irritating beast. Still adjusted for the darkness, her eyes made out Rose's position reclining against the wall at the head of the bed. Dax reluctantly joined her. The heat that had built inside her was gone, but the growing flush in her cheeks provided enough warmth to counter the cool temperature in the room. The awkwardness continued to grow, forcing Dax to dip her chin to her chest, making it impossible to look Rose in the eyes.

"You have nothing to be embarrassed about, but I'm glad we stopped. I still want your first time to be special," Rose said.

Dax couldn't make out the expression on Rose's face, but she was sure it was soft with honesty. The soothing tone told her so. "I do too."

"Then we wait."

Dax kissed the back of Rose's hand, grateful for their history. Rose understood her uncertainty and had turned doubt into confidence in three words. "Go back to sleep. Charlie will be here soon with May's brace. Then I have to get the place ready to open."

Rose flipped the covers back, exposing her legs. "Not on your life. If May is out of commission, you're going to need me. I've opened a restaurant more times than you can count."

"Can you cook?"

"I filled in plenty of times for Morris at Ida's, fixing the basics. My specialty is baking, though."

"Well, then. I might keep you around for a while." Dax let an impish grin form on her lips.

With a matching grin on her face, Rose straddled Dax's outstretched legs. "You don't say?"

Dax leaned forward, positioning herself upright until her lips were inches from Rose's. "You're making it hard to wait."

"That's the point." Rose scooted closer, rubbing her bare bottom against the skin of Dax's legs and stoking the heat between them again. "I want you to have sweet fantasies until then."

"That's been happening for years." Dax flattened her palms against Rose's back, stroking the muscles up and down through the cotton fabric. The image of their clothes flung to the floor and their chests pressed together caused a powerful ache to shoot through her. She captured Rose's lips in a kiss that was hot enough to melt a hole through the floorboards and send them tumbling to the restaurant below. Soft and moist, Rose's tongue entwined in graceful, fluid moves with hers. It was as if they were the only two dancing in a grand ballroom, twirling round and round until the rest of the world was a blur.

Nothing else mattered at that moment. Not Riley. Not Grace. Not even May. Only Rose and how she made Dax's heart sing as magnificently as she imagined Rose did. No one else could make her want to stay like this until her heart gave out and she took her dying breath. Even if she had all the money in the world, she could think of no better way to leave this life than to be in Rose's arms with their lips pressed together in an unfading kiss.

Then the sound of water pushing through the pipes downstairs broke the perfect moment in time, signaling that May was awake. Dax begrudgingly returned to the present and ended the kiss. "May is up. We have to get going."

"Good thing because I have to pee." Rose pushed herself from Dax and the bed and headed out the door.

"Way to ruin the mood," Dax yelled as Rose turned down the hallway toward the bathroom. Her tone was lighthearted, but when she thought more about it, her playfulness came to a screeching halt. Not once in her many fantasies did Dax consider her time of the month. How would intimacy work when one or both of them were bleeding? Dax flopped back on the bed with a thud and without an answer. Clearly, she had a lot of learning ahead.

Dax traipsed down the stairs minutes later, feeling a smidge more optimistic about how the next few days might unfold than when she walked up them last night. With Rose pitching in, she wasn't worried about keeping the restaurant running until her cut had healed and May's brace was in good enough shape to use.

Unfortunately, that was the only worry off her plate. Dax's primary concern was finding the money to replace the broken windows before a storm came through. After that, she had to get May a new brace. Compounding the problem, she already owed Charlie twenty dollars for her share of the materials they'd bought to fix up the basement. Sadly, she had no idea how to pay for everything.

At the bottom landing in the kitchen near the swing door leading to the main dining room, Dax stopped to turn on all the lights on the main floor. Before she flipped the last switch, Rose wrapped her arms around her waist from behind, resting a cheek against her back. Dax melted into the embrace in an instant. It contained the promise of a future she had dreamed about for years—one where they hugged like this every morning. But the staff would arrive soon, so Rose's show of affection would have to be their last until they returned to the solitude of Dax's living space upstairs.

Dax brought one of Rose's hands to her mouth and kissed its back again. "Thank you for helping."

Rose squeezed tighter. "I'd do anything for you, Dax. All you have to do is ask."

Dax spun around, discovering in Rose's eyes the same gleam she'd seen following the alarm clock debacle, assuring Dax that her offer was genuine. Though Rose didn't specifically say it, Dax was sure Rose meant money. But that was a line Dax wasn't willing to cross. Love may have dictated her actions with Rose, but pride ruled her equally regarding money.

Tracing Rose's jawline with her index finger and saying "Thank you" were the only responses that seemed appropriate to Dax.

"Ahem." May had apparently opened her bedroom door some time ago and stood in the doorway with her cane. "Sorry to interrupt, but I need to start prepping."

"That's why I'm here." Rose gave Dax a wink, grabbed the apron hanging from a nail on the wall next to the storage closet, and tied it around her waist. "Until you're back cutting a rug, May, you have yourself a personal assistant." Rose snatched a knife from the wooden block on the center table. "Shall I start with the peppers?"

"How did I get so lucky?" May clasped Rose's forearm as a rascally grin formed on her lips. "But as long as you're my helper today, how about the onions?"

"Nothing like starting on the bottom rung," Rose replied with a nose-scrunching smile. She handed May another apron and pulled out a stool at the chopping block.

When May tied the apron around her waist, an envelope fell from the pocket. Dax swooped in and picked it up. The return address on the front caught her eye. "When did you get this? What did Logan say?"

"It came yesterday." May snatched the letter from Dax's hand. "It says nothing we don't already know. He can't find a job, can't sell the house, and blames you for his misery. In other words, he's not coming. We can't rely on him for anything." She stuffed it into her pocket, limped heavily to the chopping block, and handed Rose a large yellow onion. "Let's get to work, young lady."

Two months ago, Dax would have never envisioned her and May running a restaurant in Half Moon Bay, but they did so efficiently without complaint. Two weeks ago, Dax would have never thought she'd see Rose again. Now, here they were, sitting in the kitchen of the Foster House together, peeling and chopping vegetables. She let the surreal situation sink in. May might have asked earlier how she got so lucky, but Dax knew she was the lucky one. The two women she loved most in the world were right here, chatting while they worked as if they'd been doing it for years. Dax had already tucked away this perfect moment in time into her memory so she could recall with ease the warm feeling that was overtaking her.

A knock on the back door shook Dax out of her reverie. She welcomed Charlie, Jules, and Brutus. Charlie removed her cap. She slicked back her dark hair, still appearing wet from a recent shower. The dark circles beneath her eyes suggested Jules had done her job and had woken Charlie up every hour.

"How are you feeling?" Dax asked as she guided them further into the kitchen. Brutus began sniffing the perimeter, looking for any crumbs May or Rose might have dropped.

"Just a little headache." Charlie raised the hand carrying May's repaired brace. "Let's give it a try."

Dax rested a hand on Charlie's back between the shoulder blades. "I can't thank you enough for this."

"Thank me if it holds." Following greetings all around, Charlie directed her attention to May. "I didn't have the right tools to replace the rod, so I welded a new one to the inside of the break, connecting the two pieces. It might rub a little against your cut, so I suggest wearing something over it."

"I have some stockings. Would that work?" May asked.

"If they're anything like the ones Jules wears, they might be too thin. Do you have any pants?"

"I'm afraid not. Logan never let me wear pants."

Dax bit back the words she wanted to say. She never liked the idea that people expected women and men to dress a certain way. It infuriated her more that a man could dictate his wife's clothes, forcing her to be someone she wasn't.

Rose patted May's hand as it rested atop the chopping table. "Logan isn't here to tell you what to do anymore. We'll take you shopping at Edith's."

Just when Dax thought she couldn't love Rose more after saying the most endearing thing in the world to her sister... If they were alone, she would swoop Rose into her arms and kiss her as if there were no tomorrow to show her how much her kindness meant.

Jules retrieved a cotton towel from the clean stack on the shelf next to the sink. She then knelt in front of May and went to work. "This isn't ideal, but it might help." She wrapped the towel around the lower leg before sliding the brace over it. "I left a few inches of the towel hanging over the strap so it won't slip down. This should get you through the day if you don't walk in it too much."

May patted Rose's hand in the same manner Rose had done moments earlier. "My trusty helper will see to it." May stood and cautiously put more weight onto the leg with the brace until she leveled her stance. "It feels snug like it used to years ago."

"That's a good thing," Jules said, nodding.

Dax offered May her arm for added support. "Let's try walking."

May took a few cautious steps, appearing more confident on the return trip. "This is wonderful, Charlie. It almost feels brand new."

"Those are temporary welds," Charlie said. "I wouldn't trust them past a few months."

"That should buy us some time until I can come up with the money for a new one." Dax helped May back to her stool.

"Maybe we can find a doctor who will let us pay for it over time," May said.

Dax opened her mouth and blurted out her biggest frustration before she could close it. "If it weren't for Riley King, I'd have the money by next week." May's knitted brow and demand for a prompt explanation made her regret her lack of self-control. More than when she ate one of May's apple pies whole in one sitting when she was twelve. It was delicious, but she had a stomach ache for hours the next day. "I mean—"

"I've been patient until now, Darlene Augusta Xander." Their mother would call Dax by her full name when she was about to unleash a verbal beating, but May's expression had gotten Dax's attention. It was the same look their mother used to get when Dax was on the verge of earning a thrashing from Papa's belt. "I know you and Charlie have been cooking up something in the basement, and that something brought Riley King here. I want the truth this time."

Dax hadn't outright lied about her bright idea, but May made her feel small enough to crawl through a keyhole as if she had. Half-truths between sisters who depended on one another for survival had taken their toll. She dipped her head, wishing she'd made better choices.

She began with a sigh. "I didn't tell you what was going on because I didn't think you would approve." She explained further about finding the whiskey barrel and the plan to sell it one drink at a time to raise money for a new brace. "We never got a chance to sell a single drink before Riley King broke up the place and took the barrel."

"I'm more disappointed that you didn't trust me than I am about you setting up a speakeasy right below my feet." The back of Dax's throat thickened at May's last words. She might as well have stuck one of the paring knives right through Dax's heart. It would have had the same effect.

"I'm sorry, May." Dax's voice cracked. "I never wanted to disappoint you. I only wanted to help."

"We help each other by being straight. I need to know that you'll always tell me the truth. Do you trust me enough to do that?"

"I do." Dax swallowed the hard lump in her throat before glancing at Rose, Charlie, and Jules. May had already earned her trust ten times over. "You have kept our secrets and, as such, deserved better."

"All right." May's serious expression turned soft. "With that behind us, we need to talk about your idea of selling whiskey."

"I know it was stupid." Dax shook her head at the repercussions of her bad choices sitting in front of her—her sister and her new best friend had been hurt.

"That's not a word I like to use, but you were foolish to not consider the dangers of running such an operation. I could see selling the barrel in San Francisco. I know of two speakeasies Logan used to frequent that would have paid top dollar for it. That would have been much easier and less risky." Dax didn't expect those words from May. She expected more of an earful on the dangers of crime and how May wouldn't accept it under her roof, not advice on skirting the law. "Having said that, this Riley character needs to be taught a lesson."

"What do you have in mind?" Dax asked.

"I'll leave that to you four to figure out."

CHAPTER TWENTY-TWO

Rose had forgotten how exhausting working in the backend of a restaurant could be. When three o'clock rolled around, her respect for May had reached a whole new level. Rose was at least five years younger and didn't have a brace on a poorly healed broken leg, yet May kept up with her, cooking one order after another.

May wiped the sweat from her brow with a forearm after flipping a dishtowel into the corner laundry hamper. "You're going to spoil me, Rose. This is the easiest day I've had since opening the place. I almost felt like I was slacking off half the time."

"If that's the case, I'm all wet in more ways than one." Rose followed May's lead by wiping the current round of perspiration flowing down her forehead.

"Don't be silly. We made a great team today. You certainly know your way around a kitchen."

"We did make a great team, didn't we?"

Arms wrapped around Rose's midsection from behind. "You sure did." Dax rested her chin on Rose's shoulder.

Rose melted into Dax's embrace, recalling the serenity that had overtaken her when Dax slid against her in bed last night. It had lasted until the first server arrived to prep the dining room for the early breakfast crowd.

The servers!

Rose's adrenaline spiked. She flinched and wriggled from Dax's grasp as if she'd been scorched. "The ladies might see."

"I sent them home and locked the door." Dax reeled her back in, holding her tighter. "We're safe here." She nuzzled Rose's neck, inhaling deeply and exhaling with a sigh. "I've waited all day to do this."

Pulse slower, breaths returning to a relaxed pace, Rose pressed her arms against those holding her. "I could *do* this all day."

"All right, lovebirds." May excused herself, retiring to her office/bedroom to place their next grocery order, shower, and catch a nap before dinner. That left Dax and Rose alone.

"Can you stay?" Dax whispered into Rose's ear, gliding her hands down to each hip. The invitation wasn't the least bit vague. But unfortunately, the battle between exhaustion and desire wasn't a fair match. Rose needed to perform, which meant food and a nap were the only items on the menu.

"I wish I could, but I need to eat and get back to my boarding house to prepare for tonight's first show."

"Problem solved." Dax kissed the tender patch of skin along Rose's neck that always made her knees buckle in surrender. "Charlie and Jules are on their way here. Jules is bringing everything you'll need to get ready."

"Another reason I love you." Rose sunk further into Dax's hold, but she had to catch herself before she did something that would guarantee a disastrous performance. "But after I eat, I need to get some sleep, or my voice will be terrible tonight."

"Take your shower." Dax loosened her grip after kissing Rose on the cheek. "I'll bring up some leftovers again."

The stairs proved a bigger impediment than they were the night before. The heaviness in her legs made Rose puff. She doubted whether she could perform two shows tonight without sounding like she'd smoked Lucky Strikes nonstop. Hoping it would help, she increased the water's temperature and stayed in the shower nearly ten minutes longer than usual to let the steam build and coat her vocal cords. By the time she shut off the taps, she was ready for a two-hour nap, hopefully in Dax's arms.

Rose dried off and considered changing into the nightclothes Dax had laid out for her last night. But then she heard voices in the living area and remembered Charlie and Jules were expected. They must have stayed for a visit instead of dropping off her things and leaving. Rose changed course. She slipped on a pair of undershorts from Dax's dresser and a button-down shirt she saw hanging in the closet. She had no idea how she appeared, but the outfit made her feel sexy.

After toweling off her hair more and running a comb through it, Rose cautiously stepped down the hallway barefooted. The voices grew louder as she drew closer, allowing her to confirm Dax's guests' identities. While Rose's attire wasn't something she'd wear in public, she wasn't concerned about what Jules and Charlie might think. Jules had seen Rose half-dressed too many times for her to count, and Charlie wasn't the type to judge, so she continued.

The three were sitting at the dining table. Dax had laid out four place settings and bowls of May's leftover mashed potatoes, steamed carrots, and roast beef, but no one was eating. Two steps into the room, Rose felt Dax's stare devouring her, one hopeful lick of the lips at a time.

"Geez, Rose. You'd stop traffic with that getup," Jules continued after Dax visibly swallowed. "Either that, or you'll give poor Dax a heart attack."

Charlie snickered but stopped when Rose hovered over Dax, toe to toe, and gave her a long, heart-stopping kiss. Rose pulled back, staring into Dax's hungry eyes. Though she lacked the energy to follow through, she prefaced her next words with a suggestive wink. "Good thing we have a nurse in the room."

Following a few beats, Jules broke the silence. "Is it just me, or did Rose turn up the heat in here?" A quick glance confirmed that Jules was fanning herself as if she was about to pass out from heat exhaustion.

"We waited for you. Feeling better?" Dax asked with a satisfied smile.

"Much. But I still need to catch some sleep before my show."

"Sit. I'll fill you a plate." Dax served Rose her food before filling plates for Charlie, Jules, and herself.

The family-style meal was a treat Rose hadn't enjoyed since leaving her childhood home nearly a decade ago. The parceling out of food from the same serving dish had made Rose feel like everyone around the table shared a bond, if only for that hour. Meals at the boarding house or café never came close to replicating that feeling, but being among her friends brought it back in spades.

The four ate and chatted about unimportant things and laughed like families should. Then, when the last person had swallowed their last bite, Rose pivoted to a topic best addressed after they'd already sated their appetites.

"What should we do about Riley? Even May thinks we need to teach him a lesson."

The carefree expressions that had predominated throughout dinner left everyone's faces as if a bomb had gone off in the middle of the room. Dax stiffened her posture. "Riley King crossed the line. He hurt Charlie and took out his beef on May's business."

Charlie remained still, but Jules nodded her agreement while running a comforting hand along Charlie's arm. "I never liked that man from the start. He's a bully, and a bully needs to be put in his place."

"I agree," Dax said. "But how?"

"If he's so hellbent on w-w-whiskey," Rose said, "we take his entire load and hold it for ransom. He'll either pay for the damages he caused, or he'll have to explain to Frankie why there's no w-w-whiskey at the club. Riley is already in hot w-w-water with him for lying to me about looking to hire another singer."

"And I thought *I* was mad at Riley," Dax said.

"He hurt my family, and there's no forgiving that." Those words tumbled from Rose's lips as if they spoke the most obvious truth in the world. Each person at that table had taken a different path to weave herself into Rose's life, but they were family nonetheless. Since the first day they met at Ida's café, Jules had been her best friend. And Charlie since the day Jules was brave enough to introduce her as her girlfriend. But Dax was more than a friend. Since the day she stood up to the playground bully, she had had her heart.

"How much money did you expect to make from the barrel he took from you?" Rose asked Dax, her voice still edged with anger.

"Twelve hundred dollars. I'd planned to split that down the middle with Charlie."

"Add that to the damage he caused last night, including to May's brace, and we need to hold his load until he pays you sixteen hundred dollars."

"Remind me to never cross you," Dax said, snickering. "I like your idea, but we'd have to know when and where he's supposed to make a pickup."

"Riley told me the ship delivers the same night every week at one of two locations. W-W-When and w-w-where did you find the barrel?"

"At Gray Whale Cove on Sunday night."

"That makes sense. Riley always left between my shows on Sunday nights. So my guess is the next shipment will be at Shelter Cove on Sunday between eight and ten."

"That means we have two days to come up with a plan." Dax shifted her stare toward Charlie. Quiet was in keeping with her character, but complete silence wasn't. Something was amiss. "You haven't said a word. What do you think, Charlie?"

Charlie's stoic expression was unreadable. She wasn't one to wear her feelings on her sleeve, but her eyes typically gave away her emotions. Rose saw nothing in them now, neither excitement nor fear. Whatever Charlie was about to say, it already had chills coursing down Rose's spine.

"Shelter Cove is on the other side of Devil's Slide. That section of road is dangerous enough during the day. But, with a full load of whiskey barrels, darkness, and nightly fog, we'll have to crawl around the curve. Toss in the possibility of foul weather and prohibition agents on our tails. I think we're asking for trouble."

* * *

Rose never considered herself the type to need a bodyguard, but once Dax insisted on escorting her to the Seaside Club after waking her from the sorely needed nap, the idea grew on her. Besides spending more time together, it had the benefit of putting Riley on the spot, considering he'd banned Dax from the club. Between his lying and his brutality, he'd earned everything Rose planned to throw at him.

"Good night, May." Rose accepted a kiss on the cheek from her. "I enjoyed w-w-working with you today. I'd forgotten how much I enjoy cooking."

"If you ever lose your voice—not that I'd wish that in a million years—I'm looking to hire another cook so we can expand our hours."

"I appreciate that."

After grabbing their coats and ensuring the blinds were drawn in the dining room, Rose pulled Dax closer by the lapels for a heated kiss. Parts of her tingled when she tasted the coffee Dax had downed before coming downstairs. She'd kissed exactly four people like this—two men and two women—but Dax was the only one capable of making her want to forget the world existed beyond the confines of her embrace. If not for her job, she would be content to linger there for days.

She pulled back, leaving Dax visibly weak-kneed. "Can you walk?" Rose asked.

"Give me a minute."

"Take your time. I need my bodyguard in top shape."

Dax pressed both hands on Rose's bottom and pushed their centers together with a force strong enough to crack a walnut. "No worries there, Miss Prissy." She released her hold. "Let's get you to the club."

The moment the door opened, Dax and Rose's safe cocoon, the place where they could be themselves, vanished into thin air. Each of their clasped hands gave a squeeze before letting go. That would have to sustain them until they were alone again. Outside, a fog followed them down the sidewalk, echoing their gloomy future in the outside world—a life of secrecy.

Rose had lived in two towns, and intolerance for people who were different was the one thing both had in common. Alameda and Half Moon Bay were teeming with people who only accepted those who acted and dressed and loved like them. To do otherwise would mean to them that they'd sinned as much as the sinner.

Thankfully, May was an anomaly. She wasn't an odd girl like Rose and Dax, but she differed from the rest of the town in the one way that counted. As a business owner, she had to be cautious in public, but in private she refused to buy into baseless teachings and prejudices. May accepted Dax, Rose, and their friends for who they were with open arms. Unfortunately, apart from Grace's husband, May was the only truly tolerant person Rose had come across. And that was more disappointing than she'd thought possible.

Rose slipped through the kitchen staff entrance with Dax by her side. The cook, dishwasher, and servers acknowledged her with a dip of the head, a warm smile, and cheery greetings. But the best reception came when she opened the storage room door.

"Rosebud. Are we ready to knock 'em dead tonight?" Lester slipped on his traditional black blazer. He inspected Rose up and down. "Someone got ready early. You look like a million bucks."

"I told her the same thing." Dax stepped behind Rose, making herself visible to Lester.

"Who do we have here?" Lester's narrowed eyes highlighted his protective nature. Over their four years performing together, they rarely socialized outside of the club, but their affection for each other extended well beyond these walls. As the only colored man in town, Lester faced bias and discrimination every day, making Rose appreciate him more. She wouldn't let closemindedness stop her from celebrating with him, going so far as to sing at his brother's wedding last year, something that was risky for a white woman.

Rose pulled Dax by the arm until she was even with her in the doorway. "Dax, this is Lester, the best piano player on the west coast. Lester, this is Dax, my oldest and dearest friend."

"Ah, Right Cross. I heard about you last night." Lester shook Dax's hand before redirecting his attention to Rose. "Does Riley know she's here? I heard he banned her."

"What he doesn't know won't hurt him."

Lester pinched his expression. "Do you mind giving us a minute, Dax?"

"Sure." Dax gestured her thumb over her shoulder while briefly locking eyes with Rose. "I'll wait in the hallway."

Lester closed the door after Dax stepped away. His normally fun-filled expression when they prepared for a show had disappeared. "What's going on, Rosebud? First, you walk off the stage before you can belt out your first note. Now, you're begging for a confrontation with our boss."

"Riley is a lying sack of manure." Rose recounted Riley's scheme to get her to marry him, bringing out Lester's protective nature again. Clenched fists and a curled lip made their rare appearance. "So that's when I socked him."

"Good for you, Rosebud. I'm glad you dumped him." Lester softened his expression while caressing Rose's upper arms. "Grace is much better suited for you." What did he say? Rose's stomach turned at the realization that Lester knew her secret. She tried to speak, but her words logjammed like they used to do when she was little. "You heard me right. I figured it out over a year ago."

"And y-y-y-you're okay with it?"

"It makes no difference to me. We're both outsiders in this town, and I figure we need to stick together."

Having a second ally in town gave Rose hope that more might be waiting in the wings. Edith came to mind, but Rose couldn't take the chance by bringing up the topic first. Until then, she was grateful to have Lester's support. "Then you should know that Grace and I are no longer seeing one another in that way."

"That's a shame. I'm rather fond of her." Lester angled his chin toward the door. "So, you and Dax?"

"Yes, and before you ask, Grace is happy for me. I've loved Dax since we were kids."

"Your secret is safe with me, Rosebud." Lester opened the door. "Let's wow the crowd."

Lester and Rose took the stage while Dax stood sentinel along the wall about twenty feet away. She scanned the room and spotted Riley at the bar, chatting with the bartender and the other thug who demolished the Foster House. She wasn't looking for a fight but was there tonight to ensure Riley didn't take out his whiskey grievance on Rose if he ever got her alone. She was there to make sure that never happened.

"…proud to present, Miss Rose Hamilton." Lester finished the introduction from his seat at the piano and tickled the ivory keys. Rose then opened her mouth. The first time Dax heard her sing when they were young girls, she couldn't get enough of Rose's soft voice. Unlike her speaking voice, it never skipped a beat. As it didn't tonight. Her tone had transformed from that of an innocent young girl to one of a sultry woman.

Dax hung on every word, unable to take her eyes off Rose. She couldn't blame the men Rose had told her about because Rose was utterly irresistible. They'd sit in the audience night after night, hoping the sexy canary would finally say yes to their regular propositions.

During her fifth, sixth, or seventh song—Dax had lost count—Rose locked her stare on Dax with concern etched on her face. Moments later, a surly man broke Dax's trance. "What the hell are you doing here?"

Dax recognized the voice but refused to give him the satisfaction of acknowledging his question. Not even a shrug. She kept her eyes on Rose, who appeared unnerved by the possibility of a confrontation.

Riley twisted Dax's lapel, repeating his question. Before Dax could rip her stare away from Rose, a vaguely familiar voice sounded from several feet to her right. "Why are you accosting my special guest?"

Rose continued to sing, hopefully without missing a note. The last thing Dax wanted was to disrupt another of her performances.

Riley pivoted his head toward the voice. "You invited her?"

"I most certainly did." Grace Parsons took a long drag from the Lucky Strike she'd mounted onto the end of an elegant foot-long black metal cigarette holder. She wagged her index finger at Dax in a "come hither" fashion. "Come, Dax. We have champagne waiting."

Dax accepted Grace's hand, thinking how easy it must have been for Rose to fall under her spell. This starlet was stunningly handsome with a mesmerizing voice. She emphasized the right syllables and added the right dramatic pauses to command everyone's attention. And that walk of hers left little to the imagination regarding her prowess between the sheets.

Dax gave Riley a scornful sneer before pushing herself from the wall. She felt his seething grow, but when he didn't make a move to toss her out on her ear, Dax knew she'd found his soft spot. He feared losing his job if he bent the nose of the wrong customer. The healthy shoulder bump she gave him as she passed conveyed her disdain and underscored his lack of power in the matter.

Grace's male companion poured a third glass for Dax when she took a seat at the table. His silent omnipresence around Grace raised Dax's curiosity. On Grace's urging, he'd politely vacated last night to allow Grace and Dax to hold a delicate conversation. Yet he hovered from a distance in quiet concern.

"We never officially met last night." Dax extended her hand. "I'm Dax, Rose's friend."

He remained in his chair and shook hands with a firm grip but didn't say a word. "This is my very understanding husband," Grace replied for him on cue as if it were common practice.

Dax acknowledged him with a nod, realizing that he was Rose's inspiration to find cover herself, but Riley was nothing like him. This man clearly understood Grace's predilections and had entered into an agreement.

"A much better choice than Riley King."

"I wish Rose would have consulted me before taking up with that vile man. I know several actors who would have jumped at the chance to pair up with her without expectation."

"Their misfortune is my blessing." If there was ever a situation where Dax was grateful for poor judgment, it was Rose and Riley.

"I'll drink to that." Grace clinked glasses with Dax and then sipped. Her gaze drifted to the stage and fixated on Rose. A deep sigh revealed a lingering connection, at least on Grace's part. It contained the bitter taste of regret but was not so strong that Dax felt threatened.

Dax squeezed Grace's hand beneath the white tablecloth. "I know what it's like to lose her." Grace clutched her hand, sharing a pain only they understood. Recalling how Rose had inhabited every facet of Dax's mind after she lost her, Dax didn't envy the road ahead of Grace.

Dax turned to meet Grace's stare when she sensed it had shifted. Neither spoke until Rose finished her final song and Lester announced she'd return in an hour. It was a shared moment of finality and of handing over the mantle. Grace broke the silence with "Cherish her every day" and then let go of Dax's hand.

"I will." Dax shifted her stare to the stage, expecting to find Rose, but she'd already left. Dax scanned the club but couldn't locate Riley either. After what had happened last night, her chest tightened at the unlikeliness of a coincidence with that man. She tried to not rush her words, but panic had forced them out. "I have to find Rose. Where does she go after a show?"

"Either her dressing area or the bathroom. Then she always goes to the bar for hot tea to soothe her throat."

Dax shot through the swinging door leading to the kitchen like a bullet, bouncing it off the wall several times. She pounded a fist on the storage room door where she'd found Rose last night. "Open up, Rose. It's Dax." She waited for a five-count, during which her heart rate reached a dangerously high level before she darted further down the corridor. The kitchen was a small operation like the Foster House with only three people in the back. "Where's Rose Hamilton?" she yelled.

The cook standing in front of the stove gestured toward the staff door Rose and Dax had entered earlier. "Bathroom, I think."

"Which direction?"

Grace had caught up. "I'll show you." She took Dax by the hand and dashed out the door, passing a sign in the main basement-level hallway with an arrow pointing around the corner toward the restrooms.

The loud voice echoing in the hallway had Dax fearing the worst. Riley's ego and face had taken a beating the last few days, and Dax feared her little show of who was in control in the club earlier might have pushed him over the edge. If he took out his anger on Rose, she would never forgive herself.

Dax turned the corner at top speed but came to an abrupt stop. It took her a few seconds to make sense of the unexpected scene.

"Open the damn door, Rose. You're crushing my hand." Riley was nearly doubled over in obvious pain with his hand wedged between the frame and the almost shut ladies' room door. Dax snorted and stepped closer.

"Not until you promise to pay Dax for the damages you caused at the Foster House." Rose's voice should have been muffled through the wood door, but it was coming through loud and clear.

"I don't have that kind of money on me."

The door flew open, stopping sharply shy of ninety degrees. Rose flared her nostrils like a bull about to charge. "Then you better get it." She emphasized her last two words like a loud clap of thunder.

Riley lowered his hand and nursed his misshapen fingers. "I'm not paying that beast one red cent. She stole from me and got what was coming. She's lucky it was just a few broken windows."

"You're lucky it's just a few broken fingers." Rose popped her chin higher. Her sharp tone underscored a fierce contempt for the man, an opinion Dax shared.

God, she's so sexy when she's mad, Dax thought. If she and Rose ever argued, Dax was confident she'd lack the ability to mount a defense, let alone concentrate on anything but Rose's fiery disposition.

Riley pivoted and plowed into Dax on his first step, crushing his mangled hand between their chests. Skin from his neck up assumed the shade of the town's fire truck. His guttural moan didn't sound human.

"One way or another." Dax formed her right hand into a fist. "I'm getting the money you owe me."

"Stop spreading rumors." Riley clutched his hand and marched away with a considerable limp. Whatever Rose did to him, it had a lasting effect.

"He's an angry one." Grace had come forward and joined Dax in watching Riley slink away. "What rumors?"

"That it sure was a coincidence he showed up in town the night the owner of the Foster House conveniently fell down the stairs and died," Dax snarled. "And that he happened to be the nephew of the man who'd been trying to buy the place for over a year."

Grace arched her eyebrows and then narrowed one eye. "Are you sure?"

"As sure as I can be." Dax shrugged, feeling her anger recede. "I know the autopsy ignored bruises that looked like someone had roughed up Mr. Foster."

"Interesting." Grace turned toward Rose, briefly holding her by the elbows. "Are you all right?" The heightened level of concern in her voice didn't escape Dax.

"I'm fine." Rose arched her back, clearly still worked up over the diverting events of the last few minutes. "That displaced farm boy thought he could intimidate me with empty threats."

"What type of threats?" Each word from Grace came out sharp as if all of this was news to her. She appeared ready to filet Riley King like a fresh ocean catch.

"The kind that made me think Dax is right about him. He was more concerned about the rumors than the missing whiskey barrel."

CHAPTER TWENTY-THREE

Spending the night at the boarding house to avoid questions from Mrs. Prescott seemed prudent last night, but the moment Rose pried her eyes open this morning, the empty space beside her had been ruefully cold. Not having Dax pressed against her all night long was a harsh reminder that she'd been partnerless far too long. Days and evenings filled with tourists, customers, and friends had kept her busy, but she was drearily alone once she closed her boarding house door at night. The handful of nights spent with Grace wasn't enough to make her feel less lonely, but being with Dax did in spades. One night in her arms and Rose felt at home.

Jules had been at work for hours by the time Rose dressed, so she exited her room and tiptoed downstairs. Thankfully, Mrs. Prescott had departed for her daily errands. She couldn't give Rose snide looks nor ply her with prying questions like she did when Rose didn't come home for the night when Grace was in town. That made Rose much lighter on her feet as she set out for the walk to the Foster House for a late breakfast.

The head waitress seated Rose at a table for two nestled against one wall. She ordered her eggs, bacon, and toast and sipped her coffee, keeping an eye on the swinging door leading to the kitchen. Minutes after Ruth delivered her meal, Dax emerged, dressed in her traditional dark pants and button-down white shirt with a white apron wrapped around her trim waist. The empty dish bucket in her hands meant she was on a mission to bring more dirty plates and cups to the back for cleaning. Rose kept her eyes fixed on Dax, following her around the dining room while she cleared tables and filled the bucket. When Dax looked up from her third table, they locked gazes, sharing a long intangible hello. Dax gestured upward with her thumb but with a wrinkled brow, her unmistakable look of worry.

Rose finished her food, laid two quarters on the table to cover the bill plus tip, and walked toward the customer bathrooms. Once down the hallway, she slipped through the private entrance leading to the upstairs residence. When Rose reached the top landing, Dax stepped forward and swept her into her strong arms, whispering, "I missed you last night."

Head to toe, toe to head, their bodies blended into one, space between them nonexistent, proving Rose's instincts right. Wherever Dax was, that was Rose's home. "I missed you, too."

Dax released her grip and pulled a folded newspaper from her back pocket—today's *Half Moon Bay Review* edition. She pointed to the headline, "Local Man's Body Found at Devil's Slide."

"Was this guy Riley's sidekick?"

Rose scanned the article. It reported a pickup truck had gone over the cliffs at Devil's Slide last night, and a rescue crew had recovered the body of James Gibbs, a Half Moon Bay resident who had recently relocated from Fresno. "I only knew Jimmy's first name, but Riley once introduced him as his high school buddy. So it must be him."

"Good." Dax smiled.

"I never like to see anyone die, but I'm glad he won't bother you again." Rose returned the newspaper to Dax.

"Then we should heist Riley's whiskey load tomorrow," Dax said. "Maybe then I can get the money to replace the windows he broke."

"Okay." Rose added a reluctant nod. She wondered uneasily if Jimmy's death was an accident, but then she shook off the thought. In Rose's nine years in Half Moon Bay, at least one person a year had met his death on Devil's Slide, though most of them were out-of-towners who weren't familiar with its inherent dangers.

"All right, then. I'll have Charlie meet us here tomorrow night before your first show to go over the plan." Dax pulled Rose closer by her waist until their hips touched, making it hard for her to concentrate on much beyond how Dax felt against her. "As much as it pains me, you need to sleep at the boarding house again tonight."

"This isn't helping." Rose pulled back until the buffer between them was enough to let her think again. She took a deep breath and cleared her head. "You're right. If Riley suspected we were planning something, he'd be on guard instead of thinking you'd learned your lesson about sticking your nose into Mr. Foster's death."

Dax pulled Rose against her again, but this time with a jolt. "I'll be glad when this is over so we can pick up where we left off yesterday morning."

Rose replied with a kiss containing enough steam to make wallpaper peel. Dax's groan alone made Rose want to drag her to the bedroom, but she dug deep and pulled back. "Go before one of the ladies comes looking for you."

* * *

The following day

Suppressing simmering anger for two days. Sleeping alone for two nights. Neither of those things contributed to Rose's peace of mind, but they were necessary to keep Riley complacent. An hour before her first show of the evening, Rose walked in the dark from the boarding house, choosing to arrive at the kitchen door of the Foster House. Dax had suggested using that entrance because it wasn't on the street and didn't have an exterior light. Looking left and right, Rose made sure neither Riley nor anyone else from the club was around before knocking. Sneaking around this way made her feel like a spy in an Agatha Christie novel.

The door opened to a darkened interior.

Before Rose could make out who was on the other side, someone grabbed her by the arm and dragged her inside. "What the—" Her pulse quickened when the door shut behind them. Then she recognized the scent of Dax's shampoo. Pinned against the wall, she surrendered to Dax's soft, hungry lips, which were devouring her neck as if it were a slice of rich five-layer cake. The day and a half since they'd last kissed had apparently seemed like an eternity for Dax too. Rose spread her legs wider by several inches, partially out of habit but also out of hope. Grace had a similar practice of surprising Rose at the door and then diving into the deep end of foreplay with a strategically placed knee. What better opportunity to teach Dax how Rose liked to be aroused?

Rose untied the belt around her jacket, providing an opening. She wrapped her arms tighter around Dax and whispered in an unmistakable, gravelly tone, "Use your knee."

Without hesitation, Dax cupped a breast with a hand and pushed a knee into Rose's center, raising and lowering it in a slow, erotic rhythm. *My, she learns fast.*

"I watched you walk past the Foster House last night," Dax whispered into her ear. "I wanted to pull you inside and do exactly this."

Rose's heartbeat reverberated so loudly in her head that it muffled a knock on the door next to her. Dax somehow found the willpower Rose lacked to pull back, and flipped on the light switch near the door, revealing her self-satisfied grin.

"We'll continue this after we deal with Riley." Dax opened the door without giving Rose a chance to gather herself. "Come in, you two." Dax glanced down at Brutus, wagging his stocky body in a charged greeting. "You three."

Rose wasn't concerned about Charlie in her current state but about Jules. She pushed herself from the wall and brushed her hair back, hoping her best friend wasn't her usual attentive self.

"You look flushed." Jules dropped her observation like a hand grenade, added a wink, and continued further into the kitchen without breaking stride. Rose dipped her chin. Nothing ever got past Jules. Ever.

Brutus gave her outstretched hand a lick on his way by. Charlie followed, greeting Rose with a single nod after removing her cap.

"Later. I promise," Dax whispered, whisking Rose to the heart of the kitchen.

"You're not helping." Rose forced herself to concentrate on the purpose of tonight's meeting and ignore the enticing hands around her waist.

"May is in her room reading. I don't want her to hear some of this." Dax gestured for the others to follow her into the main dining room. She turned on the lights and guided the group to a booth in a corner furthest from the kitchen. Brutus lay on the floor beneath a nearby table, licking mud from his front claws.

Jules plopped down next to Charlie, rubbing her hands together as if studying a table full of delectables. "This is exciting. I've never been part of a gang before."

Charlie rolled her eyes while Rose gave Jules a soft kick to the shin. She loved how Jules had a unique way of lightening the mood, but categorizing themselves as a criminal organization didn't do the trick. "We are not a gang. We are four women who will get Riley to pay for the damages he caused, including May's brace that broke when he tore up the place."

"Exciting all the same." Jules snuggled closer against Charlie, entwining their arms.

Charlie laced their fingers together before kissing the back of Jules's hand. "Let's clam up and listen."

"All right," Dax said. "While Rose keeps Riley busy at the club, Charlie and I will head to Shelter Cove and wait for the shipment to come ashore. We'll take only the twelve barrels intended for the Seaside Club, load them into my truck, and bring them to Charlie's garage."

"Right," Charlie said. "I've emptied the storage room beneath the stairs that lead to the second floor. It should be plenty big enough to hide the barrels. We can move a tire rack in front of the access door in case Riley comes sniffing around."

"Good." Dax redirected her stare to Rose. "What's your plan to keep Riley there?"

"Grace. I'll ask her to invite him to his table during my first show. He won't dare turn down Frankie's most important customer."

"Good thinking," Dax added.

"What about me?" Jules asked. "What's my role?"

"I don't like leaving May alone at night." Dax looked at Jules squarely, knowing her sister would be in good hands. "I need you to stay here and keep an eye on her."

Jules leaned against the back of the booth in a huff, crossing both arms over her chest. "I hope your sister likes to play gin." The last time Jules pulled out her pouty lips in front of Rose was when the washing machine at the boarding house had broken down and she had to do her laundry by hand on her day off.

"Be careful what you ask for with my sister and cards," Dax said. "But thank you, Jules. I couldn't do this unless I was sure May was taken care of."

Once they finalized the plan, Dax walked Rose and the others to the kitchen to exit through the back door in case Riley was on the street. To Rose's surprise, May had come out of her room and had warmed up enough leftover meat, potatoes, and green beans for the entire crew.

"Whatever you four have cooked up for tonight, I thought you should do it on a full stomach."

Dax kissed her sister on the cheek. "Do you want to know the specifics?"

"Is that pill going to pay for my windows, or is he going to give me squat?"

"After tonight, he'll gladly pay up," Dax said.

"Then teach that young man a lesson." May patted the stool next to her. "Sit with me, Rose. Let's put some meat on those bones."

"I'd love to stay, but my show starts soon."

"Well then, the show must go on, but take a few biscuits." May wrapped some reheated rolls into a paper napkin and handed them to Rose. "Since I'm not as tired at night these days, maybe I'll come to your show this week."

"I'd love that. I'll make sure you get a front-row table."

Dax walked Rose to the door. With May a few feet away, they paused at the threshold. Neither said a word, and neither did more than grin and dip their head.

"Just kiss her goodbye already," May quipped.

"You heard the woman." Rose let a toothy smile form.

Cupping Rose's cheeks with both hands, Dax gave Rose a brief yet passionate kiss. "Stall him for as long as you can."

"And you be careful driving back." Rose pecked Dax on the lips once more and stepped into the chilly night air. A clap of thunder sounded the storm's arrival on the dark, watery horizon. Her hands shook at the realization that the odds of her worry becoming reality were high tonight.

Rose made her way to the street on the balls of her feet like a cat on the hunt. Reaching the front of the Foster House, she checked up and down the sidewalk before turning toward the Seaside Hotel. No Riley. She then assumed a normal stride, clutching her biscuits until she slipped through the employee kitchen entrance and peeked around the swinging door leading to the club. She locked stares with Grace seated at her traditional front-row table and waved her over.

Grace whispered into her husband's ear before pushing herself from the chair. Her walk never failed to catch Rose's eye. Her teasing hip sway was still sexy, but it didn't affect her as it once did. Dax occupied that space in her head and would until the day she died.

When Grace reached the door, Rose pulled her by the hand into the storage/dressing room, where Lester was changing into his stage jacket. "Do you mind giving Grace and me a minute?"

"Sure thing, Rosebud. I'll see you on stage." Lester walked out.

Rose closed the door and leaned against it. She was confident Grace would accommodate her, even if she asked for a marching band to perform at her birthday party. "I need a favor."

"Anything for you. Do you want me to have that bum strung up by his toenails?"

"Maybe later, but he first needs to learn a lesson and pay Dax what he owes her."

"He really has ruffled your feathers."

"You have no idea."

The determined look in Grace's eyes was the same one they had the first night she seduced Rose. "How can I help?"

"Keep him busy. He can't leave the club until after my second show."

"So he won't see what's about to hit him? Consider it done." Grace kissed Rose on the cheek but didn't let it linger. No longer lovers, they were still friends, and her kiss was nothing more than a friend saying yes.

When Rose finally took the stage and started her set, Grace summoned Riley to her table with a snap of her fingers. He scurried over like a pet on the end of a leash before sitting in the seat next to Grace—the one her husband had occupied earlier. With no one else at the table, Riley had no other choice but to engage in quiet conversation, which put Rose at ease. Grace had the ability to craft a story that would have anyone within the sound of her voice mesmerized for hours, and she didn't disappoint tonight. She had Riley hanging on the edge of his seat for the entire first show.

When Lester and Rose departed the stage and escaped to the hallway leading to the kitchen, his expression took on a look of curiosity. "Did you and Grace have a falling out over Dax?"

"Of course not. Why would you ask?"

"I've never seen her that rude, talking through your entire show."

Rose let out a self-satisfied laugh. "All you need to know is that was her helping me."

"Some days, I don't think I'll ever understand women." Lester hung his suit blazer on a hook on the wall. "I'm going to snatch some dinner. Hungry?"

"A sandwich would be nice. Oh, that reminds me." Rose retrieved the paper napkin May had given her earlier in the evening from her locker and carefully unwrapped its contents. "I saved you a homemade biscuit from the Foster House."

Lester rubbed his hands together as if Rose had offered him a brand-new baby grand piano. "Ooh, ever since they reopened, they have the best biscuits in town."

"That's because of May Foster, Dax's sister."

"Well, tell her she has my approval." Lester bit off half of the biscuit, waved goodbye, and headed to the kitchen.

Rose changed into more comfortable shoes and peeked into the club through the little glass window in the swinging door. Riley was still seated, and servers had brought dinner plates to Grace's table—steak, creamy mashed potatoes, and asparagus, most likely. As a special guest, Grace had certain privileges, and when she was in town, the kitchen stocked her favorites beyond what they served from the menu. Besides the intriguing conversations she had shared with Grace, Rose would miss the thick cuts of filet she had enjoyed during their regular visits.

Rose stepped past Grace's table, giving her a secretive wink. Grace returned it in kind. Riley looked up between bites, wearing a hard-to-read expression, but if Rose had to guess, she and Grace intimidated him. That gave Rose great pleasure, something, thank goodness, Riley never did.

At the end of the bar, Jason had Rose's hot tea with lemon and honey waiting. She thanked him and let the warm liquid soothe her tired vocal cords. On her second sip, Rose pivoted on the stool to watch the actual show of the evening—Grace making Riley nervous. The second act was nearly as entertaining as the first.

When dessert came at Grace's table and Rose had finished the sandwich Lester had a server deliver, Riley checked his wristwatch for the fourth time. His hand appeared swollen, but his fingers seemed to be in working order. *Darn.* He then tossed his cloth napkin on the table and pushed himself from the chair. *Oh no.* It was only eight thirty. Dax could have been done by then, but Rose couldn't chance she wasn't. There was no telling what Riley might do if he caught Dax on the beach.

Rose locked eyes with Grace, who mouthed, "Sorry." She couldn't let Riley leave yet, so she leaped off her stool, cut Riley off before he stepped away from the table, and spouted the first nugget of truth that came to mind. "More floorboards are loose on the stage, and I nearly tripped. How do you expect me to perform if I'm worried about falling flat on my face? I can't believe Frankie put someone with no experience in charge of the club." She pointed toward the back of the stage. "Go find the hammer and nails and fix the damn thing before I give your uncle an earful about the dangerous conditions I'm forced to work under."

Riley narrowed his eyes. "You couldn't have told me this before taking your break?"

"I'm telling you now." Rose assumed her fighting stance, her hands on her hips, using on him the same bullying tactic he used on her last night. "If you expect me to perform a second show tonight, you better fix those boards."

He stomped toward the stage, mumbling one curse word after another loud enough for half the room to hear.

"You're very sexy when your dander is up." Grace raised her champagne glass, honoring Rose's quick thinking. "Well done."

"I bought us a few minutes." A long list of horrifying outcomes flooded Rose's head at the prospect of Riley leaving too early, making it impossible for her to concoct more diversions. "I'm out of ideas."

"I have an idea." Grace gestured for Rose to sit to her left, leaving Riley's chair unoccupied. She poured Rose a glass of champagne. "You look as if you need this." Rose never drank alcohol between shows because it made her voice hoarse, but she took Grace's offering and swallowed it in one gulp. "Slow down, tiger, or you'll slur your way through your next performance."

"Can you blame me?" Rose extended her glass for a refill.

"Not when a certain someone's safety is at stake." Grace obliged, and Rose downed the glass's contents in one long drink. "He's coming."

Rose straightened her posture and tightened her expression to feign another brewing tantrum. "Well?"

"All fixed." He wiped the perspiration from his brow. Rose would bet a week's pay that his sweat was more about fear of losing his job than the few minutes of labor. "Now I gotta go."

"Before you do," Grace said. "Be a good chap and fetch my other cigarette case from my suite."

"I'll send someone up."

"That won't do." Grace gave Riley a look stern enough to make every man in the room quake in his loafers. "I am Mr. Wilkes's most valued guest, and I won't have just anyone pawing through my things. I trust only you."

"Fine." Riley lowered his chin until it nearly bounced off his chest. "Where is it?"

"On the nightstand next to my bed."

Rose followed Riley with her gaze until he exited the club before turning her attention to Grace. "I really appreciate everything you've done tonight."

"I love you. Of course, I'd help. I've had more excitement tonight than I did making my last movie." Grace placed a fingertip on Rose's forearm as if they were the only two people in the room—an out-of-character, attention-getting public move among a sea of patrons. Her expression turned more serious than the situation dictated. "I need to tell you something."

"What is it?" Rose tucked her arm beneath the table with one question in her head: What brought on the unnecessary risk? She had long wondered if the times Grace had said "I love you" surpassed the boundaries of friendship. The pain behind the dark eyes staring back at her suggested that might be the case.

"Not here. Perhaps the next time we're alone."

"Maybe after all of this is over."

A bellboy dressed in a traditional maroon uniform with shiny gold buttons and a distinctive black-brimmed cap dashed up to Grace's table. "Your cigarettes, Mrs. Parsons."

Dread settled into Rose's gut when Grace accepted the case and the young man scurried away. Where was Riley? "He left. I have to warn Dax, but I don't have a car."

"Take mine." Grace waved her husband over from the bar.

"I don't know how to drive."

"Then I'll drive." Grace extended her hand to her husband when she approached. "We need the car."

He dug into the front pocket of his tuxedo pants and handed Grace two keys linked together by a short wire strand before kissing her on the cheek. "Remember, the clutch sticks a bit. Shall I have breakfast delivered for two or three?"

Grace glanced at Rose and then back at him. "Just two."

"I'll grab my things." Rushing to the back, Rose picked up her purse and coat and told Lester an emergency had arisen that needed her immediate attention. She kissed him on the cheek. "I'm sorry, but I have to go. It could be life or death." She shivered when she said those last three words, hoping they sprouted from an overactive imagination.

Minutes later, she dodged wind and rain before slipping into the passenger seat of Grace's two-tone red and maroon 1929 Packard Roadster. She'd ridden in it once along the coast during Grace's previous trip.

Grace slid behind the wheel, inserted the key, and turned on the fuel pump before pulling out the choke. She then gave the gas pedal a few pumps, hit the starter, and pushed in the choke a fraction to get the engine revving at the correct speed. "Where to?" she asked Rose before popping the clutch.

"North to Shelter Cove."

"Isn't that past Devil's Slide?"

"Yes. Now hurry."

CHAPTER TWENTY-FOUR

Dax stepped on the clutch and downshifted to begin the steep incline through Devil's Slide, her headlights providing the only illumination in the night storm. The wiper was working hard to keep the windshield clear, but the pelting rain obscured the coming hillcrest and its tight curve. She gripped the steering wheel extra tightly and cautiously slowed at the peak, keeping her pickup between the faded lines on the road.

When the last of the ocean cliffs were in the rearview mirror, Dax relaxed her grip and finally glanced at the panting dog wedged between her and Charlie. She'd learned her lesson the previous time Brutus tagged along for a car ride and had placed towels on the seat and floorboard to catch the constant stream of drool. Once Dax reached the bottom of the hill and the road straightened, she gave Brutus a healthy rub between the ears, thinking she'd love to have a dog of her own, especially one that liked to ride in a car as much as this little guy.

A few yards past the city sign for Shelter Cove, Dax pulled off the highway and onto the gravel parking area that stretched the length of the beach. Before dousing the headlights she checked the wristwatch she'd found in old Mr. Foster's bedroom. It was almost seven o'clock; Rose should be taking the stage in a few minutes for her first show of the evening. Then, if all went to plan, Grace Parsons would occupy Riley's time for the next hour or two.

Now they waited. And now Dax hoped Rose had guessed correctly that the Canadian ship was waiting offshore for the local whiskey boat runners to make their drop at Shelter Cove. The howl of the wind and rain came in waves of varying strength and duration, making the wait tense. Brutus's persistent panting ensured that the windows were soon fogged.

"At least he's keeping us warm." Dax used one of Brutus's drool rags to clear a portal in the windshield to see through and then returned her stare to the beach, watching for the smugglers.

"He has a knack for keeping the bed warm on nights when Jules isn't there." Charlie matched Dax's stare toward the ocean.

"It certainly is nice having a warm body against you all night."

"Does that mean you and Rose…you know?"

"We came close, but no. We're waiting until it can be special." Dax flashed to the night Rose slept in her bed. Being next to her all night perfectly previewed what life together as lovers could be like. She'd never felt more content and wanted that feeling every night.

"Sometimes, I wish my first time would have been more special than on the beach. I was battling sand in the most awkward places for days."

Dax roared in laughter. Charlie joined her, and so did Brutus with a full-body wag.

Headlights shone in the back window of Dax's pickup, bringing the laughter to an abrupt halt and drawing out a deep bark from Brutus. Dax checked her side mirror. She couldn't see inside the automobile with the light shining directly at her truck, but the driver's and passenger's side doors were open.

"We have company." Dax eyed two men in suits stepping toward their pickup with guns drawn but pointed skyward.

Charlie looked in her side mirror until the visitors were even with the truck bed. "Prohis."

"Prohis? They ate at the Foster House today." Dax's mind raced at likely reasons Prohibition agents were at her restaurant. Were they on to her basement operation? Did Riley point the finger at her?

"Did they see you?"

"I don't think so," Dax said.

"You talk to them. They know me. I fixed their flat last month." Charlie lowered her cap to the bridge of her nose.

"Me?" Dax's mouth went dry. "What do I say?"

"Anything but whiskey."

Dax swallowed the hard lump in her throat when an agent knocked on her side window. "Prohibition agent. Open up."

Her hand shook so hard she barely budged the hand crank. "Wait a second. The window sticks." Once Dax lowered the window, she steadied her breathing long enough to ask, "How can I help, officer?"

A fedora and dark trench coat completed the look of a mysterious federal agent. However, his square jaw and hollow, sunken eyes made him appear more like the gangsters Dax had read about in the papers. He thankfully kept his gun pointed toward the clouds and not Dax. "What are you doing here?"

"We were driving north but had to pull over." Dax shifted enough in her seat to give the agent an unobstructed view of Brutus with a giant slobbery strand of drool hanging from his jowls. "The dog threw up everywhere. The twists and turns must have made him sick." She gathered a towel drenched with drool and moisture from the fogged-up window and shoved it toward his face. Saliva glistened atop the cotton strands. "See?"

The agent drew his head back, curling his lip. "Put that away." He holstered his gun. "If you know what's good for you, you'll clear out. It's not safe along the beaches at night, especially for women."

A gust of wind whipped through the cab of Dax's truck, bearing a sharp chill. Brutus shivered and let out a gooey sneeze, spraying every knob on her dashboard. "As soon as the dog feels better, we'll be on our way, officer."

The agent checked his wristwatch as if the time mattered. "Not too long." He and his partner returned to their vehicle.

Dax rolled up her window as fast as her arm could crank. Pulse beating as quickly as the wind, she kept her stare in the side mirror until the agents took off south toward Half Moon Bay. "That was close."

Charlie snickered. "Nice cover story."

Never so happy to have such a messy dog around, Dax took Brutus's head into her hands and squeezed. "Who's a good boy, sneezing on cue?" She used a playful voice as if praising a toddler.

"He's always cold with that light coat of his." Charlie threw the towel over Brutus's back and gave him a vigorous rubdown. "I think we should go. Maybe come back next week."

"Do you think May can wait another week to get those windows fixed and a new brace?" Dax intentionally phrased her question to solicit the answer she wanted to hear but instantly regretted it. "I'm sorry. I shouldn't try to guilt you into helping me."

"No, you're right. May can't wait. That temporary weld won't last forever. Besides, if the prohis come back, we can play dumb and say we were taking the barrels to the sheriff's office in town."

Dax gripped the steering wheel and twisted her hands tight. "You're a good friend, Charlie. Thank you."

They sat in silence, splitting their attention between the beach and the road. Soon, shadowy figures appeared at the waterline—two motorboats with two or three men each in them. Dax sat higher in her seat. "They're here."

The darkness and light rain made it difficult to discern the activity on the beach, but the men appeared to work at a furious pace, unloading their cargo beyond the tide line onto dry sand. They were back aboard their boats and motoring out to sea in less than two minutes. *Impressive*, Dax thought. They were a well-oiled machine. No wonder this crew was still operating nearly a decade into Prohibition.

"Last chance to back out." Dax felt obligated to offer Charlie another opportunity to call this off. She would be disappointed if she did but would respect her decision and head back to town empty-handed.

Charlie didn't hesitate to say, "We both need the money, so let's do it."

Once Dax repositioned her pickup at the edge of the gravel so the tailgate faced the beach, Charlie let Brutus out and ordered him to stay by the truck. "Guard, boy. Let us know if anyone comes." Brutus dutifully swayed his way to the back tire and sat against it, still panting and drooling.

Work gloves on, Dax and Charlie trudged toward the section of beach where the smugglers had left their load. Each stride through the wet sand was, thankfully, half as burdensome as dry sand. They surveyed the area, and Dax counted twenty barrels, more than she had expected. She did the math in her head. Potentially twenty-four thousand dollars was lying on the beach. If Dax wanted to go that route. But the agreement with Charlie and Rose was to hold the load until Riley paid for what he damaged and stole.

"We take only twelve. The rest is for another runner," Dax reminded Charlie. Each barrel weighed nearly fifty pounds and required both women to carry it across the uneven sand. After moving the first, they figured out the easiest method was to walk side by side quickly with the barrel between them. Fortunately, both were strong and in good shape, and with the wind at their backs while carrying each load, they didn't need a break between runs.

Despite the cool, damp conditions, both had worked up a sweat worthy of a full day's work on a summer day. After placing the last barrel into the truck bed and lashing the load down with a tarp and rope, Dax checked her watch. It was quarter after eight, which meant Rose and Grace might have run out of reasons to keep Riley occupied at the Seaside Club.

"We need to hurry." Dax wiped the mixture of sweat and rain from her brow.

"Come on, boy." Charlie opened the passenger door and let Brutus board before she scooted into her seat.

Dax started the engine, turned on the headlights, and popped the clutch to put the truck in drive. She pulled to the edge of the highway, looking left and then right. Headlights appeared around the curve in the road in the northbound lane and moved closer at a high rate of speed. *Good timing*, she thought. She would wait until the car passed to pull safely onto the road and not attract attention. When it came even with the gravel parking area, though, it skidded, slowing but not stopping. The backend wobbled, and the car crossed the path of Dax's headlights.

Riley was driving.

"That was Riley." Dax shifted gears, turned south toward Half Moon Bay, and punched the gas but not hard enough to spin the tires. She couldn't risk knocking the load in the bed loose.

"Did he see us?" Charlie asked.

"I don't think so, but once he figures out the barrels are missing, he'll come looking for the truck he saw, and we're the only two on the road. Is there anywhere I can pull off and hide?"

"Just Shamrock Road, but that's closed because of a landslide. That leaves only pullouts on the side of the road until we get closer to town. Once we pass Devil's Slide, I know plenty of spots where we can lose him," Charlie said.

Dax sat taller in her seat and gripped the steering wheel with the ferocity of a lion clamping onto its prey. She figured she had another minute or two before Riley figured out his whiskey delivery was missing. Until then, she needed to put as much distance between her truck and his, but safety was paramount. Darkness, wind, rain, and wet pavement made an already dangerous road downright treacherous.

Dax hit a straightaway and gunned it, leaving Riley behind in the darkness. After a quarter mile, she slowed to avoid spilling her load, letting her headlights take the lead through three consecutive sweeping turns. A check of her rearview mirror confirmed Riley still hadn't caught up to them. Dax downshifted when the road began its steady climb at the Pedro Point Headlands. The lower gear would provide the extra power needed to reach the peak at Devil's Slide without overstressing the engine.

The next turn pointed their pickup toward the ocean, leaving only two gentle turns that climbed to the summit before Dax had to slow to a crawl at the point where the road hugged the cliffside. She considered herself an expert driver, but the fact that there were only three feet between their right wheels and the sheer drop to the rocks below left little room for error. After the first curve, she checked her mirrors. The road behind her was still clear. She glided into the second turn, periodically glancing into the side mirror.

There was a loud pop.

The road grabbed her front wheels as if Dax was steering through deep sand. She took her foot off the gas when a rhythmic thumping reverberated in the wheel well, confirming she had a flat tire.

Charlie pointed toward the northbound lane on the opposite side of the road. "Pull over against the hillside and leave the lights on."

"Against the traffic on a curve?" Dax was no stranger to flat tires, but she'd always pulled over in the same direction of travel. Charlie's suggestion seemed counterintuitive and inherently dangerous.

"Would you rather be pushed into the hill or over the cliff?"

"Good point." Dax coasted to a stop so close to the hillside that she couldn't open the driver's door. Following Charlie out of the cab, she discovered the truck's passenger side extended at least a foot into the roadway. The position of the vehicle wasn't ideal, but Charlie was right. It was better than hanging their rear ends over the cliff during a windy rainstorm.

"I'll get the spare. Stay in the truck, Brutus." Charlie shimmied beneath the truck bed where she'd mounted the extra tire Dax had ordered weeks ago.

Rain soaking her clothes, Dax faced north and stood guard, looking for Riley. A distinctive sharp metal clank suggested Charlie had the jack out to replace the blown front roadside tire. A minute later, a glow appeared at the curve. "He's coming," Dax yelled over her shoulder. Then, headlights emerged, jerking around the turn. They wobbled up and down, left and right. Whoever was driving they were nearly out of control. It had to be Riley.

The lights leveled, pointing straight at Dax.

Brakes screeched.

The oncoming car bobbed and kept coming. If he didn't correct now, he'd go over the cliff. Then the headlights turned, pointing toward the hill. The vehicle went sideways, veering toward Dax's truck.

"Charlie!" Dax crouched and grabbed her friend by the collar. She dragged her across the pavement until she fell on her backside in the center of the road. The amplifying sound of skidding tires told her she didn't have time to move further, leaving her with a slim hope she'd done enough. But she couldn't look. Dax curled her body around Charlie, shielding her from certain death.

Crash! Metal hit metal.

Charlie squirmed and yelled, "Brutus!" Dax rolled off her. Before either had time to assess the dangers, Charlie dashed toward the pickup. Shaking off her daze, Dax saw that the other truck had careened off the side of the hill and had come to rest sideways against the back of Dax's truck after slamming into it. Its front end faced the hillside with one headlight not working. Her truck and whiskey were intact, save a section of the bed and a few barrels smashed on the ground. Riley's pickup was a different story. The passenger side was crushed in, eerily similar to how Logan's old Model T had been when May had been hurt.

Charlie flew to the passenger door of Dax's pickup and opened with enough force to pull it from its hinges. She emerged from the cab, cradling Brutus like a heavy sack of potatoes. His legs were stiff beneath Charlie's arms but didn't move.

Dax gasped. This was all her fault. If she hadn't guilted Charlie into helping, Brutus would still be alive. Her heart sank. Throat swelled. Tears formed, one after another, as if someone had opened the water taps and broken the valves. The rain fell faster, making it impossible to tell how many tears Dax let fall.

"I'm so sorry. Brutus was the best dog." A glistening string of slobber dangled from his mouth and dropped to Charlie's shoe. Dax dropped to her knees, unable to take in a full breath. She scooped up the patch of goo. "I'm going to miss his drool."

"Disgusting, Dax." Charlie curled her lip.

"But he's dead."

"He's not dead. He gets scared stiff when he's terrified." Charlie placed him on the pavement next to Dax and slapped his rear end. "Snap out of it, Brutus." He shook his head first and then his entire body, punctuating his resurrection with three hefty snorts.

"Brutus!" Dax enveloped him in her arms, visceral joy oozing from every pore. Her thoughts jumbled, bouncing between relief that he had survived and guilt for nearly causing his death. "You're alive. I can't believe you're alive." She rubbed his ears and kissed his wet, wrinkled face from nose to eyes, grateful enough to not dry heave when she sucked in some slobber.

"You won't be alive for long once I get my hands on you." Riley had crawled out of his truck and circled it, still clearly dazed from the accident. Hunched over, he weaved like a drunk at the Seaside Club.

Dax's joy transformed into anger the moment she heard his voice. He'd been behind everything that had gone wrong since she had set foot into Half Moon Bay. The lesson he needed to learn would start now. Dax sprung to her feet and let the first punch fly, landing it on the already well-bruised eye and sending Riley stumbling backward.

"Get Brutus in the truck." Dax looked over her shoulder at Charlie and pointed toward the cab. She turned around in time to duck a poorly thrown punch that failed to get within a foot of her. A car door creaked and slammed shut while she dodged a second and third better-placed swing.

A glow came into view from the south, distracting Dax long enough for Riley to tackle her, launching her several feet backward before she fell to the ground. Her head hit the gravel shoulder dangerously close to the cliffside. The air was driven from her lungs as his full weight landed atop her, momentarily paralyzing her. She struggled to break free, but he was too big to overcome.

A car skidded. Headlights illuminated the area.

Charlie pounced into action. The way Riley's head jerked backward, Dax suspected Charlie had grabbed a handful of his sandy brown hair. He shoved Charlie, sending her stumbling to the slick pavement. Dax then windmilled her arms, hoping a few punches would land and do some harm, but Riley deflected all but a few.

"Get off of her," a woman's voice called out from the direction of the third car. Then the woman's arms and fists flew, pounding Riley on the head and shoulder as he kept Dax pinned to the ground. Finally, Riley released one hand from his hold on Dax and shoved the woman. Her feet wobbled on the gravel.

"Dax!" she yelled.

Dax looked up. Her heart stopped. It was Rose.

Rose flailed her arms to gather her footing, but her feet slipped against the wet gravel, and she continued to lean backward. Dax reached out, desperate to grab her, but Riley's weight constrained her. "Help her. Help Rose," Dax yelled.

Dax had lost a lot in her young life but never due to death. Everyone who had left her had the possibility of coming back like Rose had. She couldn't bear losing Rose forever. She squirmed to break loose, but Riley landed a punch square on her jaw, forcing her to close her eyes for an instant to absorb the blow. A sharp pain radiated through the left side of her face. She pried one eye open only to see Rose lose her precarious toehold and begin a terrifying fall. Her head dipped below the ground line, and then a hand reached out for her from the direction of the third car.

"Rose!" Grace lunged to the ground and clamped onto Rose's wrist. "Hold on!"

A second punch landed on Dax's face, delivering the distinct coppery taste of blood into her mouth, but she refused to let the pain take over. Adrenaline spiked. She arched her upper torso from the ground and bit down on the lower arm that was pinning her down. She tightened her jaw like a vise, digging deep until a section of hairy flesh bled into her mouth. She jerked her head when he screamed, ripped off a section, and spit it to the ground.

Riley straightened his posture, placing his punching hand over the new gushing wound.

A loud grunt drowned out Riley's moaning, and Dax glanced in its direction. Charlie was approaching rapidly, wielding a tire iron, with a calm look of determination on her face. She wound up and clubbed Riley under the chin on the upswing, sending him tumbling off Dax and over the cliff. His scream faded into the dark abyss.

Dax turned over and crawled toward Rose, clawing frantically at the gravel. Grace's face grimaced as she battled the pull of gravity. She held Rose's life in her hand and looked like she had but seconds of strength remaining. Less than thirty seconds had passed since Rose went over the cliff, yet she hadn't uttered a word. Not a single scream. Riley, though, feared his death all the way to the bottom.

Dax flattened herself and peeked over the edge. Rose was dangling over a two-hundred-foot drop that ended at the bottom of the rocky cliff. "Give me your hand." She reached down in the dark, feeling for Rose's other hand. One, two, and then three seconds passed until Rose's fingertips finally grazed hers.

"I can't hold on," Grace's voice strained.

Dax pushed her torso further over the edge to extend her reach an extra six inches. Her hand searched desperately again until she hit Rose's wrist. She clenched tightly. A fraction of a second later, Grace let go, and Rose's full weight jerked Dax further until her chest hung across the edge. Both were on the verge of hurtling down the cliff.

"Charlie!" Dax yelled as her body continued to slip along the damp gravel. "Grab me."

Dax and Rose had caught only brief fear-filled glances until now. They locked stares now, and at that moment, Dax calmed. The wind and rain and the surrounding chaos slowed to a fraction of their normal speed. Dax's chest inexplicably filled with confidence despite her continued slow slide off the edge. She reached her other hand down and smiled. "It's okay, Rose. Grab my other hand."

Rose smiled and flung her other hand up until it met Dax's. If Rose fell to her death, Dax wanted to make that final journey with her. They were soulmates, and what better way to leave this world than together?

A hand grabbed Dax by the ankle. Then a second encircled her other ankle, stopping Dax's slow slide toward death. Both pulled, in unison, tugging her backward one inch at a time. When Dax's breasts scraped against the gravel, she was sure their date with death would have to wait. She retightened her grip as reassurance.

Rose's frazzled hair appeared from beneath the edge, then her face. Her smile was strangely still, and so was Dax's. Their gazes were stubbornly locked, refusing to acknowledge the rest of the world existed. The glow from the headlights disclosed the emotions in Rose's eyes—trust, love, and gratitude. Dax returned them in kind and continued to grip her hands because their lives depended on it. Not until Rose's feet cleared the gravel did Dax finally let go.

Both rose to their knees and fell into each other's arms. Dax's heart should have beat wildly, but it had settled the moment she and Rose locked eyes. She expected Rose to be trembling, but she was as steady as the rocks forming the cliffs below.

Dax loosened their embrace and wiped the strands of hair that had covered Rose's face to the side. "Hi."

"Hi." Rose's smile took on a greater brilliance. "I knew you'd save me."

"I hate to break up this lovely scene, but we need to get out of the road before someone comes." Grace brushed dust and gravel from her tuxedo.

Dax pivoted toward Grace and took her hands into hers. "Thank you for saving Rose."

"We both did, my dear Dax."

Dax turned. Charlie's face glowed in the headlights, pale as ocean whitecaps. "Are you okay?"

Charlie raised both hands even with her chin. They shook. "I killed a man."

Dax gripped Charlie by her jacket at the upper arms. "You had no choice. Rose and I would be dead if you hadn't hit him."

Charlie shifted her blank stare to look into Dax's eyes. "I've never killed anything, not even a bug. We have to tell the police."

"We are not telling the police anything. The sheriff is in Frankie Wilkes's pocket." Dax's mind raced, evaluating the options at her disposal. Only one thing made sense. "Listen to me. We're going to roll Riley's pickup over the cliff. The sheriff will think he went over with it."

"But what about the whiskey?" Charlie asked, her color coming back to her.

"We keep it and hide it like we planned. Then, we come up with a plan to sell it out of town or something." Charlie gave Dax a nod that said she still wasn't convinced. "We can do this, Charlie. You shouldn't go to jail for saving Rose's life."

Charlie only nodded.

Dax redirected her attention to Grace. "I need you to take Rose back to town and act as if nothing happened. Can you do that?"

"Of course," Grace replied.

Once Charlie and Dax rolled Riley's truck off the cliff, they picked up the remnants of the whiskey barrels that had shattered in the crash. "Wait," Grace said. "It might be better to leave a breadcrumb."

"You're right," Dax replied. If anyone from Frankie's club came looking for Riley, some wood from the broken barrels would lead them right to him. It would be better to have them find him right away than to have the mystery linger, so Dax left several pieces in the gravel near the cliff.

Dax escorted Rose to Grace's car, settling her into the passenger seat. Its luxury didn't escape Dax, but Rose had already made her choice and Dax trusted no amount of money could change her mind. She ran a fingertip down the side of

Rose's face, staring into her eyes. The loving look Rose gave her reinforced her trust.

"I'll see you in town."

Once Grace and Rose drove off, Dax and Charlie shifted the remaining load in the truck and went to work changing the tire. The blowing storm slowed them, but it also played to their advantage by keeping the locals off this treacherous stretch of road. Half an hour later, they tied down and tarped the load. Brutus joined them on the bench seat, and they drove straight to Half Moon Bay like nothing had happened.

CHAPTER TWENTY-FIVE

The nine barrels that had survived the collision were now safely in their temporary home—a hidden storage space beneath the stairs of Charlie's garage. If sold by the glass, that stash was worth over ten thousand dollars. With that kind of life-changing money at stake, lives were as well. The whiskey needed to remain a secret beyond those already in the know: Dax, Charlie, Rose, Jules, May, and Grace. But its location needed to be controlled even better. The fewer people who knew where Dax had stashed it, the better. Sure, after tonight's events, it was clear that Grace loved Rose, but that didn't mean she wouldn't fight for a piece of the pie—or all of it, for that matter. There was no way Dax would put blind trust in Grace Parsons. Heck, Dax didn't even want May to know where she'd hidden it. Trust was there, but she didn't want to put her sister at risk.

The final touch was sliding the tire rack in place to hide the grease-stained crawl door.

Charlie pulled a red bandana from her rear pocket and wiped the sweat from her brow. She wasn't the talkative type, but she'd been withdrawn since they left the accident site, uttering only a few words while they stashed the whiskey. Dax tried to put herself in Charlie's shoes and imagine the weight she carried, knowing she'd killed someone. That another human being had taken their last breath because of her. Justified or not, the guilt would overpower her.

Dax pulled two rusty metal chairs from the rickety metal card table that doubled as Charlie's dining set. "Sit." Charlie sat and bowed her head. Dax sat beside her. "I can barely imagine what you're going through, but if you hadn't done what was necessary, Rose would have died and likely you and me alongside her."

"I didn't have a choice, but that doesn't make it easier to swallow."

Dax placed a hand on Charlie's back and rubbed in small, gentle circles. "I know it doesn't, and I'm sorry I put you in that situation. What can I do to help you through this?"

Charlie finally locked eyes with Dax. "I don't know."

"You shouldn't be alone tonight. Why don't you spend the night at the Foster House? We have two extra bedrooms upstairs."

"Thanks, but I don't want to leave the whiskey unguarded all night until we know no one is on to us," Charlie said. "Besides, this way I can repair the back of your truck before anyone can see it."

"I hadn't thought about that. How about I send Jules over? Besides, I think she's much better suited to give you what you might need tonight." Dax gave Charlie a friendly shoulder shove, eliciting a long, overdue grin.

"I'd like that."

"It's settled." Dax rose from her chair, and Charlie followed. "The Foster House is closed for the next two days, so I'll be by in the morning to plan what to do with the whiskey."

The rain had finally stopped, and the clouds had continued their eastward course, leaving behind an extra chill and a sparkling night sky. The quiet and crisp intake of air on the walk home gave Dax time to clear her mind of the chaos that had bombarded her for the last hour and focus on what still needed doing tonight—telling May the truth.

Dax entered through the back door, using her key. The kitchen lights were unexpectedly off, so she flipped the switch near the door. She considered calling out, but after the events of the evening, her gut told her something might be amiss. A quick glance at the open door leading to May's room confirmed it was unoccupied. That left the dining room.

Dax cautiously opened the swinging door to the main part of the restaurant and stepped in, discovering the most entertaining sight since she'd arrived in Half Moon Bay. May and Jules were seated at a booth against the wall, and May had flipped a card on the table as if she were swatting a fly. "Gin." May broke into her version of the Charleston, done from the waist up, waving her arms like a true flapper.

"That's five in a row." Jules slammed her cards on the table. "Are you chiseling me?"

"Oh, quit being a pill." May gathered up the cards into a neat stack. "Whose shuffle is it?"

"Mine." Jules let out her pouty lip, earning a smile from May. Cute. So cute. Both of them. "I hope you take credit." Jules snatched up the cards and shuffled.

"How much has she taken you for?" Dax asked as she stepped further into the dining room. Both women cocked their heads toward her. May's toothy grin suggested the answer to her question was: a lot.

"More than I can afford." Jules put the cards down.

"She's a pro at it, which is why she got to choose what was on the menu every week before we moved here."

Jules casually turned her head toward May, giving her the stink eye. "Played a few times, my ass."

May snickered. "Where are Charlie and Brutus?"

"Back at the garage." Dax turned her attention to Jules. "She's expecting you." When Jules narrowed her eyes, Dax continued, "I'll walk you out."

As Jules gathered her coat and bag, she turned to May. "I'll have to work off that fifty cents I owe you."

"Consider it prepayment for when Dax cuts her hand again." May stood to give Jules a hug.

"Stay right here, May. I'll be right back." Dax walked Jules out through the front door and closed it behind them.

"What's wrong? It's not our night together?" Jules asked. Rose was right. Nothing ever got past Jules except for May's hidden talent.

"Things went haywire tonight." Dax swallowed the sorrow stuck in her throat and held Jules by the upper arms. "She's really upset. Let her explain what happened without asking questions. Just listen and be there for her."

"You're scaring me, Dax. Is she hurt?"

"Not on the outside, but she is on the inside."

Jules nodded firmly and disappeared across the street in the dark. Dax was certain Charlie wouldn't get over what happened tonight anytime soon, but having the support and comfort of Jules would begin the healing.

Dax returned to the dining room, locking up before she rejoined May at the booth. She locked eyes with her sister for several beats, dreading the story she had to tell.

"Something bad happened, didn't it?" May asked.

"Yes, but Rose, Charlie, and Brutus are safe." Dax explained the harrowing events of the evening, including Riley's fate. She choked on the part where she nearly lost Rose and considered glossing over the detail of her almost slipping over the edge but remembered her promise. "If not for Charlie and Grace each grabbing an ankle, I would have gone over the cliff with Rose. And if she did, I didn't want them to save me." Two sets of eyes filled with tears. "I learned tonight that I can't live without her."

"How is Charlie taking it?"

"Bad, which is why I sent Jules. Charlie shouldn't be alone tonight, and Jules is the right person to help her through this."

"What about the liquor?"

Dax hesitated with a sigh. But, risky or not, she would keep her promise. "We hid it in Charlie's garage until we can figure out what to do with it."

"How about selling them in the city to the speakeasy Logan used to frequent?" May asked.

"Maybe two or three to get the money for the windows and your brace. But the rest? We're sitting on a gold mine, May. Charlie and Rose think we could get ten thousand dollars selling it by the glass."

"Ten thousand? That's crazy."

"That's how desperate people are to drink. I was thinking about Logan's bleak letter," Dax said. "We have to face reality. He's never coming back for us."

"I think you're right. After Mr. Portman put the word out, no one will hire him and no one will buy our house. He blames you for his misfortune and me for defending you."

"Which is why we have to plan for our future. Reopening the basement speakeasy could mean life-changing money even after splitting it with Charlie. We could hire someone to run this place and get a proper house of our own."

"With room enough for Rose?" May asked with a smile.

"I hoped you'd say that."

"She's welcome here anytime for as long as you want her here."

Dax extended her hand across the table and clenched her sister's strong, loving hand. "Thank you, May."

A knock on the main door interrupted the tender moment and made Dax jumpy. With the windows boarded up, she couldn't peek to see who was out there after eleven o'clock at night. Was it the prohibition agents who had rousted her and Dax at Shelter Cove? Had the police come to arrest her? Was it Frankie Wilkes out for revenge?

Dax couldn't be too careful. She stood at the door, a hand on the knob and her feet shoulder-width apart if she needed extra balance. She nervously called out, "Who is it?" She leaned into the door, bracing herself if someone on the other side tried to kick it in.

"Dax, it's Rose."

Every tense muscle relaxed at the sound of Rose's voice. After tonight's frightening events, seeing her again was exactly what Dax needed. She whipped the door open, dragging Rose inside by the arm. A moment after Dax shut and locked the door, she whisked Rose into her arms. The thought of going through life without this woman made her tremble and hold on tighter. Images of Rose hanging off the cliff flashed in her head. If Grace hadn't jumped into action at that precise moment. If Dax hadn't been strong from her carpentry work. If she'd initially reached out for Rose with her injured left hand and not her right. If Grace and Charlie hadn't worked as a team, Rose would be dead.

Dax buried her face in the crook of Rose's neck, unable to shake the dreadful image of the events at Devil's Slide turning out tragically different. "I almost lost you," she cried.

Rose pulled back and pushed a few locks of Dax's bangs toward her ear. "You saved me."

"Ahem," May cleared her throat. She'd gotten out of the booth and stepped toward Dax and Rose. "I heard you had quite a scare tonight. Can I get a hug?"

"Of course." Rose released Dax and accepted May's giant bear hug. The type of hug May typically reserved for family and loved ones and one that made Dax smile inside. They were already a family.

When May finished squeezing the stuffing out of Rose like a Raggedy Ann doll, she kissed Rose and then Dax on the cheek. "I'm heading to bed. You two take care of each other tonight."

Alone. They were finally alone. Dax extended her hand, which Rose accepted, and without uttering a word, guided her upstairs. Each step brought into clarity how deeply she loved Rose and that this was the right time. Dax stopped Rose at the threshold of the bedroom door and cupped her face with both hands. Looking into her eyes, she was sure they would make their first time special.

Dax kissed Rose, gently and briefly at first, to show her affection. Rose displayed as much with an adorable smile when she pulled back. The second kiss went deeper and lasted longer to show her love. Rose responded by draping her arms over Dax's shoulders and bringing their bodies together until they became one. Nothing formed a barrier between them. Not Riley. Not Grace. Not their parents or the church. The third kiss had fire behind it, and soon neither of them could contain their desire. Arms cradled dampened coats. Moans escaped and entwined in the air as a prelude to them becoming lovers. The fourth kiss would have to wait.

Dax took Rose by her hands, walking backward toward her bed. She removed her coat, shoes, and socks as Rose did the same. Then her shirt and pants found the floor along with Rose's sequined stage dress, which had been ripped during the night's ordeal. That left Dax in her undershorts and sleeveless undershirt and Rose in her slip. Dax's eyes drifted from Rose's smooth porcelain shoulders to the hint of tantalizing cleavage and past her waist to the slip's trailing edge.

Dax's breath hitched. Rose's knees and shins were scraped and dirty, but the bleeding had stopped. "You're hurt." She guided Rose to the side of the bed. "Sit. I'll get a towel to clean your wounds."

She walked calmly to the bathroom because no other speed seemed appropriate. The danger had passed, Rose didn't appear to be in pain, and the mood they'd set with those kisses guaranteed a future as lifelong lovers. Neither of them was going anywhere, and neither was in a hurry. Dax could say her only thought was tending to Rose's wounds, but her mind had focused on what would happen afterward. And every sexy scenario ended with Rose in her arms, warming her body until the sun came up.

Dax wet a bath towel and grabbed the hydrogen peroxide and another small towel before returning to the bedroom. Rose had scooted deeper across the bed so her legs were flat on the mattress. Her slip had hiked deliciously higher up her thighs. Unsurprisingly, shallow breaths accompanied Dax's route back to her position on the bed.

"Does it hurt?" Dax skimmed the wet towel over the dirtiest section of Rose's left shin.

"Not anymore."

"But it did?" Dax continued to clean the other leg.

"Frankly, I was so scared that I hadn't noticed they were scraped until the drive back to town."

"You didn't let Grace clean you up?" Dax raised her head enough to display her impish grin.

"She offered, but I wanted to leave that task for you."

"Why, Rose Hamilton!" Dax's grin widened and her tone got more playful. "If I didn't know you so well, I'd guess you were trying to seduce me."

Rose leaned forward until her lips were a whisper from Dax's. "Your guess would be correct."

The fourth kiss still had to wait. "After." Dax leaned Rose back to her original position. "This is going to sting." She poured a smidge of hydrogen peroxide onto a corner of the small towel and dabbed the deepest gash. Rose flinched. "I'm sorry, but we can't risk an infection."

The dabbing and flinching continued until Dax had cleaned each significant wound. When she was done, she placed the first-aid items on her dresser. She then removed the rest of her clothes, foregoing her routine of folding or putting them in the laundry basket. They remained wherever she dropped them. Turning toward the bed, she found Rose in a trance, mouth agape. Dax had never thought much about her body, but she knew she was fit. Apparently, she was also desirable, at least if Rose's fixed stare and hungry eyes were an accurate barometer.

Rose scooted from the bed and turned down the blanket before removing her slip and brassiere. Dax had thought Rose's breasts were alluring when they were kids, but they'd become downright intoxicating in the intervening years. Then Rose slipped off her underpants, and Dax could barely draw in enough air to remain on her feet.

Rose glided into bed.

Dax's pulse sped faster and faster with each step she took toward her. She'd dreamt hundreds of times, if not thousands, about lying skin to skin with Rose, but the reality far surpassed anything she'd conjured up. When they were positioned breast to breast, every inch of Dax tingled, even those parts not touching Rose, as if lightning had struck close by.

Legs entwined. Hands roamed patches of forbidden skin. Their lips collided in a sizzling passion-filled fourth kiss. Right then, Dax realized her mother and childhood pastor were dead wrong. Heaven wasn't some place not of this earth. It was right here. It was in the bliss of sharing bodies and hearts.

The hesitation that was present the night Rose had stayed overnight was gone. Dax knew how to please Rose, and she could honestly say that she always knew—Rose held the answer. She broke the kiss and whispered, "Tell me what you want."

Rose shifted to her back and grasped the hand Dax had drifted to her breast, gripping it by Dax's index and middle fingers. She guided it past her belly. "Inside."

Dax smiled, and so did Rose. Like on the cliff, the implied trust was all Dax needed to be confident that whatever happened next, whether she made a mess of things or was an expert at it, they would love each other forever. So she followed her instinct.

Her expectations of what sex with Rose would feel like didn't come close to its reality. A warmth radiated through her and activated every nerve ending in her body. She discovered the most delectable sensations and tastes in the world and was left completely drained by the discovery.

Their bodies sated, Rose covered them both with the blanket and nestled her body beside Dax, draping a leg and arm over her. Dax wrapped an arm around Rose but lacked the energy to do more than let it drop on her like a dead fish. Finally, a thought of *Will I ever breathe normally again?* entered Dax's mind. It was more than mental note-taking on her favorite parts of the night. It was the culmination of a decade of loving this wonderful creature whose words never got stuck around her. *I need to ask Rose to live with me.*

CHAPTER TWENTY-SIX

Rose Hamilton hadn't counted on still having a job singing at the Seaside Club once the sheriff fished from the sea Riley's truck and his body, or what was left of it after ocean predators had nibbled on his lower extremities at the bottom of Devil's Slide. She'd expected the police to ask Dax or Rose or Charlie questions because of their public altercations with him, but no one did. Thanks to Grace Parson's keeping her word and not involving the authorities, the sheriff wrote up Riley's death as an accident, omitting any mention of a connection with the illegal liquor trade. The official report concluded that he'd likely driven too fast during the storm and went over the cliff notorious for taking the lives of many reckless drivers.

Now, a month following Riley King's death, Jason, Rose's favorite bartender, was proving to be a much superior club manager. Unlike Riley, he understood the restaurant and nightclub business and kept it running more smoothly than before. Most importantly, he still had Rose's hot tea waiting for her after every performance. Lester still played the piano twice each night, and Frankie Wilkes still stopped by regularly to get his fill of the hotel's principal attraction. It was as if Riley never existed, or so Rose hoped. Nevertheless, a piece of her feared someone, like the prohis who had spotted Dax and Charlie on the beach, would come looking for everyone who had been on that deadly stretch of road that night. She envisioned getting a bullet between the eyes or being thrown behind bars for the rest of her life.

Rose tucked that fear away the moment she woke in Dax's bed. Two nights a week away from the boarding house like Jules wouldn't raise the wrong eyebrows. Better the town thought them whores, sleeping with customers from the club, than lesbians.

Dax's side of the bed was empty this morning, and the shower was running. Correction—the shower had just stopped running. A sliver of the sun had crept over the coastal mountains to the east, marking the beginning of another day with Dax in her life. Rose stretched her naked body across the mattress to work out the kinks, letting a satisfied smile build on her lips. Dax's technique had improved dramatically since their first time together, enough that Rose's arms and legs felt like rubber every night they spent together.

"Good morning, beautiful." Dax appeared in the doorway, wrapped deliciously in a towel at the waist with a second draped around her neck covering her breasts. The compromise of covering herself how a man would with the modesty of a woman was quintessential Dax.

"You know, you could do a lot less laundry if you use only one towel after a shower. You could wrap yourself like I do."

"And walk around in a dress? Never." Dax kissed Rose on the lips. "We need to get going soon. May has to be at the hospital by eleven."

Rose threw back the covers. "Give me ten minutes to shower."

Dax eyed the length of Rose's body as if it were a piece of fine art. "If you don't put something on, we're going to be late."

Today was an important day for May and Dax. If not for a looming departure, Rose would have Dax demonstrate her newfound expertise again and likely again. "We can't have that." Instead, Rose politely put on the robe she started keeping here following their second night together as lovers and kissed Dax on the cheek on her way by. "I'll see you downstairs."

Once Rose dressed and was smelling like a fresh rose, she headed downstairs to the alluring smell of sausage and onion. One incredible benefit of having a restaurant manager as a lover was the food. Besides never going hungry, Rose was learning from May how to cook a multitude of dishes not on the menu.

"Good morning, May," Rose said. "Can I help with anything?" May was packing a picnic basket with fruit, raw carrots, cheese, and bread, everything that would keep for a long road trip.

"Good morning, Rose." May gestured with her chin toward the sink where Dax was washing the dirty pans May had used to cook the egg casserole cooling on the center butcher block. "Can you fill us a few jugs of water?"

"I'm on it." Rose grabbed two one-gallon glass jugs from the shelf, placed them on the counter next to the double sink, and took a position next to Dax. "Mind if I steal your faucet?"

Dax kissed her on the cheek before swinging the faucet to Rose's side. "What's mine is yours, so it would never be stealing."

Rose started filling the jugs. "In that case, I'd love to wear some of your clothes one day."

"You in knickers and suspenders?"

"Why not?" Rose inched closer to Dax until they touched shoulder to hip. "I think they're sexy."

"I don't think I'd survive seeing you in those." Dax grinned.

"Now you know what I go through every time I see you."

"All right, lovebirds," May chuckled. "Let's eat before the casserole gets too cold."

* * *

May took the arm Rose had offered to help her out of the truck and to the curb. Once Rose closed the passenger door, Dax pulled away from the main hospital entrance and took off toward the parking lot. Rose supported May's arm as they walked through the doors to the lobby, May with her cane.

"Thank you for including me in your big day. It means a lot," Rose said.

"I wouldn't have it any other way, Rose."

Dax caught up with Rose and May moments before they reached Doctor Shephard's office, slowing to match May's pace. "Good. I didn't miss anything."

"I wouldn't have started without you. You're the reason I'm getting my new brace today." May squeezed Dax's hand. They were sisters, but they'd clearly become much closer from their shared journey. There were words for men like Logan who abandoned their crippled wives, but even those slurs seemed too kind. It was no wonder May hadn't sent word to include him in this momentous day. They were better off without him.

Fifteen minutes later, the nurse escorted May, Dax, and Rose to the exam room, where the doctor was waiting with May's new brace. Dr. Shepard walked in. "Have a seat, May. Ready to make your life a lot easier?"

"I sure am."

"And who do we have here?" he asked. "I remember your younger sister, Dax, but this other young lady is new."

"This is Rose Hamilton. She's family." May's warm reference tickled Rose's heart. Though they'd reconnected only two months ago, the feeling of family went both ways.

"All right, then. Let's try it on." Doctor Shepard carefully removed May's old brace and attached the new one. He demonstrated the optimum position before tightening the upper and lower straps. "You'll like this one much more than your old one. Padding has gotten so much better in the last four years. And if you wear slacks over the brace, you shouldn't chafe at all."

"Slacks. I've never worn pants in my life."

"Doctor's orders." Dax positioned herself behind May, placing both hands atop her shoulders. "We'll go shopping before we leave the city."

"Ready?" Doctor Shepard stood and extended both hands, which May accepted. "Take it slow until you get used to how it feels. The double rods on each side make it stronger and stiffer."

"I'm familiar with double rods. A family friend added one when she repaired the old brace."

"She?" Doctor Shepard cocked his head back. "Please tell her she did an outstanding job. If she's ever looking for work, she'd be in great demand with the hospitals in the city."

"I'll pass that along." May stood, testing the brace's sturdiness by shifting more and more weight to that leg. "It feels so much softer."

"I still think you're a candidate for reconstructive surgery," he said. "If we put in the newer rods and plates, you might not need a brace."

"Maybe when we get the money." May took several decisive steps. Her limp was still prominent, but her smile suggested the new brace was a long-overdue necessity. Rose shifted her gaze to Dax. Tears had streaked each cheek. Everything Dax had gone through, from Riley sabotaging and vandalizing the Foster House, to building a speakeasy of her own, to taking a beating that resulted in Riley's death and nearly hers and Rose's, now seemed like a price worth paying. Pure joy filled the room and Rose's heart.

Three shopping bags occupied the truck bed. Each lady walked out of the clothing boutique with several sets of slacks, knickers, blouses and shirts, shoes, and pairs of suspenders for Rose and Dax. Even after the spending spree, the doctor's bill, and the brace, Dax still had some leftover cash from the sale of two whiskey barrels at Logan's old watering hole. But that money, Dax had said, was earmarked for something special she had in mind for her and Rose.

They crested Devil's Slide at a virtual crawl, and as they did, Rose reached across May for Dax's hand. They clasped hands and squeezed. The minute or two she spent hanging over the cliff, contemplating her death, marked the most terrifying event she'd lived through. The memory of that night haunted her, but never when she was with Dax or simply thinking of her. Dax had the power to make her feel safe no matter the circumstance or distance.

"It happened here, didn't it?" May asked.

"Yes, it did." Dax released Rose's hand and pointed at the apex of the curve in the road. "Right there, but all of that is behind us. Riley can't hurt us anymore."

When the road flattened and hugged a series of beaches, Dax pulled her truck onto the gravel parking area next to a sign marked Gray Whale Cove. This was the spot Riley had taken Rose when he tried to impress her with his high-risk job as a whiskey runner.

"I thought we could celebrate with a sunset picnic on the beach," Dax said. "Do you think you're up for a short walk, May?"

"Up for it? I've been dying to walk on the beach." The sparkle in May's eyes and the near giggle in her voice were breathtaking. May's disability had limited her to a few stairs and walking short distances and had deprived her of so many of life's simple pleasures. Walking on the beach was one of them.

"Let's do it." Dax exited the truck and retrieved a jug of water, two blankets, and the picnic basket May had packed.

Rose got out and offered her hand again, but May politely waved her off. "Let me try on my own." May scooted to the edge of the bench seat and swung her legs out the door opening. She then lowered both legs to the exterior step and held onto the door. Surprisingly, she led with her braced leg. Following a brief wobble, she dropped her other leg to the ground. "This is amazing, Rose. This is the first time I've been able to get out of this thing by myself."

"I'm so happy for you, May." Rose glanced at Dax. She had stood silently, witnessing May's newfound independence.

"I am too, May." Dax's smile stretched to her eyes. She led the group to the beach, picked out a spot on the sand, and spread out one blanket.

Rose followed, helping May when she said the soft sand made her stride unsteady. They spread out a blanket, nibbled on the food, and took in the sun as it dipped lower on the horizon. It was a shame they were the only ones there. A beautiful beach sunset should be enjoyed every time nature presented one.

The temperature had dropped, so Dax bundled May in the second blanket. "Do you mind if Rose and I take a walk to the rocks?" Dax asked her.

"Not at all. Take your time. I'd forgotten how nice it is to sit on the beach."

"Thanks, May." Dax led Rose across the lumpy sand toward an outcropping of rocks. When they got closer, she directed them to a small L-shaped formation backed by the cliffs and opened to the ocean. The side walls were tall enough that a passerby would need to peer around them to know someone was there.

Dax pulled them to a sitting position on the sand and kissed Rose with a passion as fiery as if they were in her room at the Foster House. Under any other circumstance, kissing on the beach would have sent Rose into a tizzy, but they were alone. The longer the kiss went on, the more natural it felt to be affectionate in public—like men and women did with great frequency.

The kiss ended, leaving Rose thinking how perfect the world would be if she and Dax could hold hands and kiss in public without being marked as sinners and put in jail for indecency. "I wish we could do this every day."

"I do too." Dax took a deep breath as if preparing to start a contentious conversation. "I've discussed it with May, and she's all for it. Move in with us, Rose. You can work with May in the kitchen during the day, and we can be with each other upstairs every night. I've even set aside enough money to get us a bigger bed." Dax took Rose's hands into hers. "Please say yes."

Rose's head spun. Dax had wrapped everything she'd come to love into a single proposal. But was she ready to give up her job? The money was decent, but her hesitation wasn't about that. Rose loved Dax and May. That wasn't the issue either. She even loved cooking, but she loved singing even more. Could she give that up?

"I—"

The Speakeasy Series continues with Whiskey War

Sometimes good needs a little help overcoming evil.

After narrowly escaping death at Devil's Slide, lesbian couple Dax and Rose look forward to a clandestine life together in Half Moon Bay. Dax's sister, May, makes the Foster House restaurant their refuge at the height of Prohibition and the dawn of the Great Depression while they sit on a gold mine of stolen whiskey from the local speakeasy.

When Frankie Wilkes, the speakeasy owner and Rose's employer, suspects Dax might have the whiskey, he makes Rose's life miserable, forcing Dax to scramble to unload the barrels before he finds them. The trip to San Francisco sparks the attention of May's husband, Logan, who abandoned her and Dax months earlier. He surfaces in Half Moon Bay, looking for money. He quickly puts a wedge in May, Dax, and Rose's idyllic life and riles up a nasty competition with Frankie Wilkes. Tragedy strikes, and Dax sees the ugly side of the illegal liquor business when left unchecked.

In comes Grace Parsons, a wealthy Hollywood starlet and Rose's former lover, with a solution to their problems. However, her bold help spirals into a violent feud that leaves no one in their inner circle untouched. How far will Logan and Frankie go to get what they want? Can Dax and Rose find a way out before the whiskey war takes their lives?

Bella Books, Inc.
Women. Books. Even Better Together.
P.O. Box 10543
Tallahassee, FL 32302
Phone: (800) 729-4992
www.BellaBooks.com

More Titles from Bella Books

Mabel and Everything After – Hannah Safren
978-1-64247-390-2 | 274 pgs | paperback: $17.95 | eBook: $9.99
A law student and a wannabe brewery owner find that the path to a
fairy tale happily-ever-after is often the long and scenic route.

To Be With You – TJ O'Shea
978-1-64247-419-0 | 348 pgs | paperback: $19.95 | eBook: $9.99
Sometimes the choice is between loving safely or loving bravely.

I Dare You to Love Me – Lori G. Matthews
978-1-64247-389-6 | 292 pgs | paperback: $18.95 | eBook: $9.99
An enemy-to-lovers romance about daring to follow your heart, even
when it's the hardest thing to do.

The Lady Adventurers Club - Karen Frost
978-1-64247-414-5 | 300 pgs | paperback: $18.95 | eBook: $9.99
Four women. One undiscovered Egyptian tomb. One (maybe) angry
Egyptian goddess. What could possibly go wrong?

Golden Hour - Kat Jackson
978-1-64247-397-1 | 250 pgs | paperback: $17.95 | eBook: $9.99
Life would be so much easier if Lina were afraid of something
basic—like spiders—instead of something significant. Something like
real, true, healthy love.

Schuss – E. J. Noyes
978-1-64247-430-5 | 276 pgs | paperback: $17.95 | eBook: $9.99
They're best friends who both want something more, but what if
admitting it ruins the best friendship either of them have had?